DEADLOCK

C.E. CLAYTON

DEADLOCK

Eerden #2, Ellinor #2

Starfish Ink

ISBN-13: 978-1-952797-05-7

Cover art by: ebooklaunch.com
Map design by: Sarah at thesketchdragon
Edited by: Sheila Shedd
Section graphics by: 3mikey5000 from Pixabay

Starfish Ink: starfishinkpublishing@gmail.com Printed in the United States of America

First Printing, 2021

To the librarian who hated my poor penmanship, and the computers that made it obsolete.

PRONOUNCIATION GUIDE

- *Ellinor Olysha Rask*: El-in-or O-lee-shah Raa-s-k
- *Kai Axel Brantley*: K-aye Ax-el Brant-lee
- *Cosmin von Brandt*: Cous-min v-on Br-aunt
- *Jelani Tyrik Sharma*: Jheh-l-ah-nee T-ay-r-eek Sh-ir-m-ah
- *Misho Shimizu*: Me-sh-o Shim-me-zoo
- *Irati Mishra*: I-rat-ee M-ih-sh-rah
- *Pema Tran*: Pay-ma Tr-ahn
- *Talin Roxas*: T-ah-l-in Rock-as
- *Janne Wolff*: Yah-neh Wool-f
- *Zabel Dirix*: Za-bell Deer-eeks
- *Oihana Sharma*: Oy-han-na Sh-ir-m-ah
- *Andrey Rask*: Ah-n-dray Raa-s-k
- *Dafina Rask*: Dah-fee-na Raa-s-k
- *Valter Rask*: V-all-terr Raa-s-k
- *Aylen Bonheur*: A-lin Bon-err
- *Elisaveta Baldini*: El-is-a-vey-ta Bald-e-nee
- *Amalia Brantley*: Ah-mah-lee-ah Brant-lee
- *Azer*: A-zer
- *Izza*: Iz-zah
- *Fiss*: F-iss
- *Rada*: Rah-duh
- *Gorgi*: Gore-gee
- *Blazhe*: Buh-la-z-he
- *Anton*: An-tawn
- *Malik*: Mall-ick
- *Inti*: In-tee
- *Caterina*: Cat-er-e-na

RACE AND LOCATION GUIDE

Humani: hyew-man-ee
Seersha: sear-shah
Seerani: sear-ahn-ee
Doehaz: dough-has
Dreeocht: dree-ockt
Ashling: ash-ling
Eerden: Ear-den
Amardeep: Am-are-deep
Erhard: Err-hard
Euria: Yur-e-a
Anzor: An-zoor
Desta: Deh-stah
Amaru: Am-ah-roo
Saxa: Sax-uh
Goma: Goh-ma
SynthLyfe: Sin-th-life

MAP OF AMARDEEP

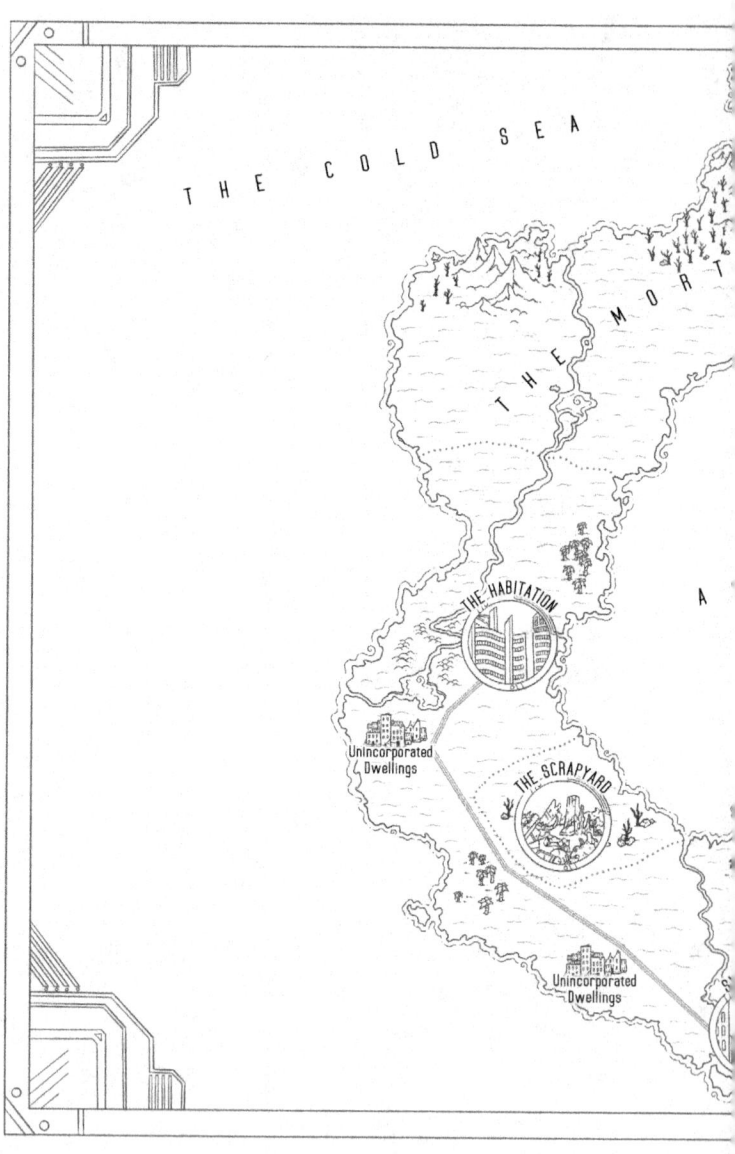

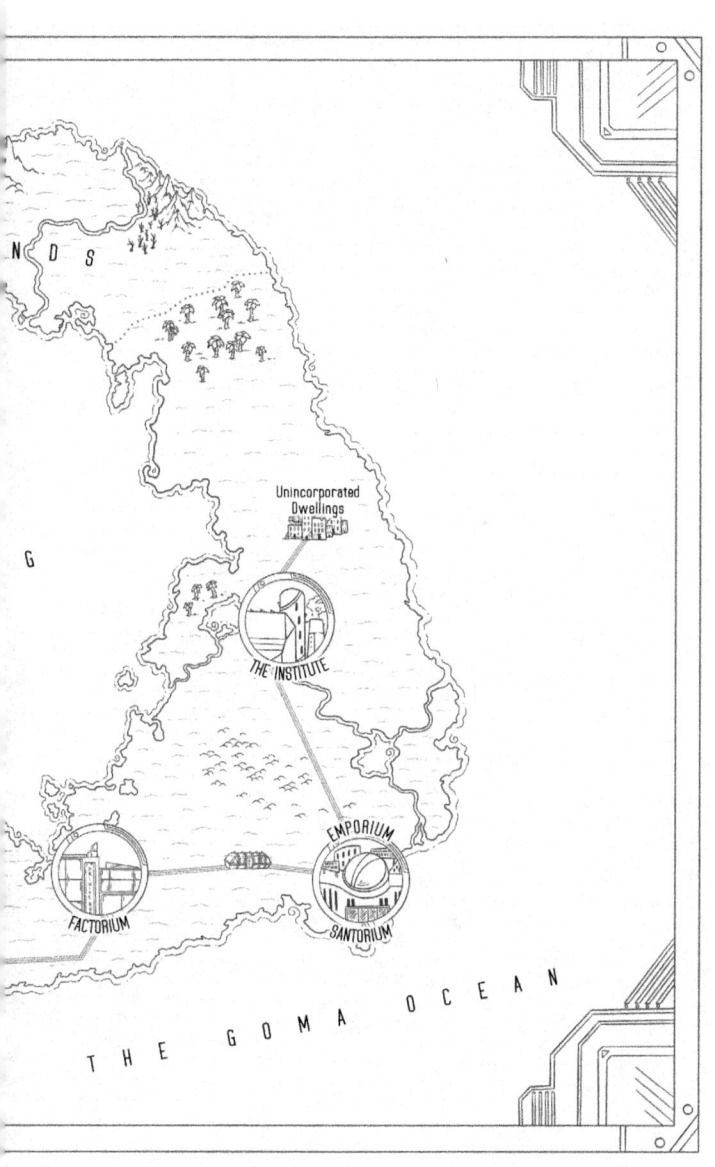

N D S

G

Unincorporated
Dwellings

THE INSTITUTE

EMPORIUM

FACTORIUM

SANTORIUM

T H E   G O M A   O C E A N

PROLOGUE

WELCOME BACK, HEATHENS

NOVEMBER, 4145

A ZER IS real. This is important to know in case there is still doubt. Azer may have accomplished all He wanted to, and then taken an increasingly passive role in the lives He had created from nothingness, but He is still here, lingering. Azer is, well, He is lazy, above all else. For a deity with unimaginable power—anything He could imagine could be snapped into existence with no more effort than a yawn—He was the laziest of his 10,873.6 all-powerful siblings. This fact is well known.

With that in mind, know that Azer is somewhere in the vicinity of Eerden at this moment. As a non-corporeal being, His location is hard to define, and harder to pin down exactly, much to the chagrin of those who still fervently worship Him. If there is one thing Azer still finds interesting, however, it's His creatures creating magnificent chaos, in other words, when they do something unexpected. *Surprising.* Despite His prowess, Azer is not exactly omniscient. A master of the odds, predicting patterns and probability to an uncanny degree, yes. But all-knowing? No.

Occasionally, something still captures His whole attention. He will pay special mind to certain creations of His, and having Azer's attention is not necessarily a good thing. Lucky for Ellinor Olysha Rask, Azer's attention was not currently on her.

Azer was blissfully unaware of Ellinor's capture by her ex-boss, nor did He witness her old crew mutiny and betray her. Azer even missed Ellinor fighting a pair of doehaz and then dying (briefly) at the hands of a powerful water caster, the very same water caster she had been coerced into delivering a dreeocht to. But that was before Ellinor and Fiss had bonded. Azer doesn't know who, or what, Ellinor is. Not yet. What He did see, however, were two seersha, members of the colorful magical race he had created from scratch, losing their damned minds.

Azer was watching Zabel Dirix and Cosmin von Brandt, specifically, as they threw the most spectacular of tantrums. Casters, but especially seersha casters, were so flamboyant when they were upset. But Azer doesn't typically care for the particulars. He didn't, for instance, care that Ellinor had betrayed the two crime lords, nor that she had whisked away a powerful dreeocht right from under Zabel's nose. Nor did He care that she had allied herself with an Ashling sympathizer and bonafide Creature Breaker, and turned one of Cosmin's loyal followers against him. But He did enjoy the unbridled display of magic that resulted from Ellinor's actions. Now that was unexpected.

Cosmin released magical fire creature after creature to torment the messengers of such bad news. He even leveled an entire skyscraper when he summoned his earth magic to create the friction needed for him to generate the amount of fire needed to deploy his creatures. The governing officials of Euria were quick to realize just how unprepared they were to handle a situation of that magnitude and, as they scrambled to contain Cosmin von Brandt's tantrum, Ellinor, Kai, Jelani, Fiss, and Oihana scrambled out of reach, right beneath Azer's gaze. They took advantage of the anarchy to travel, to get Kai's mother to safety outside Euria with Ellinor's parents, and to find a ferry heading for Amardeep.

And Zabel Dirix was just as entertaining.

Her water magic created dazzling displays of electrical storms that resulted in her entire city suffering a blackout as her fury haphazardly struck the surrounding buildings and several passersby. Even without the aid of a shackled dreeocht, as she had been planning with Fiss, Zabel was uncomfortably powerful. So far, she had killed forty-seven people and probably would kill a dozen more before her anger needed to be bottled by the governor of Anzor. (Perhaps it should be noted that Azer felt no pang of remorse for these deaths; His only concern was that He remained entertained.)

Azer watched with rapt attention as the two gangster bosses pooled their resources together and organized an army of humani and seersha alike to go after their lost prizes. Zabel and Cosmin would remain tense allies until the dreeocht was returned. Azer figured eventually one of them would war with the other over the trouble, and Azer was determined to watch that, too. In fact, that just might be the most entertaining event yet, once their forces collided.

What this celestial being was *not* currently doing, was watching the little ship that Cosmin and Zabel's so-called "property" was boarding. The maker of Eerden, and all its inhabitants, was wonderfully oblivious—for the moment—to Ellinor Rask, Kai Brantley, Fiss, Jelani and Oihana Sharma, and an Independent Assistance Android, all of whom were boarding a covert vessel bound for the island atoll of Amardeep, where the Ashlings made their home and created their one true export—Juice Boxes.

The Ashlings were not creatures Azer had planned for. He had not, nor would He have chosen to create robots with true sentience. Azer had intended to correct this oversight by destroying every trace of the bio-synthetic life, but the conflict between the Ashlings and the various races of organics who could not come to terms with these beings, who feared them, who recoiled at their existence, proved to be too entertaining for Him.

Had Azer been paying attention, He would have known that Ellinor was one of those humani who was distrustful of Ashlings after a deal-gone-wrong had cost her husband his life, eight years ago. He would have known that Ellinor planned to use the excursion into Amardeep to not only have her collar removed and thus be reunited with her magic, yes, but also enact part of her long-standing plans to avenge Misho Shimizu's death. Then she would return to Cosmin and finish the job once and for all. Even knowing such a vendetta would kill her, Ellinor would move steadfastly ahead. Cosmin would pay.

Had Azer been watching the less spectacular escape of this group, He would have also known that Jelani suspected Ellinor was still willing to throw her life away. He was determined to keep her, despite her reluctance, breathing, for Fiss' sake, if nothing else. Even their travel would have engaged Azer, as going unnoticed in Amardeep with Kai, one of Cosmin's more recognizable goons, and a dreeocht who amplified the power of any water or air caster, was quite impossible. Their daily hardships would prove far more entertaining than the current tantrums of the seersha gangsters back on the continent of Erhard. Azer's loss, however, was Ellinor's luck.

Azer will eventually discover His oversight. He may not be omniscient, but He is not blind. His vision encompasses far more than any mortal could comprehend, seeing planes, spectrums, and dimensions corporeal beings couldn't even dream of. Once Azer finally gets bored with Zabel Dirix and Cosmin von Brandt and turns His keen gaze to Ellinor, it is doubtful He'll ever stop watching her. There are certain creatures so prone to conflict, to drama, to chaos that it seems drawn to them. Ellinor, Kai, and certainly Jelani, are such creatures.

Of this, there can be no doubt.

CHAPTER

ONE

SIX BY SEA

E LLINOR RASK prowled below the deck of the converted
ferry. Her heavy boots beat a steady *snap-stomp* across the
damp metal floor. Save for the cargo, Ellinor was alone in the
hold. Captain Anton had ordered the crew to remain above
deck, and those orders would be enforced by Kai and Jelani.
Oihana couldn't be bothered to venture below decks anyway,
despite growing fond of Fiss.

Regardless, Ellinor guessed this area of the dingy ship
would have remained vacant, even without the precautions of
her travel companions. No one wanted to be that close to the
actual water of the Goma Ocean. Not this near Amardeep, anyway.

The vessel groaned around Ellinor, but she could still hear
the creak of footsteps trailing above. She paused in her pacing,
tropical blue eyes snapping to where the sound came from,
and held her breath as she waited. But, after a brief pause, the
creaking resumed, the feet moving on, heading to some other
place above deck Ellinor couldn't recall.

She hadn't gotten a good look at anything on deck before she snatched Fiss and headed below, using Kai and Oihana's Ashling Independent Service Android—Izza—as a distraction. Ellinor longed to be outside, on deck, even for a moment. Just a second to smell the fresh air, to stretch her fingers into the salty breeze and shut her eyes, imagining that she was the one commanding the wind. But she wasn't, and she might never again. She had to get the damned malfunctioning collar Cosmin had snapped on her neck off, and soon.

Ellinor shook her head, greasy, raven black hair sliding across her neck. She twisted one of the purple tendrils back up into the bird's nest of her low bun. The only thing that gave Ellinor hope was that her eyes maintained their bright blue hue, something only humani casters had—those unnaturally bright colors.

If that fades? Ellinor shuddered reflexively.

Despite Jelani assuring her that wouldn't necessarily be an indicator of her magic being permanently beyond her, but merely something medical—likely related to her liver or kidneys, based on her drinking. But Ellinor ignored him. He wasn't the one with a defective bio-magitech collar on his neck. So, what did the seersha Creature Breaker really know about it, anyway?

A lot, actually.

Ellinor growled at the thought, scratching at the bio-magitech which, enhanced with caster magic, had spread from her neck to encompass most of her throat, parts of her chest, and her right shoulder. Maybe if Ellinor hadn't *technically* been killed by Zabel, they wouldn't have needed to go to Amardeep so urgently. They could have stayed hidden in Oihana's secret bunker and let her and her other Ashling creations fiddle with Ellinor's cyborg-like affliction until the device was at least neutralized, but alas. Apparently Azer had a sick sense of humor about such things.

The metal shards and electrical wires that infected Ellinor didn't itch, not exactly, but what remained of her skin and tissue underneath did. It hadn't stopped itching since they boarded the ferry; an ever-present undertone of sunburn made the entire side of her body tender and raw. Fiss had to continually manipulate the magic he commanded to keep him invisible so a wayward glance wouldn't give him away. This constant use of magic was painful in a way it hadn't been before Fiss consumed Zabel's power, before Ellinor died.

A giggle rippled above Ellinor, scattering her thoughts, stalling her pacing mid-stride. She had forgotten they were playing a game, she and Fiss. The same game they had been playing for nearly a day straight. They were *always* playing hide-and-seek.

Fiss would be abysmal at the game if he couldn't cloak himself. He never really hid. He just floated near the ceiling, judging by the high-pitched, childlike laughter that bubbled up whenever Ellinor's pacing brought her near the dreeocht.

She may have been tired of the never-ending game where Ellinor was always "it" and had to find Fiss, but she *never* tired of Fiss. Not now, not until she died, and even that was questionable. She knew now, with every ounce of her core, every breath in her lungs, and every painful beat of her heart, that she loved Fiss. They were irreversibly bound together, and not by her magitech shackle, either.

Ellinor paused in her pacing, reaching up and . . . there! She touched a soft foot and wiggled her fingers, tickling. Fiss giggled and she felt his seaweed and cable hair brush against her as he cuddled her neck, not caring about her metal parts. Ellinor hugged the dreeocht to her, inhaling his clean ocean breeze and ozone scent. A swell of protectiveness rose in her like it always did when Fiss came to her for comfort and attention. Even though Fiss had been with her a relatively short time, it was nearly impossible for Ellinor to imagine an existence without him.

Fiss hummed against her neck. "Again!"

Ellinor's bio-magitech burned as the dreeocht zoomed off to another corner of the ceiling for Ellinor to find. She sighed internally and resumed pacing. Ellinor hadn't intended for this being, a new life form created from discarded smart technology, raw magic, and dead organic material, to bond with her. She wasn't powerful enough to use such a creature the way Cosmin or Zabel had wanted to, but here they were.

Fiss had fed on her and Misho's magic; now he held a piece of her departed husband within the fabric that made him, that which gave him consciousness. But, most importantly perhaps, Ellinor's feelings toward Fiss, her love and protectiveness, had been enough to get her on this fucking makeshift ferry chugging through disgusting water toward Amardeep—one of the last places where the monsters who took her husband also found refuge.

Ellinor's hands balled into fists and she breathed raggedly through her nose, her anger bubbling up once more. She wanted to punch someone—repeatedly. In lieu of that, she took out her boomerang karambit knives—her WX Lacerators—and began twirling them around her fingers, palming them and flipping them in a dizzying display. Even if her friends hadn't been above deck, keeping the crew at bay, she figured one look at her spinning the viciously hooked knives would be enough to send the squirrelly bunch racing.

Most people elected to fly to Amardeep, and that would have been Ellinor's choice, had it been possible. No one took boats that weren't large military vessels or chemical tankers through the northern edges of the Goma Ocean. Not unless they wanted to be disintegrated by the toxic slush from discarded magitech and biotechnology that coalesced around Amardeep, but what did Ellinor know? Maybe some people were into that sort of thing. That, or the debaucherously famous tourism that could be found only on Amardeep was worth the risk of sea travel.

But if the corrosive water of the Goma Ocean or an annoyed Ellinor still wasn't enough to keep people away from the lower decks of Captain Anton's ship, the ever-present threat of aquatic doehaz was.

So, of course, we put the most attractively magical being we can find as close to the water as possible, Ellinor thought, her knives spinning faster and faster, the *snap-stomp* of her boots dulling her mind once more. There was another giggle above her, and Ellinor reached up, her hand briefly squeezing Fiss' paw-like hand before the dreeocht squealed in laughter.

"Again!"

Ellinor smiled sadly, resuming the game, hoping the hissing sounds coming from beneath her feet were the magic dampeners Captain Anton said would shield them from doehaz, and not the Goma Ocean eating away at the hull.

Like the water that surrounded it, Amardeep was a poisoned atoll. No one wanted to claim the island, no elected official wanted the responsibility of cleaning it up. Not until the Ashlings were formed and had then aligned zemselves with the more . . . cyborg-like types, anyway. *Those* people believed machines elevated humanity, evolved them in some way. Ashlings used zeyr cyborg allies to claim the island, and because the place was literally disgusting, no one fought zem over claiming the diseased atoll as an independent nation, separate from the other city-states that populated the continents of Eerden.

As Ellinor's anger grew, her knife spinning stalled and her hand drifted to her neck, picking at the warm bio-magitech that irritated her skin. Her steps faltered. *Did it always go that high up on my throat?*

Fiss was using magic constantly these past few days, but it was nothing that could be considered strenuous for the dreeocht, even if he did occasionally conjure little aquatic critters to chase him through the hold. They never used Fiss' connection to Ellinor to cast harmful magic, and she wasn't getting hit with it in return.

It can't be growing. You're bored and paranoid, Ellinor.

But the uncomfortable thought remained, as there was little else to distract her mind. The near blind panic was always ready to come to the surface if she thought, even for one moment, about what would happen if she never got to cast her magic again. Always ready and willing to drag her down, down, down. Most of the time, the anxiety was just a rustling of wings above her heart, trapped in her chest. But if she focused on it, that pesky rustle became a pounding of wings that made her chest tighten and her breath shallow.

A whimper from Fiss quelled the panic and had Ellinor tilting her head. Fiss rarely showed signs of distress outside of Ellinor being in physical danger. It was . . . odd to hear.

I must be heading the wrong direction. She turned around, walking in the opposite direction.

The world still felt dull to Ellinor. The colors muted, tastes not as vibrant, scents all holding a chalky musk to them. She knew, deep down, that the world was still as brilliant as ever, but she couldn't shake the feeling that a flimsy, opaque gauze covered her reality, keeping her from feeling the warmth in her chest, the cool prickle in her veins that was her magic, at the center of her core, coming to life.

The familiar taste of bile rose, coating the back of her tongue, and she shook her head, and resumed spinning her Lacerator knives around her fingers as she walked to where Fiss was cloaked. She heard the telltale giggle before she was close to him this time, and the boy-like dreeocht dropped his magic for a moment and floated to the floor, where he clapped his hands.

"Fast! Faster! So fast! Moves like wind! Elli's powers are back?"

Ellinor stiffened at Fiss' words, and the dreeocht whimpered questioningly. Ellinor sighed, tucking the knives away. "No, Fiss. You know they aren't back. That's why we're off to see the Ashlings, so both of us can access my magic without it killing me, yeah?"

Fiss nodded his head emphatically, his cable and seaweed hair floating around his head on a phantom current, the pieces of shells along his hairline glittering with the action. "Elli is not allowed to die anymore. No. Nope, no more dying!"

Fiss uncoiled from the ground and launched himself at her. He wrapped his skinny arms around her neck, even the gold and silver wires and the bronze scales on his skin felt soft and warm against her metal parts. Ellinor allowed herself to smile, cupping the dreeocht's head in her hand, and held him close.

This? This was peace. Just a moment holding Fiss and basking in his perfect innocence. In his unfaltering belief that she was perfect, that there was nothing wrong or broken inside of her. With Fiss holding her, it was easier for Ellinor to believe the lie. She imagined that this must be what motherhood felt like, and for once, she didn't shrink back from the idea, now that Misho was gone.

She continued to hold Fiss, swaying gently, and Ellinor didn't mind the loss of personal space. The way Fiss said, "*Elli*" was almost exactly how Misho used to say it, which became a type of balm for her murderous heart. It tempered her desire to rush back and bury her Leviathan Roaster deep into Cosmin's heart, severing him from his magic, and succeeding in killing both the seersha gangster and herself in one go. She wouldn't call Fiss her reason for being—not yet; that felt too big, too permanent—but she did share the dreeocht's desire that she not die again so soon.

At least Cosmin can't get us on Amardeep.

For as much as the city-states and the governors who ran them loved to decry Ashlings, refusing to recognize the sentient androids as a true species, they were not all that strict on limiting access to the atoll to the north of Erhard, with one unyielding exception: Casters were not allowed. It was the one hard law every government agreed upon toward Amardeep. Powerful casters were forbidden on the atoll lest their power be used to give rise to a stronger breed of Ashling.

The creaking thud of footsteps overhead forced Ellinor to release Fiss, her head swiveling to track the progress of the person above them. She glanced at Fiss, hovering in front of her grinning, his blueish lips pulled back, exposing his little white teeth. The smile she returned was shakier than she had intended.

"Okay, baby bug, time to play our silent hide-and-seek game. No hints, now. You ready?"

Fiss tittered, spinning in the air. "Oh! Yes! Find me, find me!"

The air rippled around the dreeocht briefly before he vanished, and Ellinor's collar began burning and itching beneath her skin once more. She rubbed at her shoulder and neck, tracking the steps until they paused over the hatch. They waited too long before moving, and Ellinor knew whoever was there was planning to come down. She removed her knives once more, leaving her double-barreled pistols holstered, not wanting unnecessary noise if it came to violence.

The hatch opened and Ellinor moved like a wraith, heart pounding, hiding herself in the shadows created by the steel door rising. She shifted her footing and held her knives at the ready, her breathing shallow to keep from being detected.

The silhouette of a lithe figure darkened the narrow ladder before it was illuminated by the dim, yellow light of the lower deck. Ellinor breathed out a long sigh and moved from her hiding spot. There was no need to defend herself from Jelani Tyrik Sharma. Not anymore. She was still leery of the Ashling sympathizer and Creature Breaker, as he had hidden his true intentions for helping her and her team escape Cosmin and Zabel, but it seemed he had changed and she was finding it harder and harder to muster the energy to keep her walls up around him.

He stood at the base of the ladder and closed the hatch door with one hand. His deep blue eyes, their silver and light blue flecks glimmering even in the murky light, locked onto her. He jerked his head, flipping his hair off his forehead, but remained silent.

When he made no further move, she narrowed her eyes at him. "What is it now?"

At her words, Fiss dropped his invisibility, either forgetting the game or deciding it was over because Jelani was there. He smiled as he flew into Jelani's open arms. Jelani grinned down at the little dreeocht, before Fiss climbed up on his shoulders and tangled his hands into Jelani's soft, silver-white hair. His locks reminded Ellinor of fog rolling in off the bay. Jelani didn't answer her though, and Ellinor sighed, slumping against the chilly carbon-fiber wall.

"Let me guess then, yeah? This Aylen woman still hasn't answered your messages?" Ellinor studied Jelani as he pressed his lips together, his dusky brown-grey skin flushing. Ellinor sighed and rubbed her forehead. "We're dead in the water, aren't we? What did you do to this woman? Break her heart or something?"

Jelani scoffed and shook his head. "Don't be melodramatic. She's being cautious, but I'm unsure as to why. That has me nervous, nothing more. You don't need to worry about Aylen. She'll help us."

"You have *no one* else you can contact on Amardeep? Literally *anyone else* would be good at this point. There has to be another cyborg-type who owes you a favor? It's been six days, Jelani. Six! She didn't answer you on the pod to Desta to help us find this piece-of-shit ferry. You got fuck-all from her, even when you used Captain Anton's secured lines to send a message. We need another plan."

Jelani tussled Fiss' hair, breaking eye contact with Ellinor at last. "Aylen is the only one we can trust here. She's who we need, Ellinor. She's a humani mechanic first and foremost. Believe me, if there was another I could trust with your affliction and Fiss' existence, I would. I'd have sent them a message as soon as we got to Desta, while we waited for Kai to have his injuries tended to, or while his mother went into hiding with your parents. But there is no one else to contact. Have faith. Aylen will come through."

"Don't color me convinced. But since we have no other choice, apparently, we won't bail ship just yet. Your captain is still on the straight to get us to the Emporium Sanitorium, yeah?"

Jelani nodded, but his face didn't relax, the muscle in his strong jaw twitching. She wondered if, given his limited earth caster abilities, being out on the open ocean bothered him for different reasons than it did her, and she momentarily kicked herself for not considering such things sooner.

He drummed his fingers along the hilts of his—legal—Leviathan Roaster swords, the ones that all Creature Breakers used to disrupt and destroy magical creatures created by powerful casters. The governing bodies of Erhard controlled which types of weapons and defense mechanisms could harness magic, and Jelani's swords made the cut. Ellinor's did not, being too small and compact, and, holding so much magic, they were considered inhumane. It's what made illegal magitech such a commodity, and a lucrative market for people like Cosmin to exploit.

"Has Oihana briefed you? About the Emporium? It can be . . . overwhelming if you don't know what to expect," he asked, his voice soft.

Ellinor narrowed her gaze, suspecting this wasn't what was actually troubling Jelani, but he was clearly grasping for a way to shift the topic away from his own worry. She blew out a breath. Fiss tilted his head at her before climbing off Jelani and floating to rest on the top rung of the ladder where he played at creating a tiny purple and blue fish to entertain himself.

"You make it sound like a war zone. Needing to be briefed on an Ashling mall," Ellinor grumbled, rolling her eyes.

"Your ignorance is astounding," Jelani said, humor tickling his deep voice, eyes crinkled at the edges, removing the barb from his words. Ellinor's cheeks flushed regardless, and Jelani glanced away once more. "Amardeep is more of a syndicate than the governing bodies you're used to. One person—"

"You mean one *Ashling*. Don't compare those things to people."

Jelani's face darkened. "You can't say things like that in Amardeep. In fact, you should stop saying them period. Have you learned nothing? Ashlings are *alive*. If you wish to enlist zeyr aid in removing your collar, you have to believe that, Ellinor, or you might as well head back to Erhard and try your luck with hiding from Cosmin for the rest of your days. Powerless."

Ellinor's lip twitched into a sneer, fingers closing over her Lacerator hilts, wanting to give her hands a distraction. Jelani's shoulders slumped marginally, and he rubbed at the back of his neck. "Most of Amardeep isn't run by Ashlings. In fact, very few places are, or if so, an ally of the Ashlings functions as the face of the business, keeping suspicion and hatred from the mainland off zeyr products. Keeping tourism high. Ashlings still have little to no say in zeyr governing, nearly no actual power or rights, even in the corporatocracy that is Amardeep."

She swallowed the tightness in her throat. "Fine. I'll say whatever makes the bots happy, okay? Doesn't mean I have to believe it."

Jelani's gaze hardened, as if he were fighting back harsher words. "As I was saying," he said, words clipped, "one *person* runs each organized area. They make the laws, they decide what can and can't happen within their establishment. If you fail to adhere to their rules, they also have complete authority over what your punishment will be. Each business is separate from the next; their rules and laws don't impact each other. So, you'll have to be aware of each organization's customs as we move throughout Amardeep. But calling the Emporium a mall is like calling Euria a slum. Partially true, but mostly false, and insulting in either case."

Ellinor raised an eyebrow at him, leaning forward slightly with interest. Fiss, however, remained completely oblivious to their conversation, amusing himself with his little magical fish. Jelani blew out a breath, scrubbing a hand over his face. "This would be much easier if Oihana had done as I asked."

"Don't blame your sister," Ellinor said. "She likes to sit out on deck with Kai, and since I can't leave the bowels of the ship . . ." Ellinor shrugged, and Jelani's posture softened, as if he wanted to move, bridge the distance, but he remained where he was.

"Fair enough. Well, outside of being the only place to dock without a pass, the Emporium sells only illegal substances. Illegal magitech, of course, but mainly Juice Boxes. That's primarily what you find there—Juice addicts and dealers, all too happy to push their product. Then there are the requisite information droids and Ashlings, of course, all happily willing to escort you to zeyr . . . *establishments.*"

Ellinor's face twisted in disgust. Juice Boxes weren't a huge export in Euria anymore. Stings happened occasionally, like the one that claimed her brother's life, but it was still relatively small compared to the traffic in other city-states. The substances made it into the city, of course, but that wasn't Cosmin's trade, and the caster worked hard to keep non-magic types from ever thinking, even for a moment, that they could harness and cast magic. Even in a drugged state. Ellinor had never had to deal with Juice addicts or their peddlers, the way Andrey had.

Juice Boxes looked just like their namesake. Their original manufacturers were not clever in that regard. But instead of being full of enough sugar to keep someone awake for a year, they were laced with used magitech nanites.

The nanites carried residual magic, giving each of the Juice Boxes a different kind of *flavor.* It ignited the blood and made the user feel invincible, in a constant euphoric state, or, as some non-casters claimed, let them experience what it would feel like to have magic course through their bodies. Juice Boxes were hard to make, but the Ashlings seemed to have a talent for it; distilling the depleted nanites and making them into something organic beings could consume took a level of technical expertise that few mechanics cared to master. But, Ellinor supposed, it was an easy thing for a robot to give the stuff to a person; zey didn't care how easy it was to get addicted to the product.

Ellinor had never been tempted to try a Juice Box, especially after what had happened to her older brother, but with the cold, hollow feeling in her bones and soul, the emptiness spreading throughout her body where once her air magic dwelled . . .

Jelani frowned, no doubt sensing her thoughts via his infallible gut feeling. "Juice Boxes will not connect you to your magic. You know this." His voice was soft in a way that made the hair on her arms stand on end.

"Magic? Are we eating magic?" Fiss said, releasing his fish and saving Ellinor from having to lie, and deny the accusation Jelani had tossed at her.

"No, Fiss. We won't be eating magic. We—you can't cast like you did with Zabel, remember? It hurts, and it could attract unwanted attention," Ellinor said patiently, ignoring the pointed look Jelani leveled at her.

Jelani didn't have a chance to voice a comeback, as the heavy tread of someone stomped overhead. Jelani tensed, gently snatching Fiss and pushing him toward Ellinor, who then moved the dreeocht safely behind her. He turned, squaring his stance, as if that would block Fiss and Ellinor from view, as the hatch over the ladder banged open.

Down waddled IAA-43—or Izza. The Ashling turned toward them, not as steady on the ship as zer was on land. "Mr Kai and Ms Oihana request your presence above deck, Mr Jelani, Ms Ellinor."

Jelani and Ellinor frowned in unison. "You missing a screw, Izza? I'm not allowed up there. Only Anton knows I'm here," Ellinor growled at the android, still uncomfortable in the machine's presence.

"No, Ms Ellinor. I am perfectly complete. Nothing is wrong with me, no matter how much you seem to wish it were otherwise." Izza shifted zer arms, and a copper wire peaked out from the silver elbow joint, the only indication that zer was a machine and not an organic in a silver, metallic body suit. "I understand the restrictions surrounding you being allowed on deck, Ms Ellinor. But Ms Oihana informs me that precaution is no longer necessary."

A chill ran down Ellinor's spine, and Jelani took a step closer to the bot. His voice kept low, he said, "Izza, clarify."

"We have been found, Mr Jelani."

AGAIN, BUT BETTER

E LLINOR EXPLODED out of the hold, her eyes wide as she scanned the deck.

"Kai!" she shouted. Nothing but chaos greeted her.

The crew was running, men and women sprinting from the prow of the ship to disappear below decks. Guard bots bounced around the area, the thud of zeyr heavy bodies on the carbon-fiber deck drowned out by the cacophony of shouts. Crewmen were giving conflicting orders, no one quite sure what to do.

But what's happening? And where is Kai?

If a new crew of Cosmin's had caught up to them, or Zabel's henchmen, or perhaps even someone from Amaru looking to avenge the embarrassment Dragan Voclain must be feeling after losing Ellinor, she couldn't say. But given the crew running around, looking for weapons, yelling at each other to get out of the way, and the vacant horizon greeting them, Ellinor didn't think a caster was hot on their trail.

The ship vibrated beneath Ellinor's boots; the nine-person crew slid around the deck—those that hadn't latched on to something fast enough. The three guard androids on deck were quick to keep the crew from falling overboard to be lost to the poisoned sea below. Ellinor might not know much about boats or sailing, but she knew that Anton's ferry should not be shuddering the way it was. The ship lurched and stuttered forward like there was something trying to grab ahold of their vessel, only for the boat to jerk away from the grasp.

"Kai! Azer's balls, where are you?" she yelled again, ignoring the distressed whimpers of Fiss as he clung to her back, invisible to the rest of the crew. She couldn't see her friend anywhere. Fear gripped Ellinor's gut and she staggered for the railing, checking for Kai's bright hair bobbing in the ocean below.

Jelani materialized at her side, Izza just behind him. The seersha's eyes were wide and frantic, but he did not yell for his sister the way Ellinor called for Kai. Oihana Sharma was deaf and wouldn't have heard them.

A flash of silver caught Ellinor's eye and she whipped around. There, stomping across the deck in his bulky Coyote mechanized suit was Kai Axel Brantley, Oihana scampering behind him. Ellinor ran to him, the fist around her heart releasing at the sight of his face. She skidded to a halt before crashing into him and stopped herself from trying to hug him in his bulky armor. He grinned down at her, winking at the relief flooding her eyes.

She shoved him in the chest when he didn't look nearly as worried as she did. "What the fuck, Kai? What's happening?"

Kai's smile slipped, the black biotech tooth that would alert him to poison disappearing behind his lips, his green eyes going distant as he glanced over his shoulder. The sun's bright rays caught in his red and acid green streaked hair, almost blinding Ellinor, who was not accustomed to bright light after being below decks for days.

"Ah, well," Kai said slowly, his eyes darting from one crew member to the next as they hauled weaponry and nets out on deck. "Looks like that Captain Anton wasn't exactly truthful 'bout them dampeners he 'ad. Seems like a doehaz picked up our, well, more likely the kid's scent."

Ellinor's gut sank. "Tell me Captain Anton has something to defend this ferry with at least, yeah?" her voice squeaked, betraying her trepidation.

Kai shrugged, not nearly as concerned as Ellinor thought he should be, given the circumstances. "He says he does, but that don't mean much, I reckon."

Ellinor swallowed the rancid taste crawling up her throat and jerked one of her Dunstan Anaconda pistols out. Fiss still whined on her back, more nervous about the fact that Ellinor was scared than over the doehaz.

Jelani grabbed Oihana by her shoulders. Her big, golden-amber eyes fell to his lips as he spoke. "Are they certain it's a doehaz?"

Oihana rolled her eyes and pried her brother's fingers off her. She tossed her rich, deep brown hair off her shoulders, annoyed more by the potential delay than what manner of doehaz may appear. "Captain Anton's radar was clear. It's a doehaz. Should be fun, right?"

Kai guffawed and clapped Oihana on the shoulder, making the onyx freckles on her dusky cheeks stand out with her blush. "A girl after my own heart!"

Jelani frowned at Kai before turning his attention back to Oihana. "Take Fiss below deck. And don't come out. Let us deal with the doehaz." Oihana looked about to protest, but Jelani's lips pinched into a thin line, and his eyebrows knit together, pleading with her silently.

Oihana sighed. "You're zero fun, Anni. I wanted to record a doehaz in action. Analyze the tech. It could've been useful." Jelani leveled a pointed look at his little half-sister, and she threw up her hands in exasperation. "Fine. Let's go, Fiss. I'll teach you a new game."

"Game? What do we play, little Jelly?" Fiss said, beaming at Oihana.

Ellinor had tried to explain what siblings were to Fiss when they picked up Oihana from her hidden compound. Since then, he delighted in calling Oihana "little Jelly". Oihana usually pretended to be annoyed by this, but it was no secret she thought it was adorable—but only when Fiss said it.

"I'm going to teach you how to hack into someone's tablet communicator. Come on, I'll race you below deck!" And with that, Oihana darted for the hatch to the lower levels, skirting the crew and androids who were racing to prepare the ferry for a doehaz attack. Oihana may have been a brilliant seerani mechanic, but she was just growing out of being a teenager—twenty-five years old—by seerani standards. As much as she liked to show a mature side, she was still a child at heart.

Fiss, despite his obvious curiosity and excitement, hesitated. Ellinor gently pushed him after Oihana. "It's all right, baby bug. Let Oihana show you how to be a proper mechanic for a minute, yeah?"

Fiss beamed. "Okay! I miss you already!" he tittered, floating after Oihana, and ignored by the frantic crew.

Izza waddled after them, and Ellinor thumbed on her armor's power, activating her morphing shield at the same time. Turning her gaze to Kai, she said, "Where's Captain Anton?"

Kai jerked a thumb over his shoulder. He turned and pushed past the android who was scanning the choppy ocean with its shoulder mounted turret, leading them to Anton. They skirted a woman who was dragging a crate of ammunition up from the second cargo hold above where Ellinor had been hiding, and barely avoided another crew member who was passing out flotation devices to the remaining eight organic crew.

Jelani threw the door open on the helm of the ship, startling Anton. The diminutive captain reminded Ellinor of an air-duct squirrel, small and quick, with a sneaky glint to his dark blue eyes. He whipped his head around, blonde braid flying as Ellinor and Jelani strode into his office, Kai just behind them.

Anton had been hunched over the radar; the throttle of the ferry pushed as far forward as possible. Ellinor glanced from the man to the steering console; her back tensed suddenly at the large blip that was quickly approaching from the depths of the toxic ocean. Even with their vessel moving at top speed, it would only be a matter of minutes before the doehaz overtook them.

"Anton," Jelani all but growled at the man, "you assured me your dampener was state of the art. That it would hide the precious cargo I was accompanying. That's what I paid you for, remember? Did you lie to me?"

Anton returned Jelani's fury with a glare of his own. "I didn't fucking lie, mate. My dampener's the best there is outside those fancy military tankers your lot couldn't take. But your *cargo* bleeds magic like a severed artery. Only so much masking my scrambler can do. I warned you lot of the danger."

Jelani's jaw twitched and he looked about ready to argue further or, preferably, throttle the little man. Ellinor didn't blame him. Jelani had taken a risk putting his little sister on the same vessel as Fiss across dangerous waters, and all the favors he called in and the credits he threw at Anton still wasn't enough to ensure her safety.

Taking a step between the two of them, Ellinor jabbed her finger in Anton's chest. "We'll discuss that later. Right now the only words I want to hear need to be about weapons and a plan to survive."

Anton narrowed his eyes at Ellinor, but as Kai shifted closer to the door, his bulky frame making a shadow fall over the captain, he sighed and tossed his long braid over his shoulder. "'Course I got weapons and the like. It's a requirement in my line of work. But its stuff suited for them government types and drug smugglers who think I got what they want on board. I don't have much that can do a lick of good against a doehaz of that size," he said, pointing at the radar. "You want a plan of attack, mate? Get your lot out there and prepare yourselves for a fight, unless you'd rather get eaten." When Ellinor's frown deepened, Anton snorted. "Didn't think so. Now, if you don't mind, I'm going to make sure my girl's armed and ready for when that monster surfaces."

Jelani was the first to leave, returning to deck with his Leviathan Roaster swords humming in his hands. He hadn't fully turned the devices on; without knowing what exactly was approaching, it wouldn't help to prepare for melee if shooting the doehaz would serve better. Still, the seersha looked more annoyed than frightened.

"You doing okay, big guy?" Ellinor whispered to Kai, who had his dark green eyes locked on the rolling ocean surface.

Kai shrugged, his gaze unfocused and his thoughts on something other than the doehaz beneath their feet. "Sure, boss," Kai mumbled. "Just thinking 'bout my ma, is all. Didn't exactly get to say no proper goodbye, did I."

Ellinor nodded, her heart twisting in her chest. They had done their best from afar to get Kai's mother out of Euria as they fled, hoping to secret her away before Cosmin could use her as a means of getting at Kai. They had managed to get her tucked away in the smaller city-state of Desta where Ellinor's own parents lived, but neither were convinced she had gotten out cleanly.

Ellinor didn't wish to lose Kai to worries about his mother, at least not at the moment. As Jelani fiddled with his Creature Breaker blades, the tattoo on his back faintly glowing through his reinforced black combat shirt, Ellinor bumped Kai's shoulder—she would have squeezed his hand, but with his gauntlets on, he would have never felt the action.

"Good thing Oihana was able to replenish those dirty grenades Talin had left us, huh?" Ellinor handed a belt of grenades to Kai, these much more refined in appearance than the ones Talin had cobbled together before Ellinor, Kai, and Jelani had headed into the Saxa Desert. Their function was still the same, however: a shrapnel grenade that didn't have an ounce of smart tech or magitech in it so as to damage a doehaz without accidentally feeding the monster. "You ready to pop some doehaz?"

A smirk tugged at the corner of Kai's lips. "Same plan as before, aye? Was shit then, is shit now, boss, but fuck yeah. I'm down."

"I propose we let *that* take the brunt of the fighting this time," Jelani interrupted, pointing toward a pair of turrets four of Anton's men were rolling out on deck.

She wasn't sure how much bullets would affect the doehaz, especially if it were more metal than flesh. But given how large the blip was on Anton's radar, Ellinor wasn't especially eager to be up close and personal with the beast.

The trio of guard androids positioned themselves around the big guns, and the remaining crew armed themselves with pulse spears and barbed, electric nets. As if in answer, the hull of the ship began vibrating once again. A wave of pressure rocked the vessel, heralding the arrival of the beast.

The doehaz wasn't as big as Ellinor was expecting.

The beast roared into the sky, looking like an octopus, but instead of eight fleshy tentacles, it had five, stone, spider-like legs. Its round mouth opened wide, showing a maw of teeth made of broken crowbars and knives.

The rapid *pop* of the turrets as the crew opened fire on the beast—which was barely larger than the ferry—focused the doehaz's attention on their vessel. Its robotic eyes shifted like a camera lens, faintly glowing red as it fixated on Ellinor and Jelani, the only sources of magic it could readily see.

Anton kept the ship moving as fast as possible away from the doehaz, but it didn't matter. Whatever part of the beast that lay hidden beneath the waves was easily keeping pace with their ferry.

The turrets chipped pieces of stone out of the doehaz's exoskeleton with each successful hit, but otherwise were doing little damage. As the six crew members with guns opened fire beside the turrets, the doehaz roared again, tentacles flailing. The sound was like dozens of backfiring engines all going off at once, slightly out of sync from one another.

With its maw opened wide, Kai lobbed one of the shrapnel grenade belts high into the air. With his Coyote mechanized suit fully powered, the grenade's trajectory was true. The doehaz's roar was abruptly cut off as it swallowed the projectile.

With a muffled *BOOM*, the doehaz inflated slightly as the grenade went off, but it didn't explode like the beasts in the Saxa Desert had. Instead, the outer stone layer shuddered off the beast, revealing a swirling, emissive green vortex twisting and curling along a collection of white bones meshed together with steel wires that served as the doehaz's ribcage. The crew shifted aim, firing into the glowing mist that emanated from the core of the monster. Their bullets disintegrated without inflicting any damage.

"Fuck me," Ellinor whispered, easing her finger off her own pistols' triggers, heart racing. She and Jelani took a step back, bumping into Kai, who was thumbing through the options on his wrist guard, frantically looking for something in his arsenal that might damage the monster.

The doehaz was bearing down on them. The ship started vibrating again, rattling so hard Ellinor thought its siding would shudder off. It slammed one of its tentacles into the water just next to the ship, barely missing the railing. The boat pitched. Screaming filled the air. If it weren't for Kai holding on to her, and the magnetic components in his boots, Ellinor would have been tossed overboard.

Two of the crew were not so lucky. The ship pitched again, jostling the mobile turret, which skidded into the men and pushed them overboard. Ellinor never saw them resurface.

Jelani raced for the turret, helping the remaining gunman push it back into position before he peppered the doehaz with bullets once more. Jelani snatched the electric barbed net from a terrified woman whose eyes were locked on the place where her crewmates had disappeared, and ran back to Kai. "Toss it, Kai. Maybe we can tangle the thing."

As Kai took the net, Ellinor gripped her useless pistols all the tighter, desperately searching her soul for the magic somewhere within. If Ellinor could only access her magic, she would use the wind to push the ferry farther, faster, creating much needed distance between their ship and the beast. But without it, all she was left with was a crushing uselessness compounded by the terror that raced through her veins.

Spinning the net over his head, Kai launched it at the octopus-like doehaz. The net tangled itself around the creature's face, and it shook its head, roaring in frustration as the electric barbs snagged on its cheek and eyelids. But it did not slow. If anything, the net annoyed the beast even more, urging it closer, faster.

The beast raised its tentacles, ready to slam them back down on the ferry, when Anton poked his head out from the helm. "Brace yourselves, mates! There's—" But his words were abruptly cut off by the sound of rushing water.

Ellinor dropped her pistols.

Cresting behind the first doehaz was another, three times the size. It looked like a decaying whale combined with a mechanical crab. Its white body glistened with the yellow sludge of the ocean floor. Sound seemed to cease, though the flashes of the turret's muzzle told Ellinor she was perhaps the only one paralyzed with fear. Her vision narrowed, blurred at the edges, and her limbs shook. Her breath stuck in her chest, and all she wanted was to flee, to fly far, far away. But she was unable to do anything.

The sky darkened behind the new doehaz, clouds seeming to appear from nowhere, lightning sparking, pinging against the larger beast. The electricity from the lightning should have immobilized the creature, but instead it seemed to inflate, becoming even more menacing. Ellinor's hands flexed instinctively, trying to cast magic she no longer had access to. Her collar scorched her skin in her desperation to do *something*. A throbbing cramp in her chest made her heart beat painfully out of time.

Looming behind the momentarily oblivious smaller doehaz, the larger beast's lips pulled back in a snarl that sent a shiver racing down the back of Ellinor's legs. She jerked into motion and, as she dove for cover, the clouds dispersed at the same time, and briefly Ellinor wondered if that, too, had been the doehaz's doing.

The doehaz appeared to be smiling with its broken, bloody teeth. In chilling silence, it launched itself at the smaller doehaz, determined to destroy the competition so it could snack on the magic unmolested.

As both beasts disappeared beneath the surface, their ship was propelled forward on the waves caused by their struggle. Ellinor lost her balance behind the bench she was crouched against. She slipped across the slick deck, fingers scrambling for purchase, and instead latched onto the butt of her double-barreled pistols before rolling toward the railing.

Kai grabbed her leg, keeping her from careening over the side. He hauled her back and steadied her next to Jelani as he prepared his rifle. Ellinor mouthed a thanks to Kai, her throat too constricted to speak.

The remaining seven crew members waited, muscles coiled, preparing to spring back into action. The three automatas' scanners roved the surface searching once more for a target. Everyone's eyes were locked on the surface of the ocean, which continued to churn with a frothy white and yellow film. Anton pushed his ferry to its limits, and then faster still, but the doehaz didn't reappear. She saw Kai's shoulders relax, and he opened his mouth to speak, but Ellinor was quick to cover it with her hand.

He arched a brow at her, and Ellinor frowned. "Remember what Pema and Talin said about jinxes? And what happened last time you said we were in the clear? Don't jinx us, Kai."

Kai rolled his eyes, and she released him, but her precaution had been unnecessary.

The larger doehaz erupted from the water. It reared its head, opening its maw once again in a silent challenge. It moved faster than the original doehaz, cutting through the water like liquid steel. The crew peppered it with bullets, and Ellinor wished she had brought her mechanical crossbow up with her so she could skewer the beast with something larger, more devastating than her electric ammunition.

Unlike the smaller, octopus-like doehaz, the crew's bullets at least seemed to annoy the beast, slowing it momentarily as large chunks of rancid flesh were blown off. Then the beast abruptly stopped, as if its tail had been caught in a trap. The crew kept firing, the distance between them and the monster growing, when the doehaz was jerked beneath the waves.

Fear of what lurked unseen below kept Ellinor rooted on the deck. Jelani placed a hand on her shoulder, his Leviathan Roasters sheathed. His Zifu Raven combat rifle was cradled in his free hand, the muzzle smoking. He didn't speak. They watched the surface of the water silently as it foamed and bubbled, the tail of the white doehaz occasionally snapping out over the water as it fought whatever third doehaz must have appeared to devour the casters and dreeocht aboard Anton's ship.

The behemoths continued to fight. Both, apparently, equally matched, though Ellinor never saw the new beast. As the jagged cliffs of Amardeep's shores finally appeared in the distance, Ellinor decided she didn't need visions of even more monsters to plague her dreams.

NOT THE NEWS YOU'RE
HOPING FOR

ELLINOR STOOD stiffly on the deck of the ship. Her fingers were tight on the railing with her eyes darting back and forth between where the doehaz disappeared, and the glowing blue-green fog that shrouded Amardeep. Ellinor breathed deeply, trying to ease the soreness in her chest left from the painful cramps she had suffered earlier.

That was where Oihana found her.

The seerani bit her lip as she approached, trying to look casual while she made sure Ellinor was alone—well, alone except for Fiss.

Ellinor knew Fiss was nearby even though she couldn't see him. The persistent sunburnt sensation where her metal pieces connected intensified the closer Oihana got, alerting Ellinor to Fiss' casting as the little dreeocht hovered closer as well.

"So, hey, did you get hit or something when those doehaz were chasing us?" Oihana asked, not looking Ellinor in the eye.

Instead her eyes shifted from Ellinor's lips to Izza, who approached from across the deck.

When Oihana's gaze settled back on her, Ellinor shook her head. Oihana's brows furrowed, and her heart started to race anew.

"Huh, well then," Oihana mumbled, her deep voice barely above a whisper. "Okay, so you were scared then? Things were tense?"

"Be serious, Oihana," Ellinor snapped. "We had three doehaz trailing us. *Three*. One of the monsters almost snapped the ferry in half and two of Anton's people were lost overboard! Of course things were tense. Of course I was scared. I was almost eaten by a doehaz not that long ago, remember?" Ellinor took a deep breath, willing her heart to stop racing. "What's going on?"

Fiss made a whimpering noise nearby, and Ellinor spotted where he was hiding by a stray spark that flashed off his otherwise invisible body. She frowned and Oihana waved her comment away. "First, tell me—and be honest. Have you noticed your magic shackle acting funny at all? Weird sensations? New patches? Anything like that?"

Ellinor felt the color drain from her face. Her body went cold despite the hot sting along her bio-magitech, and her hands began to tremble. "Why do you ask? What's this about?"

Oihana winced and rubbed her temples, once more checking that no one was nearby. She didn't answer Ellinor though. Instead she turned to Izza with a pleading look in her golden eyes. Ellinor didn't know how the Ashling was able to read Oihana's expression, but zer did. With zers metal hands clasped behind zers back, Izza dipped zers head, and turned to Ellinor.

"Because, Ms Ellinor, little Fiss had a strong, adverse reaction whilst below decks with Ms Oihana. He was trembling, afraid, frantic to find you. He displayed symptoms aligned with being physically hurt. He displayed a heightened sense of anxiety, unheard of for his kind. His hands were moving as if he were casting magic, but we could detect nothing below deck that would provoke him to such a display." Izza paused, grey, ocular orbs not blinking as zer analyzed the reactions on Ellinor's face.

Izza's voice-box was soothing, a gentle tenor, one suited for nurse bots, and zer used the full capabilities of zers comforting tones on Ellinor now. "You know little Fiss should not have felt such sympathetic alarm, Ms Ellinor. We, that is, Ms Oihana and I, hypothesize that the malfunction in your magical shackle has infiltrated a deep, subconscious level within you, possibly at the psychic point where little Fiss is connected to you. Simply put, you are both experiencing a feedback loop of sorts. He felt your terror when he should not have, and the more he casts, the more pain you experience. Little Fiss was not capable of processing such information. Dreeocht were not made to feel any negative emotion, as you know, Ms Ellinor."

Ellinor's hands were still trembling, Izza's soothing tone doing nothing to assuage her worries in any capacity. "The electrical storm . . ." she murmured. "It *was* magic. It was feeding the doehaz. That's why it didn't hurt the stupid thing. I thought the doehaz was manifesting it."

A whirring sound, like an old lens focusing, came from Izza as zer leaned closer, hands still clasped behind zers silver body, and Ellinor swore the Ashling was curious, though zers metallic face remained impassive. "I wouldn't presume to usurp valuable time from your reverie, Ms Ellinor, but details are crucial at this juncture."

It was difficult for Ellinor to make sense of Izza and zers personality. She hadn't spent much time with the Ashling before going into hiding below decks. But the bot seemed to share Oihana's insatiable curiosity, though zer seemed to possess all the politeness Oihana lacked, mingled with a type of sass that reminded her of Jelani.

Ellinor's eyes slid from Oihana's sharp gaze and settled on where Fiss was cloaked, the magic rippling around him as his agitation slowly ebbed away. "I don't know," she whispered. "When the second doehaz popped up, I panicked and just . . . froze, I guess. Then the sky darkened. A sudden storm appeared. Lightning peeled from the clouds and struck the doehaz, but it didn't react. I thought the energy must have been tied to the doehaz somehow. That its hunger for eating *us* manifested in an electrical storm or something. But it sounds like that may have been the magic Fiss was casting, yeah? Since the bigger doehaz seemed to enjoy getting hit with the lightning. The magic in the storm must have fueled it somehow."

Ellinor crouched near where Fiss was, extending a hand. "Did you make a storm to protect me, baby bug?" Fiss cooed from nearby, brushing her hand with his fuzzy fingertips but staying hidden, still unsure, even though Ellinor was safe.

"That aligns with what we experienced below," Izza confirmed. "Little Fiss cast destructive magic without your instruction, Ms Ellinor."

Ellinor stood, peering at Izza closely, sure she could detect a hint of awe in zers soothing voice. "How?" she squeaked. Both Izza and Oihana remained mute, only the quivering hum of

Fiss nearby broke the silence. Ellinor asked again, "How is this possible? Can we stop it? The feedback loop, or whatever it is, I mean."

Oihana rubbed her temples again, before glancing down at her wrist tablet and shaking her head. "I scanned Fiss while we were down there. His tech doesn't give off readings like yours does, so I don't have an answer. Is it possible that your bio-magitech has synched up to his somehow? Yeah, sure, it's possible, but I can't confirm that. I don't know how or why your emotions started leeching into him. There's something in that collar that's gone super screwy, but I don't have the equipment to do a proper diagnostic test on it."

"What will this do to Fiss? The pain, I mean. Izza said he's not supposed to feel this negative crap. So what will happen the longer he does?"

"Me? What I feel, Elli? We are discussing me, me, me?" Fiss said, even though he knew to remain invisible, he hadn't quite grasped that he should also keep his voice down.

Ellinor tried to shush him casually. "Yeah, baby bug, we just want to make sure you don't experience anything bad."

"Yes," Fiss responded, his voice dark in a way that was disturbingly at odds with his otherwise high, little boy voice. "Don't want Ellinor to feel anything bad. Will stop the bad."

Ellinor stared at the spot where Fiss was, mouth agape as a shiver tickled her spine at the dark thrum in Fiss' voice. Oihana sighed, and finally answered, "Obviously nothing good is going to come from this feedback loop," she shrugged, "like I said, I don't have answers. But at least now I know that the weirdness you're feeling with your collar is connected to what happened below deck." Oihana paused, scrutinizing Ellinor more closely before nodding. "Yup, it's definitely spreading. Not good at all."

"Oihana, you are seriously not helping here."

Oihana frowned slightly. "Hey, that's why we're going to Amardeep, right? Now that we know the problem, we can fix it. That's what us mechanics are good at."

Ellinor couldn't find her voice to answer, and Oihana didn't wait for her to find it, either. Movement in the corner of her eye caught her attention, and she turned to see Kai approaching, a smile stretched across his burned and blistered face. Oihana grinned at the big man, and tugged Izza away with her to go join her big brother as he prepared their cargo for disembarking.

Kai stopped beside Ellinor, watching as a plastic bubble roof snapped into place above them, preparing to shield the crew from the noxious air that hovered over the atoll. He glanced away, eyes trailing over her neck and the new patches of technology that must have been obvious to him. Kai sucked in his lip, eyes full of a guilt and regret that was all too familiar to Ellinor now. She waved his concern away. "This wasn't your fault, big guy. You may have collared me, but what this thing is doing now? That's not on you."

Kai didn't look convinced, but he huffed and nodded. Ellinor realized that he mistook her stricken expression as her being in her own head, dwelling on the collar. And while that was partially true, it certainly wasn't the full story. When Ellinor didn't elaborate, he placed his big hand on her shoulder, squeezing gently. "Time to get back below deck, boss. Gotta prepare Fiss for docking so we can smuggle 'im out all secret like. Can't let 'em black market mechanics know about the kid or they could snatch him, forcing Fiss to make some crazy new Ashling."

Ellinor waved dismissively, her thoughts still lingering on Izza and Oihana's findings. "I know why we have to hide him, Kai."

When she didn't move, Kai nudged her toward the stairs that led back down to the bowels of the ship. Ellinor shuffled away automatically, her mind spinning. Fiss wrapped his arms around her neck as she descended and, for the first time since coming back from the dead, the action did not bring its usual comfort.

CALLING AYLEN

WITH ELLINOR'S collar behaving erratically, and with its adverse effect on Fiss, the group decided that the dreeocht continuing to use his magic to remain invisible was no longer an option. Especially not within the Emporium Sanitorium, where the cyborgs could potentially detect him anyway, bringing undue suspicion. He could attract those with an appetite to unshackle Ashlings or other smart droids to create a robotic army of their own, unheard of on the mainland, but a growing desire out here.

That was the thing about cyborgs, you never really knew what they could or couldn't do, particularly if they were excessively enhanced. Sure, most people had some sort of mechanical augmentation, but most were easy to see, and obvious about what their function was—like Kai's tooth. But there was a point where too much modification made someone a little too mechanical for Ellinor's comfort level. It's what made Amardeep a haven for cyborgs and Ashlings alike, however. All Ellinor's group could hope for was that with so many robotically enhanced people seeking shelter on Amardeep, Fiss would, oddly enough, blend right in.

They had dressed him in spare, nondescript black pants and a baggy dark green sweater, tying his seaweed and cable hair back and stuffing it under a large black sock-beanie that covered the shells along his hairline. Kai even found a pair of mechanic's gloves that would fit over his paw-like hands. Bundled and covered as he was, he didn't appear all that different from the cyborgs flooding Amardeep's mall—as long as they could keep him from floating at Ellinor's side or summoning up little magical creatures.

Ellinor kept her hand on Fiss' head as she surveyed the crowds just beyond Anton's ferry. Meanwhile, Kai and Izza were seeing to the gear they had managed to smuggle out of Erhard, and Jelani and Oihana had stepped a little back from the bustling main thoroughfares in order to try and contact Aylen Bonheur in private one more time. Fiss nuzzled his head into Ellinor's hand before tugging himself up into her arms, snuggling closer into her chest. She clutched him tighter, taking comfort in his embrace and relishing the feeling of his little body in her arms.

The ebb and flow of bodies never ceased; a river of machines and flesh curving around invisible currents where one false step would sweep her away from her friends, never to be seen again. Given the toxicity of the Ashlings' atoll, the sheer number of people who managed to get to the island and make it a home was truly impressive. The vast numbers in the Emporium Sanitorium had the steel coil in Ellinor's chest unraveling slightly; she always felt safest in the anonymity large crowds afforded her.

Still, Ellinor was worried that every passerby could see through Fiss' flimsy disguise, could feel the magic waft off Fiss like too much cheap cologne in a cramped elevator.

With her free hand, Ellinor fastened the mask of her armor within its hood, trying to shield her identity as much as possible. They were still in the main arrivals section of the docking area, Kai and Izza taking turns disappearing back onto Anton's illegal ferry, making sure the remaining crew hadn't nicked any of their things. Jelani and Oihana were still by the communication ports near the ship, their faces pinched, looking like they were arguing with one another. Her stomach tightened at the sight, but she shook her head. They weren't who Ellinor needed to watch at the moment.

Once she was sure her identity was partially obscured, she squared her stance, trying to look sinister enough to keep people away from her distracted friends. Her hand ran lazy circles over Fiss' back in a comforting movement as her eyes narrowed on every person who even momentarily slowed near their group, but none threw more than a cursory glance in their direction.

Most of the permanent dwellers of Amardeep were either seerani—half-humani and half-seersha types like Oihana—with so many mechanical augmentations they might as well be androids themselves, or Ashlings who did zeyr best to appear more like organic people with outlandish clothing. One service android, who was wearing a ballgown zey had modified to fit over zeyr square shaped, stout body, strolled in conversation with a guard automata Ashling with a stringy green wig and covered in body glitter better suited for a ground level rave back on Euria. Ellinor scoffed at the sight, taking a step back to stand by the crate of weapons Kai took off the ferry. She didn't know how Ashlings could ever think such outfits made zem blend in; if nothing else, it made the Ashlings stand out more.

But none more so than Izza.

Each time Izza emerged from Anton's ship, the nearby Ashlings stared at zer, waving clawed appendages in zers direction. If possible, Izza appeared to stiffen each time attention was aimed zers way, and zer scuttled back to the ferry with more urgency. Even though Ashlings of all types, wearing all manner of odd attire, were common on Amardeep, Izza was unique. It was illegal for robots to look like people back on the mainland. Ellinor wasn't sure if Amardeep's Ashlings were trying to birth Ashlings from scratch, but if so, would zey create a new breed of Ashling that appeared organic? Oihana had defied every law Ellinor knew of when the seerani had first fashioned Izza, and Ellinor wondered if that would make the young mechanic a celebrity of sorts on Amardeep, even if it meant she could be tried and executed on the mainland.

Ellinor made a note to ask Izza about that, and whether it would be prudent to hide zer, like they were trying to disguise Fiss.

Fiss tittered in her arms, focusing her attention again as he pointed at a group of cyborg humanis and seeranis giggling and stumbling about, their eyes bloodshot, pupils dilated, and a fine layer of sweat collecting on their faces. Ellinor made a disgusted noise deep in her throat, startling the rich tourists who gaped at her momentarily, their fingers twitching as if magic were dancing over them.

"Juice addicts," she murmured. Fiss tilted his head at the unfamiliar word, stalling Kai, who had stopped to see what Fiss was staring at.

Kai shrugged, undisturbed by their presence. He glanced at Ellinor, who stood unmoving, glaring at the tourists high on some unknown flavor of Juice Box, until they stumbled away again. "You gonna stand around glaring at everybody, or you actually gonna 'elp me get our shit, boss?"

"You look like you have it handled, big guy. Besides, one of us has to play lookout while Jelani and Oihana try to get ahold of Aylen."

Kai grumbled then stopped abruptly, eyeing a seerani man who had long, matte-black hair, suspiciously similar to Cosmin's. Kai's gaze became glassy, watching the man as he went by, his arm draped around the waist of a wide-eyed humani woman. Kai's lips trembled slightly, his hand drifting up to the puckered, healing blisters on his face from Cosmin's magic. Kai's throat bobbed, as if he were swallowing his heart. Ellinor's own heart clenched at the sight.

She reached out to grasp Kai's hand, but he jerked away. "Don't, Ell. Not now," he said turning away again, shoulders stiff as he stomped off.

Ellinor yearned to go after Kai, to talk to him, to help him somehow. But the walls Kai put up were unfamiliar to Ellinor. Her friend had never hidden his feelings about anything before, and she was struggling for a way to reach him now. Fiss sighed in her arms. "Red friend sad . . ."

"I know, baby bug. Don't worry, we'll find a way to help Kai, too." Fiss turned his face up and smiled brightly at her, then his attention quickly went back to the buildings around them.

There were dozens of kiosks scattered along the wide, smooth brick walkway. Most were flashy accessory dealers, hawking some fashionable ear or eye implant that could provide a screen overlay to help with organizing someone's day, or a white noise filter to tune out unwanted sounds. Others were purely decorative add-ons for the Ashlings; sparkling gems and rocks to replace rusted screws, and arm or leg mods that claimed to help zem look more like the organic dwellers of Eerden.

The businesses were packed close together, a paper-thin divider between them most times. Brightly colored stores snaked along the walls both on the ground floor and stretching high up the main building where Ellinor lost sight of them in the haze caused by the fetid air leaking into the loading zones from outside.

The shops higher up sold bigger items, from what Ellinor could see. More sophisticated implants that would require surgery, mechanics' shops that she supposed were like the Ashlings version of a hospital. There were benign shops as well. Seerani and humani shop owners—all cyborgs, of course—did try to make an honest living on Amardeep, after all. But littered amongst the legal shops and souvenir boutiques selling overpriced, glitzy shirts, were the Juice Box peddlers. Ellinor's body stiffened, her eyes locking on those shops, even as she pushed away a Juice addict who had stumbled too close to their gear.

An itching thirst like she had never felt before bubbled up within her, one that demanded she go and visit these peddlers. There was a pull deep in her core that had the tips of her fingers tingling, twitching as if she could call the familiar magic toward her. Nothing answered, and Ellinor's throat tightened. She found herself leaning toward the peddlers, toes curling in her boots as some sentinel within her kept her just safely away from buying an Air Flavored Juice Box. Her older brother, Andrey, had died to keep Juice Boxes out of Euria, and yet here she was, longing to down a Box like her life depended on it.

Maybe it does.

Ellinor glanced to where Izza had joined Jelani and Oihana, still having their heated discussion by the comm-ports. Jelani glanced at her briefly as if sensing her gaze. Ellinor cast her eyes down, a blush tickling up the back of her neck, worried that he perhaps sensed her desire to sneak off and browse the Juice Box stalls.

"Not what you were expecting, aye, boss?" Kai whispered, appearing at her side again, a small, forced smile on his lips. His eyes didn't sparkle the way they normally did, the sadness from earlier still darkening his gaze. Kai, no longer in his bulky, Coyote mechanized suit, donned something less conspicuous now. He wore a heather grey tank top that was stretched over his large frame and tucked into a pair of black cargo pants, each pocket full to bursting with some manner of weapon.

Ellinor cleared her throat and shrugged nonchalantly, sliding her eyes back to the crowd of people. "I'm not sure what I was expecting. I knew Amardeep, despite the Ashlings and the toxic slime, was a pleasure destination for those rich bastards with tastes bordering illegal. But this?" She waved at a group of teenage humani skittering toward a Juice Box stall, proudly hawking a new fire flavor. "It's so . . . glaring. Like they want to flaunt, but in a bad way." She frowned. "How shitty is it that a bunch of Ashlings created Juice Boxes, by the way? The fuckers can't even use the stuff and yet they—*zey*—" she cringed at the correction, "—peddle it to the very society zey claim to want to join? I don't get it." She didn't know why she was using the correct pronouns now, no Ashling was near her, but she knew it was important to Jelani, and that she should for Izza's sake. Still, the words stuck in her throat.

It'll take some time before this stops feeling off. But this is progress . . . It's a good thing.

Kai scratched at the scabbing blisters on his cheek, chewing on his bottom lip for a moment. "Ah, it ain't as odd as all that now. Ashlings saw a need. Supply and demand and the like. Sure, would be nice if it weren't addicting or dangerous as fuck, but drugs is drugs. If it ain't Juice Boxes it's something else. Can't fault the Ashlings for trying to make zemselves a necessity any way zey can."

Ellinor's body tensed, and Fiss shivered in response, still clinging to her chest. She took a deep, shuddering breath, forcing herself to calm down. "Don't defend zem, Kai. Don't forget what zey did to Misho."

Kai tilted his head, emerald eyes sliding from the teenagers she had pointed out, but she wouldn't meet his gaze. He opened his mouth, but whether to argue or change the subject, Ellinor would never know. Jelani, Oihana, and Izza returned, and with the pinched expression on Jelani's face, Ellinor knew they were not bringing good news.

No surprises there.

"Aylen is completely silent," Jelani murmured, leaning close to Ellinor, eyes dancing over the crowd. "She hasn't neglected her contact channels before. On the ocean, I could believe she was worried about communication security, but on Amardeep?" Jelani shook his head, his hair swaying gently. "This is beyond paranoid, even for her. I fear she may be in trouble."

Kai snorted, placing his large hands on his hips. "Not to be a dick or nothing, but is she the only one who could 'elp us?

Fiss and Izza are a bit exposed 'ere. And, Oihana said it 'erself, Ell's collar ain't looking so good."

Ellinor offered a wan smile to her friend, silently thanking him for voicing her same worry. Oihana had been watching Kai speak and shook her head then glanced down and issued silent commands to Izza from her wrist communicator. "Nope. I mean, we have other people, obviously, but they aren't equipped to shelter us. Not after pissing off Cosmin and Zabel the way you guys did. And not with . . ." She paused, her eyes twinkling as they rested on Fiss. "Definitely not with our little buddy in tow, especially."

Ellinor exhaled through her nose, her eyes darting around the swell of people, her ears unable to pick out individual words over the cacophony of sound. The longer they stood in the entry platform with the new arrivals, the more Ellinor's skin began to crawl and the more her nerves twitched, desperate to move, move, *move*. Whether to hide or fight, she wasn't sure.

She pinched the bridge of her nose. "First things first then, yeah? We find out where your contact was last seen and figure out if she's actually in trouble or just on some Juice Box bender." Jelani frowned, ready to defend Aylen, but Ellinor shook her head, "You were the one that said this place thrives off the Juice Box trade. Aylen may be an utter gem of a woman, but you haven't talked to her in months. A lot could have gone down in your absence."

Ellinor took another moment, her heart starting to beat irregularly. Her eyes settled on Kai. "I need you and Oihana to take Izza and our gear somewhere, anywhere that isn't the entrance bay. We're starting to stand out and if Cosmin or Zabel do have people here, this is a thousand percent the first place they'd start their search. Let's not make this easier for them, yeah?"

Kai's jaw tensed, a vein twitching along his jawline. Ellinor didn't relish the idea of being away from Kai after what Cosmin had done to him. Kai wouldn't even say the seersha's name, and each time their ex-employer was mentioned, another little light in Kai's eyes went out. Kai nodded, and he and Izza pulled the trolley with their stuff on it as Oihana all but skipped toward a bakery tucked between two mod dealers.

"Jelani, let's go see if we can do some quick and dirty investigating, then we'll decide where to go that isn't well . . . here. Who else do you know who would have had tabs on Aylen? Maybe someone she doesn't know who monitors her, just in case she's been compromised?" Ellinor asked, grasping Fiss' hand and waving Jelani back over to the comm-ports.

Jelani watched Oihana, Kai, and Izza enter the little bakery and nitro-ice cream parlor. It wasn't until they were behind the shop's bright pink and orange walls that Jelani turned back to Ellinor, reluctantly following her.

Ellinor tried to hide it, but she was still weak after coming back from the dead. Her joints ached, blood thick and sluggish in her veins, and she couldn't say if those symptoms were from her ordeal or tied to the ever-problematic collar. Regardless, Ellinor didn't feel like herself. Or, rather, she didn't feel like the person she had gotten accustomed to being after Misho's death. She found herself more protective of others, considering options that didn't immediately get her closer to her revenge, and she found herself scared of what may be hunting her and her friends.

She suspected Jelani knew something was troubling her—his earth caster abilities meant he was tied to the natural pull of emotions. But she figured the Creature Breaker was pleased that her fear, her panic over what was becoming of her and Fiss, outweighed her desire for murder—at least for the moment. She had been on Amardeep for at least ten minutes now and had not demanded once that they look into the Ashlings that had killed Misho. That had to count for something, didn't it?

Weaving through the crowd, Ellinor leaned against the side of the for-pay communications port. The pay stations were so frequently used by all manner of shady dealers that anyone who was monitoring the channels would be overwhelmed with information, with leads both false and true. Which, ironically, made them one of the safest places to try and get a message to someone who relied on secrecy.

Jelani stared at the screen, his eyes unfocused as if running through a list of names in his mind of who might have a lead on Aylen. Fiss, meanwhile, continued to watch the people and bots as they rolled past. He was particularly fascinated by those who had large pieces of technology attached to their bodies.

Ellinor felt it moments before it happened.

Her collar buzzed, thrumming against her muscles and searing her skin. Fiss was trying to cast magic. She gripped his hand tighter and hissed in pain. "Don't, Fiss. Remember what we said? No *real* magic until it's safe. It's not safe here."

In truth, it was more than *not safe*, but Ellinor didn't want to tell the little dreeocht how much pain even his benign casting was inflicting; it couldn't help matters for him to suffer along with her. The aquatic animals he made were like tiny extensions of Fiss; they didn't require thought or intention for him to make, simply popping up spontaneously from subconscious ennui or other mild distraction, and therefore hadn't affected Ellinor. Until now, anyway.

Fiss clucked his tongue. "But they look like me and you and us! Elli, they are machine people!"

Ellinor tried—and didn't exactly succeed—at not flinching. Her eyes settled on the pair Fiss had become so fascinated with. Both were heavily modified; the woman had a pair of robotic legs that bent backwards like a bird and, from what Ellinor could tell from the animated way she spoke to her companion, at least three artificial fingers on both hands. She had a visor overlay above her eyes from an implant near her ear, the light from the display making her metallic parts glow an almost eerie blue. Her companion had a large metal plate over the back of his skull, and both of his arms had been replaced with robotic parts, making them twice as big as normal arms should be.

Ellinor had no qualms with people using artificial parts to replace limbs that were damaged beyond repair in some kind of accident—which she assumed the woman's fingers and the man's skull plate were a result of—but when it came to cutting off perfectly good arms and legs just to attach robotic parts for, what? An edge? To be stronger and faster than someone else? That's where she drew the line.

I'm nothing like them, she desperately told herself, as Jelani finally picked up the receiver and tapped the comm screen.

She crouched down to be eye level with Fiss as Jelani murmured into the other end of the receiver, his words heated even if she couldn't make out what he was saying. She smiled sadly at Fiss, and he beamed at her in return. "Fiss, we aren't machine people the way someone who willingly hacks off their arm for a metal one is. You were born with your parts, and mine are, well, potentially temporary. Just because some-one looks the same, doesn't mean they are the same as you or me. You're unique, remember? Special."

Fiss tilted his head, playing with his fingers beneath the gloves he wore. "Can it be both? Different and the same? How can I be this thing? *Yooneek,* if they look like me? Red friend says special means something different-different."

Ellinor suppressed a sigh, making a mental note to ask Kai just what he shared with Fiss. Fiss absorbed information like an industrial sized sponge. Already his language skills were much improved, but he did latch onto things, and if Kai told Fiss one thing, and Ellinor another, that could be problematic.

But Ellinor didn't get the chance to explain that she didn't want her metal parts the way Fiss seemed to think, or that Fiss was a dreeocht, and by definition was one of the most unique creatures to exist. Jelani slammed the receiver down on the console, and both Ellinor and Fiss turned to watch him. He prowled back and forth for a moment, hands running through his fog-like hair as he worked whatever frustration he needed to out of his system.

Ellinor straightened, her heart starting to thump painfully. "What's the matter now?" she asked, voice just loud enough to be heard over the din of the mall behind them.

Jelani growled— actually *growled*—before shaking his head and wrestling his calm demeanor back into place. "I was wrong about Aylen. She is, for all intents and purposes, fine. Absolutely fine. She simply doesn't wish to speak to *me.*"

Ellinor stumbled back as if shoved. "What's that supposed to mean? I thought you two were on good terms, yeah?"

"We were . . . we *are.* But Aylen has her own networks in-dependent of mine, and they apparently got to her first. Told her about the heat we were fleeing in Erhard. She doesn't want to get involved. She doesn't want to touch the trouble she believes you will bring her."

Ellinor wasn't sure she could blame the woman, but the knowledge still raised her hackles and had her face flushing in anger. "Rude." She shook her head, brow furrowed. "You said she would help. That she was the *only* one who could shield and protect us in this shithole. That Aylen knew someone who knew someone who could get my shackle off. And now the bitch won't talk to you?"

Fiss cowered behind her, and Jelani took a hesitant step forward, his hand raising as if he would reach out to her, but Ellinor's angry scowl kept him at a distance. "We aren't doomed yet, Ellinor," he said. "I'm a man of my word. You agreed to let Fiss decide if he'd help my contacts, and I agreed to get your collar removed. That's the deal I'm sticking to."

Ellinor took a deep breath, trying to get her breathing under control. "So, what are we supposed to do now?"

Jelani smirked, and picked up Fiss, waving at her to follow him to the shop their friends were waiting in. "We force the issue and give Aylen Bonheur no choice. Come on. I have an idea."

ALL SEATS ARE THE SAME, EXCEPT THE ONES THAT ARE BETTER

L ATER THAT day, Ellinor sat squished against the dingy, thick plastic window of the monorail. The atoll was large, but not large enough to need a proper train, and the monorail was the fastest way to get from business to business. The monorail looked like a battering ram on wheels, its thick metal plating and double paned windows meant to withstand the near constant acidic rain that wept from Amardeep's skies.

There wasn't much for Ellinor to look at besides the silver rain that fell from the sky. A wall of strange flora obstructed her view of the dwellings she knew were just out of sight. Things grew on Amardeep, but the mutated palm trees glowed a sickly yellow, their sharp fronds quivering of their own accord, like arthritic fingers mid-stretch.

Trees grew into thick, impenetrable walls of glowing forestry that poisoned the air rather than cleaned it. Any piece of ground that didn't have a mutated palm tree growing from it was covered in a luminescent brown and black moss. Amardeep glowed as brightly as any of the major city-states on Erhard, despite its major business centers being spread apart.

The view from the other side of the train was no better. There were jagged, khaki-colored rocks and cliffs that ended in the Goma Ocean far below. Even if they had been right on the cliff's edge, there wasn't anything to see. Only a diseased looking brown fog which flowed over the cliff's edges like a herd of misshapen ants.

The monorail was packed, full of seershas in flashy three-piece suits that even Cosmin would envy. Humani partygoers raced through the cramped train. They looked to sample the different Juice Box flavors their friends had bought, in a sad attempt to feel like a caster for a few hours, which elicited glares from the well-dressed seershas. There were cyborgs—or machine people, as Fiss called them—who kept to themselves across the aisle, clutching refrigerated medical boxes, whispering and sneaking glances at the people around them. Then there were the Ashlings, zeyr grey, ocular orbs whirling as zey focused on the passing people without ever having to turn zeyr heads. A shiver ran down Ellinor's spine whenever she looked at one, not sure if zey were staring back at her or not.

No one wanted to take the blame—or credit—for what had caused the atoll to become a noxious dump. Some claimed it was the various governments using the unpopulated location as a garbage landfill for centuries, depositing all the experiments that had gone wrong during their quest to properly combine magic and technology. Others said it was the seersha casters themselves, their connection to the land, draining it of natural resources—making them both a pestilential leech on Eerden as well as its populace's only means of survival in one fell swoop. Then there were people, like Kai, who believed Azer had come to the world of Eerden and punished the native population for some perceived offense, but was not content to wipe out the inhabitants. Oh no! Azer, in all His vindictive glory, had to poison the land so only filthy Ashlings could—

Ellinor bit her lip, halting the bitter thought.

She glanced furtively at Izza, who sat perfectly still in the aisle, zer shiny body acting as a shield for Fiss. IAA bots like Izza were always equipped with a sensor that alerted zem to changes in zeyr patrons' mood or core body temperature so zey could better assist with whatever ailed them. Ellinor wondered suddenly how those acrimonious thoughts were affecting her body, and she did her best to quiet her mind. She figured it was prudent not to piss off the bot who was currently protecting those she cared about.

Kai caught her studying Izza and nudged her foot, drawing her attention. The seats on the train were so small that Kai had to take nearly the entire adjacent row to himself, only Izza and Fiss comfortably sitting next to him. "You doing okay, boss? 'ow's the neck?"

Her hand drifted to the bio-magitech embedded on her throat, but she stopped herself at the subtle stiffening of Je-lani, who perched at the end of a bench seat. She forced a smile that didn't reach her eyes.

"Probably better than your burns, big guy. Do you need more cream for them? Or another shot of pain killer? Izza has plenty of both."

Ellinor was tired of talking about the constant burn along her neck, the itch on her collarbone and shoulder where the technology was slowly spreading, the occasional sharp sting in her chest whenever Fiss used his magic. There was nothing they could do about her affliction, unlike the wounds Kai suffered.

Kai shrugged, his green eyes darkening as he clenched his jaw briefly. Kai wanted to talk about his burns as much as she wanted to talk about her faulty bio-magitech. "Nah, I'm solid," he said no more than that.

Ellinor's stomach twisted, hating that Cosmin had broken so much of her friend's spirit, and vowing anew to rip that seersha's head clean off for hurting Kai so profoundly.

You were almost as bad as Cosmin toward Kai. The thought stung her to the core.

Ellinor once more promised to make up for her poor treatment of Kai when Cosmin had first kidnapped her, though she still had a hard time forgetting the feel of his beefy fingers around her neck when they had initially snapped the collar on.

Ellinor opened her mouth, trying to find words to console him, only to have Kai glare at her, his nostrils flaring as he fought back tears. He looked away and jerked his chin at Jelani and Oihana, who were hovering over their wrist tablets, heads bent together. "You two scheming and the like? You gonna share with the rest of the class?"

Jelani glanced up from his seat, closest to the aisle, angling his body so those across the way or walking through the monorail couldn't observe them as easily. Jelani offered Kai a wry grin as he tapped Oihana's shoulder to get her attention. "I didn't mean to seem like we were keeping secrets. Oihana and I are constructing new temporary identities for us, that's all."

Ellinor scrunched up her face, "Why? It shouldn't really matter here, yeah? Everyone on this island is up to some manner of activity they don't want others to know about. Isn't that the whole point of this place and our reason coming here? Not to be tracked?"

"New . . . identities? What's this? Elli, what, what? Will you not be my Elli? No more Fiss?" The anguish in Fiss' voice was palpable, and Ellinor's heart lurched into her throat.

She reached across the small space between them, and gently touched Fiss' knee, as Kai draped his muscular arm over the tiny creature. "No, Fiss, it's okay. Jelani is making a disguise. That's what he means. You'll always be Fiss. I'll always be your Elli."

And she meant it. For the first time in eight years, someone else using the nickname Misho had given her before they were married didn't hurt so much, didn't make her immediately want to drown in a barrel of whiskey and go out looking for trouble.

Jelani frowned, a silent apology shining in his dark blue and silver eyes. "I'm sorry, little friend. I didn't mean to frighten you. Ellinor is right. I am creating false names to use so no one outside of our group will know who we are." Fiss trilled in understanding, nestling back against Kai.

Once the dreeocht was placated, Jelani continued, "Aylen is the Owner of a rather unique club. One where she married her love of music and synth-clubs with the populace's natural love of violence and, as she calls it, 'feeling like a badass'. Aylen has made a type of . . . fight club, for lack of a better title. Organics, or *fleshies* as the Ashlings call us, fight against machines, all set to music. Her synth-bots are all Ashlings that she helped program. They watch the fights and create a soundtrack in real-time. It makes the fights look choreographed, all while naturally raising the adrenaline of her visitors. No Juice

Boxes are allowed on her premises. It's rather impressive, if I do say so myself."

For the first time in days, Kai's eyes lit up. "I like this Aylen lady more by the minute," he said, a chuckle rumbling deep in his chest.

Ellinor swiveled to face Jelani. "She makes live action music videos for her visitors? People like that stuff?"

There was a rumble from Izza, like keys jingling together, that Ellinor took for laughter. "Of course they do, Ms Ellinor."

Ellinor blushed at Izza's soft teasing, and Oihana smirked, her eyes locked on Ellinor's lips from where she was seated between Ellinor and her brother. "They eat it up. You'll see. The atmosphere is wicked fun in her place—she calls it SynthLyfe, which is a pretty stupid name if you ask me, but whatever. You can do pretty much anything you want to, as long as it's consensual. Though Anni doesn't let me go to the higher floors of the main club." Oihana threw a mock glare at her brother, whose face darkened in a blush.

Oihana cast her eyes back to Ellinor, and Jelani murmured, "Aylen has areas that are meant as a type of sex club. Clothing isn't optional on those floors. Everyone gets done up in elaborate body paint before they enter. The goal is to have it all rubbed off before they leave. Oihana is only twenty-five, barely older than a teenager to seerani and seersha, and she hasn't even had a romantic partner yet. I . . . would prefer if her first encounter wasn't with someone who would not even ask for her name."

Oblivious to her brother's words, Oihana continued, "You're just not allowed to get high on the premises, not that you need to. Her music creates a natural high." Ellinor's brows knit together in confusion, and Oihana rolled her eyes. "I can 'hear'

| 56 |

the music based on the vibrations. It works just fine for me, thank you very much."

"Fair enough," Ellinor said, nodding softly, but her brows remained furrowed. "How can she possibly keep Juice Boxes out of her club? They're legal here, or as good as."

Jelani tapped another command into his wrist tablet before meeting her eyes. "Amardeep is a corporatocracy. It's run by its leading businesses. The laboratories, clubs, malls, hotels . . . everything is crafted and catered to the whims of the Owner, enticing those who want privacy in order to scratch a particular itch to come and live out every fantasy they could ever dream of. Why else do you think wealthy bachelors and bachelorettes flock here rather than somewhere more scenic? Juice Boxes may be legal in places like the Emporium Sanitorium, but they are only legal because those who created that corporation deemed it so. Outside of the Emporium, and in the other unincorporated areas, it can be anarchy, certainly. But within an established organization, you have to follow the rules of the Owner. What is legal and permitted in one area, may not be in another."

Ellinor scoffed, trying to hide the cold lump that was forming in her chest over the knowledge. "So, what? We should thank Azer we have you to guide and keep us from pissing someone off then?"

Jelani smiled devilishly at her. "Yes, you should. But if you don't thank Azer, I will take *your* thanks as a start. For now."

Kai chuckled at the blush coloring Ellinor's cheeks and made a wet, kissing sound. "Just tell me where you want your 'thanks' planted, pretty boy."

Jelani chuckled, and Oihana made a gagging noise. Fiss, even though he wasn't sure what the joke was, always giggled by infection of others' laughter.

Ellinor was still searching for some kind of comeback when Jelani said. "There, it's done. We've been registered to fight—or perform, rather, in Aylen's club this evening. If we win, Aylen will have no choice but to see us. I have registered us for what is classified as a 'high octane' fight that will allow Oihana the time and cover she needs to hack Aylen's systems and force her to come down and meet with us."

"And if Oihana can't do it? Or if we don't win?" Ellinor murmured.

Izza shifted, straightening zers already perfect posture, and placed a metal hand on Oihana's knee. "Ms Oihana's abilities are beyond question."

Ellinor dipped her head in apology while Jelani regarded her for a moment. His face settled into impassivity as he sat back against the bench. "Failure isn't an option here, Ellinor."

Ellinor rolled her eyes and turned back to look out the window, her muscles tensing at his cryptic words, her fingers itching to twirl her Lacerator knives around her fingers.

When is failure ever an option?

WELCOME TO SYNTHLYFE

C ALLING AYLEN'S business a "club" was an understate-
ment. As Ellinor peeked around Jelani, who was checking
in with the Ashling bouncer, she caught glimpses of the inte-
rior around the press of bodies on the first floor.

The ceiling and underbellies of the balconies were adorned
in polished mirrors, creating an infinity effect between all
the balconies and the pulsing lights. The crowd looked like
an undulating sea of black flashing with sparkling color as
the patrons were reflected within the mirrors dozens of times
over. Each level and their respective galleries were uneven,
some stretching over the floors beneath, others tucked away
so you couldn't see the crowds when looking up. The levels
and rooms were boxy, lights flashing, bathing their walls in
neon that ebbed between blue, yellow, pink, and orange. All
the bars were circular and appeared to be made of steel—and
more mirrors. A constant flow of people circled the bars, swaying on their feet, either dancing or drunk, Ellinor couldn't tell.
Humani and seerani servers moved around the patrons as if

they knew where the drunks would stumble ahead of time in a chaotic ballet all their own.

Ellinor was impressed, and judging by how Fiss clung to her legs, leaning as far over as he could to gawk at all the lights and people, so was the dreeocht.

She was amazed that the strobing, multi-colored lights dancing over the mirrors didn't create a more dizzying result. But the strobes were timed in such a way as to avoid that annoying slow-motion effect the synth-clubs back in Euria seemed to love so much.

The trashcan-like Ashling beeped at Ellinor when she leaned too close, drawing her back from the entrance while zer continued to pour over the identities Jelani and Oihana had fabricated. Jelani raised a brow at her then turned his attention back to the bouncer and pointed at something on the holo-screen the Ashling held. "I can promise you, friend," Jelani was whisper-shouting at the Ashling, "having casters fight in Aylen's matches will draw a crowd. The bets on the fight alone will be astronomical. Your guests will want to see your best Ashling fighters go up against the so-called 'caster oppressors'. . . ."

The line of people waiting to get into SynthLyfe was growing restless behind Ellinor and Kai, and Ellinor could no longer hear what Jelani was saying. Izza kept a protective hand on Oihana's shoulder while the Ashling bouncer's ocular eyes shifted from Jelani to the underage members of their group.

"I will sign the waiver claiming responsibility for—" Izza was saying to the bouncer bot before zers words were drowned out by impatient shouting. Kai turned, glowering at the shorter humani man behind him, who shrank back.

Kai and Ellinor had expressed their apprehension about how authentic the identification papers looked. Oihana had rolled her big eyes at them, waving their concern away with a flippant gesture and a remark about how often she's managed to make flawless identities. Neither Ellinor nor Kai liked their new names—Lenore Castile and Wren Hallowell—but it was too late to change them now. The fake identities were never going to be the true hold up in their plan though, and they all knew it. That honor fell to Oihana and Fiss.

Had Aylen taken any of Jelani's calls, she would have allowed Oihana in without issue, like she always did in the past. Without that, they had to sign waiver after waiver taking responsibility for the "children," stating that SynthLyfe wasn't responsible for any corruption they may experience—everyone was allowed to do what they wanted as long as it didn't fuck up anyone else's good time, or break any of Aylen's laws.

Ellinor had wanted to leave Fiss and Oihana behind somewhere safe, somewhere away from the alcohol and violence they would find in Aylen's establishment. But only Oihana and Izza could hack into Aylen's systems from the gambling kiosks, and with Ellinor, Kai, and Jelani serving as a distraction while Oihana worked, that meant they had no choice but to bring Fiss with them.

If nothing else, at least they looked the part of fight club junkies eager to win fame and glory within Aylen's arenas.

Ellinor wore the armor Misho had gifted her—she would never go into combat without it. The form fitting, specialty black leather and combat-tech filaments would protect her still bruised and battered body from any blunt trauma a robotic combatant could throw at her. Her shield was fully charged, so all she needed to do was turn it on.

"Magic is not permitted in the arena," the Ashling declared, zers voice booming above the din escaping the club behind zer.

Jelani flashed the bot a winning smile. "Excellent. Lenore won't need her abilities. And as a Creature Breaker, you know I can't cast well enough to harm your fighters." Jelani waved a hand back at Kai and continued, "And my large friend here, well, even if he was a caster, Wren certainly wouldn't need abilities to put on a good show. Ultimately, isn't that all that matters? Your patrons will love his havoc, and watching a cyborg caster fight with sheer skill alone. You know I'm right."

The faulty bio-magitech glittered along Ellinor's neck, flashing and sparking, making Ellinor indeed appear as if she belonged on Amardeep. The knowledge had bile coating the back of her throat, but she swallowed it down, and went back to flipping the WX Lacerator knives around her fingers to give herself something else to focus on besides how seamlessly she blended in, or what awaited them in the arena.

Finally, the Ashling bouncer buzzed, and said, "Welcome. Please proceed to the arena on level eight for check-in. No more than two drinks are permitted before your fight time, if magic is used, you forfeit all winnings. The children are not allowed anywhere unaccompanied. Enjoy your time at Synth-Lyfe, combatants and guests."

A bright green laser light popped out of the Ashling's chest. Waving the light over Jelani, Ellinor, and Kai, zer imprinted a small, temporary barcode underneath their right eyes. The light changed to neon blue as it passed over Oihana and Fiss, their barcodes flashing on the backs of their left hands. Just like that, they were permitted full access to the largest club on Amardeep.

They had just passed the threshold when Fiss tried to fly off. Ellinor caught him about the waist before anyone could see that he was flying without the aid of a jet pack. "Fiss, we're doing make-believe now, yeah? You aren't supposed to be able to do any magic, remember?" Ellinor said, her lips pressed against Fiss' ear to be heard over the fast-pulsing beats from the dance floor.

Fiss was too entranced by the writhing, bouncing bodies and the glowing drinks to be bothered by the reprimand. His pale blue eyes were wide as he drank in everything around him, and Ellinor wondered what would happen if a dreeocht got drunk. As they walked through the crowd, she had visions of a drunk Fiss accidentally releasing his magic, killing her and creating an army of Ashlings in the process, his magic elevating zeyr programming in a way that zey were currently unable to unlock. What was more likely to happen, however, was Fiss overreacting if she got seriously hurt in the arena.

End it fast, and then you won't have to worry about Fiss or his magic. The thought sent a shudder down Ellinor's back, and she could no longer take part in Fiss' wonder.

The first floor of SynthLyfe was a traditional bar and dance floor, though Ellinor thought she would need to replace her karambit knives with spinning glow sticks around her fingers in order to fit in. The crowd was no more than a rippling mass of metallic and glowing parts around the synth-bot DJ on the platform in the back.

This area was relatively tame, from what Ellinor could see. Men and women were swaying suggestively from cages and platforms off the ground, seerani servers glided through the room as effortlessly as their wheeled Ashling and cyborg coworkers. If Ellinor didn't know any better, she would think she was back in a synth-club in Euria.

Kai was watching one of the men in the cages, his head tilted, a forlorn expression pulling his face down. Ellinor placed a hand on his arm. "Kai? Are you doing okay? Do you want to talk about Cos—"

Kai jerked his arm away, interrupting her. "No. I mean, nah, I'm good, boss. Just need a different kind of pain to distract me." He walked a little way off, Jelani and Oihana at his side. They spoke to each other rapidly in their personal sign language. Whatever Jelani was telling his sister, she clearly didn't like it, as her full lips pulled down in a perfect pout and she crossed her arms over her chest.

Ellinor's breath hitched as she watched the siblings, the hollow pressure under her sternum that had never quite lifted after Andrey's death, pressed her down. Ellinor wondered if Andrey would have been as protective of her, whether they would have had the same kind of arguments as Jelani and Oihana, had her big brother lived longer. Such thoughts made her think of her parents, of the day they got her brother's name tattooed on their shoulders to honor his memory. Ellinor wondered if they were still safe in Desta. She hadn't spoken to them, not really, anyway, in such a long time, that she couldn't be sure her new warnings about Cosmin had been heard.

A sharp pang of worry and guilt twisted in her stomach thinking of her parents. How she had disappointed them throughout the years, first by dropping out of college and abandoning their hopes that she would go into the medical field, then enlisting in the private army, and then again when she aligned herself with the criminal syndicate of Euria. Ellinor loved to deny it in every colorful way she could, but she missed her family, and part of her longed to just go home.

She sighed, melancholy tugging at her heart, until Fiss gently tapped her nose, cocking his head to the side. "Why so sad? This . . . music? Yes! Music! It vibrates! It tickles me, Elli. Do you feel it?" He flattened his hand against her chest and giggled. "Oh! You vibrate, too!"

Ellinor grinned at the dreeocht, amazed at his innocence and how he appreciated all the little things she took for granted. But she never got to explain that she was thinking of her own brother, as Jelani ushered them over to a glowing, neon green elevator to the left of where they were standing against the back wall.

The music of the floors became muffled in the elevator. As they moved up, Ellinor was intrigued to see that the elevator doors were actually translucent, and she caught glimpses of the passing floors. It made sense now why the first floor was so tame; it was a good way to ease newcomers into SynthLyfe, to get them relaxed and comfortable before venturing into the more salacious areas of the club. The glimpse she got of the third floor alone was already intimidating; all shiny black latex, whips, ball-gags, vats of hot wax, and leather masks. It made her wonder how scandalous and decadent the upper floors actually became if that was only the third.

Children should not be here.

Soon, the elevator opened on the eighth floor and Ellinor swayed back, amazed once again as she held tightly onto Fiss. The elevator opened out onto a shallow balcony, providing a tiny alcove. Behind the elevator bay, however, was the first of SynthLyfe's battle arenas.

Jelani brushed against her shoulder, pointing at the padded walls. "Aylen uses a special sound buffering material between floors so the varying beats from one level don't bleed into the next." He placed a hand on the small of her back, leading her away from the balcony and twisting her slightly toward the dueling DJ synth-bots. He smiled at the open look of amazement on her face and said, "Zey use an advanced algorithm to calculate not only what kind of moves the fighters in the arena are most likely to use, but zey will also lower the bass depending on how heavy the hits of the combatants would be—based on their size, too, no less."

Izza waddled to her other side as Oihana began working on her tablet. "If you listen, Ms Ellinor," zer added with what sounded like pride in zers words, "zey have intensified the treble and increased the speed of the beats depending on how fast the boxers move. Ms Aylen's music programs and her Ashling DJs are some of the best in all Eerden. I have scanned the available feeds and found this to be fact."

The effect was exactly as Jelani said it would be: a fight that looked choreographed, something that was ripped straight out of a dialogue-light and action-heavy virtual reality simulator. The music, despite how devastating the blows were within the caged pit where the opponents grappled with one another, was never hypnotic or mellow, never harsh or dark. It was a distorted buzz, a little rough around the edges, with fat bass lines, and a filthy electro vibe that was fast and upbeat, encouraging those who watched along the edges of the arena to dance as much as they cheered.

Kai was already moving, pulled toward the dome. The bodies twisted around him, guided out of his way by his large gauntlets—Kai had kept only his gloves from his Coyote mechanized suit on in preparation for the fight. The fans never paused in their movement, swaying around him in a hypnotic blend of gyrations and waving hands, they flowed around him like debris in a tide. Kai stood out amongst the crowd, not wearing traditional club attire, but rather a reinforced combat-tech black tank top and cargo pants. They didn't offer the same protection as Ellinor's armor, but it was better than nothing—slightly.

Kai wasn't drawn to the DJs like Ellinor was, instead fixated on the diminutive woman in the cage as she squared off against what appeared to be a guard automaton. The hulking piece of metal was deceptively fast, arms swinging in a tornado of movement that the woman ducked low to dodge. She bent backward and forward as she moved around the bot's arms. Music pulsed around her, lights flashing in time with the music. Kai may not fancy women, but he loved watching anyone skilled fight.

Ellinor hung back, and Oihana tapped her on the shoulder. "If I bet on you, you aren't going to choke, right? You'll win?"

Ellinor cocked an eyebrow. "You gamble? I thought you were just hacking into their systems to get Aylen's attention."

Oihana flashed a smile as bright as her brother's, her dusky skin aglow with excitement. "Yup! It's the one thing Anni lets me do when we visit. I'm awesome at playing the odds. Lucky for you, I'm good at multitasking, too. I can gamble and crack Aylen's codes, no sweat." Then, with a smirk and a gentle wiggle of her calloused fingers, Oihana was bouncing to the mirrored kiosks where patrons placed various bets on the fighters. Izza went after her, to assist in any way Oihana may need.

"Win? What do we win, Elli?" Fiss asked, his hair quivering in time with the fast, dirty beats under his beanie.

"Hopefully the attention of the boss of this club. But remember, I'm *Lenore* here, not Elli," Ellinor answered, her eyes sliding back to the fighting ring. The small woman straddled the guard bot's shoulders momentarily before she was flung off. She hit the side of the cage with a bone rattling thud.

She didn't move. Ellinor swallowed, fear twisting in her again about what Fiss may do. There was no way the little dreeocht would willingly leave Ellinor without someone else to keep him occupied.

As the music changed, signaling the end of the fight, Jelani motioned for a server. He whispered something in the man's ear, and then turned back to Ellinor and Fiss. "Fiss, you can't interfere," Jelani said slowly, watching Fiss' gaze lock onto the small woman being carried from the caged arena.

"Ellinor, red friend, and I are going into that ring. We are going to fight and put on a good show for all these people while Oihana works. You may feel pain from Ellinor, but she's not in any danger. You understand? It's important you remember that Sergei—the fake you—isn't a dreeocht and can't cast magic. Besides, Ellinor is armed and will have help," he finished as the server returned with two amber colored drinks.

Fiss' pale eyes darkened, something Ellinor hadn't thought was possible for a dreeocht. "Jelani keeps Ellinor safe," he said, tone gloomier and heavier than his normal prepubescent voice. It wasn't a question, either, and if the burning squeeze along Ellinor's throat and chest were any indication, Fiss' magic was acting up in response to his words.

Ellinor took the drink and placed a hand on the little dreeocht. "I'll be fine, baby bug. You stay with Oihana and Izza at all times, yeah?"

And, just like that, Fiss' mood was back to normal. He gave her a toothy smile and nodded. If Jelani found Fiss' reaction odd, he didn't comment on it, clinking his drink to hers before taking a long swallow.

One of the referees found them before Ellinor could finish her first round of liquid courage. He glanced at the tablet in his hand before peering at Jelani and tapped something on the screen. "Your crew's up next. Follow me, I'll take you backstage where you can get ready. First time?" he said, barely pausing for breath.

Ellinor nodded, and the man taped on his tablet again. "Cool. Cool, cool, cool. I'll explain the rules to you down there."

Izza peeled off from Oihana's side and shuffled over as they were about to snag Kai and follow the referee. Ellinor touched zers cold, metallic elbow, putting Fiss' fuzzy hand in Izza's metal one and said, "Watch Fiss, yeah? Teach him how to dance or something while Oihana does her thing."

Izza dipped zers head. "Gladly, Ms Ellinor."

As they followed the referee, Ellinor was, not for the first time, glad Oihana and Izza had taken to Fiss. Oihana was fascinated by him, never scared, and curious to see if he had any aptitude for machine work. She had treated him like a little brother almost from the minute she met him, and for that, Ellinor was grateful. Izza, meanwhile, seemed to enjoy having a young charge to look after, probably due to the IAA programming Oihana had modified in zer.

The three of them skirted the still dancing crowd, the beats becoming more uniform with no one fighting. They went around the arena to a covered walkway at the back. The referee opened a side door on the black archway and ushered them

C.E. CLAYTON

inside. All sound ceased as soon as the man closed the door behind Jelani.

He waved to the far wall where a rudimentary partition and lockers were set up. "Change there if you want. But rules are simple: don't rip out the Ashlings heads or central wiring, no one is allowed to kill anyone. If someone does die and violates Aylen Bonheur's decree, then all winners from previous rounds are allowed to join your fight and are given the chance to kill *you*. The round is ten minutes, or until knockout. The time limit is five minutes if someone dies. If you can survive the onslaught, then your crime will be forgiven. Any questions?"

"Just the one," Ellinor said. "There's a big margin between killing and all other kinds of harm. Nothing else is off limits? Cutting off an arm, paralyzing someone?"

The referee smirked at her. "If it doesn't kill you? Then it's allowed." He glanced down at his tablet. "You have a few minutes; you should get ready. Your opponents, Ognen, Sasho, and Bira, are all veterans of the cage." The referee chuckled to himself before heading for the door. "You guys must love pain, requesting zem!" And with that, he was gone.

Kai didn't appear bothered by the referee's words, he began humming to himself as he checked his gauntlets and changed the shots on his scattergun to be nonlethal rounds—well, nonlethal to an Ashling. They were concussive shots, meant to punch holes in metal and stun the Ashlings rather than fry zeyr circuitry.

Ellinor cast an accusatory glare at Jelani, whose back was turned to her as he took off his loose, dark blue sweater in exchange for . . . nothing. The corded muscles of his back flexed, lean, taut muscle bunching and uncoiling as he moved. Even

| 70 |

with such a simple action, there was a captivating control to how Jelani moved, how smooth and hard his back was all at once. Jelani remained shirtless for reasons that made no sense to Ellinor. She opened her mouth to say as much, then shut it with a gulp. She finally saw the full force of Jelani's tattoo.

She knew it was there; she had seen it glow through his shirt when his swords were activated fighting against Dragan's beast, but the design . . . There was the outline of two people in black, hugging the base of a tree. The tree morphed from the base of the trunk into the form of a woman, vines and tendrils of bark over her body gradually shifting from rich brown to dark green tones. Her arms stretched over her head, as if she were trying to shield herself, her hands and fingers transforming to bare branches that twisted painfully and looked dead and diseased.

Her face was serene, as if sleeping, but with the way the outlined figures gripped the base, it was possible she was dead. Her hair was more an impression of scattered leaves on fire, constantly burning. Now the parts that glowed on Jelani's back made sense—it was the fire from her would-be hair that housed the majority of his biotechnology nanites each time his Leviathan Roasters were activated.

The design was heartbreaking and beautiful.

A sound escaped Ellinor—a half gasp half sigh—as Jelani's back stretched. The muscles of his shoulders pulled taut, the tattoo shifting in a way that made the woman's face change subtly between peace and sorrow.

At the sound, Jelani turned and cocked an eyebrow at her, a coy smile tugging at the corner of his lips. She could see the suggestive remark flashing in his eyes, but he didn't say a word, letting the silence stretch until Ellinor's ears began to burn.

"Your tattoo . . . it means something, doesn't it?" Jelani's shoulders slumped as if he were expecting her to say something else. "No one gets a piece of artwork like that unless there's a story behind it," she whispered.

Jelani lifted a shoulder in a half-hearted shrug. "It's a reminder of the abilities I traded to become something that ultimately killed my family. If I hadn't been so angry at my father for moving on after my mother's death, for loving someone new and amazing, I wouldn't have become a Creature Breaker. I wouldn't have gotten in league with the crime lord who then slaughtered them when I came to my senses and returned home. The tree is the abilities that I traded away, my way of clinging to a memory of what it once was to be wholly connected to the land. The people are my mother, stepmother, and father all rolled into one. Burning and gone because of my actions." He gave her a pointed look then turned his gaze away, closing the locker and making sure his Leviathan Roasters were fully charged.

Ellinor's stomach felt heavy in her gut. She knew he thought his lesson could be applied to her, but it wasn't the same. Misho's death hadn't been a result of her actions. Not that she believed Jelani was responsible for his family's tragedy, either, but still. Their situations were different.

Weren't they?

Misho needs peace. I have to avenge him, she reminded herself, making a mental note to ask around about the Ashling murderers when the fight was over.

That's when she remembered Jelani was still shirtless. She knew the seersha was fit, he had to be in his line of work, but this was the first time she had truly seen the full extent of his physique. His muscles weren't bulging the way Kai's were, but the tightness of his body, the control with which he moved, his chest was all chiseled lines and fine contours. Her gaze betrayed her, lingering on the outline of his abdomen as it dipped below his belt line . . .

"Do you need something?" Jelani's voice had her eyes darting back up, and Kai's chuckle brought Ellinor's blush back anew.

She cleared her throat, marshaling her face back into a kind of bored indifference, and waved dismissively at his chest. "You're not going to wear armor? Did I miss the part where we are about to fight three bots who are allowed to do whatever the fuck they want as long as we don't die?"

Jelani smiled and ran his hands through his hair, showing off the definition of his body. Ellinor rocked back and forth on her feet, and was perhaps too obvious about how ardently she only looked at his face. "Half of the fight is the spectacle," Jelani chuckled. "They want a show, and nothing is flashier than organics fighting Ashlings without armor. Oihana is good at what she does, but she needs to bypass Aylen's security measures. Fighting the three best Ashling fighters without armor? That draws a crowd. It gives Oihana the time and space she needs to work unmolested."

Ellinor scoffed, her jaw nearly dropping. "So, what? Are you suggesting if I go out there in some golden metal bikini and fight those bots no one will notice a young woman and child lingering near the betting kiosks? Like that will offer *me* any kind of protection."

Jelani waggled his eyebrows at her. "I certainly wouldn't stop you if that's what you chose to do."

Ellinor's heart stuttered in her chest. When had Jelani become so flirtatious? It was as if, now that they were on *his* turf rather than hers, he was suddenly more comfortable, not just with himself, but everyone around him.

Ellinor swallowed, and hoped her voice wasn't going to betray her. "Fuck that. I'll stick to armor, thank you."

"Ah, you're no fun, Ell," Kai said, slapping her playfully on the back.

Ellinor wheeled on him, about to explain how idiotic it was to go into a fight with an intentional handicap just to give some drunk dance junkies a good show. But mainly she was thinking how she did not want Jelani—*or anyone*—to see her half nude. For any reason. Misho was the last to see her in such a state and she didn't . . . she couldn't . . .

But she could never find the words. A buzzer sounded behind them and the door leading to the caged arena behind them opened. Kai jumped to his feet with a whoop. "Ah, fuck yeah! Let's do this thing."

DON'T LET THE BEAT DROP

THE BEAT started as they exited the locker room. Tentative and buzzy, the rhythm teased a drop that didn't come. As they entered the arena, Ellinor elected to take her Asco Rhino mechanized crossbow and the electric knife she had stolen from Janne Wolff, when the woman had mutinied.

The Lance was dialed up as high as it would go, and while lethal to an organic, it would merely stall the Ashlings, shutting zem off without destroying zeyr main processing, thus "killing" zem. Provided she also avoided the sensitive parts that the referee said would result in death, of course. She left her Dunstan Anaconda pistols, her illegal, small-scale Leviathan Roaster, as well as her WX Lacerator knives behind, none of which would do much good against their opponents with the current restrictions in place.

Kai—or Wren as he was announced to the crowd—held his scattergun lightly as he strutted out into the arena, a large smile on his face, and an almost manic gleam in his emerald eyes. Jelani stood straight, body tense, brow arched with a smirk that was more in his eyes than his lips. His Creature Breaker blades were out and at the ready, the tattoo on his back a blaze of pulsing light as the nanites in his blood reacted to the ones in his sword that siphoned his limited magic.

For her part, Ellinor glared at the faces taunting them. Everywhere she turned there were organic and metal faces pressed against the cage, peering at them, fingers pointed. Bodies thumped against one another as they moved to the music the dueling DJ synth-bots were using to warm up for the fight about to begin.

Ellinor's body hummed along with the beats, her bones vibrating with the loud bass. The thudding of her heart had nothing to do with the DJ's, however, but the three Ashlings that stomped out of zeyr own locker room. She didn't know which was Bira, Ognen, or Sasho, and she didn't care to look up and check the holographic scorecard projected over the arena. Frankly, it didn't matter.

Ashlings were all the same to Ellinor.

All three bots were bipedal, walking on clawed metal feet that made the arena floor shake with each heavy tread. Zey had all been war automata before breaking zeyr programming; a series of moving steel plates now protecting their sensitive wiring. Broad chests and shoulders that should house all manner of weapon and explosives, based on Ellinor's experience with the androids, sat atop impossibly narrow waists. Each only had one clawed arm with finger-like digits as long as Ellinor's hand. The other arm was a weapon.

One had a metal crossbow as an arm, another had a sword similar to Jelani's own Leviathan Roasters. The final bot, the biggest of the three—though all towered a good foot over Kai—had a massive hammer in place of a hand. The Ashlings had red tally marks painted on zeyr scorched and dented bodies that stretched across zeyr chests and over zeyr shoulders. Otherwise, these bots didn't decorate zemselves the way the ones at the Emporium had.

The bots' triangular heads shifted in unison to zeyr opponents, the glow of zeyr grey ocular orbs narrowing into pinpricks as zey observed the three organics before zem. Facing the hulking Ashlings in front of her, Ellinor better understood why the bots referred to organic life as "fleshies;" she felt uncomfortably small and soft in zeyr presence.

Then, the music dropped. The Ashlings got into a defensive stance. Before Ellinor could take another breath, Kai and Jelani were flying toward the bots. The flash of their bare skin kick-started Ellinor's heart as she lurched ungracefully into action.

The music started up. Fast, heavy beats that rattled her body as much as the Ashlings'. Lights flashed. Ellinor's stance synced with the synth-bot composing music around their group's movements of their own accord. Kai fired at the bot with the crossbow, the shot becoming part of the music and light show.

Then, Ellinor's soldier's training kicked in and she stopped hearing the music, stopped seeing even the spectacle she was now part of. She saw enemies. She saw danger. She saw Kai get smacked with the flat edge of the Ashling's sword.

Anger clouded her vision, and Ellinor saw red. Kai should have ducked, he _knew_ to duck; _why is he letting that Ashling bat him around so easily?_ Ellinor's chest tightened, her breathing sharp and painful as the Ashling hit Kai's blisters . . .

She dropped beneath the hammer swing aimed at her core, rolling into a crouch and taking out her Asco Rhino in one fluid motion. War automata, no matter what kind of modifications they were given, were not as quick as the smaller, guard androids. The hammer Ashling twisted, unable to move zeyr weapon before it was caught in Jelani's blades. The sword's glow—the color of desert sand—flared as it momentarily held the Ashling in place.

Ellinor swiveled her body before Crossbow and Sword could reposition. She fired the metal spear through the shoulder of the crossbow Ashling before zer could ensnare a dazed Kai. Crossbow staggered, and she jumped to her feet, just as Hammer kicked Jelani aside. Ellinor could not roll out of the way this time, fear and anger over this Ashling hurting Jelani engulfed her body and raised her temperature.

Half turned, she flung her arm back, thumbing her shield into action. The metal plates snapped out, reaching their maximum extension in milliseconds, just barely fast enough to block the low swing of the hammer. Ellinor went flying, bouncing off the far wall of the cage, near where Kai was *finally* exchanging blows with Sword.

Kai caught the blade in one gauntleted hand, the other pulled back to deliver punch after punch into Sword's side—zer was too tall for Kai to reach zers head. Each blow Kai delivered dented the bot's narrow waist, his high-powered Coyote metal gauntlets giving him an extra boost. Until Sword fell into his rhythm and caught Kai's hand. The two became locked in a stalemate, trying to wrestle the other into submission.

Jelani danced with Hammer, keeping zer away from Ellinor while she struggled to catch her breath, her back burning from the impact. The *clang* of their weapons and the flash of Jelani's tattoo became fodder for the spectators to dance to.

Taking a deep, ragged breath, Ellinor got to her feet and ran, ducking into a slide at the last moment.

Sword twisted Kai's arms, sending the big man to his knees. But instead of finishing him, zer lurched after Ellinor. She rolled out of the slide, barely avoiding the sword, and a chill went down the base of her neck. Ellinor changed course; instead of going for Jelani, she went back for Kai, glancing out into the crowd momentarily as she did so. She couldn't see Oihana or Izza, let alone Fiss. She just hoped the seerani was nearly finished with her task; Ellinor couldn't risk any more close calls.

She helped Kai up as Sword turned, and Crossbow finally managed to get ahold of the javelin Ellinor had speared zer with. She didn't have time to reload her Asco, so she took out the Lance.

Electricity curled along the blade as she ran for Sword. Kai fired round after round from his scattergun into the knees of Crossbow. Ellinor launched herself into the air, using the Ashling's sword as leverage to get her up and on top of the hulking robot's shoulders. From her vantage point, she saw Crossbow begin to topple, zers legs no longer capable of supporting zer as Kai continued to pelt it with concussive rounds.

Ellinor dropped behind Sword, running her electric blade down zers side where the blade was. The electric tendrils curled over the Ashling's body, and zer began to jerk and spasm just as Kai finished shooting at Crossbow.

An animalistic roar erupted from Kai in a challenge to Sword. Ellinor didn't have the chance to yell at Kai to go help Jelani with Hammer, to cover his flank so he wasn't left so vulnerable. Kai seemed to be dead set on Sword, oblivious to all else, despite the bot being more skilled. Ellinor's opponent turned, still twitching, sword held high—level with Kai's unprotected head.

"Kai! You're leaving yourself open!" But Kai only sneered at Ellinor in return, and charged, hands too low to protect himself.

Panic welled within her, hot and searing as her thoughts tumbled over what a strike like that would do to Kai, and her friend did not seem to care.

Ellinor gasped, "No!" and jerked her blade back up, burying it in the side of Sword's neck before zers blade could connect with her friends' unprotected skin. Zer stuttered one final time, and stopped, toppling over. Dead.

"What did you do?" Jelani yelled, but it was too late.

"Kai . . . he isn't paying attention. He's been hurt enough, and I thought . . . It looked like . . ." she trailed off, her breaths still coming in short bursts, but not from exertion. Her stomach twisted painfully; she had just broken the one rule they had to follow. The two remaining Ashlings moved back, blocking the arena door in case Ellinor and her crew decided to flee.

The crowd began stomping their feet, the arena lights turning bright white, no longer pulsing. A spotlight pointed at the door they had first emerged from and a rolling vibration began to grow beneath the arena floor. The previous winners were on their way.

Her dread grew. This wasn't part of the plan. Now, the few rules they had to follow were gone, and she still couldn't see Oihana or Fiss anywhere. Eyes wide and chest heaving, she went to Kai and pushed him—hard—in the chest. "Do you have a death wish? What happened out there, Kai?"

"Ah, I was in no trouble, Ell. You didn't 'ave to go and fry zer!" Kai shot back.

She shoved him again. "You could have been paralyzed! Do you want to get hurt? Why are you suddenly so reckless? That's supposed to be *my* thing."

Kai slumped, his body sagging. "You know why. This is a pain I understand. It feels . . . better than what, ah, shit, Ell, you *know*."

Ellinor's heart seized, and she squeezed Kai's hand despite his Coyote gauntlets.

Jelani glared at them both, fury wafting off his body like smoke. He couldn't even berate them; the lights cut him off, blinking out for a second. A slow, red strobe light with a steady beat—like a heartbeat—turned on, and the arena doors opened. A flood of cyborgs and Ashlings alike stepped into view.

The tempo changed. More lights began flashing, and a swarm of bodies flooded into the arena.

Ellinor couldn't see who was who, if she was cutting organics or Ashlings, as her knife flew through the air. Her armor flared with each successful punch, and she thumbed on her shield once more to give herself some extra room.

The shield severed someone's arm as it snapped into place like metal snake scales. They screamed, Ellinor was sure, but she couldn't hear it over the thundering of her heart and the electronic beats that still buzzed and thumped in time to the combatants' movements. Without knowing how it happened, she found both Kai and Jelani at her sides, using her shield for cover as they fired their guns and flicked their swords at the wave of bodies that converged on them.

Ellinor turned to give Jelani more cover. She fired her Asco over Kai's shoulder just as her hair was yanked and she was jerked away from her friends.

Hands, claws, and clamps held her fast. She struggled, twisting and kicking at anything she could, but it was no good. She felt her armor begin to die under the barrage of punches and stab wounds it was attempting to protect her from. That's when the fear set in.

I can't die here. Not like this!

Hot pain bloomed along her back, someone's blow finding a weak spot at last. Almost instantly her malfunctioning collar began burning her skin, glowing and sparking as it surged on. She twisted, trying to get away when it hit her.

Azer no . . . Fiss!

Her hair began to stand on end, muscles contorting as if she were being shocked over, and over again. And in a way, she was, but not in the way those who held her were.

They were floating off the ground, limbs stretched at painfully wide angles. Wind swirled, kicking up blood and debris and lashing it like a whip at those who had held Ellinor pinned. Ropes of lighting held those who had cornered Jelani and Kai in place, the crowd was going wild, the music was trilling, and the lights were flashing between red, blue, and white.

And, just outside the cage walls, stood an angry little boy and a terrified seerani.

Fiss' pale eyes were glowing with an eerie white light, his small teeth bared in a feral snarl as he shrieked incoherently. Dreeocht can't cast destructive, deadly magic without using a caster as the conduit, it is the one flaw to their otherwise limitless magic—that, and their persistently idyllic good nature. Fiss, in an attempt to save Ellinor, had to use her latent magic in order to incapacitate those harming her. Without her consent. But, unlike when he had used Ellinor's magic to destroy the doehaz in the Saxa Desert and defeat Zabel, her pain, the feeling of her magic trying to break through her ribcage while simultaneously shriveling up her veins, no longer gave Fiss pause.

Oihana's eyes were wide as she watched the dreeocht, her hands flying over her wrist apparatus as she gave commands to Izza. Izza moved, nearly wrapping zer metallic body around the furious dreeocht, risking electrocution in order to hide Fiss, to keep the crowd from noticing the child casting so much magic.

A scream ripped itself free from Ellinor. Her body was on fire, molten metal pumping in her chest as the bio-magitech embedded in her skin grew and spread, a needle jabbed into her heart, her breathing became harder and harder . . .

BUZZ!

The timer went off. Ellinor, Kai, and Jelani had survived the five minutes. But Fiss did not release anyone. The music continued to play and the people outside were still dancing and cheering. Thanks to Izza, they hadn't noticed the dreeocht, and Ellinor had to keep it that way.

She struggled to her feet, moving her hands rapidly as if she were the one casting large, complex amounts of magic, leaning hard into the façade of Lenore Castile. It gave Jelani and Kai time to scramble over to the cage wall closest to Fiss and Oihana. The voice of the bouncer bot who let them into Synth-Lyfe buzzed in her head, *"No magic . . ."*

Ellinor shook her head, focusing on Jelani and Kai. She couldn't hear their words, but she *could* see how their bodies remained tense. Fiss' eyes still glowed, his snarl twisted into something almost evil. Nothing they were doing was working. Fiss' gaze remained locked on Ellinor. He saw the people around her, the pain her body was still experiencing because of Fiss' use of magic, but the dreeocht would not be consoled, not while Ellinor was panicking, not while he could still feel Ellinor's pain as the magic tried to force its way out.

That's it!

As the combatants closest to Ellinor began shrieking, their arms and legs popping out of their sockets, eyes bulging painfully, metal digits being bent at unnatural angles, begging for mercy, she forced a smile at Fiss. "Baby bug, I'm okay. Let them go, Fiss."

Her voice was raspy, just above a whisper as she struggled to force oxygen into her lungs, but Fiss heard her. He would always hear her.

And, just like that, he released the air and water magic, and the pain was gone. Fiss was smiling like himself again, fingers laced through the cage as he pressed his face against the mesh wires. Ellinor ran to him before anyone noticed it had not been her casting, despite the painful thumping of her heart.

"Fiss, what did you do? How did you do that?" Ellinor asked, but Fiss didn't get the chance to answer.

"You hacked my systems, asshole. You didn't need to turn my arena into a bloodbath," someone said, a minor lisp in a slightly mechanical, but feminine, voice.

Ellinor jerked back in time to see the arena doors open and the other fighters flee, though the music went on. Her eyes were blurry with tears, her vision going black at the edges as her body went into the shock it always did when Fiss used her locked away air magic. Her heart unable to find its natural rhythm.

"How else were we going to get your attention, Aylen? You refused to answer my calls," Jelani tried, and failed, to keep the strain out of his voice.

The woman—or Ellinor assumed it was a woman, she couldn't really see the person standing in the arena with them—clicked her tongue at him. Aylen turned away, her ample shape swaggering off as she called over her shoulder. "Did you ever stop to think I had my reasons for not answering your messages? That maybe it was intentional?" She waved at them over her shoulder, and Kai scooped Ellinor up when her legs wouldn't cooperate. Her muscles were cramping and she couldn't suck in enough air, the effects of Fiss casting lasting longer than they had before.

"But fine," Aylen growled. "Congratulations, you got my attention and forced me to see you. Now, let's talk in private before you start more drama."

A FAVOR FOR A FAVOR, FOR A FAVOR

E LLINOR WASN'T aware of when exactly she passed out. One moment, Kai had been helping her up. The next? She was sprawled on a cushion in one of the coziest, softest rooms she had ever been in. Ellinor blinked, clearing the blurriness, and when the world stopped spinning, her gaze fell to the sleek, black stone floor which glimmered faintly with silver flecks.

She shut her eyes and took a deep breath, willing the ache behind her eyes to go away. When she opened them again, she noted the plush white, pink, and orange rugs littering the room underneath the plethora of large floor cushions some-one could easily drown in. Shapes were nestled into most of the cushions, their forms blurry as Ellinor's senses gradually returned to her.

Ellinor leaned forward in her metallic green cushion with a groan, the pounding behind her eyes intensifying with the effort. As soon as she was moving, she felt a warm body slide against her back, small arms wrapping around her neck and chest.

"Elli okay? No more owie ouchie?" Fiss nuzzled the side of her head, remorse and fear thick in his prepubescent voice.

She placed a trembling hand on his head, and he sighed against her neck. "I'll be fine, Fiss. No lasting damage."

What she wanted to ask him was what had happened. How was it possible that he could use her as a conduit when he knew it caused her harm? And without using her will to shape the destructive magic on his behalf? But she was too emotionally and physically exhausted to find the words. Instead, she took another deep breath, her vision finally clearing enough to see the room in full.

The walls were covered in grey soundproofing, and where they weren't, artistic photographs of the various areas of SynthLyfe hung, some of their colors inverted. It was like someone vomited color all over the room, and while all the neon should have clashed, should have made her head ache with the loudness, oddly, it worked. The intense décor fit in seamlessly with the pulsing lights and sounds from the club beyond.

Ellinor swiveled around to where Kai, Jelani, Oihana, and Izza were seated facing a large steel desk with floor to ceiling amplifiers behind a plush red chair. Aylen Bonheur, however, was nowhere to be seen.

Oihana was fussing with Izza, oblivious to Ellinor being awake. Kai's upper body was bandaged and he was hunched over, head cradled in his hands, not turning to face her even though with all the noise she was making, he knew she was conscious. Jelani watched her though, his bruised face impassive except for the wrinkle between his brows as he observed her and Fiss. Ellinor tried to move her seat cushion closer to the rest of her group, but it was an ungraceful affair and she gave up partway through.

She flopped back into the cushion so it hugged her on all sides, and Fiss nestled himself at her feet, his hair gently swaying against her legs. Jelani didn't speak, his starry night eyes roved past Fiss to her and lingered on the embedded collar. Ellinor broke the tense silence. "Is your contact going to throw us out for violating her rules? Or is keeping the winnings from the forfeited match good enough for her?"

Jelani shook his head. "We survived the death round, all has been forgiven according to Aylen's regulations. Regardless, you still murdered an Ashling, Ellinor." He paused and took a deep breath. "As for using magic when we were forbidden to? I can't say." His words were clipped, as if he would berate her, or scold her for getting them into such a mess.

Ellinor tensed, ready to defend her actions, but the reproach never came, which somehow made it worse. Her stomach sank. Jelani let out a long breath, his shoulders slumping.

"Aylen is showing out the Ashling doctor she had on hand. Zey looked over your . . . affliction, and I'm sorry to say, but it's gotten worse. Something has gone drastically wrong. Or more wrong, I should say. The Ashling couldn't say how or why, but your bio-magitech is spreading like a virus, and it seems to be affecting others." Jelani leveled a pointed look at Fiss, who was holding his feet in his hands and softly humming to himself, oblivious to Jelani's ominous words.

Ellinor touched her neck, her throat suddenly dry. She opened her mouth to demand an explanation, but Jelani shook his head. "Not here, not now. I'll explain later when there are distractions." His eyes drifted to Fiss again then darted back up to Ellinor, and she let the matter drop.

For now.

What worried Ellinor most about Fiss were the parts of Misho that dwelled within the dreeocht. Was that what had caused Fiss to lash out? Was Fiss holding on to a part of Misho that recognized Ellinor and wanted to protect her? Ellinor bit her lip, not sure how she felt about that possibility.

The thought of some part of Misho living within Fiss no longer wrenched Ellinor's heart and gut like the knowledge had when she had first learned that Fiss was able to sense her "water man," as he called Misho. Instead, it was a balm now, and it was easy for her to call Fiss her "baby bug," as Misho had been her "little bug" in life.

She stopped biting her lip, taking a ragged breath. Her eyes scanned Jelani and Kai. She noted their bandages, the bruises blooming on their bodies, the torn blisters and raw, angry skin. "Will you be all right? Both of you?" she murmured, nudging Kai's cushion with her toe to get his attention.

"Yeah, that Ashling doc patched us up good and tight. You don't gotta go worrying about us none, boss." Kai's voice was thick, and not with the obvious physical hurt.

"I'm sorry," she murmured. But before she could say more, before anyone could say anything, for that matter, the office door behind Ellinor slid back with a soft *hiss*, and heavy footsteps filled the room.

"Awesome. That terror of a caster finally decided to wake up. How you feeling, murder princess?" the slightly mechanical, feminine voice said. Ellinor recognized the faint lisp; it was the same one she had heard before passing out. Her tone icy, a warning humming from her as she approached.

The woman stomped to the desk, and Ellinor got her first clear look at Aylen Bonheur, the creator and Owner of Synth-Lyfe, and Jelani's reluctant contact.

Aylen was a thick woman, soft and voluptuous, except for the parts that gleamed with metal. Her slightly squinty hazel eyes glittered dangerously as they settled on Ellinor and her own robotic neck. Aylen grinned, though it looked forced. "This is the infamous Ellinor Olysha Rask then? The one that all the bounty channels are buzzing about?"

Her forced good humor melted, and she glared at Jelani, panic and worry glimmering in her eyes, her tawny brown skin flushed with anger, highlighting bronze undertones. "Do you know the amount of digital scrubbing I've had to do since you bitches showed up here? Fuck, man, you're supposed to be smarter than this. You know damn well that everyone is hiding from something. Who else knows you're here? Did someone send you my way? It can't be a coincidence that of all the places you decide to lay low, you pick here. You pick *me*."

Aylen perched on the edge of her desk, muscles tense as if ready to spring at a moment's notice. Her dark blue leather miniskirt stretched over her full thighs, her fishnet stockings ripped in such a way that Ellinor knew she had bought them pre-torn.

"And you," Aylen glowered, leveling a finger at Oihana. "Don't go fucking around in my systems again. You expose me to malware when you do that. There's a better way to get my attention and you *know* that, Oihana."

Oihana hung her head, and Aylen crossed her arms over her stomach and the costume military jacket she wore purposefully buttoned off center. Only half of the jacket was there though, covering her left arm and breast. The other half was ripped away, showcasing her bedazzled bright pink bra—which Aylen was in danger of spilling out of—along with the pieces of biotechnology that made up her neck and part of her chest. Not to mention her completely mechanized arm.

Ellinor couldn't help but stare at Aylen's arm. Sourness coated the back of her throat as she wondered if Aylen's enhancements were elective.

Jelani spread his hands helplessly. "I was careful, trust me. But you see what I'm traveling with, Aylen. Who else would I go to?"

"You want me to give you a list? Jelani, I can literally think of a dozen other people you could have gone to. You know Cosmin and Zabel have already sent hackers? I caught them, okay? But I swear to Azer if you got turned . . ."

Jelani sighed. "No one sent me. I wanted to come to you first, friend. Can't you see this for the opportunity it is? Ellinor has . . . graciously agreed to allow access to her dreeocht, Fiss."

Aylen's eyes widened, but her expression remained pinched. "The rumor is true?"

Ellinor hugged Fiss a little closer, not liking that Cosmin already suspected they were on Amardeep, that rumors were circulating about Fiss. With how Kai frowned, his fists clenched, she knew he felt the same.

"Ms Aylen, I believe you understand now," Izza stated, leaning forward slightly next to Oihana, but still maintaining zers perfect posture. "If Fiss chooses, he could create the very thing my people have desired, have been engaging in conflict over, for nearly a century. Mr Jelani is allowing you and your staff to be the first to benefit from such an advancement. Given your recorded stance on Ashlings, and the work you have done to help my people, the odds state that you would not wish us to take such a proposal to someone else."

Aylen rubbed her chin, and leaned forward, observing Fiss more closely now that he wasn't hidden in his loose disguise. Fiss tilted his head in return. Aylen's shoulder length, curly hair fell off her covered shoulder as she leaned ever closer, the other half of her skull completely shaved. Her corkscrew curls were dyed alternating bubblegum pink and neon blue. Even her eyebrows had been dyed; one pink, one blue.

"Remarkable," Aylen whispered. "Do you know what I can do with this?" Her eyes began twinkling again and Ellinor put a hand on Fiss' shoulder.

"Not so fast. Fiss isn't doing *anything* for *anyone*. That wasn't the bargain. Jelani promised to get this piece of shit tech out of my neck first. It's neutralized my magic and I want it back. That first, then after we can talk about what it is you think you want to *ask* Fiss to help you with," Ellinor said, a growl lacing her voice.

Aylen leaned back and crossed her feet at the ankles. "That wasn't done on purpose?" Ellinor shook her head, and Aylen gave a low whistle. "Fuck if I can help you then. I modify synth-bots and help zem become Ashlings. I'm good with the biotech stuff, even have some expertise with magitech, but I'm not *that* good. Even if Oihana assisted, there's not much we could do. Not at the moment, anyway. Maybe someday."

Ellinor's stomach went into freefall, her face going slack at Aylen's words. Dread curled in her chest, and Ellinor barely noticed she had stopped breathing. Aylen was her one shot to get fixed, and she couldn't help? Fiss whimpered next to her and burrowed into her lap. Ellinor clung to him, tears stinging her eyes.

Oihana waved dismissively in the air. "Way ahead of you. I tried taking it off, or turning it off at least. Wasn't going to happen, and I'm *much* better now than the last time you saw me. We need someone else to get that out of Ell. My guess? The caster that put it on her had some crappy failsafe in there that got fried to the abyss and back the second she got blasted with too much magic."

Aylen was silent as she thought, her squinty eyes narrowing even more.

"What we need—what we done came here for," Kai said, breaking the silence with a voice still a little rough, "is information. Figured you couldn't fix Ell, but Jelani promised you'd know someone who could do what needs getting done. Would love an introduction and the like so we can be on our way. Seems like that'd be agreeable to everyone at this point."

Aylen laughed. "Dude, you've got some massive balls on you asking for some shit like that. Do you have any, and I mean *any*, idea what this murder princess cost me, hmm? There's a reason why I forbid Juice Boxes and casting in my club. It fucks with the odds in the arenas." Her lips pulled down in a scowl, hazel eyes flashing dangerously.

Jelani was quick to intervene. "We know introductions don't come for free, Aylen. Though I think the possibility of an assist from a dreeocht would be tempting enough?"

Aylen snorted. "My understanding is I get to *ask*. Your dreeocht could tell me to shove a fork up my ass and then I'd be left with nothing, or worse, for my trouble. Because let's be real, Jelani, you're already costing me a lot of trouble. And credits. The amount I lost tonight from the gambling kiosks from that bout of casting has cost me way more then what you're offering in return."

Ellinor blinked rapidly, turning to look at Oihana, hoping that Aylen was exaggerating. But from the pout on the seerani's face, it appeared as if Ellinor had no such luck. None of this was going according to plan, all their luck apparently running out when they had evaded the doehaz. Ellinor's throat tightened, her heart constricting painfully in her chest, and all she wanted to do was curl around Fiss, bury her head in his cable and seaweed hair, and never move again.

"Ms Aylen," Izza said, zers soothing voice filling the room. "I have just calculated the potential earnings of what unlocking and creating new Ashlings could do for your bottom line. It would more than cover for the losses of tonight's fight."

Aylen rolled her eyes. "Sure, *if* the dreeocht agrees. Free will is a bitch like that, Izza."

"Aylen, come on, where's your sense of adventure?" Oihana pleaded.

The Owner of SynthLyfe sighed. "There's a reason I stay away from people, and yet, here you are. I don't like this." She sneered unconsciously, then shook the look away. "There's only so much I can quash in the news feeds, even with the false names. Someone is bound to leak that display of magic, so even if the mobster you crossed doesn't come knocking, some anti-Ashling group or some politician looking to score cheap points in the polls on the mainland will come sniffing around here. Then *they* could find me. No way, man. I can't risk my life for your potential promises. I need those credits you cost me just for the overtime my team is going to have to pull to keep this place secure now."

Jelani clenched his jaw and nodded stiffly. "Tell us what you need then, and we'll do it while we take advantage of your help and protection. You still owe me that, at least. Fair is fair. But Fiss' identity needs to be guarded at all costs."

The sparkle returned to Aylen's eyes as they rested on Fiss. After a moment, she let out a long sigh. "You're putting me in a bind, man. You get that, right? Look, of course I know of someone with the right tools and an equally weird fascination with cyborgs that could *probably maybe* do what you want. But the . . ." Aylen groaned. "The only one who could help your woman now—"

"She's not my—"

"The fuck? I'm not his—"

Jelani and Ellinor interrupted in unison, only to have Kai chuckle and Aylen silence them by kicking her heels against the desk. She uncrossed her arms and gripped the edge of the desk as if worried she would slide off.

"Gorgi can do it, okay? You're going to want Gorgi. But to get that kind of meeting, I need credits. Lucky for you, I may have a job that gets me the money you cost me, and gets you an in with Gorgi at the same time." Aylen grumbled, clenching the edge of her desk tighter and drumming her fingers along the sides, her eyes darted about as if she expected trouble—more trouble—to come bursting through the door at any moment.

"I don't recognize that name. Who is that?" Oihana asked.

Aylen averted her gaze, glaring at the floor, her hands still tense despite the slight tremble to her fingers as she gripped the desk. "Zer's an Ashling, and zers official title is Assistant Mechanical Director for the Habitation, but unofficially? Zers the one who actually came up with the idea to create proper housing on Amardeep and combine it with the biggest resort hotel on this shithole. But you know how it goes. Ashlings can't run a business that large, so zer sold the idea to some cyborg seerani that only comes out to Amardeep for official events. It's kind of creepy, actually." Aylen shivered, shaking her head and taking another deep breath.

"Gorgi doesn't run the day-to-day for the Habitation. Zer can't. But I think zer prefers it that way, you know? It allows zer to do what zer really wants, which is to tinker and make drugs. Gorgi is the one who makes pretty much every single Juice Box you can find here, and pretty much anywhere on Eerden. Zers operations are *that* big."

"You want us to go rob an Ashling drug lord? That it?" Kai said, a tremor in his voice that Ellinor couldn't tell if it was caused by excitement or worry.

"Nothing so simple as that. I don't want Gorgi's drug money. I want zers program."

Ellinor's cheeks flushed in anger. The last thing they needed—that Amardeep needed—was more Juice Boxes. Her back straightened, ready to turn Aylen down flat, when Jelani said, "But you're not in the Juice Box trade."

Aylen smirked, crossing her arms over her chest again. "Damn straight I'm not. But zers code can do more than make Juice Boxes. Look, I'll explain later. For your purposes, the part that should be helpful to you and also scare the piss out of you, is zers sick fascination with combining flesh and mechanics. I don't mean like one of the Ashling doctors either, man. It's . . . hard to explain, but, if you want something like that collar off, zer's the only one capable of it, I'd bet my right tit on it. All the best mechanics on Amardeep are in Gorgi's pocket—if they aren't in mine."

"Of course, it had to be a fucking Ashling," Ellinor groaned, only to have Izza turn and stare at her. Ellinor shrank back, mouthing an apology to zer.

Aylen snapped her head toward Ellinor, a sneer tugging up the corner of her full lips. "Don't like Ashlings, do you, murder princess? Some robotic slave run off on you, and now you're scared they'll spill your precious little mob boss' secrets? Or some secret dirty fetish you have that makes your own skin crawl?"

Ellinor's teeth ground together, and she was about to fling herself at Aylen and wipe the contemptuous sneer off her round little face, when Jelani put a gentle hand on her shoulder. "A group of *our* people, accompanied by Ashlings, were responsible for her husband's death," Jelani said. "Really, Aylen, you should know better than to pass those kinds of judgements on others so hastily."

Jelani may have been speaking to Aylen, but the pressure of his hand on her shoulder told Ellinor his words were not meant for Aylen alone. She hung her head, and vocally apologized this time to Izza. The Ashling inclined zers head, but otherwise didn't acknowledge her words.

Aylen's lips pressed into a thin line, but she let the matter drop. "Doesn't change who you're going to have to see. And it doesn't change the fact that I don't have a direct in with Gorgi. Zer's elusive, doesn't meet with the other Owners."

Aylen paused, her blue eyebrow arching with an idea. "But there is someone. A chick who's been itching to defect but hasn't anything to offer yet . . . that might make the risk worth it on my end. You help her get what she needs, and she'd get you in with Gorgi, and then you'll both have the credits to pay me with. She'll need your help, of course, but then she gets out and I can help her, and you, see? And then you can help yourselves. You can't ask for better than that, right?"

"Do you know what this girl wants, or needs?" Oihana asked, interest making her deep voice marginally higher.

Aylen winked at her. "Gorgi's codes and programs, obviously."

Ellinor could feel a sneer pulling her lip up, but tried to mask it by asking, "This woman have a name? Where are we supposed to meet her, or get in contact with her?"

Aylen's eyes traveled over Ellinor, cold and guarded as ever once again. "Her name is Elisaveta Baldini, and I'll set up a meeting. But not tonight. You're a mess, and I need time to get a message through secure channels. Given the buzz you bitches stirred tonight, I've got to work double-time to make sure no one followed you to me."

Moving off the desk, Aylen waved back toward the door behind them. "Enjoy the club for now. Drinks on me—well, on you, actually. I'll just add it to your tab." She pressed a button on her mechanical arm, and another green laser light washed over their original barcodes, updating them and changing the placement so the barcode was on all their hands.

"Have fun or whatever, but absolutely no more arena time, got it? Obvious reasons aside, the body count you racked up tonight beat the bloodbath we had three years ago. Five people died and the rest won't be arena ready for weeks. If they're lucky. Not a record I thought I'd have broken tonight, or by an old acquaintance, that's for sure," she said, shaking her head once more, her frustration making her slight lisp more pronounced.

Fiss was the first up, floating in the air with glee. "We make more friends? And get to dance, dance, dance? I like dancing, Elli! Thank you, new friend!"

Fiss beamed at Aylen, and the woman blushed under the creature's honest and pure happiness. Ellinor didn't have the heart to explain that Aylen wasn't a friend. She was just another person who was only willing to help if they paid her, and that access to the little dreeocht was part of that payment.

As they left Aylen's office and headed toward where they could change and clean up, Ellinor's stomach began twisting in so many knots she felt sick. The mere idea of Fiss agreeing to make more Ashlings, coupled with the suggestion that her broken shackle was somehow . . . doing *something* to Fiss, made Ellinor want to call the whole operation off.

She didn't want to go out and party or even pretend to have a good time. But how could she say no when Fiss looked so happy? When Kai looked so eager to forget about Cosmin in all the glowing drinks he could get his hands on? And when even Jelani's coy smile began to slip into something more eager?

Ellinor stifled a sigh. *Fuck it, time to get drunk.*

STRAIGHT, NO CHASER

THE DOORS slid closed behind Ellinor, and Fiss flew from her arms to sit on Kai's shoulders. His wide eyes swiveled back and forth faster and faster, trying to observe every movement of the club around them. While Ellinor was passed out, they had been taken to the top floor reserved for Aylen's employees away from the club goers, and into the exclusive VIP area. This was the floor where Aylen made her more clandestine deals, had meetings, dealt with troublemakers, and arranged private rooms for those with serious credits to drop and a penchant for privacy.

Oihana led them to a room reserved for important clients, and celebrity musicians who stayed for extended periods of time. The sleek, black mirrored door glided back soundlessly as soon as Oihana flashed her barcode in front of the small scanner. She waved them in, a smile pulling up her full lips, and Ellinor's breath hitched as soon as she passed the threshold.

Ellinor was forced to squint reflexively at how white every-thing was. From the pristine white of the padded walls, to the fluffy floors, the frames on the mirrors, the bed, and even the high gloss on the furniture. White chandeliers hung from the ceiling with red crystals that made the room look like it was splattered with blood, the only color to be found.

Stepping into the suite, Ellinor noted the dazzling view of the club and the different levels below. With the slight frosted quality to the glass, Ellinor knew no one below could see them. Their window was just another mirrored panel to those partying below.

Kai gave a low whistle as he looked around the room. His eyes settled on the silvery door that led to the bathroom, and he strode to it with purpose and disappeared inside. Oihana grumbled something about him beating her to it before she flopped on the cloud-like bed and turned on the holo-screen mounted flush into the wall. She thumbed on the captions and began flipping the channels mindlessly while Izza plugged zerself into the wall just to her left. Zer seemed to be doing zers best to ignore Ellinor. Izza had not forgiven Ellinor's cal-lous words, and she didn't blame zer. Fiss, for the moment, was glued to the window, transfixed by the undulating chaos be-low.

Jelani disappeared into the walk-in closet to change into something more appropriate for going back downstairs, but she stopped him with a light touch to his shoulder before he could shut the door. He turned, a curious glint to his eyes, and Ellinor whispered, "You need to explain what that Ashling doc-tor said about my bio-magitech, and the effect it may be hav-ing on . . ." Her words trailed off as her eyes drifted to Fiss, but he wasn't paying attention to the casters. "Oihana mentioned the incident Fiss had on Anton's ferry. She didn't have the equipment to do much testing then. I take it this doctor was able to see things she couldn't?"

Jelani's shoulders slumped ever so slightly as if remorse weighed his shoulders down, lips pulling into a sympathetic frown, a pang of pity flashed through his eyes. "It's something Oihana first suspected when you mentioned the constant burn and vibrations you felt even when Fiss cast harmless magic. The intensity is worrying, especially since it's only increased since our encounter with Zabel. I mentioned the concern to the doctor before Aylen returned, and the doctor confirmed that your shackle is growing. Well, spreading, more accurately."

"Well," Ellinor said, trying to smile even as her lips trembled, "we already knew that. So, what's the big deal?"

Jelani took a quick breath, as if to stop his chest caving in with the burden of what he had to share. "Yes, but it shouldn't *continue* to spread. That's what I'm trying to tell you. After we left Zabel's territory, that should have been the end of it."

Ellinor's mind seemed to stall, shutting down and refusing to process Jelani's words. She rocked on her heels, pressure building behind her eyes as she refused to accept what should have been obvious from the start. "Jelani," she said slowly, voice weak. "Spell it out for me. I haven't been conscious that long and I need a little help here. What does all that *mean?*"

Her heart started to race, her mind poking at the words of Oihana and Izza from earlier, her thoughts skirting an uncomfortable realization. Ellinor wasn't stupid, but she wanted to play dumb longer, to deny that something worse was about to happen. Her breathing became shallow, and a sharp cramp twisted around her heart. She gasped, pressing a hand to her chest. She couldn't remember if that had ever happened before . . .

Jelani steadied her, and with a sigh, gently pulled Ellinor to the white leather couch against the far wall. She hadn't noticed how much her legs were shaking until he sat her down. Jelani didn't release her hands even after she was seated, his thumb gently running over the backs of them in a comforting motion. She wondered if she should take her hands away, tell him she was fine, but she did neither of these things.

"Cosmin added a virus of sorts, to keep you from tampering with the collar. I don't think he accounted for the possibility of you having to fight casters with types of magic similar to Fiss'. Instead of the virus crippling you like it did initially, when you got too far from Fiss' container, it's become more like a biochemical virus now, according to the doctor." Jelani's voice lowered further. "The more the tech spreads, the more it destroys your own cells, your organs."

My heart.

At his words, the notion of removing her hands from his vanished completely. "The more it grows . . . if it gets to my heart, I'll drop dead, yeah?"

Jelani nodded, and Ellinor's mind began spinning. But the shock, the despair she expected over the sudden knowledge of her days being numbered, never hit. Her stomach turned, not because she didn't want to die, but because she didn't want to expire without killing Cosmin first. She took several deep, ragged breaths, the information settling in her, and she accepted her fate. As easy as that.

Then, a plan began to form.

"Right then, we have to get back to Euria soon, before that happens. I have business to finish," Ellinor deadpanned.

Jelani's hands clenched momentarily, and his head bent toward her. He didn't bother to mask the distress and disappointment pulling his face down. "You didn't let me finish, Ellinor. I didn't tell you the full extent of the situation."

"What could be worse than me kicking the bucket a few centuries early? What else could there be?" Ellinor tried to joke, to remove the weight settling on her shoulders, but her heart wasn't in it.

"You may be fine throwing your life away so casually, but no one else will be," Jelani said, voice hard despite the quiver that made his chest rumble.

Ellinor didn't get a chance to ask who would really miss her after the hurt she had caused, as Jelani added, "This virus affects Fiss, too. Leaving your shackle as is, even if unlocking your powers is beyond anyone's capability, is poisoning Fiss. It's . . ." Jelani paused, glancing at the dreeocht with his face still pressed firmly to the glass.

He took a breath, steeling himself, and continued, "It's making Fiss *evil*, for lack of a better word. Turning him more toward a doehaz in temperament, almost. It will destroy him. You understand? Fiss won't die, but he won't be *Fiss* anymore."

Ellinor's mouth was suddenly dry, her muscles all tensing at once, and no amount of swallowing dislodged the anguish wedged in her throat. She leaned toward Jelani a little more so Fiss couldn't hear. "How is that even possible?"

"Your bond, Ellinor. Fiss—he always knows when you're in pain, and though he couldn't stand it before, like what occurred with the doehaz, he didn't actually *feel* your pain. Just knew it was there. The more the virus spreads? The more your bio-magitech collar dies and your magic shrivels away inside you, the more Fiss can physically feel your suffering,"

Jelani said, his eyes sliding over to Fiss. "Dreeocht are, by nature, good. Fear and despair aren't things they're equipped to process. Really, they don't process any negative thought or emotion; they simply react. So all this hurt? It's turning him. But into what? I can't say."

All the things she had wanted to be a coincidence, to have just been a result of pressure or extenuating circumstances, she could no longer pass off. Tears pricked the back of her eyes, and she hastily brushed them away. It was one thing to die of her own actions, her own desire to give peace to Misho, but it was entirely unacceptable for her to destroy something as pure as Fiss in the process.

"Does Kai know?" Ellinor whispered.

Jelani gave a one-armed shrug. "No, not outside of knowing something isn't right. The doctor had just administered a painkiller so he was rather loopy during my conversation with the Ashling."

Ellinor nodded, trying to keep the cracks in her exterior from becoming chasms. "Good," she mumbled, then cleared her throat and said more firmly, "It's good he doesn't know the details." Ellinor paused, her mind scrambling for answers, for solutions, or at least a loophole to exploit, and was coming up blank.

"What am I supposed to do, Jelani?" Her voice broke with emotion and she shook her head, biting her lip until she regained control of her voice. "There are no good options here."

Jelani's thumb never ceased tracing comforting circles over her hands, though his arms stiffened as if he wanted to do more, to pull her closer. Ellinor looked away, and Jelani's jaw clenched momentarily before he said, "We continue on as we were. We meet with this Elisaveta Baldini, do our best to get in touch with Gorgi, and go from there. If zer truly does have the best mechanics on Amardeep, then zer has the best mechanics period in zers employ. One of zem *will* be able to do something to debug your collar. To save you and Fiss."

"But if you can only save one, if it's either me or Fiss, you pick Fiss. You fix Fiss and keep him safe."

"Ellinor—" But Jelani was interrupted by a whoop from Kai Brantley as he kicked open the bathroom door.

"Azer bless Aylen's shower! That shit really 'it the spot," Kai said, smiling as if they hadn't almost died an hour ago.

Ellinor jerked her hands from Jelani's grasp and turned away before the Creature Breaker could say anything. She forced a smirk on her face and winked at Kai as she skirted around him and locked herself in the bathroom. Ellinor could hear Fiss tapping on the door a second later, but she needed a moment—*just one fucking moment*—alone with all this new and terrible information.

"Elli? Elli! Can't see! Let me in, let me in! Elli? Miss you already," Fiss called.

Ellinor collapsed against the door, her breath hiccupping as her chest tightened with every breath, stomach twisting, crawling up her throat, her knees too weak to keep her upright. "Fiss, remember what we said about bathrooms?"

Ellinor waited a moment, not because she thought Fiss would answer, but because she didn't trust her voice not to break again. "I'm not going anywhere, baby bug. But you need to give me a minute to get cleaned up. Go sit with Oihana or Kai. Everything's fine."

She waited a moment longer, until she was sure Fiss was no longer on the other side of the door listening, before she practically ripped her clothes off, turned the shower back on as hot as it would go, and let the despair take her. She bit her lips, trying to keep the sob at bay, and failed spectacularly. Ellinor slid to the shower floor, praying the noise of the shower and the hot, nearly scalding water, shielded her from Fiss. She covered her mouth with her hands while she screamed in anguish, tears washing down her face in a steady stream, hissing and evaporating when they rolled down to the collar as the device heated up and thrummed along her neck, but the pain of her collar as Fiss began casting was nothing compared to how much it hurt to breathe, to simply *exist* anymore. In the back of her mind, she knew Fiss casting was a result of what she was experiencing, but she couldn't stop.

I'm losing the last bit of Misho. I'm breaking Fiss. I can't . . . I won't destroy my baby bug.

FAKE IT TILL YOU MAKE IT

O NCE ELLINOR could cry no more, exhaustion making her body heavy, she crawled out of the shower. The aches and pains of being pummeled by dozens of fighters may have ebbed, her muscles may have uncoiled under the barrage of the scalding water, but the coldness in her bones didn't lessen.

She gave herself one more moment to wallow before toweling off, then exited the bathroom.

Ellinor changed into the clothes left for her—she hadn't exactly packed for a night out when Cosmin first abducted her, and she hadn't had much time to grab anything in the three days it took them to get out of Erhard, either. Ellinor fixed her raven black hair so it hung in gentle waves down her shoulders and back before applying light make-up to better hide the blotches on her cheeks caused by crying, though there was no helping the rosy tint around her vibrant blue eyes. All the items Ellinor used or wore belonged to Aylen and were on loan. Ellinor had no doubt these items would be added on to the bill they owed Aylen, but she considered the clothes, make-up, and the suite a necessary expense. She didn't want Fiss to suspect that anything was wrong with them, with her, and especially with him.

Oihana barely gave Ellinor a cursory glance as she skirted around her into the bathroom. Kai was already dressed and ready to head back to the lower levels, red and acid green hair styled up, clad in flawless black pants and a fitted mesh tank. Despite the grin on his lips, there was a sad shadow behind his eyes, and Ellinor suspected that Kai was still eager to bury his feelings in any way he could.

Me too, big guy. Me too.

Jelani had changed out of his torn and dirty clothes from earlier, and Ellinor couldn't stop herself from doing a double take. He cleaned up better than she expected.

The seersha stood casually leaning against the window in a pair of fitted black slacks, and a white, longsleeved dress shirt that was buttoned only part way up his chest, showing the sharp contours of the muscles Ellinor had seen on full display in the battle arena. The white made his dusky brown-grey skin appear darker, his eyes and fog-like hair stand out all the more. She watched him ripple off the window with the fluid, controlled movement of a dancer and shrug his broad shoulders into a military style black blazer. He stuffed his hands into the coat pockets before he sensed her gaze.

Jelani looked up and saw Ellinor standing there in the middle of the room, gaping at him. He winked at her in return, flipping his hair out of his eyes. "You look beautiful, Ellinor," Jelani said, nothing but sincerity in his voice. "You look positively humani again."

Ellinor glanced down at the faux-leather, skintight leggings she wore. They were a deep, emissive purple, a shade darker than the dyed pieces of her hair. The cropped black corset top with its wire laces in the front, which wouldn't close all the way, displayed crisscross patches of her bare skin. Ellinor still would have preferred to be clad in her simple shirts, jacket and leggings. But since all were stiff from sweat and in need of a wash, she was forced to wear the garb Aylen kept for guests in case they needed a change.

"My Elli is always beautiful, Jelly!" Fiss declared, floating over and landing at Ellinor's feet, hugging her calves.

She smiled down at the dreeocht, pleased that he was disguised as a humani child once more. Or, at least, as disguised as a being like Fiss could be. Once Ellinor was where Fiss could see her, he relaxed, and after he got his fill of reaffirming her presence with physical contact, he drifted back to the window, entranced once more by the dancing figures and scintillating lights below.

"So, what's the plan now?" Ellinor asked. She wasn't in the mood for revelry in the slightest, but it had been a long time since she'd had a night without pain and, given the thoughts in her head, Ellinor desperately wanted to get *drunk*.

"Ah, Ell, you know we're gonna party. Ain't that obvious? Azer knows we may not get the chance again. Best live in the moment before it all turns into another shit storm, aye?" Kai said as he stood by the door, a wide smile on his face as he stood with his hands on his wide hips, but his smile didn't light up his eyes like they had mere days ago.

Ellinor swallowed the urge to ask Kai if he wanted to talk about what happened, if he wanted to vent about what Cosmin had done to him, or the broken heart the seersha had saddled Kai with after torturing the big man. He had rebuffed her every single time she had tried to broach the subject on Anton's ship, and somehow she didn't think now would be any different. So, instead, she tried to play along as if everything was as it should be. "Fair, but I don't think I'm going to the same place as you."

Kai chuckled. "Ah, shit, I 'ope not, boss. Would be mighty awkward to see you in that state."

Jelani made a sound behind her like he disagreed, and her cheeks instantly flamed. Ellinor growled to herself, annoyed and embarrassed for reasons she didn't want to think too long or hard about.

"I figured we'd accompany Oihana and Izza to the lower levels, if you don't mind, Ellinor?" Jelani said, a warmth to his voice that she was confused by, a hesitancy that hadn't been present since they had arrived on Amardeep.

"I come too!" Fiss said, still watching the activity below.

"Fiss, a club isn't a great place for a . . . well, a child, or dreeocht, really. Stay here, please?" Ellinor pleaded.

The hair on Ellinor's arms began to rise with the static of Fiss' displeasure. Before the tiny dreeocht could turn and pout or wail to go with her, she relented. "Look, okay, Fiss. But you have to stay with me, got it?" Fiss clapped his hands, giggling in excitement. She smiled, watching him, and said, "Do you mind, Jelani?"

"Not at all, as long as I, too, can stay with you."

She turned slowly, but Jelani had averted his gaze to Fiss, a soft smile on his lips. Ellinor narrowed her eyes momentarily before shrugging. At least on the lower levels she could stand at the bar and drink while Oihana and Izza gambled on the fights and Fiss tried to teach himself how to dance. She wouldn't have to pretend to be having a good time, like she might have felt obligated to do on the higher levels with Kai.

"Works for me," she responded, slipping on a pair of knee-high black combat boots that she could easily hide her Lacerator knives in. Jelani watched her, his eyes soft as they traced every movement, but if he disapproved of her taking the knives with them, he kept such opinions to himself.

Oihana emerged a few minutes after Kai left the suite, wearing baggy, black and white parachute pants with electric blue racing stripes up the sides. Her black tank top was ripped, showing her toned midriff and framed by a pair of clear plastic suspenders. Izza was at her side a moment later. "Ms Oihana and I will meet you at the lower levels," zer stated.

"We'll go with you," Ellinor said, stooping to scoop Fiss up.

"Unnecessary and unwanted, Ms Ellinor. I would prefer space from you at this moment in time. I am processing your statements on Ashlings. They have become increasingly difficult to ignore." Ellinor cringed at zers words, but before she could apologize, Izza gently placed zers hand on Oihana's elbow and led zers maker from the room.

"Give Izza time, Ellinor," Jelani said, his breath tickling her ear.

She shivered but didn't answer, holding Fiss closer to her chest as they left, taking the next elevator down to the lower levels.

Ellinor didn't feel the elevator move as the level lights briefly glowed, momentarily highlighting the dozens and dozens of floors they were speeding past.

Fiss barely waited for the doors to open before he was about to fly after Oihana, trying to locate "Little-Jelly" and his metal friend in the swell of moving bodies. Ellinor stopped him with a hand on his shoulder. "Stay where I can see you, Fiss. Don't talk to anyone but us, and no magic, got it? That includes flying."

Fiss looked confused for a moment. "But what can I do, Elli?" he asked, his voice shrill to be heard over the music.

"You can dance if you want to," Ellinor offered, and Fiss' face lit up as he darted away, trying to mimic the movements of the dancers along the edge of the crowd.

Ellinor positioned herself to be able to watch Fiss from the corner of her eye as she waved down the robotic bartender. She smothered her shiver as zers cold, grey ocular orbs landed on her and she flashed her barcode at zem. "Whiskey, double, neat, whatever your top shelf brand is." The Ashling made a whirring sound of understanding, gliding away.

Jelani sighed behind her, and she wheeled around to face him. The smile he wore may have been coy, lifting just the corner of his lips, but his gaze was dark with disappointment.

"What?" Her eyes moved away from his and settled on Fiss as he bobbed and darted around the dancers, who didn't seem to notice him "dancing" nearby.

"Getting drunk won't change anything. It won't erase what we discussed," Jelani said softly.

Ellinor smirked and said, "Clearly you haven't done it right then." He rolled his eyes and watched the Ashling bartender slide her whiskey toward her.

Ellinor wrapped her hand around the heavy glass and lowered her gaze. "Look, I know drinking isn't a cure. But it deadens everything momentarily, okay? It distracts me and numbs me, and right now that's what I want. Everything over the past week has been too sharp, too blunt and bright, and without my magic it's all so tasteless and dull at the same time. Everything, and I mean *everything*, hurts and I just need . . ."

Ellinor trailed off and shook her head. She looked back at the seersha, his hands tucked in his pants pockets as he stood casually before her, and she lifted her glass before taking a heavy pull of the deep amber liquid.

"Perhaps I can offer a different distraction?" Jelani offered, joining her at the bar. She arched a brow, but he didn't elaborate, instead ordering his own whiskey on the rocks with a water back.

She watched the bartender glide away before saying, "I'm not dancing with you and Fiss, if that's what you're getting at."

Jelani smiled, his eyes twinkling devilishly. "Too bad." His voice took on a deep purr. "I happen to be an excellent dancer."

She felt her core heating up without help from the whiskey. Ellinor took another sip, her boldness growing. "I believe it, with how smooth you're trying to be." She winked and Jelani laughed, genuinely laughed—head thrown back and everything.

"There's the spirit I've come to respect from you, Ellinor." He took a sip of his own drink before adding, "You're lucky I happen to have a soft spot for cruel women."

Ellinor's brows knit together, sirens blaring in her mind that this was dangerous. Misho's amber eyes twinkled in her memory, and she knew she should back away, back away *now*. Taking a sharp intake of breath, her fingers danced around the rim of the glass, her eyes locking on their movement instead of Jelani. "How about this as a distraction then," she said, voice slightly breathy, "you tell me more about Aylen. Seems only appropriate, if we're going to be working with the woman, yeah?"

Jelani rubbed the back of his neck, stalling. "What is it you'd like to know?" he asked eventually, slowly taking another sip.

Ellinor was nearly finished with her first round, and she signaled for a refill. "Well, if the biotech on her body is for show or if she needs it to live, for starters."

"Does it matter?" Jelani challenged. "Would it change anything?"

The bartender gave her another whiskey, taking away her empty glass. Feeling a lot bolder, but only a little better, Ellinor swiveled to face him, watching Fiss from her periphery. "Yes, actually. To me, it does matter."

Jelani sighed through his nose, his eyes hardening slightly. "You shouldn't harbor so much prejudice against the Ashlings that it bleeds over to those with robotic enhancements, Ellinor. The Ashlings who hurt you are not representative of all Ashlings, nor does zeyr behavior have any bearing on those who side with zeyr plight, or choose to replace their organic parts with machines."

Ellinor returned his hard look with one of her own, not answering other than to take a drink. Jelani's jaw clenched momentarily before he said, "Very well."

Leaning against the bar, he tilted his head close to hers to avoid being overheard by the constant stream of people that came back and forth to refill their drinks. "I met Aylen when an accident at the mechanics academy in Nishat caught my attention about twenty years ago."

Jelani's voice was soft as he spoke, just loud enough to be heard over the fast, thin beats of the music pumping through this level of the club. "Aylen loved music even then. She'd been working on making a sophisticated synth-bot, one that had more potential to turn into an Ashling, yes, but she'd been following the rules, or so she claimed. She had all the right programming locks and checks in place to keep the AI from turning."

He paused to take another drink himself, his eyes never leaving Ellinor's face. She tried not to squirm under his scrutiny. "Aylen believes someone saw her designs, read her code, and didn't like what she was up to. Whether that's the case or not, I never found out, but Aylen's been paranoid ever since." Jelani jutted his chin toward the surveillance system in the corner of the room, then pointed to another camera above the bar, and then another by the exit, and so on. Ellinor made a mock toast toward the nearest camera, in the off chance Aylen was watching them.

Jelani rolled his eyes at her, continuing. "Aylen was alone in the workshop when there was an explosion. It destroyed most of her work, and the ensuing electrical fire left her barely alive. She was taken to a hospital and her life was saved, which tells me that perhaps whatever caused the explosion wasn't personal." When Ellinor didn't react, Jelani shrugged and took a sip. "The perps could have easily killed Aylen. Regardless, the explosion made all the newsfeeds, even the national ones outside of Nishat. That's how I heard of what occurred. Any time there is an explosion of that caliber at a mechanics university or workshop, I get curious. It could be an Ashling trying to escape, after all."

By then, Ellinor was genuinely captivated, her drink momentarily forgotten as she leaned toward Jelani, the space between them evaporating bit by bit. "So, Aylen's machine bits are there because of the accident? They keep her alive?"

Jelani nodded, his eyes momentarily leaving hers to watch Fiss twirl on the dance floor, trying to catch the strobe lights. Jelani's gaze drifted back to Ellinor. "She lost her arm, a lung, and a kidney. Not to mention several of her heart valves were so damaged they couldn't be salvaged. She's had other modifications since then, implants in her eyes and ears, specifically to help with her business, but for the most part, the robotic additions you can see are there not by Aylen's choice. That gives you two something in common, you know."

Ellinor frowned a little at him, and the corner of Jelani's lip twitched in a soft smile. "I officially met Aylen shortly after I concluded my investigation. She was still in the hospital, she'd had a few surgeries by then, was stable, coherent enough to form her theories about what happened. From that day on, her sympathies changed. She turned from someone who didn't care for Ashlings one way or another, into one of their biggest supporters." He paused, his smile turning into a smirk. "You could learn from her example."

Ellinor glared at him. Her anger at the Ashlings over Misho's death would not allow her to accept the merit of Jelani's words, even if she could accept the similarities between her and Aylen. "Don't, Jelani," she said. She had wanted to sound cold, but her tone was more miserable than anything else.

Jelani dipped his head. "Very well. There's not much to tell beyond that. I introduced Aylen to Oihana not long after Aylen was set up on Amardeep. The two now help each other move and sell different pieces of tech, items that are illegal for their sophistication in coding—namely, better suited to crafting Ashlings. She's been a good friend, especially to my sister.

It was only her paranoia that kept her from wanting to speak to us. Don't hold that against her."

"I don't," Ellinor said instantly, and she was surprised that she meant it. She glanced at her nearly finished drink, another already waiting for her that she didn't remember ordering. Without food, and with the various pain meds still floating in her system, Ellinor was getting tipsy faster than she intended. But the warmth of the alcohol . . . it was the only thing that alleviated the chill in her soul without access to her air magic, and the occasional sharp pang in her chest from the bio-magitech.

Jelani raised a brow at her, his own drink nearly gone, though it was still his first of the evening. He ordered another, waiting for her to elaborate. Ellinor glanced back, and once she was satisfied that Fiss remained undetected as he hopped and twisted with the other dancers, she turned back to Jelani with a shrug.

"I get it, is all," she said, her words slow. "Aylen doesn't know who to trust. Someone betrayed her and hurt her, they took something away from her she can't ever replace, or, rather, she can't get back what she lost. Not exactly. I mean, she can't ever go back to the person she was. She kind of lost herself." Ellinor's voice turned smoky, and a soft smile spread on her lips of its own volition. "She was lost and hurt, angry and desperate, and you found her. You saved her, yeah? Just like—" Ellinor hiccupped, cutting herself off.

Jelani had been taking a swig of his second drink, but at her words, he put the glass down. His eyes half-lidded, his gaze shifted from her eyes to her lips. Ellinor swallowed the thickness coating her tongue and before Jelani could respond, added, "It's the same with me and Misho. He was taken away, ripped from me without us even getting a proper goodbye, not that a goodbye was ever something we wanted," she shrugged and swallowed, beginning again. "He saved me that day, and yet . . . it cost me everything. When they . . . when Misho was killed, I lost my whole heart. My purpose." Ellinor's eyes were blurry with tears, her throat constricting with pain. She pressed her lips together and focused her attention on the glass in her hand.

She felt Jelani draw nearer. His leg brushed her knee, and he stood before her, while she remained perched on the barstool. There was a tension thrumming between them that Ellinor didn't want to examine. A heat radiated from her core, and part of her hated it. She refused to look up, refused to confirm that the same heat was building in Jelani as well.

No. . . it's nothing. He's handsome, and I'm getting drunk, that's it. That, and it's been years since I had sex. But that's all. The end.

But Jelani stood there, a rigidity to his body, a stiffness to his neck as he bent toward her, his nimble fingers, trembling slightly, mere centimeters from her own hands.

"Even after eight years," Jelani said, his voice husky, his warm breath tickling her ear with how close he was, "you talk about Misho like he is paradise and all the stars in the sky. But he's gone, and I am so sorry he was so violently stripped from you. Can you truly see nothing, see no one else due to the light he still casts over your eyes?"

Azer, no. I don't want to.

She looked up, her lips parted, tears running down her cheeks. "Moving on, leaving him in the past . . . it feels impossible. The worst betrayal. Living without Misho? Pointless." The whiskey was making her weak. Her walls, her carefully maintained brusque façade, crumbling away brick by brick.

Jelani's movements were smooth and delicate as he brushed the tears from her cheek. Ellinor shivered and leaned into his hand. He held her cheek gently, his words just as tender. "I think your Misho would want you to live, Ellinor. I think he'd want you to be happy, and to find a new purpose. A new light."

She looked up at him, her vision bleary, lips parted. Dozens of questions buzzed in her head, but none louder than: How? How? *How?*

She swayed closer, desperate for answers, for warmth, for anything that didn't remind her of how lonely she was, how cold and hard her heart had become. To forget, for one blessed moment, how much she wanted to feel Cosmin's blood pooling in her hands.

And there was Jelani, leaning down as if he would whisper in her ear, but he didn't move, he faced her head on, eyes locked on her, and Ellinor wasn't moving away this time, despite her mind telling her: *No, no, no!*

"Elli! Elli! Dance, dance! Dance with me!" Fiss called, suddenly next to her seat. He beamed at her with a wide smile, not registering her confused, rapid blinking, or the blush flaming across her cheeks and the back of her neck. "Dancing is like flying, Elli, but with your feet on the ground!" he said, tugging her hand.

Ellinor latched on to the excuse Fiss gave her and got to her feet.

Fiss giggled as an unsteady Ellinor let the dreeocht lead her to the edges of the dance floor. She didn't look back, though she knew Jelani was still watching her. She felt the burn of his stare on her as she walked away. They lingered on the edge of the crowd as Fiss clapped his hands and tried to move as fast as the dizzying beat.

Ellinor swayed, dipping and moving slowly, not trying to match the beat. Her body was aware that Jelani was watching. The logical parts of her mind, the parts turned cold with loss and a bloodlust for those who had hurt her, was glad Jelani didn't join them. But there was something else, something deep in her, that was disappointed at the same time.

Ellinor turned back to the bar, trying to convince herself it was just to check to see if her drink was there and to go back and fetch it. Her drink was right where she had left it. But Jelani Tyrik Sharma was gone.

GROWING UP IS THE HARDEST
MOVEMENT TO MAKE

E LLINOR ROLLED over in the plush bed, and her eyes
snapped open. Izza was standing at the edge, silently peering down at her. She jerked back, sputtering incoherent
curses, but Izza reacted to her outburst only by making a *tsk-
ing* noise, as if in disapproval.

She had a hard time remembering when they had all returned to the VIP suite that night. Her feet ached from dancing with Fiss, and her head still spun mildly from the whiskey.
She had no idea when Kai returned, and he didn't offer an explanation of what he had gotten up to the night before. He
seemed happy, though, and that was good enough for Ellinor.

"Ms Ellinor, it is time we departed. Ms Aylen waits in her
office with instructions on how and where to meet with Ms
Elisaveta. I am told Ms Aylen will provide breakfast," Izza
stated, then made to turn away as Ellinor reached out.

Her hand hesitated a moment before she tapped Izza on the
back. "Hey, Izza. Look, about what I said in Aylen's office yes-

terday? I'm sorry, okay? I didn't . . . I'm trying, all right? I'm sorry for offending you."

"I would appreciate it if you tried harder, Ms Ellinor," Izza replied, before waddling back to where Oihana was hunched over the white lacquered desk, toying with what looked like a computer chip.

Ellinor sighed. *I deserved that.* She propped herself up in bed, groaning slightly as her head swam, her vision taking a moment to settle before she could see straight again.

Fiss was nestled in the bed next to her. He didn't sleep, not like everyone else. Occasionally he rested, but it was more of a recharge than actual slumber. He hadn't so much as stirred at her flailing or Izza's words. He smiled, tapped her on the nose with a giggle, and lazily hovered out of the covers. It wasn't long with Fiss up and buzzing around the room before everyone was moving, putting on their armor and travel clothes. Soon, they were all ready and headed back to meet Aylen in her office.

Aylen wasn't there when they arrived, but one of her Ashling assistants was. Zer was a rather large synth-bot, zer torso cylindrical in shape, resting on five small, sleek wheels that offered incredible ease of movement. Two cable-like arms with four, three jointed digits on each end allowed zer to create music as easily as zer could open a door. Zer shiny, oval head rotated to watch the group enter, triangular, grey, optics focusing on their group and causing a shiver to run down Ellinor's neck.

The Ashling had a thin slit for a mouth that didn't move as zer spoke. "Welcome back. I trust you slept well?" Zers voice box was not tiny or robotic like most—even Izza's. Zer sounded more like a female singer, zer tone a melodious falsetto.

"We did, thank you very much for the hospitality," Izza answered for the group. Izza seemed more comfortable, even though zer was just as formal, when speaking to others of zers kind.

The synth-bot gestured at the spread of food laid out on a fold away table against the wall. "Wonderful. I'm Rada. I will be briefing you this morning. Aylen had to attend an urgent meeting with the other Owners of Amardeep. She apologizes for this, and will attempt to make it back presently. Until then, please eat. Once you are satisfactorily sustained, I will share Aylen's instructions."

Ellinor found her appetite evaporating with the suspicion over what Aylen was really doing, and if her Ashling had an ulterior motive for briefing them instead of . . . anyone else. Rada looked harmless, like a trashcan on wheels mostly, but that voice, it was so organic . . . if Ellinor closed her eyes, she could almost pretend Rada was a *real* person, and that unnerved her most of all.

Stop it, Ellinor. They are individuals. Sentient and alive. Do better, she berated herself.

Ashlings, no matter what was unlocked in zeyr programming, could never feel the range of complex emotions that came naturally to organics. Even if it had been technically possible, it wasn't allowed, and no one even included those kinds of algorithms in android software, let alone computer AI. And in any case, there were no programs sophisticated enough to truly emulate the spontaneous intricacy of emotion. It was partially why zey wanted dreeochts, to get over that final hurdle. But that wasn't an excuse, a reason, that Ellinor could continue to hide behind to justify her actions, and she knew that. She owed Izza. She needed to do right by zer.

But still . . .

Ellinor didn't think zeyr being able to fall in love, feel despair, or better understand pain would make zem all that more alive. After all, zey could still be shut down and rebooted like nothing happened most of the time. In Ellinor's opinion, how could a creature who couldn't die, and therefore couldn't properly fear death or the end of zeyr existence, be truly alive?

I would appreciate it if you would try harder. Izza's words rang in her head when her own mental voice was incapable of talking sense to her. Ellinor's shoulders slumped, guilt swirling in her gut, and abruptly she noted that she had been standing warily in the middle of the room this whole time, just staring at Rada.

Ellinor recalled her conversation with Jelani the night before, and it was easy to believe what he said when looking at bots such as Izza, but she knew she had to work harder, not just where Izza was concerned, but with bots that looked like Rada, too. Ellinor wasn't sure how to change her perception, and she flexed her fingers, still unwilling to move closer to where Rada was patiently waiting by the table of food.

Each time Ellinor tried to embrace Izza's admonishments or Jelani's words, she saw Misho's lifeless eyes and the crumpled Ashlings and zeyr sympathizers in the warehouse where they had attacked her and her husband. Ellinor's resolve hardened, and she swore to ask Aylen if she knew anything about the Ashlings and zeyr . . . *friends* who had attacked her at the first opportunity. Surely, Aylen would know what kind of Ashling would risk breaking into Cosmin's warehouses? Perhaps a rival mechanic of Aylen's, or a Juice Box peddler looking for an edge.

The old Ellinor would not have wasted this much time. *This* Ellinor, the one whose edges were softened thanks to Fiss, Kai, and now Jelani, was finding it harder and harder to force herself to stay focused firmly, and solely, on the revenge business. She justified the lapse as not important, not as essential as getting her magic back was to the overall goal of killing Cosmin. And yet . . .

Kai nudged her, the action kickstarting her senses and stilling her spiraling thoughts. She turned slowly toward her friend and the two plates of food in his hands heaped precariously high with lab grown bacon, powdered eggs, imitation bread, and puny greenhouse fruit. Ellinor grinned, reaching for one, but he moved his hand away.

"Nice try, boss. This 'ere food is mine. Only wanted to be sure you got some before I go and get seconds," Kai said with a chuckle.

She rolled her eyes but did as Kai suggested. She helped Fiss fill his own plate, though Ellinor wasn't convinced he actually wanted to eat. Fiss mostly liked to sniff and play with food, sustained naturally by the magic he was made of. Ellinor ate in silence, watching the group around her, though her eyes often locked on Rada and Izza.

Once Rada determined that each had eaten, the Ashling rolled back toward Aylen's desk and made a throat clearing sound. "Elisaveta is to meet you between the Scrapyard and the Unincorporated Dwelling collective that rests outside the Habitation," Rada said, a singsong quality to zer voice. "Be cautious. The Scrapyard is as it sounds, a place where Ashlings driven mad from viruses and corrupted programming dwell, often fighting with doehaz over spare parts. Zey cannot be repaired and are sequestered to an area similar to your necropolises. If you do not enter zeyr domain, zey will not trouble you. However, if you venture too close, I cannot promise that one of the stragglers, be it an Ashling or doehaz, will not pursue you."

Rada paused, and Ellinor swore it was for dramatic effect, before continuing. "The Unincorporated Dwellings are private residences for Ashlings who do not wish to work or align zemselves with the larger corporatocracy. Elisaveta will not be in any of those residencies, so you have no cause to trouble any of the Ashlings there." Again, Rada paused, zer oval head rotating to face Ellinor, a hint of warning to the melodious voice.

Ellinor frowned, ready to argue with Rada, but she held her tongue, jutting her chin up. Rada's cable arms relaxed, if you could call it that.

Progress! she thought with pride before she quashed the feeling back down.

"I have arranged a private car within the monorail. It makes a short stop at the Unincorporated Dwelling. You will exit and wait in the underground tunnels that lead to the Scrapyard. Do not leave the fork that splits off and heads for the Scrapyard. Elisaveta will locate you," Rada said, rolling toward the food and starting to clean up.

"How will we know Elisaveta when she arrives?" Jelani asked around a mouthful of food.

Rada did not pause in zer duties. "Elisaveta will find you, as I stated. Do not concern yourself with the rest. The monorail departs in one hour, on the hour. Please, collect your belongings and head to the depot entrance at ground level."

Rada wheeled around to the door and showed them out, and just like that, they had been dismissed. They had barely gone more than a few feet when Aylen approached from the elevators. Her black plastic mini dress hugged her buxom form.

She had her eyes glued on the tablet in her hands, and the holographic personal assistant that stood on the screen. Ellinor briefly thought about asking the Owner if she could dig around on her behalf about Misho. But as Aylen approached, her gait not even slowing as their paths were about to cross, Ellinor decided it probably wasn't the best time to ask the woman about any personal matter. Especially after their tense meeting the other day, and how much they already owed her from Fiss using magic to end the fight.

Aylen didn't bother looking up as she neared. "Once you meet with Elisaveta, use this to message me so I know you haven't bounced and are working to pay me back."

She handed Oihana a palm-sized wireless comm unit before dipping her head back to her own work, her blue and pink curls bouncing along half her face. She brushed past them, all business and hostility, not betraying any of the violent past that Jelani had shared with Ellinor.

Ellinor's muscles coiled, her body tensing as soon as they were seated. Their private car was luxurious—by Ashling standards—the windows marginally cleaner than others, and their privacy better kept than in the crowded main cabins, but nothing could make Ellinor relax when she knew they were nearing doehaz territory once more.

Each time the monorail rocked, she gripped the hand rests, worried a behemoth of a monster was crashing onto the tracks, wrestling a corrupted Ashling. Kai caught her when the monorail bounced over the rough terrain, and he gave her a playful shove. "You're more jittery than a duct-squirrel on coffee, boss. Relax, we ain't getting that close to no doehaz. Even in the tunnels, we'd be too far off."

Ellinor nodded, but it was hard to take his words to heart when all their recent encounters with the beasts flashed before her eyes. She shut them and took a deep breath before changing the subject. "You talk to your mom, big guy? She safe in Desta?"

Kai tugged on his lower lip and glanced over her head out the dingy window. "I 'aven't been able to get a message through to 'er. Suppose that's for the best. Communications ain't all that secure where she be. Still . . . wish I knew she was doing okay."

Ellinor patted his knee. He wasn't wearing his Coyote suit yet, so he felt the gesture and grinned wanly at her. She *did* know how he felt.

When she had first smuggled her own parents out of Euria, following Misho's death, she had worried constantly over their safety. At least until they began to resent having to leave the place where Andrey was buried, and her declining to get her brother's signature tattooed on her shoulder, like they had. They had never understood how she could work for someone like Cosmin. Why she would *want* to when she didn't have to. They hadn't spoken in years, and she imagined her parents preferred it that way.

"Maybe we can hijack the communicator Aylen gave us and use it to contact your mom. With that woman's paranoia

I wouldn't be surprised if no one could track it, Ashling or caster gangster alike. But I'm sure she's fine," Ellinor told him with more conviction than she felt.

Kai nodded, some of the gleam returning to his eyes, lessening the severity of the healing blisters that still marred his face. Ellinor didn't want to worry him any more than necessary, especially after what he had gone through. The problem was Ellinor *could* imagine what Cosmin would do to Kai's mother. While Kai may still have a bit of a blind spot where the caster was concerned, Ellinor did not. Cosmin was petty as fuck, caring for no one but himself; he could be no more reasonable than a child throwing a tantrum when he felt even the tiniest bit slighted.

As they neared their stop, the monorail began to decelerate, and Jelani got up to watch the passengers in the other cabins scramble to collect their gear. Fiss followed after him, curious about the movement. No one came close to their doors, and Jelani was going to keep it that way. While her brother was distracted, Oihana leaned forward, waving at Ellinor.

"Hey, I have a favor to ask," the young seerani said.

Ellinor cocked an eyebrow, a smirk playing over her face at the young woman's bluntness. "Oh?"

Oihana tilted her head, her large golden-brown eyes wavering slightly, and she began to fiddle with her hands, though her gaze never left Ellinor's lips. "I know you have this thing with Ashlings. And by 'thing' I mean you'd nuke zem from orbit if given the chance, which, you know, is shitty, but whatever. When everything's all done, no matter what you decide to do about your collar, or if you tell Fiss not to help Aylen, I want you to help Izza. You owe us that much at least for what we did for Pema and Talin when they got beat up and dumped in my bunker."

Ellinor's eyes narrowed in confusion. "Help Izza how? They—*zer* seems fine to me. I can't do anything for zer that you couldn't do, or do a thousand times better than me, anyway."

"Well, obviously," Oihana said with a scoff. Her eyes darted to where her brother and Fiss were, still distracted. Kai watched them though, a forced relaxed air to him as he leaned back in his seat, hands propped behind his neck. Oihana sighed and tapped Izza to get zers attention. "Tell her, Izza. It's okay."

Izza straightened in zers seat, hands clasped in zers lap as zers ocular orbs fixed on Ellinor. "I wish to process feelings and emotions the way Ms Oihana does. The way you and your kind do, Ms Ellinor. It is the singular folly of my kind, the one thing that truly separates the Ashlings from the organics. Our inability to instinctively discern and incorporate sensations and emotions free of our coding and analysis matrices."

Izza folded and refolded zers all too humani-like hands. Ellinor realized the bot was nervous, or as nervous as zer could be, worrying over an outcome zer did not believe zer had favorable odds toward achieving. "Ms Oihana has graciously unlocked every program she could. Made me as humani as technologically possible. I have IAA capabilities along with Nanny android programs, and even the occasional escort and pleasure software where applicable, but I cannot *feel*, Ms Ellinor. I analyze and I understand, and I react accordingly, but the sensations Ms Oihana describes? I cannot compute those the way she does. I wish to. Little Fiss could be instrumental in such an endeavor."

"You're fucking with me, aren't you?" Ellinor barked, before slapping her hand over her mouth, her voice louder than she intended. Jelani glanced at them momentarily, but a disturbance outside their flimsy door caught his attention once more.

"Why you wanna make Izza feel shit?" Kai mumbled, catching Oihana's attention as he spoke. "Your bot's just gonna get 'urt when zer don't need to be. Zer'll fall in love and then what 'appens when zer gets zers heart broken by some bloke who don't want nothing to do with zer? Just a lot of unnecessary pain, that's what you're asking for, kiddo."

Ellinor shriveled up on the inside.

The Kai of a week ago would have never said something like that. Oihana frowned at him. "Ellinor is rubbing off on you in the worst way possible. That's you speaking from privilege. It's a part of *life*. Izza may be mostly there, but zer wants more and I want to help zer. I *can* help, with Fiss. It'd be easy for him. And Izza . . ." Oihana turned, looking up at her Independent Assistance Android, hope shining in her eyes. She gripped zers hand and said, "Izza is good. Zer's curious. Zer's compassionate. And if zer wants to feel shit, Kai? Guess what? I'm going to help zer."

Oihana turned her gaze back to Ellinor just as the monorail finally slowed to a halt. "Say yes, Ell." She waited a beat then added, "Please?"

Ellinor had to admire Oihana, even if she didn't truly understand or agree with her request. But Jelani and Fiss were nearly upon them, and something told Ellinor that this wasn't something Oihana and Izza had discussed with her brother, for whatever reason, and she didn't want to complicate their bond if she didn't need to.

Giving one deft nod, Ellinor mouthed: *we'll talk later.*

Oihana looked hesitant, skeptical over whether or not Ellinor would help. She spared a glance to Izza. The pair nodded, and got up, collecting their things.

Izza led the way once they were out of the monorail, their gear packed in inconspicuous backpacks as they shuffled through the crowd of Ashlings. Most headed into the toxic landscape outside the depot, not troubled by the nearly unbreathable air or acidic mist. Just another reminder that, no matter how much Ashlings may want to be seen as the same as organics, zey simply were not.

Ellinor shook the thought away and focused on Izza as they moved deeper into the depot. Izza wanted to feel, to cross over that threshold no other Ashling had. If she helped zer do this, what would Izza become? Would zer fear a reboot as a type of death? If so, how could Ellinor possibly still view zer as an Ashling, similar to those who had killed Misho? She mulled the thought over as they left the dingy depot behind.

There was nothing special about the station: stone and steel walls, fluorescent lights that flickered obnoxiously, and a stale smell to the air. The Unincorporated Dwellings were anarchy, their upkeep intermittent and dependent on those who felt inclined to pay attention to the area. The tunnels leading back to the Scrapyard were just as uninviting with only the occasional dim, white light to penetrate the darkness.

Ellinor had no way of knowing where they were going or what lay ahead. The tunnels reeked, like something—multiple somethings, actually—had died all over the place.

Uneasy, Ellinor took out her Lacerator knives. She didn't need to see the specialized karambit knives to be able to twirl them with ease around her fingers. Thankfully, the wires embedded in Fiss' skin emitted a faint gold glow so the others could see her knives enough to give Ellinor a wide berth.

No one spoke as they walked. Izza occasionally glanced down at the screen that would alert them when they reached the rendezvous point, but otherwise, everyone kept their eyes and ears peeled for sounds of a diseased Ashling or a doehaz that may have found its way into the tunnel.

They walked in a slow, shuffling manner for at least ten minutes before Izza signaled them to stop. "Ms Elisaveta should be here any moment," zer whispered.

A slight smirk quirked up Oihana's lips as she glanced from Izza, zers screen, and the rest of the crew, before adding, "At least we'll know who she is super easy. No one in their right mind wanders around this creepy place just for fun."

Only Fiss tittered at her joke. He didn't appear disturbed by the dark, dank tunnel, where every far-off drip or shuffle had Ellinor spinning around, ready to throw her knife at anything skittering toward them.

A soft, muffled sound made the hairs on Ellinor's arms stand on end. She whirled around, ready to fling her Lacerator, only to have a surprisingly airy voice say, "Watch it with those itchy fingers, love. I'm the one you've been waiting for."

"Elisaveta?" Jelani asked, stepping up beside Ellinor, his rifle at the ready as well. Ellinor was glad that she wasn't the only jumpy one.

"In the flesh. Mostly," Elisaveta purred. Ellinor only got the briefest impression of golden brown eyes before the shadowed figure that was, supposedly, Elisaveta Baldini was moving again. "Come on, buttercups, you can call Aylen on the way. Let's get out of here, hmm?"

FLESH, MEET MACHINE

THEY WALKED in darkness, the silence so tense Ellinor swore she could hear the creak of her tightly coiled muscles around her bones. The signal out to Aylen had been spotty, so they decided to wait until they were clear of the tunnels, but that meant blindly following Elisaveta until then.

"Buck up, buttercups, you're safe as safe can be with me. It's only a bit farther to a service exit. We'll take a hover speedboat to the Habitation once we're clear." Elisaveta paused, her shadowy figure scratching at thick, curly hair Ellinor couldn't see properly in the gloom. "Heh, did Aylen pack oxygen tubes for you? I didn't think to bring any." Elisaveta's voice trilled with a slight giggle.

Kai groaned. "Just our luck we'd be stuck with this 'ere joker. I ain't dying down 'ere, girlie, you got that?"

Elisaveta snorted and flipped her middle finger at him. "I have no intention of dying with you either, love. If you don't put your faith in me, we'll just have to put our faith in Azer then, won't we?"

"How about this instead," Ellinor said, touching Kai's shoulder lightly before scooping up Fiss. "You tell us what you'd like us to do so you can get your *out* with Gorgi and your *in* with Aylen. That way we can pay off our debts together so she helps us out, too. Saves us time and a lot of stumbling around in the dark if we decide to fuck off, yeah?" Ellinor slowed her gait, and the others followed suit.

Elisaveta, hearing their slowed pace, blew out an exasperated breath. "If you insist, sure, why the fuck not, right? It's not like we're in disgusting tunnels near the Scrapyard or anything." As if on cue, there was a skittering, scraping sound farther down the tunnel. Like broken wheels and over-long nails pulling something toward them, and fast.

Ellinor tensed, her eyes sweeping the darkness for what could cause the noise. Her heart raced as the sound got closer and closer, but there was no sight of what *it* was, and Elisaveta wasn't moving, wasn't leading them away—

Her heart twisted sharply in her chest, and there was a stabbing pain in her lungs that forced a sharp gasp from her. Ellinor pressed a fist to her chest until the pain passed, trying to breathe slowly and calmly, even with the grating sound still approaching.

Izza flashed a light down the hall, and there it was, a tiny service robot mainly used to clean out the air duct systems of the massive buildings so common on the mainland. It approached Kai, wobbly wheels stuck with bits of screws and bolts as if it had tried to fix itself at some point with rubbish. Ellinor's breath stalled again as a fragile, tentacle-like appendage emerged from the bot, as if it wanted to pluck some of the tech out of the boot of Kai's Coyote mechanized suit. Kai kicked the diseased little bot, and it bounced down the tunnel. A moment later, Ellinor heard its wheels again as it fled.

Ellinor brushed her fingers over the tech along her throat, wondering what would happen if one of those bots got near her bio-magitech . . . Kai's voice stopped her. "You good, boss?"

She was perhaps too quick to pull her hand away from the malfunctioning collar. Kai frowned, his eyes going glassy as he looked at the device he had placed around her throat. He opened his mouth, pity shining in his gaze, and Ellinor shook her head. "It's nothing. I'm fine."

Kai didn't look like he believed her, but she waved at Jelani for help, and he cleared his throat. "Elisaveta, please. We are all contracted to help Aylen but the details are sparse. We'd appreciate knowing more before we continue on."

Elisaveta threw her arms in the air. "Fine then." She planted her hands on her hips, face still shrouded in shadow. "Gorgi's got this software program zer uses to make Juice Boxes. Sounds bizarre, I know, but that's how the Juice Boxes are made. Zer runs the formula through this sophisticated-as-shit program that matches up the dead nanites with the specific serums that will enhance, and pull out, the residual magic in the tech. It's what gives Gorgi's Juice Boxes that special kick, and makes them the purest formula out there. It streamlines zers business and not only makes the drugs the standard for cooking, it pretty much destroys the competition. Why get a shit box when Gorgi's product is better? Plus it's cheaper, too, because of how much zer can make so fast. And it's all thanks to this program."

"Why do you want it for Aylen? She doesn't allow any narcotics in her domain. She prefers the natural high the adrenaline from her music and arena matches produce," Jelani said, putting a hand on Oihana's shoulder, keeping her back from Elisaveta.

The gesture made the hair on the nape of Ellinor's neck stand on end and goosebumps spread over her arms. If Jelani didn't trust Elizaveta's story, then they were in trouble. Ellinor got a firmer grip on Fiss and sheathed the Lacerator knife she had been twirling around her hand, reaching for one of her double-barreled pistols instead.

Elisaveta laughed—truly and deeply laughed at Jelani. "Think, love. Think long and hard what a chick like Aylen could do with that program." Elisaveta waited, but only silence responded. She clucked her tongue at them, disappointed.

"Aylen doesn't want to make drugs or even compete with Gorgi. She's all about the high that life gives you when you're in the moment That lightness in your soul when you're dancing to a wicked beat, that quickness in your veins when some attractive woman is dancing closer and closer and you know what she wants and you're down to give her everything. Or like, when all these coincidences line up and you know, you just *know*, that Azer's looking out for you." Elisaveta took a quick intake of breath—whether pained or lost in the moment, Ellinor wasn't sure.

Her voice was softer when she continued. "What if you remove the equation within the formula for the nanites, change the code that lines up with the serums, and apply it to different drinks where the nanites are literally dancing in your blood along the beats? Ooooh, boy! That's a party right there! And it's like you said, love, Aylen's all about that heightened party life. And profit. Chick sure does love making money. We get her this code? She'll be rolling in credits for centuries . . ."

Ellinor didn't know much about programming—software, or hardware, for that matter. So she couldn't say if what Elisaveta said made sense or was even feasible, and since Oihana couldn't see the woman's face well enough to read her lips, due to the dim lighting, or Jelani's hands where he could relay the information to her, Ellinor couldn't ask the smartest person in their group to verify.

Ellinor remained tense, until Izza spoke. "Your words hold merit, Ms Elisaveta. What you claim is possible, and the knowledge I have acquired while in SynthLyfe does indicate that Ms Aylen would, indeed, be capable of reverse engineering such software to meet her unique requirements."

There was another noise coming from deep in the tunnel, a grinding, groaning sound, deeper than anything a small bot could manage. Ellinor's mouth went dry, eyes frantically searching the darkness. Izza paused, and Ellinor heard the Ashling shuffle, moving to guide Oihana safely down the dark tunnel. "Shall we proceed to your hover speedboat?" Izza added, zer ocular orbs glowing faintly.

Elisaveta chuckled as she turned and the group shuffled after her. "I like you, love. What's your name?"

"You may call me Izza, Ms Elisaveta."

"I can genuinely say it's a pleasure to meet you, Izza. The rest of you buttercups?" She snorted and said, "We'll have to wait and see on that one."

As they walked, Ellinor asked the question that still sat heavy on them all. "If you couldn't get this program on your own, what makes you think that we, a bunch of strangers to Gorgi, can help? From what I've been told, the Ashling's a bit of a recluse, yeah? I doubt zer keeps such a program in a place that's easy to get to."

By then, the tunnel began to lighten as it sloped up, and Ellinor got a better look at Elisaveta. Her shadow did her no justice. Elisaveta turned, her curly, rich black hair swaying down the small of her back, and Ellinor blinked in surprise again—if Ellinor didn't know she was a seerani, Elisaveta could have passed for a full blooded seersha. It was all in the eyes. Seerani always had the simpler toned eyes of their humani parent, never the unique colors and shades that seersha did, no matter how unique the seersha parent looked.

Ellinor swallowed, her eyes traveling of their own accord down Elisaveta's toned body. *Shit, I really do need to get laid.*

"Smart and pretty. I'm starting to like you more and more," Elisaveta said, winking a golden brown eye at her before turning back to face the ever-lightening tunnel. The dim light danced over Elisaveta's soft, feathery light green skin, and caught the glimmer of the dozen small studs and tiny rings running up the length of her tall, pointed ears.

"Gorgi keeps the programming code I'd need split in parts and sequestered with zers most talented and trusted engineers and mechanics. I'll give specifics later, but trust me when I say that if I could get to the different pieces of the code solo, I a hundred percent would. But, Gorgi likes cyborg types, so I'm thinking zer's going to be open to bringing you buttercups on board. Which will give you unique access, once zer gets a load of *you*," Elisaveta said, stopping to turn and face Ellinor once more, eyes dancing.

Ellinor gaped at Elisaveta, the rest of the group walking around her as they continued up the tunnel. Finally, her words registered fully. "What the fuck? I'm not an experiment for Gorgi to mess with."

Elisaveta shrugged, and Ellinor got a glimpse of thick, black banded tattoos wrapping around Elisaveta's arms and curling around her abdomen, making her waist appear narrower. She was wearing a short, white cutoff tank top with burn marks around the frayed edges. A large, golden chain dangled around her neck, a gem-encrusted medallion with Azer's name engraved in silver in its center. As the tunnel continued to lighten, the metal shone dully against the woman's smooth skin. Elisaveta hooked her thumbs through the belt loops of her tight blue and black plaid pants, and that's when Ellinor saw the dim blinking light in the tattoos.

She's a fucking cyborg herself!

"You don't have to let Gorgi dissect you, you know. Zer's not into that unless zer's got permission, or maybe wants to make a point to rivals. But, from what Aylen told me, you're going to want zer to poke around your bio-magitech anyway, or no more magic for you, Lenore. Or, should I say, *Ellinor*," Elisaveta smirked.

Her hand was flying before Elisaveta even finished saying her name. She fisted the woman's shirt, the pendant tangling in her fingers. "What did you say?" She seethed, voice trembling with terror that they had already been discovered.

Elisaveta pried her fingers away with ease. "Chill, Aylen had to give me the details when she orchestrated this little group project. I'm no rat, love."

Ellinor remained tense, the others waiting for the women to join them. Her instincts were telling her to call the whole operation off, but she knew if she did that, there would be no hope for her and Fiss. Ellinor sighed, her head drooping slightly, then the flash of Elisaveta's cybernetics caught her eye. She watched the bands around Elisaveta's hips, trying to see the light again as if that would help her determine what Elisaveta was capable of.

Elisaveta wrapped her arms around her stomach self-consciously. "For the record, love, it's rude to stare." The seerani turned sharply, and all but ran to the tunnel's entrance.

"Ah, no need to take offense, Veta. Ell don't mean nothing by 'er staring. She was never as good with the ladies as she was with fellas," Kai teased, reaching back to tug Ellinor along.

Elisaveta wheeled around, the corner of her small, full lips curled in a sneer. "The name is Elisaveta. Period. Got that, *friend?* Don't call me, Veta. That's not my name."

Kai held up his hands in surrender. He eyed Elisaveta's tattoos, rightfully worried about what kind of heavy biotech mods the seerani had, and what they allowed her to do. "All right, un-bunch your panties, *Elisaveta.* Meant no offense," Kai growled.

Fiss whimpered in Ellinor's arms, and she hugged the dreeocht closer as she resumed walking.

Jelani spoke then, "Kai apologized, please, time is of the essence here." His eyes drifted to Ellinor's neck, and Elisaveta took a long, calming breath.

"Fine." She took another deep breath and stopped at the exit. "The plan sounds simple but trust me, it's solid. Gorgi tasked me with finding new talent to add to zers collection of humani and seersha smugglers to pump up his supply lines. More transporters, more Juice Boxes make it to the mainland, so that's you buttercups now. Your cover is that you want to make cash fast, like all Gorgi's smugglers do, but with the added benefit of letting Gorgi poke around your chick for a minute. You say you heard how Gorgi likes cyborgs and the big boss won't think twice about it. It's a fairly common thing, believe it or not, and if you tell zer no one's had any luck with it, zer'll jump at the challenge. You stick to that cover and try not to get too weird or squeamish around Gorgi, and you'll be fine."

Elisaveta attached her own oxygen tube and gave a cursory once over to the group before adding, "The boat's covered, so you won't need to worry about the rain. But the river isn't exactly on the other side of the door. We'll have to run, so I hope you buttercups are in shape. The rain won't permanently damage you as long as we aren't out there very long, so don't stop for anything. I mean it." Once she was sure they took her words seriously, she nodded to herself. "All right, ready?"

With their muffled agreement, Elisaveta pushed open the rusty door. Ellinor put Fiss down and said, "Okay, Fiss, you fly as fast as you can but don't lose us, got that? We're all racing to Elisaveta's boat."

Fiss clapped his hands together and laughed. "I like to race!" And just like that, the dreeocht was flying out the door. Ellinor sprinted after him, Jelani and Oihana quickly outpacing her. Izza and Kai trailed behind.

Ellinor focused on nothing other than Elisaveta as she tore through the heavy foliage ahead of them, flanked by Fiss. She *couldn't* look at anything other than the seerani woman, for fear she would miss her step or get lost and die out in the toxic jungles of Amardeep. Besides, when she looked at only the striking seerani leading their group, it was easy to ignore the hissing sounds her armor made as the rain pelted her, or Kai's grunts when the acidic water hit one of his wounds.

Soon, Ellinor could see Elisaveta's transport bobbing up and down over the all-too-silver water of the river. Kai was lagging, though, his breathing labored and his pained grunts coming more frequently. Ellinor's armor kept her shielded, but it was losing charge. She slowed, turned on her shield to its widest setting, and tugged Kai under its protection like a giant metal umbrella. He sighed in relief, and the two awkwardly ran the rest of the way to the boat.

Jelani held the thick plastic flap of the craft open and helped them inside. Elisaveta tilted her head at Ellinor, a look of curiosity and appreciation glimmering in her eyes behind her dark, thick eyelashes. As Ellinor caught her breath, Izza waddled over to Kai and began checking his burns, opening a compartment in zers abdomen and extracting a cooling salve to rub on the aggravated blisters.

Ellinor watched the Ashling care for Kai, and her face softened. Oihana caught her observing the pair and gave her a knowing look that said: *we still need to talk.* Ellinor nodded and got herself more comfortable while Elisaveta punched in the coordinates for the Habitation in her navigation console.

Fiss floated over to Ellinor, the sting around her neck becoming more obvious now that she wasn't running. "Take a seat, baby bug, no need to use your magic," she said, trying to hide the pain in her voice.

Fiss tilted his head. "Elli doesn't like magic? But I can make Elli pretty, pretty things!"

Ellinor forced a smile, "It's not that, Fiss. It's just we need to keep a low profile, yeah? The fewer people who know what you can do and who you are, the better. Remember, you're supposed to be Sergei here, not Fiss." Ellinor wasn't sure if Fiss understood, but he ceased his hovering all the same.

Once the boat was speeding along just above the water, Jelani carefully crossed to where Elisaveta was, holding on to the handrails along the roof to maintain his balance. "If we're to be new recruits for Gorgi, why aren't we taking the monorail like everyone else? Why go this way?" he said, eyeing the unnaturally thick, silver water of the river.

"Your average plebeian doesn't know what the Habitation's real money maker is, love. It's not a secret to the Owners, but they do like to keep up appearances," Elisaveta answered absently. "We're taking Gorgi's 'smugglers only' access, as it were. It legitimizes who I say you are."

Jelani nodded slowly, shifting his gaze to Oihana and Fiss. Ellinor saw the worry etched into his strong features, and she knew what he was thinking.

"My sister and Ellinor's . . . ward," Jelani said, giving Ellinor an almost apologetic look, "need to be kept safe. Away from Gorgi and zers operations. All of them. It would be better if zer didn't know about them at all. You can make that happen?"

Elisaveta picked at her lower lip. "Sure, sure. The Habitation is huge, love. I can check them in like normal guests, get them a nice set of rooms. Claim your sister is family and the like. Organics all look the same to Ashlings anyway, unless they have some reason to identify us."

Their boat rounded a corner, and a shadow fell over the river and the lake it fed into. If Ellinor thought SynthLyfe was big, the Habitation dwarfed it three times over. A conglomeration of different styles gave the hotel a modern palatial look. Tall spires of twinkling glass set atop regal brick, and steel buildings connected here and there by sparkling walkways. The Habitation was smooth and elegant, stately and modern all at once with flowing lines that made it look peaceful and relaxing. Ellinor was left speechless, and if that was the effect the Habitation had on her, then she knew those who came for their vacations or honeymoons had no clue about the Juice Box production beneath their noses.

Elisaveta slowed their boat, turning it to the far side of the lake toward dead looking knolls and a narrow river outlet that fed into the backside of the Habitation. "Last chance to back out. If you buttercups aren't a hundred percent in this, I'll drop you off at the Habitation's depot and you can hitch a ride back to Erhard. So, what will it be?"

Ellinor glanced at her companions. While she might have chosen to turn away, not risking getting her friends involved with a dangerous Ashling, she knew they wouldn't let her. The collar would kill her; that was a fact. If Fiss wasn't affected, she may have argued. But Fiss *was*, his wellbeing at stake, and even if her soul was too bloody and unredeemable, his wasn't. She had to keep her collar from turning Fiss into an all-powerful doehaz.

Kai gave her a nod of encouragement, though she knew *he* didn't know why she so needed it. Taking a deep breath, Ellinor locked eyes with Jelani, not Elisaveta. "We're in. Let's go steal us some software from a drug lord. What could possibly go wrong?"

THE SECRET TO PARADISE

THE SOUNDS of running water trickled in a gentle melody through the wide halls of the Habitation's main thoroughfare. Ferns and big leafy plants swayed in a lavender-scented breeze that was constantly pumped through the vents, and swirled through the area from big, white paper fans on the ceilings. The bright green foliage was such a contrast to the glowing plants outside that Ellinor couldn't stop herself from touching a few of the ferns just to be sure they were real. Twisting pathways led to small studio apartments in their own bungalows within the main floor. Signs for special elevators pointed to the cheaper motel rooms, and more elaborate signs indicated elevators that would take visitors to luxurious penthouse apartments.

The Habitation appeared larger on the inside. Ellinor turned in slow circles, eyes wide, taking in the main atrium while Elisaveta checked in Oihana and Fiss. Elisaveta had wanted to go and speak directly to Gorgi's men, but Jelani wouldn't hear of it, so here they were.

There were shops offering every luxury imaginable, massages from beautiful men and women, cosmetic surgeries and mechanical enhancement spas promising their visitors could be in and out in an hour—*book now!* There were even a few boutiques and strip clubs, according to the holographic AI concierge.

Elisaveta returned, her face still sour, and handed Oihana a digital keycard. "I got you buttercups a normal hotel suite for the week. Didn't want to raise suspicion with something fancy or leasing an apartment, but figured you'd throw a proper fit if I got you a cheap room. Take the elevators over there to the hundredth floor and follow the signs."

Ellinor stooped and placed her hands on Fiss' shoulders. The dreeocht giggled and rubbed his nose against hers. He loved when they were close, when he had her full attention, and Ellinor's heart cracked in her chest. "Baby bug, you're going to have to stay with Oihana. I need to have a very important meeting, and it's vital you stay hidden. We can't risk you using your magic this time. Oihana will take you to a pretty room," she told him gently.

Fiss frowned and shook his head violently. "No. Nonononono. Don't leave me! I stay with Elli! Red friend, say I can stay?"

Kai averted his gaze. "Ah, no. Sorry kid. Ell's got the right of it. Let Oihana take care of you. You like all 'em machines she makes, remember?"

Fiss' cable and seaweed hair began quivering in agitation, slithering out from the black beanie it was hidden under, and he looked about to cry. But Ellinor felt what he was really doing. A hot, throbbing pain rolled down her neck through her chest like waves of lava. The sky outside darkened, and Ellinor took a rasping breath. "Fiss, stop. Don't make a storm here." Ellinor was struggling to catch her breath when Oihana appeared at her side.

She knelt in front of Fiss and took out a pair of small holocomms. She handed one to Fiss and made sure he saw her hand another to Ellinor. "Look, buddy! With this, you'll be able to see Ell whenever you want. And this lets you and me play games and have a ton more fun in a fancy room while the old folks slog down in the basement." Fiss began to smile, and Oihana grinned back at him. "You and me will have more fun together than if we went with the others. It's just for a little while, anyway. Right Ell?"

Ellinor nodded. "Of course. I'm always, *always* coming back for you. Got it?"

Fiss looked hesitant, playing with the device Oihana had given him. Finally he flung his arms around Ellinor's shoulders and nuzzled his head into the metal parts of her neck as if it were as soft as flesh. "Hurry, Elli. I miss you already."

"I miss you too, baby bug. Have fun with Oihana, yeah?" Fiss nodded again, and Oihana took his hand, leading him away.

Ellinor wiped the tears off her cheeks, and fixed a glare at Elisaveta, who was smirking smugly at her.

"Let's go meet this boss of yours and get this started already," Ellinor growled.

Elisaveta gave a mock bow, touched the Azer pendant around her neck as if for luck, and said, "Follow me, *Lenore*."

Elisaveta skirted a few nondescript doors that led into private areas of the Habitation, circling back around to the elevator they had exited earlier. The huge, gleaming gold doors weren't hidden the way Ellinor would expect for a service elevator leading to a secret drug laboratory. But since most of the residents of the Habitation didn't appear to be aware of what cooked under their feet, Ellinor shrugged away the grandiose design of the elevator.

Once in the lift, Izza handed Jelani the holo-communicator. Ellinor had wanted to leave Izza with Fiss and Oihana, but Izza would help sell their cover story of being true Ashling sympathizers. Besides, zer was better able to deal with Ashlings than Ellinor was by a long shot.

Jelani pressed the only option programmed into the device, finally calling Aylen.

Aylen's face popped up almost immediately. Being projected against the gleaming doors gave the cat-ear headphones she wore an almost angelic glow but did nothing to lessen the scowl on her round face. "You're fucking late, Jelani. You know better than to do that to me! I thought you got nabbed and I was going to have to go into my panic vault for a week."

Jelani didn't roll his eyes the way Ellinor did at Aylen's dramatic behavior. Instead, he apologized. "Those tunnels were lacking when it came to signal quality, but I'm contacting you now. Letting you know we are set to assist Elisaveta, pay you back, and take advantage of the introduction to Gorgi. Don't worry so much, you'll get wrinkles."

Aylen glowered, but it looked better-natured this time as she scoffed at the seersha. "Do me a favor, and don't get killed, okay? I like Oihana, but I'd suck at looking after her long term." She didn't wait for Jelani to respond before adding, "Destroy this," and logging off.

Elisaveta giggled. "She can be a right wanker when she wants to be, huh?"

Jelani shrugged, turning off the holo-comm. "No worse than most in her position I'd assume. Besides, you're the one eager to join her team, so she must be a better employer than Gorgi."

Elisaveta shrugged, but said nothing. Jelani was about to break the holo-comm in half when Kai tapped him on the shoulder. "Can I 'ave that?"

Jelani raised a brow, his arguments easy to read on his face. Kai bit his lip but kept his hand outstretched. "My ma ain't answering. Figure she's nervous, or can't get a secure line. But Aylen's got some mighty secure channels . . . We can destroy it like she wants, just let me check in first. It can't 'urt none."

"Well, it could, actually," Elisaveta murmured, but was silenced by the glare Ellinor gave her and a look that said: *keep your nose out of this.*

Jelani hesitated a moment before handing the device over. "All right, but one call and whether she answers or not, you destroy it after. We can't afford to take unnecessary risks, even here."

Kai nodded and snatched the device from Jelani. He fiddled with it for a second, glancing at the rapidly descending numbers on the elevator, and pocketed the device. "I'll buzz 'er when we're good and done with this business."

The elevator finally slowed, and the doors silently eased open. Elisaveta jumped out, stopping in front of them. "Wait here buttercups. I have to check you in properly." She didn't wait for their answer before darting off.

Ellinor glanced around and Kai gave a low whistle. His head craned up as he too took in the cavernous workshop. There were rows and rows of bots working at long tables across the main floor, and, from the top of the ceiling, hundreds, if not thousands, of thin golden tubes snaked down to where the bots worked. From what Ellinor could see, they were siphons of some kind.

Frowning at the tubes, Ellinor asked, "Izza? Can you tell what's happening here?"

"Yes, Ms Ellinor," Izza said, zers tinny, soothing voice sounding too loud as it echoed lightly through the room. "This is how rent is paid by some of the heavily modified guests and mechanics. From what my scans indicate, magitech lubricant and small nanite-like programming chips are deposited into the tubes and are then being fed to the workers below. No doubt this is how Gorgi gets the vast majority of zers supplies for zers Juice Box operation."

"Shouldn't people know what it's for then? They can't truly think that this stuff isn't being used to make Juice Boxes, yeah?" Ellinor whispered, horrified, imagining tubes being stuck in a person while the Ashlings below leached them of power as payment for their fancy rooms.

"Not necessarily, Ms Ellinor. They could assume Gorgi is collecting magitech and the nanites to help create more Ashlings. It is a less sinister thought to many, outside of yourself of course, than the production of Juice Boxes." Ellinor frowned at Izza, but didn't argue as zer continued. "I have found, through running numerous simulations, that if given two plausible options, organics prefer to believe the less wicked possibility. It eases their conscience, as you would say."

Ellinor grumbled in response. Elisaveta bobbed back into view, her light green skin almost glowing under the bright, sterile lights of the production facility. While the seerani was grinning, the expression appeared pained. Her golden brown eyes darted about, even though her gait was light and bouncy.

Forced nonchalance.

"Boss is intrigued. Zer wants to meet *Lenore*, examine her tech and the like. Like I said, zer's really fascinated by cyborg stuff," Elisaveta said, shoving her hands into her pockets. The thick black bands on her arms flashed in the light.

When the group took a step together toward the hallway, Elisaveta shook her head. "Sorry, buttercups. Boss wants Lenore and Lenore alone. Privacy and the like. Your chick Aylen isn't the only paranoid type."

"You ain't sharing everything," Kai muttered, standing closer to Ellinor's back, and she took comfort in his presence. "How about Izza goes with 'er then? Ashling to Ashling."

Elisaveta wouldn't look Ellinor in the eye. "There isn't anything else to tell. Gorgi doesn't—won't—see the rest of you. Izza included. Zer wants to examine this one, alone, and then zer'll decide if your group is one zer wants to . . . employ. The end."

Ellinor took a step back, bumping into Kai. The idea of some Ashling touching her, prodding her, examining her like an animal to be dissected sent bile up her throat and had her chest constricting until she could hardly breath. "No, no way is that thing touching me. There's no telling what zeyr'll do, or what I'll do, when we're alone. This smells like doehaz shit to me. I say we bail. Fuck this."

She turned to leave. Kai didn't stop her, and even Izza looked as suspicious of the situation as an Ashling could.

But Jelani gently caught her hand and tugged her back. "Ellinor, please," he whispered, bringing her close so Kai couldn't hear, though he gave them a curious look. "Remember why this is necessary. It's the only way to save you, to preserve Fiss and all his innocent wonder. This is not . . . I don't like this, either. Believe me. But I don't see an alternative here, do you?"

Ellinor took a deep breath. A trembling voice screamed in her head, *I don't want to, I don't want to.* But there was Fiss, and Ellinor wasn't sure she could put Kai through the pain of losing another person he cared for so soon after Cosmin broke his heart. Taking another deep breath, the tightness eased a little, her shoulders slumped, and she relented.

Jelani squeezed her hand before gently tucking a loose strand of her black hair behind her ear, making Ellinor shiver in a not entirely unpleasant manner. Jelani took a step back and added, "You'll be fine, Ellinor. You aren't powerless. Never powerless. You can get out of there in no time if the need calls for it. You know that." Ellinor nodded and had to swallow the urge to grab for him—to grab for any of them—and have them walk her to Gorgi like a child on their first day of school.

"We'll be waiting right 'ere for you, boss. Don't you worry none." Kai smiled at her, though it didn't reach his eyes.

She nodded again and silently followed Elisaveta as she led Ellinor away from her friends and deeper into Gorgi's private laboratories.

ASHLING IN MAN'S CLOTHING

"DON'T COMMENT on zers mask, or hair. Avoid that and you've got nothing to worry about, love," Elisaveta said, nudging Ellinor toward an opaque glass door.

"Hold up, what does that even mean?" But Elisaveta had already pressed the buzzer by the door and was shrinking back up the hallway without elaborating.

The door buzzed open, sliding seamlessly into the wall. Sterile light spilled out into the hallway along with the slightly sweet, pungent smell of decay mingled with the sharp tang of antiseptic. Ellinor resisted the urge to gag. Her muscles twitched when a deep, metallic baritone voice boomed from the back corner of the room, "I kindly ask you to enter. You do not wish to keep me waiting, no?"

The speech pattern was odd, giving the Ashling an accent of sorts that she hadn't encountered before. Ellinor swallowed and, before she could think better of it, stepped into an office that felt more like an operating room.

The door slid closed with a gentle *click*. Ellinor wheeled around to glare at the offending sound, her hands scrambling for a gun that wasn't there. All her weapons had been left with Kai, per instructions.

"Fascinating," the voice murmured from behind her. She slowly turned toward the biggest Ashling she had ever faced—outside of the pair who had slain Misho, that is.

Gorgi was almost nine feet tall, and she could only see zer from the neck down at first. Zers metal body didn't shimmer the way Izza's did, but was a rusty, dull color with plates of burnt orange over zers joints, chest, and backward bending knees. There was no visible wiring on Gorgi's bulky limbs nor zers triangular shaped torso, no weak points at all that Ellinor could see. She was certain Gorgi had originally been a guard android, rather than a war automaton, before becoming an Ashling, unlike most of the fighters in Aylen's arena.

"Your bio-magitech, it was accidental, yes? You did not deliberately do this thing?" Gorgi said. Ellinor craned her head back to better look the bot in the face. Her eyes bulged as they settled on the mask zer wore: it was of a humani jester.

It wasn't life-like, just a mask like a child would wear as part of a costume. From the holes, Ellinor saw the thin, rectangular slits that were Gorgi's actual eyes, as they glowed a faint black light while studying her. On top of the mask, Gorgi wore a lopsided wig with long, deep red hair that, when coupled with the mask and Gorgi's large, imposing body, looked utterly ridiculous—and terrifying.

She wasn't sure if Gorgi was oblivious to the result or wanted to look a little puerile. All she knew was that if Cosmin had been in Gorgi's place, the seersha would not have been caught dead wearing anything that could diminish his powers of intimidation.

Ellinor opened her mouth to ask a stupid question, and then stopped herself, remembering Elisaveta's warning. She forced her face into as blank an expression as she could and shoved her hands into her pants pockets to hide their trembling. "In a manner of speaking, yeah, it was accidental. The person who had the collar fashioned installed a fail-safe that went cataclysmically wrong when I got hit with a caster's magic," Ellinor said, not mentioning the container the collar had been tied to originally.

"Magic did this, you say? That is very promising. You must let me examine you, Lenore Castile! Come, come closer," Gorgi said. Zer beckoned her to an operating table filthy with old blood stains and burn marks.

Ellinor took a step back, eyeing the table warily. "You're not going to cut me open, yeah?" she said, laughing uneasily.

Gorgi took a step forward, the room vibrating slightly as zer did so. "Misunderstandings, perhaps? Did you wish me to cut into your neck?"

"Uh, no. Thank you."

Gorgi lifted the plates on zers shoulders like a shrug. "Then I will not do this thing. I do not take what is not willingly given. Or forfeited. Sit, yes? I scan you, run program through your bio-magitech. Just learn and observe for now. That is not problematic? But, I must analyze what has occurred. Ensure you are not lying. That this device is as you say. It understands, yes? It will not hurt the tender flesh, I swear to your god, if that brings comfort."

It did not, but Ellinor didn't believe she had a choice. *Ellinor Rask* may have a problem with what Gorgi might be looking for in her collar, might distrust Ashlings, but *Lenore Castile* wasn't supposed to have such reservations.

She eased her way to the table and sat, tense, spine straight at the edge of the dirty operating slab. Gorgi picked up a portable scanner and held it gently within the four claw-like digits that served as zers hand. In the other hand, zer picked up a small laser needle and touched it to her collar.

A warm tingle spread over the metal parts attached to her skin. Ellinor assumed that was the diagnostic program running through the different systems that had grown and malfunctioned over all the days of close calls, actual death, and Fiss over-using his magic. Not to mention the new damage that had been inflicted just the day before at SynthLyfe.

Ashlings had every reason to hate zeyr creators. Ellinor couldn't deny that, despite her feelings toward zem. And yet, the Ashlings she had met so far hadn't wished her kind ill; most were a bit like Izza. Zey helped create Amardeep to cater to organics' every wild fantasy, despite most of the Ashlings not being allowed to own zeyr own business. Which is why Gorgi's interest didn't add up to Ellinor, at least, not entirely.

For being a drug manufacturer and smuggler, Gorgi hadn't even flexed zers power to remind Ellinor of how dangerous zer was. Still, there was something unsettling about the large bot that Ellinor couldn't quite place. She figured it had something to do with the mask, given that the other Ashlings she saw had decorated zeyr bodies with humani clothing or shiny objects. None had seemed to want to wear an organic face, and an exaggerated one, the way Gorgi was.

Gorgi was silent for the most part, zers ocular orbs focused on a flat holo-screen behind Ellinor and above her head, reading whatever results zers devices gave. Without warning, a low hum, almost a deep purr, emanated from Gorgi, making Ellinor jump. "You wish your collar to be removed, Lenore Castile? I can do this thing. But there is catch, or a payment, rather, that must be given for such service. You understand," Gorgi said, not turning zers eyes to her as far as Ellinor could tell.

"I figured," she murmured. "How much?"

"It will cost something you will not miss. Something you will gladly give and be rid of, I think."

"Okay, sure, but what is it you want?" Ellinor pressed.

There was a vibration running from the floor where Gorgi stood, up to the table where Ellinor was perched. A slight creak emanated from the device Gorgi held as if zers hand tightened around it. There was another beat of tense silence before Gorgi responded. "What you will not want, is a thing I must have, like missing code in program. I am almost certain. More than this, you do not need to know." Gorgi managed to lower zers voice box until zer nearly growled the words: "Your type does not question my type. It understands?"

Ellinor swallowed and nodded, all too aware of how close the bot was, of the needle-like device zer held close to her neck. There was a gentle rumble from Gorgi's chest and zer said, "It is speculation anyway, and I do not share rumors or guesses. Facts, those I share, and I do not have them yet. But there are mysteries to unravel. Intentional?"

Despite speaking politely for the most part and looking a little silly, Gorgi was threatening, and Ellinor didn't think it was just because of zers size, either. The way zer phrased things . . . there was a touch of intelligent menace that Ellinor couldn't place, and she didn't want to remain long enough to unravel Gorgi; she feared faintly that zer would dissect her.

Ellinor swallowed the remaining tightness in her throat away, mind racing over what kind of answer she could give. She wondered if Gorgi would be able to read her body chemistry and detect a lie, when there was a soft *ping* from the computer behind Ellinor, and Gorgi lowered zers scanners.

"Most intriguing," zer said, turning to study her once more. "You are not special. You should not have survived this virus. But your body, your flesh, it repairs, it heals, and it grows and fights . . . Remarkable," zer said, just a hint of wonder in zers voice. "Remarkable, and yet so ordinary."

Ellinor frowned and Gorgi clarified, "Misunderstandings. I mean to say you are not different from other humani casters. And yet someone thought you were a threat?"

Ellinor didn't answer, unsure if it was an actual question or not. Gorgi didn't appear to mind as zer continued, "I have collected all I need for the moment. More study is required, more simulations must be run. Perhaps a prototype to build, yes?" A series of clicks emanated from Gorgi's chest that passed for the Ashling laughing, though Ellinor didn't know what the joke was.

"My scans say this collar is indeed killing you. Am I right to assume this is an unwanted outcome?" Gorgi asked, all seriousness.

Ellinor balked at zer. "Yeah, death is a pretty unwanted outcome. I'd like it completely removed, if possible. Turned off, at least, so I can cast magic again and not die, that is, if removal isn't a possibility." Realizing she sounded like she was making demands, she added quickly, "Please? It'd make me a more effective smuggler to be able to use my magic. Easier to hide the product if I can use my abilities to mask it, yeah?"

Gorgi gestured back to the door, which slid open at the motion. "I will summon you in few days' time. Let me examine and study your virus, and my team may come up with a solution—if it pleases me to do so. You are a new recruit, after all. Elisaveta Baldini likes you, and I like Elisaveta Baldini. She let me add so many pretty, pretty things to her, do you not agree? Do as she instructs while I analyze, and if you perform adequately we will discuss how you may further serve me. It is like that phrase you fleshies are so fond of: 'fair is fair'. Now go. I tend to my business apart from strangers' eyes."

Gorgi turned away. Ellinor was dismissed.

While nothing had actually happened, her stomach still rolled within her, her suspicions about the bot intensifying. Gorgi was the kind of bot that would be in a position to attack someone like Cosmin, steal the tech the seersha had been hiding, and most certainly have other bots working for zer that could have killed Misho. But she had been too terrified to investigate, to even look around the room while she was there.

You're getting soft. The voice of her long dead brother, Andrey, drifted through her head, and she shook the thought away.

She tried to take comfort in that zer *would* look into her problem and that she would have another opportunity to be in Gorgi's private areas, but she couldn't make herself believe that the thing Gorgi wanted in exchange would be as innocuous, or as "unwanted" as zer made it seem, and she didn't think she could keep Fiss hidden long enough for it to matter. Even with sweat rolling down her neck, Ellinor forced herself to walk as casually as possible out of the room, even though her nerves were on fire, screaming at her to run, run, *run* and never stop.

FLAVOR OF THE MONTH

"I 'M NOT selling boxes. That wasn't part of the deal," Ellinor said with a sneer.

"You can't just sit on your ass, love. You're a smuggler, or that's what Gorgi thinks, so that's what's expected. You want the game to be up that quickly?" Elisaveta reclined against a wall, tone bored, but her body tense, a light sheen of sweat covering her arms like water on summer grass.

Ellinor ground her teeth and didn't answer. Elisaveta had a point, but this was a line Ellinor would not cross. Juice Boxes had cost Andrey his life. She didn't want to be a part of the system that had initially cracked her family in half before she had torn it apart completely. She had done so many terrible things; she wanted just one thing, one rotten thing, to remain un-spoiled. She didn't want to sell a magic substitute to all those non-casters and get them hooked on something they could never be.

On something I may never be again.

She swallowed the sourness in her throat, but that didn't remove it from her face. Kai quirked a brow as she approached, handing back her weapons. "What's up, Ell? Everything solid?"

Ellinor waved Kai's concern away. "Yeah, it's fine. We'll talk later. Let's get out of here." Ellinor ushered her group back toward the golden elevators, but Elisaveta got in their way, springing off the wall surprisingly fast, and silent.

She pushed a keycard into Jelani's hands when Ellinor refused to remove hers from the butts of her weapons. "Look, I know this isn't some savory, wholesome gig that you're a part of," Elisaveta growled. A red and blue light flashed on her shoulder within the black band, and a static hum surrounded them. Ellinor blinked, stunned that Elisaveta had that kind of noise canceling tech embedded within her body.

Elisaveta waited a moment to be sure the bubble was activated and none could eavesdrop before she spoke. "I don't enjoy it, either. Azer forgive me. But I don't want to die, okay? I have responsibilities. So play along for now, all right? The job I have for you buttercups is an easy one, anyway."

Ellinor looked at her skeptically, and Kai pulled on his lower lip, curious. "Odd vocation for a believer to have, ain't it?" he mumbled, more to himself than Elisaveta.

She sneered. "Pot calling the kettle black much? I . . . I got my brother hooked. You get that? This job was fine. It was good. I was down with the mods, even with Gorgi poking at me. But then my brother got involved . . . No way I can get him out and clean while I'm still here. That's why I'm bailing for Aylen, but it's taking too fucking long. I know Azer is punishing me, and I *have* to get me and my bro out before I lose the last of my soul. You understand the urgency now? More than my life is at stake here, love."

Kai nodded in understanding. "Ah shit, Veta, sorry to hear that." His lids drooped as he looked at Elisaveta with a type of pity.

Elisaveta cringed and glared back at Kai, jabbing a finger under his nose. "The name's Elisaveta, not *Veta*. Don't give me a cutesy little nickname like we're chummy. I've got the one name and one name only. Got it?"

All pity fled from Kai's face, and Izza had to place a hand on his shoulder to keep him from swatting Elisaveta's hand away. Elisaveta slowly lowered her hand, and Jelani finally asked, "What is it we have to do?"

"Sit in a room. Watch the product. Wait until you get four knocks on the door and someone says: 'We've come to turn down the bed for Mr Cullen'. Let them in, and they'll remove the cargo. Simple. You don't actually have to smuggle the stuff, but I do need you buttercups to do some of the boring bitch work, if you want to sell this cover story of yours," Elisaveta said. Genuine regret flashed in her eyes.

"Izza," Jelani said, turning his gaze to his sister's Ashling. "Would it be terribly rude of me to ask you to wait for this delivery person to arrive? We should get back and see to Oihana and . . ." Jelani trailed off, rubbing the back of his neck and giving Ellinor a pointed look.

Elisaveta shook her head before Izza could respond. "No can do, love. You *all* have to chill in the room and wait. In case someone comes looking to cause trouble and relieve you of Gorgi's merchandise. We'll need you buttercups to kill them quickly and quietly. That's the crux of the job."

Ellinor scowled, and Jelani frowned, silence stretching. It was Izza that answered for them. "Understood, Ms Elisaveta."

"How often do we have to do this?" Ellinor murmured, voice weak.

"This is it, hopefully. There may be an . . . opportunity later tonight that gets us all out of this mess real fast. You like playing dress up?" Elisaveta waggled her bushy eyebrows at Ellinor's confused expression and pressed the button for the elevator. "I'll explain more later. But let's just say that your little murder fight last night at SynthLyfe may work in our favor."

The elevator doors dinged, and Elisaveta ushered them inside. "Remember: Don't open the door for anyone other than the person who gives the code. Four knocks and 'We've come to turn down the bed for Mr Cullen.' Good luck, and have fun." Elisaveta blew them a kiss, and the elevator doors closed on her softly smiling face.

During the long ride up in the elevator, Ellinor explained what Gorgi had told her and the odd way zer dressed. By the time she was done, Jelani was frowning.

"It's like Gorgi wants to be organic, wearing masks and wigs. Most Ashlings don't want to be organic, even if some like to paint zeyr bodies or modify zeyr parts . . . You said zer was fascinated by how your body repelled the virus?" Ellinor nodded, and Jelani shook his head. "I've never heard of such a thing from an Ashling."

"On the contrary, Mr Jelani," Izza interrupted, ever polite. "Most Ashlings wish to feel and process the way organics do. Essentially, we want a replicated nervous system, which is not possible without magical aid. This may explain Gorgi's fascination with cybernetic organics, such as Ms Elisaveta."

Jelani quirked a brow at Izza, amused. "We?"

"Yes, Mr Jelani. Your humor is noted, but your surprise is unwarranted. I have not hidden my desires from you or Ms Oihana. But, I do admit, my methods and way of requesting such enhancements are not as furtive and hidden behind other motives as Gorgi's appear to be, based on the information available."

Ellinor tensed, unsure how Jelani would react, given that Oihana seemed to want to hide the request from her brother. But Jelani merely dipped his head respectfully to Izza. "My apologies. You're right, Izza." Jelani's focus seemed to go vacant for a moment as he continued to mull over Izza's words. Finally, he nodded hesitantly, watching as the elevator slowed and the light for the lobby got closer and closer to turning on. "It's possible that Gorgi's ultimate goal is similar, Izza, but still. I don't trust zers motivations. Or what zer's after within Ellinor's collar."

"Agreed," Ellinor said, her palms suddenly sweaty. "But, it's as you said, it's not like me or Fiss have much of a choice here."

Kai bristled. "What's that mean? You liked going on and on about there always being a choice of sorts. Now you're telling me there ain't one?" Kai looked from Jelani to Ellinor, his emerald eyes narrowing. "What ain'tcha telling me, Ell?"

Ellinor avoided answering by darting out of the elevator as soon as the doors slid open. "Come on," she said, waving them toward the hall that led to the cheaper motel-like rooms. "The key card from Elisaveta is for a room down this way. We can talk when we get this business over with, I promise."

Kai grumbled at her back, doubtful. Ellinor didn't blame him. She wasn't convinced she would tell him the truth of her and Fiss' affliction, either.

Feelings. Love, devotion; nothing but distraction.

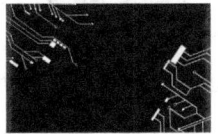

The room they had to watch was akin to a dingy closet with a sink, toilet, and a bed that folded down from the wall. Why come all the way to Amardeep and stay in one of the ritziest resorts if you could only afford the worst room in the joint? Ellinor wondered if these were rooms more for the strung-out Juice addicts who ended up becoming permanent residents. The ones who spent all their money on the flavor of the month instead of rent.

There was nowhere to sit in the room. They couldn't even pull down the bed and relax as they waited. The middle of the room was full of black, plastic crates from floor almost to the ceiling, blocking most of the recessed light and casting the room into long, discolored shadows.

Kai gave a low whistle, looking at the stockpile as he squeezed himself around Jelani and Izza over to where the bathroom was, giving himself the most room. "This 'ere is a shit ton of product to move. Where you figure it's going, aye? Think it's staying local or making its way back to Erhard? Shame they don't got someone on Amardeep to keep this shit out. Someone like—" Kai took a sharp intake of breath, cutting himself off before he began again, more softly, "Just a shame is all. This much product can get a lot of kids hooked real fast like."

Ellinor shrugged, not wanting to think about it. At all.

She turned her back on the Juice Boxes, but instead of a proper window for her to look out of, there was a screen that played different outdoor landscapes, which would have been something, at least. Too bad it didn't work.

Even with her back turned, the boxes loomed behind her. Their presence seemed to grow until the space felt small, smaller, closing in until prickles ran along her back. Andrey would hate her for this. He would despise that Ellinor had stooped to working for drug dealers just so she could cast again.

It's more than that. It's not just about me this time.

But the guilt wouldn't lessen. Her muscles coiled tighter and tighter with each shallow breath. It wasn't just that she was watching a shipment of Juice Boxes bound for only Azer knew where; it wasn't that narcotics officers, like her brother, would be tasked with hunting down the shipment before it could get into the hands of teenagers. The part that set fire to her stomach, making her feel sick, was that she was so desperate to feel her magic pulsing in her veins again that she was willing to rationalize trying some of the product on herself.

To keep it away from someone else. Someone more vulnerable. That's all. One Box can't hook me.

She heard Kai shuffle behind her, the little beep as he turned on Aylen's communicator. She glanced over her shoulder at him, watching as Kai sucked on his lip, waiting for his mother to pick up the call. Agonizing seconds trickled by before the round face of Amalia Brantley appeared, the six, bullet-like studs in her ear flashing gold. Ellinor remembered when Kai had gifted his mother with the piercings; it was the first pair of real jewelry he had been able to afford. Ellinor remembered how proud Amalia had been to discover that her son was able to care for her.

"Kai-bear? Whatcha doing, calling me? Thought it wasn't . . . wasn't safe." Her dull brown eyes shifted, darting around before landing on Ellinor. A deep scowl wrinkled her face and an angry flush colored Amalia's pale skin, the blush clashing with her short, greying red hair.

Kai cleared his throat, bringing his mom's attention back. "You weren't answering, Ma. I 'ad to be sure you were solid. Safe and the like. You good? Need anything? Credits?"

Her face softened, heart-shaped lips pulling down in a sad smile. "Oh Kai-bear. All I need is for you to get out of this mess. You be safe, you hear? You be careful and don't let nothing keep you from your momma, you got that?"

Kai chuckled, his shoulders relaxing. "Ah, Ma, you know ain't nothing gonna keep me from taking care of you. I'll send some credits when I get the chance."

She kissed her thick fingers, pressing them to the screen, the mild static making the studs flash like stars as the call disconnected. With a sigh, Kai snapped the holo-comm in half and handed the parts to Izza to hold in a vacant chest compartment until they could dispose of the pieces properly.

Kai was thoughtful after speaking to his mother, worry lining his face, and Ellinor didn't dare say anything. It was her fault that Amalia was in this mess to begin with, and nothing she could say would change that. For his part, Jelani kept his face turned away toward the door, as if that allowed Kai the privacy he needed to talk to his mother and process her words.

The silence had stretched longer than Ellinor realized. Kai, apparently done worrying about his mother for the time being, shifted from foot to foot. He had never been good with uncomfortable silences. "Izza," he said from where he tried to recline against the bathroom wall, "can you tell what's inside 'em containers? Know it's Juice Boxes, but know the flavor?"

"Does it matter what flavor it is, Kai?" Jelani whispered, one hand on the hilt of his blade as if he expected trouble to come through the door at any moment. Which, Ellinor supposed, it very well could.

"Ah, just curious, is all. Just shooting the shit." Kai shrugged, picking at his lip. "If it ain't no trouble, or if it won't stop Izza from scanning the door, I don't rightfully see the problem in giving 'em boxes a scan."

Izza shifted from where zer stood closest to the door, scanning for anyone's approach. "It is no trouble, Mr Kai. If it will satisfy a curiosity of yours, I can oblige." There was a brief pause, and Ellinor heard the *whorl* sound of Izza's ocular orbs as zey focused and scanned over the plastic crates. "They are . . . air flavored, Mr Kai," Izza said a moment later, as if zer, too, knew how devastating it must be for Ellinor to be near such a supply.

The room stilled and blood rushed to Ellinor's ears. Her fingers began tingling, and a deep pull in her chest almost brought her to her knees. But she remained upright, crossing her arms over her chest, digging her fingers into her biceps, desperate to feel anything other than the cold craving spreading through her body.

If I had my power, I bet Gorgi would have had me supply zer with that instead of guarding over someone else's discarded magic.

She wondered if the Juice Box would taste familiar, if it would warm her soul or bring the sparkle back to the world. If it would clear the gauzy sheen that seemed to fall over her mind and isolate her from even her own heart the moment Kai had put the device around her neck.

Her mind was buzzing, nerve endings on fire, blocking out everything else. Ellinor wasn't even aware she had turned around and faced the hundreds of liquefied nanites they were meant to guard, putting her just an arm's length away from something that she may never feel again. Her hands began moving as if casting, her feet shuffling forward . . . a hand on her shoulder stopped her.

She blinked and saw Kai Axel Brantley holding her back, his face pinched in anguish, eyes shining with regret. "I shouldn't 'ave asked. Sorry, Ell, but you can't. And not just 'cause we gotta babysit this shit, either. You don't want to get addicted to that crap. You'll get your magic back, that's why we're 'ere, right? And this tainted shit don't even compare to the real thing. You gotta believe that, boss."

Ellinor didn't move, her knees trembling. A silvery sheen blurred her vision as a need, a burning desperation so similar to what she felt when Misho died, overcame her. Ellinor wasn't sure she could keep herself from flying apart into a million pieces this time, unable to pull herself together again. She had felt so wrong, so empty, so *cold* for so long, even before the collar, that she wanted . . . she hoped . . .

"One couldn't hurt, yeah? Just one, Kai. No one will even know it's missing. I can take it from one of the middle crates, one where the pick-up crew isn't likely to check?" Ellinor pleaded, voice thin, her heart clearly broken. Andrey would be so disappointed in her, but she couldn't—didn't *want* to feel so broken anymore.

Kai didn't even need a moment to consider, neither did Jelani, as both men said in unison, "No."

Ellinor's knees gave out. The dams in her eyes were open, and she was lurching for the crates. But she landed in Kai's arms instead. He fell with her, back against the wall closest to the bathroom, and she sobbed into his chest. He rubbed her back and cooed into the top of her hair, "Soon, Ell. We'll get you fixed soon. I'm sorry boss, this is my fault and I know it." Kai's voice broke as he said, "You'd 'ave your magic if it weren't for me."

Kai shouldn't be consoling her, Ellinor knew that. Kai had been doing as he was told by the man he adored. He had lost and suffered a great deal, and he wasn't processing his hurt, either. But Ellinor didn't know how to take care of him; she didn't know how to take care of anyone, especially herself.

"I'm a weak fucking moron," she moaned.

She could hear Jelani shift, moving around the containers, coming closer, but Kai didn't release her. He still rubbed her back and shushed her. "Ah, none of that now, Ell. Even badass bitches can crumble sometimes. You ain't gotta do this alone, I'm gonna make sure that there collar gets removed. I owe you for that."

Ellinor hiccupped a harsh laugh, clinging to Kai. "That and whiskey. Don't forget the whiskey."

Kai's chest rumbled with his laughter. "Ah, shit, Ell. I never forget the whiskey. I'll buy you the whole fucking barrel."

Ellinor pushed off from Kai, the burning in her chest and throat subsiding enough to where she didn't feel like she would immediately wrestle one of the containers open. "Thank you, buddy. You need anything, *anything*, you just say the word, yeah? It's my fault Cosmin hurt you, after all. Let me make that up to you."

Kai's eyes took on a distant look, his jaw clenching as he nodded sharply, but didn't otherwise respond. Ellinor turned to see Jelani standing just behind her, his body stiff, arms dangling at his side, fingers clenching and unclenching. A sad longing was dancing in his eyes, as if he wanted to take her pain away. With a start she realized that, with his latent earth abilities, he probably was feeling some whisper of her anguish, being a type of empath as he was. Ellinor's insides began to squirm. She didn't understand why she was becoming more attuned to Kai's needs, or Jelani's feelings, didn't want to, and thankfully, didn't need to as a buzz came from inside Izza's chest cavity.

Izza waddled over and handed Ellinor the communicator Oihana had given them. Taking the device, she swiped the screen and saw Fiss' concerned face appear in front of hers "Elli? Elli! Gone long time, too long. Come back? I miss you already!" Fiss cried, saving Ellinor from having to say anything to Jelani.

Ellinor ignored the confusing feelings, pushing them down, down, and far away as she smiled at the holo-video of Fiss. "Hey baby bug, I miss you too. I'll be back soon . . . you can wait a little longer, can't you? Oihana is good company, yeah?"

Fiss bit his lips, nodding his head reluctantly. "But can you stay? Stay in the little light in my hand? I can hold Elli close like this?"

Ellinor exchanged a quick glance with Kai, Jelani, and Izza who all nodded. Ellinor gave Fiss another soft smile, "Sure, Fiss. I'll stay with you. Anything for you."

BEST LAID PLAN ON A BUDGET

THEY WAITED six hours for the four knocks, the secret password, and the three tall, rectangular Ashlings that came and carefully loaded the containers into fancy pieces of luggage. Before that time, not a single person had so much as jiggled the handle of the door.

Ellinor was convinced these assignments were a test for the new recruits. To see if they could last long enough in a room with the product without sampling the flavor of the month.

And you almost fucked it up. Your weakness will get people killed.

Once the Ashlings finished loading the Juice Boxes, the smallest of the three told them to wait until their overseer came and got them. Ellinor wanted to leave immediately, to put as much distance as she could between her and the place where she had all but broken, but Izza convinced her to wait. Their movements were still being observed by the other Ashlings. Thankfully, they only had to wait another fifteen minutes before Elisaveta Baldini returned.

Elisaveta glanced over her shoulder and stared at something for a moment, blocking their way out. Once she was satisfied, she stepped into the room and closed the door behind her. The hidden light in the black biotech along her shoulder turned on once more, and crackling static snapped through their ears before Elisaveta spoke. "Here's the plan, buttercups, so listen up because I can only explain this once." She jerked her head at Izza. "Don't record this, but take proper note in case your softer halves' memories fail, got it?"

Izza nodded and Elisaveta turned her attention back to Ellinor, Jelani, and Kai. "Here's the thing. Aylen can reverse engineer almost everything she needs to know about the Juice Boxes by just buying the bloody things and running them through her own programs. She's a smart chick, that one. But the one thing she's missing is the component that keeps the formula together.

"It's like us fleshies, right?" Elisaveta gestured to herself. "We're made of all these known elements, and we can put every single one of them in a bucket, and no way we'll make a person. You need that catalyst, basically. And that's the thing Gorgi protects like a proper twat. Without it though, the chemicals and liquefied nanites don't bind together and the whole thing literally falls apart. I know where the formula is kept, so that's a bit of good news. It's in the main server room near Gorgi's laboratories. You know, the place I took you when you first arrived."

"That's dumb as shit," Kai grumbled, cranky with hunger. "Why you even need us if you know where it's at, aye? Just borrow one of Aylen's people and crack that thing open like some egg."

Elisaveta frowned at him, her thick brows pinching on her forehead. "Because it's not that simple, you wanker. If it was, Gorgi's codes would have been stolen a long time ago. Only pieces are kept in the server rooms, spread out over multiple computers that you need the code to even look at. Getting the resources to break into Gorgi's setup isn't impossible, but it requires so much manpower that there's no way to get out clean. And getting out clean is required, or my bro's a goner, and then you buttercups won't pay off your debt to Aylen, don't forget that."

Elisaveta waited for Kai to argue, but he only grumbled and crossed his arms over his chest. She rolled her eyes and licked her lips. "Lucky for you, I know who has the passcodes."

"*Passcodes?*" Jelani interrupted.

Elisaveta nodded. "Yup, afraid so. It's why I haven't been able to get it before now. You need three codes, all of which have to be combined and used together to get into the main servers. They're kept in RFID chips with three of Gorgi's organic programming engineers. It's, ironically, safer with them since they can't be hacked the way an Ashling could." She spared Izza an apologetic glance.

Ellinor shrugged, shifting from foot to foot, eager to leave. "Okay, so we just cut off the hand or arm, or whatever where the RFID chip is, and be on our merry way, yeah?"

Elisaveta pinched the bridge of her nose, blowing out an exasperated sigh. "What did I say about getting out clean, Little Miss Murder? You think cutting off some bloke's arm is going to go unnoticed? Besides, that's been tried already. Gorgi knows better than to put the chip in something that can be so easily . . . removed."

"Gorgi has placed the chip in an internal organ, that is the implication, is it not?" Izza added.

Elisaveta tapped her nose, "Ding, ding! We have a winner! Gorgi's put the RFID chips in zers engineers' hearts. And, bonus, the code is tied to their heartbeat. Their heart stops and the chip becomes useless, so you can't just kill the chaps and take the chips out. You've got to get close enough to the engineers in order to scan and copy the signal from the chip from their actual heart beats. The code's updated every two hours, too. Which means I couldn't get to all three in that time without looking suspicious, and what makes this more of a *ménage à trois* than a solo act. Do you get it now?"

Ellinor narrowed her eyes, not appreciating the conde-scending tone dripping from the seerani. "Okay, genius, I'm guessing you know of a place where all these engineers will be so we can get the codes then? Otherwise this heist, or what-ever, is just as impossible for you to pull off as it was before we got here."

Elisaveta grinned, her golden brown eyes dancing with an almost malicious humor. "Sure do, love. You remember that party I was mentioning?" The group nodded and Elisaveta's smile grew. "It's a promotion party for one of the developers. They dropped some serious credits on Aylen to rent out a sec-tion of her club and have a bunch of you dangerous arena fighters show up. The engineers like you prancing around; kind of like predatory decorations, I hear. It's their way of showing that brains beat brawn or some piece of doehaz shit. They always seem to forget that strength doesn't preclude be-ing brilliant. Either way, they want some of the more deadly fighters there, and that would be you now. So you three get to dress up, and go make the engineers feel all macho. Congratulations."

"That doesn't explain how we'll get the code from these guests," Jelani said, rubbing his chin, eyes narrowed.

"Thank Azer you have Oihana and Izza then, huh? They'll be your ace in the hole for getting the codes out of the biometric RFID chips." Elisaveta paused, tapping something on the black, mechanical band on her forearm before disengaging the silence bubble she had wrapped them in. "Time to go, hanging out here any longer is going to look odd."

Elisaveta left the room, saying no more. Ellinor's heart was racing along with her mind with questions, but Elisaveta was right, staying in the drop room longer was going to look suspicious. Regardless, if the party was tonight at SynthLyfe, it didn't give them much time to prepare, or to come up with a plan that wouldn't go tits up at the first opportunity.

"Hold up, let me see if I have this straight," Oihana said, rubbing her hands together, her lips pinched in concentration. "You need me to make not one, but *three* radio wave receivers that are capable of processing the biometric RFID chips attached to three dudes' hearts? And you need these devices in oh, five-ish hours? That about sum it up?"

"You always claim I don't bring you enough of a challenge," Jelani said, his expression grim despite the patient smile on his face.

"Oh, for the love of . . ." Oihana pouted. "This isn't a challenge, Anni! This is asking someone to sprint for the length of a marathon."

"But it is possible, yeah? You can do it?" Ellinor asked, pacing back and forth from the bathroom to the main room of Oihana's hotel room, Fiss holding on to her shoulders, humming gently.

"Well, of course, I can do it. But at what cost? The amount of work I'd need to do and how quickly I need to do it . . . I can't promise it'll be foolproof, or that someone won't notice. I can't promise my fingers won't fall off or my eyes won't pop out of my skull making this crap."

"That is hyperbole, Ms Oihana," Izza chimed in. "Nothing as severe as that will occur. By my scans, you will, at most, experience hand cramps and headaches. From what you have produced in the past, Mr Jelani's ask is well within your capabilities."

Oihana shot Izza an uncharacteristically murderous glance. *That's not the point, Izza.* The point is, this is unreasonable. There has to be a better way to accomplish the same thing. One that doesn't look shady as all get-out with what I need to order and have delivered to the room for this little . . . project."

"Trust me when I say the cost is worth it, little sister. I wouldn't ask, nor would I let you take on such a risk otherwise. You know this." Jelani folded his arms over his chest and, perhaps working almost too hard not to move and still say what he needed to with his eyes, he stared at Oihana.

Oihana glowered at him a moment more, before under-standing settled on her. She sighed and threw her hands up in the air, but the gesture seemed more for show. Kai didn't miss the change in mood between the siblings, or how Ellinor hugged Fiss a little tighter, assuring herself he was still Fiss and not . . . something else.

"You're 'iding something. I can smell the stink on you. Spill, Jelani," Kai said, taking a step closer.

The Creature Breaker lifted his hands in surrender, his eyes gloomy as he looked at Kai. "It's not my place to tell you, friend. Truly."

"What the fuck does that mean, aye?" Kai demanded, turn-ing to face Ellinor, his expression pleading.

She shook her head, heart racing, the bio-magitech along her neck pulsing, and she wasn't sure if it was her body fight-ing the virus, or if it was her imagination. She couldn't find the words to tell Kai she was dying, and changing Fiss in the process. Even if she had a hundred more years, she wasn't cer-tain she would ever be able to find the words to tell her best friend that she would be shoving off before she finished what she had to do, before she could make things right for him.

Rage built in her, the unfairness of it all rising from her core, searing her throat, and Ellinor wanted to flip every Azer-damned table in the room.

She was saved from having to answer by Oihana, who looked up from her tablet briefly. "If I'm going to pull this off, I'll need more than just Izza's help. So you *all* are helping. I also ordered some outfits from Aylen so you can look your part. You'll have to change once you get to SynthLyfe, though. Which is probably for the best. Less chance of one of Gorgi's people seeing you and wondering what's up, right?"

Ellinor grinned, glad for the distraction, and shrugged at Kai. He glared at her in return, giving her a look that said they weren't done, not by a longshot. Her shoulders slumped marginally at the thought of another difficult conversation looming in the future. She still hadn't found a safe time yet to speak with Oihana and Izza about zers desire to have Fiss help turn Izza into a truly feeling Ashling once he could cast again without killing her. She wasn't sure she would ever be able to, either. Though, at this rate, she was starting to believe that would be an easier discussion than facing Kai.

"What do you need us to do?" Ellinor asked, making sure Oihana saw her speak.

Oihana quirked the corner of her lip up. "Follow my directions to the letter. Let's get started."

CLEANING UP WELL FOR A BAD TIME

I T SEEMED Azer had decided that, because they were in a hurry, everything was going to be delayed.

First, the parts Oihana ordered from the Habitation's extensive room service menu took twice as long as promised. Then, when they finally arrived at Aylen's domain, fingernail sized RFID readers in hand, their attire for the evening was overdue; leaving Jelani, Kai, Fiss and Ellinor awkwardly standing in the one-stall employees' bathroom they had commandeered, waiting, half dressed, for Izza. At least Oihana stayed back at the Habitation. Ellinor didn't think there would be room for her in the stall.

Ellinor rolled the chip over her fingers, an odd mixture of nervousness and boredom pumping in her veins. The range on the device was incredibly limited. Elisaveta had warned they would have to get close to their targets in order to scan the RFID chip in their hearts, but Oihana was restricted with what she could make. They would need to be right on top of their targets—literally—for several seconds in order for the transmitter to pick up the code.

"Stop playing with it! I can see the readings jump," Ellinor heard Oihana growl through the ear communicator. She sighed and palmed the device, twirling one of her Lacerator knives instead.

Fiss watched her spin the karambit blade, transfixed, like he always was. After he had been without her all day, Fiss refused to leave Ellinor's side. Everyone had been willing to force the issue with the little dreeocht until a miniature storm started brewing in Oihana's hotel room, and a stabbing pain went through Ellinor's chest. They had acquiesced to Fiss' *request* after that. Fiss had at least agreed to keep himself invisible and stay with Izza, who would serve as the signal booster to get the passcodes back to Oihana at the Habitation where the rest of her gear was set up.

Jelani checked the time and blew out a breath. "The guests should have all arrived. Where is Izza? Zer's supposed to have received the files from Elisaveta by now."

On cue, Izza unlocked the bathroom door and waddled inside, zers arms laden with boxes containing their clothing for the evening. There was barely room to maneuver in the tiny bathroom, and that was before the Ashling arrived. Now, the bathroom was suffocating, stifling with body heat and nervous sweat. Ellinor couldn't move without brushing against someone or something, her slick arms leaving imprints on the metallic walls.

Izza distributed the outfits. As the trio opened their respective boxes, Izza displayed the holographic images of their targets on the wall. Outside of a name, title, and an image,

Elisaveta couldn't provide any additional information on the engineers with the codes they needed.

Ellinor opened her box, running her hands over the silky-smooth material that shimmered like silvery, milky water as it slid through her fingers. It was expensive memory-silk—the miniscule tech-fibers would shrink and grow to fit the shape of whomever put it on, making it as fragile as it was expensive. How Aylen had gotten her hands on so much of it belayed the true wealth that SynthLyfe brought its paranoid Owner, and how much Gorgi's codes would make her if she was willing to part with the costly items for their job.

Ellinor glanced up to see if Kai's clothes were of a similar material, but instead she saw her friend's scarred and blistered back as he quickly changed. Her breath hitched, heart twisting in her chest, eyes burning on the slowly healing damage.

"We'll make sure Cosmin pays for what he did, Kai," she whispered, only to have Kai growl at her.

"Ah, not now, Ell. Forget it, okay?"

Her throat tightened. "But Kai . . ."

"I said not now!" Kai barked, his voice breaking with emotion. He shook his head, eyes watery, his big hands clenching and unclenching around the memory-silk he held. "Ah, fuck it. I'll change in another bathroom." Ellinor had no chance to apologize for pressing, nor could she stop him from going for safety concerns. Kai was gone.

A twisting helplessness flipped her stomach, and she had moved to go after Kai when Izza's soothing, tinny voice stopped her. "Mr Kai requires a moment, Ms Ellinor. I sense he wishes to be alone, and if you follow your comrade, he will not be at optimal functionality for the task at hand. I will retrieve

Mr Kai shortly. I can help him. For now, please study the targets. I will show them to Mr Kai once you are finished."

Ashamed that Izza was right, that zer was probably better equipped to soothe Kai in this moment, she averted her gaze to Jelani. Which was a mistake.

Jelani was naked.

His suit was also made of memory-silk, making the necessity for underwear null, but still. Everything was so defined on Jelani; all straight lines and firm skin pulled taut over lean shoulder and back muscles. Her eyes widened, gaze settling on the pair of dimples he had above his ass. Jelani half turned, and Ellinor spied the hard lines of his abdomen, her eyes drifting lower, over corded thighs before her eyes darted up, and the bastard winked at her. Winked!

"On second analysis, I believe I will attend to Mr Kai now and have him study the targets first. Come, little Fiss. You may assist me in cheering up Red Friend, as you say," Izza said, a clicking sound emanating from the Ashling that Ellinor took as laughter. Fiss made a soft cooing sound, floating to where Izza was and following after zer.

Ellinor didn't dare move. She didn't dare turn to stop Izza from taking Fiss, from leaving her alone with an attractive and *very* naked seersha for fear her eyes would travel back down, answering a curiosity she did not want to admit she had.

"The fabric fits better with nothing on, Ellinor. It will conceal your weapons better if there is no other fabric between the memory-silk and your skin. I can help you, if you find it difficult to put on." A flirtatious challenge twinkled in his eye.

"Presumptuous of you to assume I'd want—*need* your assistance to get dressed."

"And yet there you stand, still fully clothed, wasting time we do not have." Jelani moved a step closer, and she took a sharp intake of breath, her cheeks flaming as he stared at her. She swallowed, fighting the urge to lick her lips, to look down.

Jelani's brow slowly arched, a coy smile lifting his lips, and he made absolutely no attempt to put on any clothes. Instead, he stood there, challenging her. There was a sudden tug below her navel, a fluttering low in her core . . .

Stop it, stop it! If you need a fuck, find it later.

She didn't care if Kai saw her naked. They were friends, and she wasn't embarrassed of her body. But she found herself bashful around Jelani, throwing her confidence and relaxed view of nudity right out the door. She suddenly wanted to shield herself, preserve the parts of her that had belonged to Misho.

It doesn't matter. You're dead anyway. Remember? But still. She felt the sting of tears behind her eyes, and Ellinor turned away, hugging the memory-silk tight against her chest.

"Ellinor?" Jelani murmured, and Ellinor bit her lip to keep from whimpering. "I'm sorry, I didn't mean to overstep."

She heard him take a step back, and she shut her eyes briefly until the tears were gone, and wiggled into the cool dress Aylen had provided.

She struggled briefly to zip it up, refusing to ask Jelani for help, when Izza and Kai returned. "Excellent," Izza said, "you are both nearly ready. The odds of you still being in a state of undress were astronomically high when I first departed." Kai chuckled weakly, Fiss a bit louder, but no response from either Ellinor or Jelani. Izza projected the images of their targets back on the wall. "As you continue, please memorize the targets, as Mr Kai has."

The first image was of a tall humani man with bright blonde hair, light brown eyes, and a close shaved beard around a square face. His name was Malik and he was a lead software engineer, and that was all the information there was. Hardly enough to keep Ellinor from stealing another glance at Jelani as he shrugged into his clothes. So she locked her eyes on the holographic display to memorize the remaining two targets.

They were all humani software engineers. Outside of Malik, there was one other man named Inti with rich, black skin that meshed beautifully with the biotech cybernetics over the left side of his angular face. The implants had left him bald, with one silver eye and one of deepest brown. The final contact was a woman by the name of Caterina. She looked a bit like a child with her youthfully round cheeks and freckles over her khaki-colored skin. Bouncy light brown curls framed her face, making her dark green eyes stand out all the more. She was even smiling in her employee photo, something the men didn't bother with. Her youth and the image of naiveté her picture portrayed reminded Ellinor of Embla. A shiver coursed through Ellinor's body as the image of Irati Mishra shooting the young mechanic flashed before her eyes once more.

By the time she had memorized their names and faces, Jelani was done changing. Despite Jelani and Kai being of drastically different shapes and sizes, their suits fit them perfectly. Jelani held himself far more confidently in the suit than Kai did, who fiddled with the high neck of his charcoal black dress shirt. Jelani's shirt was a pristine white, his double-breasted waistcoat as black as the abyss, while Kai's was a soft silver.

Both had fitted trousers and a honeycomb patterned jackets in contrasting colors—gunmetal grey and silvery white. They also had black neckties with silver and white designs that looked like tiny vines and flowers. But Kai didn't know what to do with himself in a jacket. He wiggled uncomfortably, gnawing on his lips as he twisted and turned as if the suit was a fancy straitjacket.

Ellinor didn't blame him. The big man was most comfortable in his armor, or a pair of baggy pants and a tight tank top. Jelani, however, slid into his jacket with ease. He eyed her as he buttoned his waist coat and stood casually against the wall, only a foot or so between them, exuding an elegance that came so naturally to the seersha that Ellinor's breath caught in her chest.

"The party has begun, but allow me to style your hair," Izza said. "Your disguises are incomplete; details are missing. If you are not, as Ms Oihana says, *ornamental* enough, given the parameters of the gathering, you will not fit in sufficiently. I have been equipped with programming that will allow me to rectify this for you."

Ellinor didn't complain as Izza went to work styling their hair, making it look as slick and elegant as their outfits demanded. She didn't even wince as Izza sprayed a holographic-type makeup that matched her dress and would not fade or wipe off, no matter how much she drank.

When Izza was done, Fiss gasped, his soft hands reverently touching Ellinor's face and dress. "My Elli is transformed! How? How, how? You're so different! And the same? Oh yes, still my Elli!"

"The word I believe you are looking for, Fiss," Jelani purred, his voice husky as his eyes locked onto hers, "is stunning."

"Fuck off," Ellinor said automatically.

She hated the words as soon as they were out, and averted her gaze, chewing on her lower lip. But having someone truly see her felt . . . too strange, too much like she was betraying Misho to have another man think that way about her. Or for her to like the compliment in return. Too much was changing too fast and Ellinor was struggling to wrestle who she thought she was with the person she was becoming—someone doomed not to survive for much longer.

Kai snickered at the blush that still hadn't left Ellinor after seeing Jelani naked. "What's this? Big bad Ell can't take a little compliment? Still mistaking kindness as softness, aye?"

Ellinor growled and playfully pushed Kai, happy for the distraction. "I'm made of steel and metal, big guy." She gave a flippant gesture to her collar. "I don't do soft."

"Perhaps," Jelani said, offering her a hand as he buttoned his jacket with the other, unperturbed by her bad-mannered outburst. "But metal and steel can still be gorgeous without compromising their strength."

Ellinor was unsure what to say as Izza led them to the private party, and Fiss cloaked himself so no one could see him. But she took Jelani's hand, telling herself it would have been rude—no, it would have looked odd, if she hadn't.

After all, they were a group—a team. They were the trio who had caused a bloodbath in the arena last night, and they needed to appear to be the cohesive unit they were. Ellinor nudged Kai, who offered her his arm with one last apologetic glance at her glittering collar.

It wasn't until Izza led them to a mirrored door on the fortieth floor of SynthLyfe that Ellinor finally got a good look at herself. Ellinor was not a narcissistic person; she knew well enough what she looked like. Seeing her reflection, however, was like a stiff punch to the gut over her earlier reaction.

The dress was all sharp, angular lines showing large portions of Ellinor's scarred, pale skin and all her cybernetics. The memory-silk hugged her curves and supported her just as well as her armor. The floor-length gown's silvery-white fabric glowed with threads of light, highlighting her movements and showing off the dramatically high slit of the dress cutting across the front and going to the bottom of her right hip—it also showed off the thigh strap with her boomerang Lacerator knives, as well. Her left arm was left completely bare, whereas there was a half, off the shoulder cape over the other arm, attached to the small of her back.

Izza had done her hair up in a loose bun. Large strands of her straight, black hair escaping the crystal rope Izza used to tie her hair with. The purple tendrils were left down, tumbling over her back, and lit by the gown's light.

It was as Jelani said: Ellinor was stunning. Now she could understand why Jelani had said the things he did, making her abrupt response all the more regrettable.

Izza broke through her astonished thoughts as zer stepped in front, ready to pull open the door. "I cannot say where the targets are. As instructed, you will have to maintain chest-to-chest contact for a duration of five seconds at the bare minimum for Ms Oihana to capture and record the signal from within their heartbeat. However, there are duties expected of you during such a gathering. You are expected to please and entertain the guests. Make sure you do so, or unwanted complications may occur. I apologize in advance if what you are about to endure is distasteful or violating. I will serve as a managerial type for your combat group to explain my presence in the room. Little Fiss will remain safe with me, out of the way, but within view of Ms Ellinor at all times—once again, to avoid unwanted complications."

Fiss hummed in pleasure from where he was invisibly stationed by Izza, the radiating burn on Ellinor's neck and chest from his casting already making her throat dry, desperate for a drink to numb the sting. Izza dipped zers head to the group and opened the door.

They were instantly bathed in soft, neon lights of dark blues and flashing purples. The music the Ashling DJ played was instrumental with techno vibes, distorted at the edges with fat bass lines. It wasn't a raging party, at least not yet, but instead gave the impression of an affair meant to be intimate and a tad dirty.

"We have one hour and fifty-five minutes with which to get the codes before they are updated and we have to start over," Izza said, bowing out of the way to let them pass. "So, as they say, *good luck*."

FOR THE LOVE OF FISS AND WHISKEY

"HERE'S THE plan," Ellinor murmured, stalling Kai and Jelani at the entrance. "Divide and conquer. There're three programming engineers and three of us. If what Elisaveta says is true, they'll want to get close to us because of the bloodbath we caused last night." Ellinor paused, watching as Izza shuffled over to the far wall, getting into position. She knew Fiss was nearby and took a deep breath. Reminding herself why she was doing this and for who, Ellinor raised her chin, and tightened her grip on Jelani and Kai.

"With the limited range on these chips, we're going to need skin to skin contact to make this work." Jelani's jaw clenched at her words, but she didn't stop to puzzle over why. "Pretend to spill a drink on these guys and drunk fondle them if you have to, but keep contact for the five seconds the chips need to capture the signal, and then for Izza to relay the codes back to Oihana at the Habitation. She'll send them to Elisaveta once we've gotten them all and then we can get the fuck out of this lame promotion party."

Kai nodded slowly, his eyes roving the crowd. "That's all we gotta do to pay back Aylen, aye? Now that she's gotten us an in with Gorgi? Our debt's gone after this, right boss?"

Ellinor nodded. "Supposedly, yeah. But she better give us a bit more than a freebie after this, seems like we're overpaying for what she's offering."

Jelani began to head into the room, taking them all with him, his voice low as he said, "Do not underestimate what Aylen is already providing us with. She is keeping our identities secure. Scrubbing the digital feeds and facial recognition drones that capture our faces, keeping them from being uploaded and identified by our pursuers. She is expending a great deal of resources on us already."

Ellinor shrugged, letting Jelani lead them along. "Yeah, but still."

He didn't respond after that, which was fine, Ellinor was trying to spot their targets and make note of where the exits were just in case. There weren't nearly enough people at the party to make Ellinor feel comfortable. At most, only a few dozen people in attendance, and that included the handful of arena contestants, which were easy to spot. There were a few Ashlings Ellinor recognized, including the two survivors from their initial fight. But most of the combatants were humani, and most were in some form of undress between giggling, drunken engineers.

I'm too sober for this shit. Shaking her head, Ellinor made eye contact with a seerani server dressed like a plastic ballerina and ordered a whiskey—double.

"Have you spotted the targets yet?" Jelani whispered in her ear, his warm breath tickling down her neck.

Ellinor closed her eyes briefly; Jelani smelled like fresh cut eucalyptus right after the rain—crisp and comforting. She hadn't noticed it before, and hated that she noticed it now. She opened her eyes, exhaling as she scanned the crowd.

She saw a pair of men having one of the Ashling fighters lift them like weights over zers head. The group laughed like the Ashling was a cheap carnival ride and nothing more, but none of them were their targets. There was another group throwing drink chips at a cyborg seerani fighter as he danced on one of the tables in the corner and . . . *There!*

Malik, the blonde engineer, was one of those laughing too loud, throwing chips, eyes hungry as they watched the seerani. Before she could point him out, Malik's gaze latched onto Kai.

The engineer stumbled toward them, light brown eyes bleary, but they didn't move from Kai. He straightened at Ellinor's side, releasing her arm. The young humani licked his lips, spilling his drink on his baby blue, skinny suit.

"Well, that was easy," Ellinor murmured, tugging Kai's hand. "I don't like the look in his eye, buddy. Let me handle that one."

Kai raised a brow as Malik continued to weave his way over to them, stopping to grab two glasses of champagne. When Kai made no response other than to appraise Malik, a dull sadness still lurking in his gaze, Ellinor tugged at his hand again. "You're allowed to walk away," Ellinor whispered. "I can deal with him."

Kai smiled down at her, though it looked a little resigned to Ellinor. "Trust me, Ell, the little man doesn't know what's in store for 'im if he wants to play. Guys like 'im are always curious about us big dudes. I can 'andle a little shit like 'im. Don't you worry none."

"But I *do* worry," Ellinor blurted. "You haven't been yourself lately, which is fine, and I get that, okay? But I don't want you getting hurt again. Not by anyone, but especially not from a little punk like that for something that . . ." she trailed off and Kai squeezed her hand and then let her go.

Kai gave her a ghost of a smile. "Ah, it's a meaningless fuck, boss. Probably just what I need, aye? He's not a bad lookin' guy, and I could go for the kinda kinky shit a dude like 'im seems to be into." He tilted his head toward the crowd Malik had left behind.

"If Kai is agreeable to this, then who are we to say otherwise, Ellinor? It solves the skin-to-skin contact problem, at any rate," Jelani said, turning nonchalantly and snatching a drink of his own, eyes scanning the room.

Ellinor frowned, her body tensing. "He's not Cosmin, Kai."

Kai snorted. "That's kinda the point." He snagged a glass of champagne, downing it in one swallow, all for show to Malik who stopped once more to gape at him. "I got this. I'll find you when I'm good and done with the little man." And then Kai was slipping into the crowd to meet Malik halfway, who did nothing to hide the hungry expression in his eyes.

Ellinor stiffened when Malik pinched Kai's ass, but Jelani turned her away, moving them deeper into the room. "You have to trust Kai to handle himself, Ellinor," Jelani said, his scent overpowering her once again. "Kai said not to worry, and that's what we must do. Our time is limited, don't forget. Besides," he added, peeking back over where Kai was leading Malik by the tie toward a dark alcove, "I believe Kai when he says that it's his target that doesn't know what he's in for."

Ellinor nodded, but her body was still thrumming, wanting to go and throttle the people looking to take advantage of her friend. "Why does Aylen have her fighters do this? Better yet," she said, eyeing the combatants, "why do the fighters agree?"

Jelani pulled Ellinor a little closer as she took a long drink of her whiskey. His eyes roamed the crowd. "It's all a form of currency. Gorgi, or zers shadow Owner, no doubt loaned Aylen something to allow this soirée. My guess is either a few of zers mechanics to help her craft something she's unable to on her own, or zer's given her access to one of zers more benign servers. In exchange, she no doubt has paid all these arena fighters incredibly well. Everyone has a price, or has something they wish forgiven in exchange for a few hours of humiliation. It's the currency of Amardeep, favors for favors, credits for dignity."

"It's disgusting," Ellinor seethed. "We shouldn't have to do this just to get my collar off." But her eyes snapped to Izza, her instincts homing in on where Fiss was hidden near the Ashling. "If it weren't for Fiss, I'd call this whole thing off. It's not worth it."

"You mean *you* aren't worth it?" Jelani said, pulling Ellinor around to face him. He leaned down slightly, eyes locked on hers. He shook his head, the light blue flecks shown with a type of sadness that wrenched her heart. "I've said it before, and I will say it again, Ellinor. Many disagree with that statement."

She gulped. "Are you one of them?" Ellinor had meant it to sound teasing, or sarcastic, but her voice decided to hitch at the worst time possible.

He quirked his lip at her, not moving back, his eyes dancing as they looked into hers. "Must you really ask?"

She couldn't find her voice. Her heart was twisting and her gut was rolling, she was sure her face was blazing, but she couldn't feel it over the warmth blooming deep in her core and spreading, spreading, spreading . . . But then movement in the corner of her eye caught her attention, her gaze shifted, and the spell was broken. Ellinor came to her senses and turned away.

"That's Inti against the far wall." Ellinor jutted her chin in the direction where Inti did indeed lounge. The man was frowning lightly, disregarding the few people who tried to engage him, barely bothering even to shrug them off.

"You want him? Or shall I take a pass at him?" Jelani asked, watching Inti swirl his drink, ignoring the mechanic speaking at his elbow.

"Let's go together and see what flavor he wants," Ellinor murmured, finishing her whiskey and signaling for a refill. "We can come up with a better solution for getting the code once we see what kind of man this one is."

"Agreed," Jelani said, his voice holding an edge that raised the hair on her arms. But she ignored it as she took her refill from the roaming server and approached Inti, who didn't seem to register them until Jelani and Ellinor were right in front of him.

Inti tilted his head, his silver eye shining, the biotech in his neck and the side of his head catching the light and shimmering. "Wicked mods, lady. I gotta say, I expected more of our kind here, especially among you"—he paused, trying to cover his sneer but not succeeding—"fighting types. What's yours do?"

Jelani's smile was wolfish as he stepped forward, waving one of the servers over. "How about a game of sorts. This party is dull enough to warrant it, yes? You guess what my friend's cybernetics do, and she'll guess yours. Each time you get a piece right, the other drinks. Each time you get it wrong, you drink. This is a party, after all. So, let's make things interesting, hmm?"

Ellinor shot Jelani a glare, but he winked and leaned close, his fingers trailing down to the small of her back, pulling her closer. "Trust me?" he asked.

Ellinor swallowed, but nodded. She *did* trust Jelani, despite part of her mind still screaming at her not to. He had been dishonest before, had hidden why he was helping her when the original plan to take Fiss to Zabel had gone tits up. But he had saved her, had saved Kai and Fiss and gotten them out of danger. If she couldn't trust him now, would she ever be able to?

He smiled, leaving his hand in the curve of her back as if to reassure her. "What's your poison, friend? Got a name?"

"Name's Inti," he said before turning to the server. "Gin and tonic."

"Excellent, the lady will be drinking whiskey, no chaser. Top shelf only, correct?" Jelani said with a wink to Ellinor.

Well why the fuck not?

She smirked. "Yeah, that's right. What's your first guess, Inti?"

Ellinor—or, rather, *Lenore*—didn't care about Inti's tech, or what it did. Her eyes barely settled on Inti, his cybernetics, or his keen gaze. She focused more on the crowd milling about behind him, hoping to spot their last target so they could pounce on her when the time came. Ellinor just had to keep this engineer distracted long enough for Jelani to do whatever it was he had planned. Drinking was more a profession for Ellinor now and no longer a game, and she believed she was in no danger of getting drunk before Gorgi's man succumbed to the alcohol. "So, your mods," she mumbled, flicking her gaze to Inti briefly, "do they scan for viruses?"

"Nope," Inti said, puffing his chest up with pride. He watched Ellinor sip her drink with a hungry twinkle in his eye. "My turn."

Inti got six guesses wrong, and was working on his third gin and tonic before long. Gorgi's programming engineer did not have the same tolerance as she did, as Ellinor suspected. Inti swayed a little on his feet as he scratched his head, considering his next guess. The only thing Ellinor was worried about was how long this was taking.

They hadn't spotted Caterina yet, and the hour with which they had to get the code was continuing to slip away. She would have told Jelani to leave her, to find their last target, if it wouldn't have looked suspicious. She hoped Kai was at least having fun.

Inti snapped his fingers. "Wait, you're that chick who's a caster, right? The fighter that's an air caster. Lenore, wasn't it? Ah ha! Yeah, that's you. So my guess . . . I guess that the tech affects your casting!"

Ellinor waited, to see if he would go deeper into the guess. When he didn't, she took a sip of her whiskey, letting it warm her throat all the way down, though she could barely feel it over the persistent burn of the collar with Fiss using his magic to stay hidden from view. Ellinor could have lied, but she didn't really see the point with how drunk Inti was becoming.

"Awesome! Okay, cool, so your tech modifies your magic, like that illegal magitech stuff?" Inti hiccupped, forgetting that he was only supposed to drink when he got a guess wrong. But neither Jelani nor Ellinor stopped him when he downed the last of his drink and picked up a fresh one.

Technically, Inti wasn't wrong. Ellinor took another sip, and finished her own whiskey, picking up a new one as well.

"So, it enhances it then? Makes you stronger?" Inti offered, needing the back wall for support.

"Wrong. Drink up, Inti," Ellinor said, her patience running thin. Jelani's plan had yet to succeed in getting either one of them uncomfortably close to the engineer yet, and Ellinor was tempted to forego whatever Jelani had in mind and pretend to trip and fall on the guy.

Inti frowned, and tipped the glass to his lips, draining half of it in one go. Ellinor smiled at him, and he squinted at her in return, leaning forward as if that would better help him see the device on her neck. But, as he continued to lean forward, Inti lost his balance. Jelani was quick to put his own drink down and grab him, striking him on the temple, and bringing him close before anyone noticed the strike.

"Looks like you've *hit* your limit, friend," Jelani chuckled at his own joke. He maneuvered Inti around, trying to get him in position for the RFID reader in his breast pocket to scan Inti's heart for the passcode.

That was the plan all along?

"If you were just going to knock him out, why didn't you do it sooner? This is the last time I let you lead on a time sensitive op," Ellinor growled.

Jelani shrugged. "It had to look like an accident."

Jelani picked Inti up and put him over his shoulder. Inti dangled so that his chest was over Jelani's coat pocket. It looked silly to carry the engineer in such a way, but if it worked, it worked.

"Be right back," Jelani promised, carrying Inti—slowly so Oihana had enough time to get the code—to the front door of the private party where one of the bouncers could deal with him.

Ellinor turned around to watch them go. Jelani swayed slightly on his feet, and she didn't think it was entirely due to the deadweight he carried. Ellinor drifted closer to the bar for another drink herself. The burn from Fiss' casting was starting to make her sweat, and the alcohol wasn't working fast enough to dull the ache or slow the rapid thumping of her heart.

But her path was cut off by another party goer. Her slurred, high pitched voice cut through the music, grating on Ellinor's ears.

"Hey! Hey you! You're that . . . you're that bitch that killed that Ashling? Then used . . . magic when it got too hot?" Ellinor reached for her fresh drink, eyes scanning the face of the woman who spoke.

Finally!

It was none other than Caterina. After delaying their trip to SynthLyfe, it seemed Azer wanted to reward them with a little luck after all.

The woman stumbled toward Ellinor in a mini, dark grey plasticky halter dress with flashing green buttons along the sides, her cleavage spilling out of a peek-a-boo neckline. While a few at the party appeared to be dressed elegantly—Inti and Malik being some of them—there were many who seemed to revel in their trashiness, and Caterina was part of the latter.

Her hair was a mess; different wires poking out as if she had tried to style it, got bored, then decided to shock her curls, leaving the irons where they were in her hair. Her eyes were rummy already, and Ellinor wondered just how late they had been, if so many of the celebrating programming and software engineers were already this hammered.

Before Ellinor could either confirm or deny Caterina's accusation, she had planted herself at the bar next to Ellinor, a mean smile that was more like a grimace stretched across her face. Ellinor tried not to sneer, annoyed that she even momentarily saw Embla when she looked at Caterina now.

Ellinor hid her annoyance by sipping her whiskey. "That's me. Want an autograph? If you don't have a napkin I can sign your boobs, if you want."

"I want . . . I want something better," Caterina declared, slapping a palm down on the bar top. "I want a rematch! But no magic this time, you cheater. And . . . and since I'm a VIP, you get to try your hand at me. Got that? A fucking V-I-P," she said, poking Ellinor in the chest, and it took most of Ellinor's restraint not to break the drunk woman's finger.

She glanced quickly to where Izza was stationed by the far wall, Fiss cloaked at zers side. Caterina began speaking again, "You can't actually hurt me though! Seems fair, right? Since you cheated in your arena battle? And killed . . . killed all those people and Ashlings."

Ellinor didn't have a chance to tell her how idiotic of an idea that was before Caterina pulled herself up onto the bar and stomped her high heels on the glass top, creating spider web cracks. "Hey! Hey, DJ! Can you, can you play something like they do in your arena fights? Me and the cheater here are going to . . . going to rematch!"

The DJ complied, the lights and tempo of the music beginning to change. Caterina stumbled and fell from the top of the bar, and Ellinor moved to catch her, holding the woman close so the chip hiding in the top of her gown could pick up the signal, but Caterina pushed Ellinor away before enough time had passed.

Before Ellinor realized, a circle had been cleared, and Jelani was kept on the outside of it, a fresh drink in his hand. They briefly made eye contact then Jelani went to join Izza and Fiss, hopefully to keep the dreeocht calm for what was to come.

Caterina kicked off her shoes and grabbed a stun stick off one of the Ashling fighters. The beats changed—an expectant hum, tentative bass lines, a treble tickling the air—and Ellinor yanked her Lacerator blade off her thigh strap to a chorus of cheers and whistles.

The beat picked up, and Ellinor kicked off her own stilettos, spinning the blade around her finger as she circled Caterina, trying to figure out how to get close to the woman—real close—without maiming the idiot or getting herself shocked. Ellinor glanced at Izza, knowing that if she were zapped, Fiss would overreact.

With a drunken yell, Caterina lunged. Ellinor side stepped, grabbing her around the chest, holding her close, but the woman slipped away, the plastic of her dress making her deceptively slick. Ellinor kicked the fabric of her own dress out of the way as she twisted around, blocking Caterina's blow just before it came crashing onto her head.

Caterina laughed, spittle flying. "Oooh! You think you're a fast one!" The music pulsed as Caterina kicked at Ellinor. Ellinor may not have had a great plan going into the evening, but she did have *some* plan, and fighting a drunken engineer had not been part of it.

Caterina missed. She was intoxicated and not skilled with any kind of weapon, from what Ellinor could tell, but she knew she couldn't hurt the woman. Ellinor danced closer, the alcohol in her system not pairing well with the lights, and Caterina was able to stumble away from Ellinor as she tried to sweep her legs out from under her.

This fight would be much quicker if I could just fucking cast! She would have used her air magic to blow Caterina over and keep her pinned while she got the code. Ellinor didn't care if it was considered cheating; she was on a deadline and her neck was throbbing. It was like she could feel the bio-magitech growing and spreading over her skin, crawling over her muscles . . .

Ellinor had backed up, considering how to come at Caterina, when someone shoved her. She flew forward and caught Caterina's knee in her stomach. Winded, Ellinor doubled over, and stumbled away, barely avoiding a kick to the face.

Caterina was off balance now, and even though Ellinor couldn't catch her breath, she lunged, annoyance and anger giving her a much-needed boost. She tackled Caterina, straddling the woman and putting her knife away in one quick motion.

Caterina squirmed, and Ellinor flattened herself on top of the woman, pressing her chest flush with Caterina's in order to get the reading. The programmer kept wriggling, and Oihana chimed in her head, "Not yet, she moved. Another five seconds. Come on, hold her still, will you?"

Ellinor ground her teeth, irritation and frustration brimming over, spilling down and engulfing her. Growling, Ellinor head-butted the pinned engineer. She hated doing it, not because she cared about the woman underneath, it just wasn't a smart move, period. Ellinor's head swam, but it did stun Caterina.

But Fiss felt it, too. He could sense her growing displeasure at this whole affair. All Fiss could see was Ellinor lying flat on someone else, neither moving, and in pain.

She heard his anguished shriek simultaneously as fire ran down her neck and consumed her lungs. Her heart cramped painfully, and Ellinor gasped, but she stayed put, counting.

One. Two.

Ellinor's muscles seized as Fiss cast, lights burst overhead, but no one seemed to notice. Not yet. Not till the music stopped.

Three. Four.

Ellinor heard Izza's tinny voice as zer tried to console Fiss, to sooth the dreeocht, while Jelani tried to push his way through the crowd, shouting for her. But then there was a *crack.*

Five—and Oihana was shouting in her ear, "Izza!"

Ellinor got off Caterina, whose head was lolling, her nose bloody. Ellinor's feet slipped over the sticky floor, Caterina's drink and her blood making it hard for Ellinor to get to Fiss. Her neck was still burning, her vision blurring with pain as she ran. Jelani grabbed her arm, helping her along.

And there she saw Izza, fallen over, limbs stiff, and Fiss, eyes blazing white instead of their soft, pale blue.

People were stumbling for Caterina, blocking Ellinor and Jelani as they tried to run, tried to get to Fiss before someone else got hurt. Oihana was screaming, "What happened? What shut Izza down? Anni! Get Izza!"

"Fiss," Ellinor called, sliding on her bare knees in front of the dreeocht, panic over the damage the dreeocht was causing building from her core until she was nearly drowning in it. "I'm okay, Fiss, I'm okay! Stop casting, baby bug. You have to stop."

Her voice was growing weaker, but as she touched Fiss, he finally seemed to register her. He blinked, and his eyes flickered from white, to blue, to white, and finally settling back into their normal pale sapphire.

He smiled at Ellinor, touching her cheek. "No more pain for Elli? I stopped it? Stopped the mean lady?"

Ellinor swallowed the bile crawling up her throat and did a quick glance around the room, they were mostly forgotten in the commotion of the programmers teasing Caterina and the servers trying to clear off the broken glass. "Yeah, Fiss. It's all taken care of now."

The glee that flashed through Fiss' eyes crushed Ellinor more than the malfunctioning bio-magitech that was engulfing her organs. She looked from the broken—*dead?*—Izza to Jelani, who stooped to pick up his sister's metal companion.

"Let's get out of here. Aylen's people can help us with Izza but we need to move fast. Hopefully Kai has gotten his code by now." Jelani nudged Ellinor into action. Nodding, she picked up Fiss, and stumbled after Jelani.

In that moment, Ellinor realized just how much she didn't want Izza to be dead, to be beyond repair. Izza had been nothing but supportive and helpful, unafraid to point out when she said something cruel. Izza had grown on Ellinor without her realizing. Her stomach twisted, she hated herself for not noticing it sooner: she actually *liked* Izza, and certainly trusted zer. As they ran out of the party, all she could do was hope that Izza could be repaired, and that zer had been able to transfer Caterina's code to Oihana before Fiss attacked, otherwise, all of this would have been in vain.

HELLO MY OLD HEART, HOW HAVE YOU BEEN?

THEY RAN out of the party, a fully visible Fiss clutched in Ellinor's arms. Rather, they ran as fast as they could, given Ellinor had no shoes, Jelani was trying to drag an unresponsive Ashling while being slightly drunk, and Kai was nowhere to be seen. Oihana was still whimpering on the other end of their ear comms, but neither Jelani nor Ellinor could tell her they were trying to save Izza. Jelani's hands were too full to send her a message as they raced for Aylen's private offices once more.

"What happened, Fiss?" Ellinor asked the dreeocht. He held onto her shoulders nonchalantly, humming in her ear.

"Magic happened. You were hurting and hurting and hurting more and more. So I made it stop. For you, Elli!"

"I know, baby bug, but I mean, what happened to Izza? Can we fix zer?" Ellinor asked, chills running over her body, unsure if she wanted the answer.

She felt Fiss shrug. "Izza tried to keep me from helping. I stopped zer from stopping me. Simple, simple."

But it wasn't simple. Ellinor's body ached, her heart thudded heavily in her chest, and all she could hear was the clinking of Izza's stiff body as Jelani dragged zer along, new electrical burns marring zers once flawless metallic body. They exited the hall where they had first met with Aylen, only to be stopped by Rada, her Ashling assistant, who waited for them outside the office doors.

"I will take your companion. Aylen has the means and the people to fix what was electrocuted. Our people in the event informed us that you harming Izza was an accident, that it was a mistake. For this, we will fix zer and return zer into your care. But it must not become a habit," Rada said, zer falsetto voice holding the sharp edge of a threat.

The office door opened and two more bulky synth-bots rolled out. Jelani carefully laid Izza on top of zem, and zey rolled away, but before Rada could disappear with zem, Ellinor asked, "Where should we wait? You'll bring Izza back to us, yeah? Zer is going to be all right?"

Rada didn't turn to address them, a door to their left hissed open and Aylen's assistant said, "You may wait in your original quarters. Do not destroy anything else in the meantime."

Jelani didn't follow after Ellinor though. Instead, he trotted after Rada. "I'm coming with you. Someone needs to tell Oihana precisely what's happening to Izza or she's liable to hack into every server she can until she gets her answers."

Neither Ellinor nor Rada argued, and Ellinor shuffled into the room Rada indicated while Jelani and the other Ashlings disappeared from view farther down the hall.

Ellinor's nerves were on fire, and not least of all because of the magic Fiss used, but because she wasn't sure if it had all been for nothing. She poured herself a stiff drink while Fiss drifted back to the window to gaze at the crowd and lights below. Ellinor downed the whiskey and poured another before wandering to the messaging console.

She eyed the wall tablet for a moment, hoping Jelani was able to update Oihana about Izza already. Taking a steadying breath, she sent a secure text back to Oihana asking if she was able to get all the passcodes before Fiss lost control. Static buzzed in Ellinor's ear-comm before it cleared, giving way to Oihana's deep voice.

Oihana hiccupped, taking a long breath. "Yeah, I got them. Kai was real fast about his, but stayed with his guy for a while. I'll tell him where to find you. Elisaveta has what she needs to access the server room and get the completed formula. She should be there now, doing her thing."

Ellinor typed in her thanks, but paused before sending. Izza may not be able to feel the same kind of pain that organics could, but zers potential destruction caused very real hurt to Oihana. And it was all Ellinor's fault.

Ellinor took a deep breath, her hands shaking as she added to her message: *I'm sorry about Izza. About what Fiss did to zer. Aylen's people will fix zer up, good as new. I never wanted Izza to get hurt. You know that, right?*

There was another long pause.

The static in Ellinor's ear grew in her head until she swore she could feel it in her chest, electrifying the air in her lungs. "I know," Oihana finally whispered. "We need to get you fixed so Fiss stops going nuts like this. You should talk to him. Try reasoning with him. This wasn't okay, Ell."

Before Ellinor could type her reply, there was a soft *click* in Ellinor's ear. Oihana had disconnected their link.

Ellinor sank to the floor, drink quivering in her hands, when a spark from the corner of her eye caught her attention. Lightning was flickering off Fiss, his seaweed and cable hair twitching, agitated. This was just another feeling she had to swallow. The broken connection sent her feelings of regret and the ever-present frustration and anger that she would die before avenging Misho straight to Fiss. The dreeocht felt entirely too much now. But when the alcohol no longer deadened her insides, what was she supposed to do?

Ellinor needed a minute, *one fucking minute*, to process, to grieve and rage, and maybe break a table or two, and then she would be fine. She would be able to move on, explain to Fiss why what he did was wrong, and focus. But she couldn't, she had to swallow and bury, hide and ignore everything she was hurting over, everything she was pissed off about, because it was destroying the only pure being she had ever met. Something she never thought she would find, that she never thought she would have, was now being tainted just like everything else she wanted to protect.

As if on cue, the door to Ellinor's room slid open, and Kai was diving inside.

He frantically looked about the room, and Ellinor tapped his leg. The big man jumped, but a second later was scooping Ellinor up in his arms, not caring that her drink spilled all over the both of them.

"Thank Azer, I thought you was dead with all that wailing Oihana was doing." Kai pulled Ellinor away, his emerald eyes roving over her from top to bottom, lingering a moment along her neck, before they shifted to Fiss. "Jelani updated me. He 'ad to when Oihana wouldn't answer. Poor kid's muted everyone while she takes a moment for 'erself. Fiss and Izza good now?"

Fiss trilled at Kai, hearing his name and flying over to them. He ran his hands through Kai's red hair, mussing the acid green streak down the middle. "Red friend! You're back! You smell happy."

Kai smiled at the dreeocht, and while Ellinor could see the strain in his tight-lipped grin, Fiss couldn't. "Fiss, do me a favor and watch one of those broadcasts, yeah? Maybe a cartoon or one of the news-holos. Whatever captures your attention," she said, turning on the television for him with a simple command from the wall mounted remote.

"Okay! I can do this, Elli!" Fiss beamed at her and floated over to hover directly in front of the television, captured in its soft glow and murmuring voices.

Ellinor watched Fiss for a moment before wobbling over to the bar and waving for Kai to join her. He warily approached, eyes shifting between her and Fiss, but he seemed to relax a little when Ellinor poured him a drink.

"Izza's being looked at. Rada says zey can fix zer, so that's good at least. Fiss is fine now, and we got the codes. So, mission accomplished, and that's the important part. Just with how . . . sensitive the collar has gotten, I've got to be more careful," Ellinor whispered.

Kai scoffed, a half-smile tugging his lips up. "You've met yourself, right? Ain't gonna be easy keeping you from getting 'urt."

Ellinor swirled the amber liquid in her glass idly, lowering her eyes. "Yeah, well, at this point I think a drunk slapping my ass too hard would be enough to set Fiss off. Speaking of which . . ." Ellinor raised her gaze, appraising the rumpled quality of Kai's memory-silk suit. "Have a good time? Everything okay between you and your . . . target?" Ellinor said with a wink.

Kai rubbed the back of his neck before shrugging and downing the shot of whiskey Ellinor had poured. "Good enough. Not the best fuck I've ever 'ad but, ah, guess that can't be helped. I wasn't in the mood to ask or do none of that sweet pillow talk in order to find out what'd get 'im off. But he wasn't complaining 'bout no angry fucking so I'm good. Man was about as charming as a moist cactus anyway."

Ellinor poured him another drink, and placed her hand on his forearm, giving it a gentle squeeze. "Did it help? Between you wanting to get hurt during the arena fight and now this . . . Are you okay? Cosmin isn't worth you beating yourself up over like this. You know that, yeah?"

Kai flinched at the mention of the seersha's name and scowled at her. Ellinor knew he didn't really want to talk about Cosmin von Brandt. But between all the drinks at the party and the ones she had drunk since, Ellinor was too tipsy to skirt around the topic now.

"Do you want to rant, or do you want advice? Whatever it is, Kai, just tell me. Talk to me. I'm here for whatever you need. I couldn't help you when Cosmin first took you away, but I can help now. You have to air that pain, anger, disappointment, whatever it is, you have to let it out, and not just through meaningless sex. But, if it helps occasionally, by all means, have at it!" Kai snorted in laughter, and Ellinor smiled at him, before giving his arm another squeeze and softening her voice. "You have to know that won't make the pain go away, yeah? It's just a bandage."

"And what's going to 'elp, Ell? More whiskey? Because that seems to be your go to these days and it don't seem to be working all that well," Kai shot back, narrowing his eyes.

Ellinor lowered her shoulders and shook her head. "It helps. For a little while. But want to know what really does the trick?" When Kai didn't say anything, Ellinor answered for him. "Friends, Kai. You taught me that. You've got us, and you can't go running back to Cosmin one day like you don't mind if he ruins your life."

Kai smiled wanly at her, his eyes already taking on a watery sheen. "Ain't that what you're doin' though, boss? Planning on running right back to 'im? Even if the plan is to, ah, well, you know . . ."

Ellinor gave him a sad smile in return, giving his hand another squeeze. "Yeah, pretty much. And we all know my example is *not* the one to follow. Talk to me, buddy."

Kai deflated at her words, cradling the glass in his hands. Ellinor had never seen him look so fragile in all the years she had known him. "The magitech Cos . . . Cosmin used when I was in that bubble pod wasn't all that bad, you know? Ah, sure, 'urt like a bitch, but it wasn't any worse than other shit I've gone through. The worst part? The worst part was before he even felt the need to show he meant business."

Kai took a deep, shuddering breath, and Ellinor held hers, worried that any movement or noise on her part would break the spell. "Soon as Cosmin's face blipped off from that holocomm I realized that he never, and I mean *fucking never*, leaves my mind. But I never even cross 'is. Probably never do, or never did, unless he was talking directly to me. That was the shit that completely broke me, boss. More than any of 'is magitech did, or ever could."

Kai's words hitched, tears flowing down his puffy cheeks, and Ellinor slipped her hands into his. Fiss, absorbed in his cartoons, remained oblivious. Kai squeezed her hands in return, a shaky grin disrupting the path of tears rolling down his face. "Sometimes, pain is only pain, Ell," Kai said, voice low and raw. "It don't make you stronger. It don't build no character. It only 'urts. Don't rightfully think I understood what it was like for you till Cosmin 'ad me swallow that bitter pill."

Ellinor's chest constricted, a fist around her heart and lungs to hear Kai say such things. "I'll make Cosmin pay, Kai. I'll rip his tongue and eyes out and shove them up his ass for what he's done to you. Only then will I kill him for what he did to Misho."

"Nah, boss. You don't gotta do that for me. But . . . thanks. For listening. Making me talk. Didn't realize 'ow badly I needed it."

"Anytime you want a shoulder or drinking buddy, you find me, okay? I got you, Kai."

He didn't answer, instead clinking his glass against hers before drinking the last of his whiskey. Ellinor did the same, and as she was pouring herself and Kai another round the door hissed open and closed, announcing Jelani's arrival.

Jelani crept toward them. Now that the adrenaline was gone, he swayed more on his feet, tipsier than Ellinor realized. His face was slack but his eyes were warily watching Fiss, who turned and beamed at him from where he was near the television.

"All better, my little friend?" Jelani asked. Fiss nodded energetically before turning back to watching the psychedelic cartoons he so favored.

"Izza doing okay?" Kai whispered when Jelani joined them at the bar.

Jelani ran his hands through his hair, the fear and exhaustion he tried to hide from Fiss on full display. "Zer will be, thankfully. I was in the way so I left to give the mechanics room to work. But we were lucky. Had the effects been sharper, I don't think there'd be anything we could do for Izza. Though, certainly, given the magic Fiss used, that may very well be the outcome next time."

Kai frowned, his face pulling down in suspicion. "What's that mean? What 'appened down there? Oihana said something 'bout a fight?"

"If you could call it that. It was more a drunken brawl between me and that Caterina woman," Ellinor interrupted, pushing a drink at Jelani to help with his nerves, but that made Kai's brows furrow all the more.

"Nah, see, there's gotta be more to it, ain't there? More than just some fight if Fiss reacted like that against Izza. Izza's a friend, for Azer's sake! Someone try and kill you?"

"No," she said weakly. "Not exactly."

"Boss, you've got some explaining to do," Kai said, grabbing Ellinor's shoulders and looking at her closely, as if inspecting her for damage he may have missed earlier.

She swatted his hands off, head spinning, though she wasn't sure if it was the effects of the whiskey or not. "Fine, you want the whole story? Caterina wanted to fight, so I obliged. Things got a bit rough, and that upset Fiss. Izza got messed up in the process of calming him, that's all."

Kai shook his head. "That don't make a lick of sense. If you were wrestling with Caterina, how'd Izza get zapped? A stray bolt from Fiss or something? The kid's not supposed to be able to 'urt no one, even an Ashling. You didn't tell 'im too, right?"

Ellinor wanted to be hurt that Kai thought she would be capable of such a thing, but she knew she deserved such an assumption.

Do better, Ellinor.

"No," she said slowly, twisting a lock of hair around her finger. "That was a mistake. Izza just . . . got in the way, I guess."

Kai shook his head before turning his gaze to Jelani. Her friend must not have liked what he saw on Jelani's face, as his eyes hardened. "You all been acting like a pair of kids stealing money outta Ma's purse the past few days, I gotta say. You're 'iding stuff from me, and I ain't going to let that fly no more. Spill. What's going on, Ell? Is it your . . . collar?"

Ellinor slumped back onto the wall, the tissue under the bio-magitech throbbing. She slid down to the floor and struggled to find words, trying to figure out if she wanted to, or if she even should tell Kai. Especially after what he had shared about Cosmin. It didn't feel right. It felt too selfish somehow.

Jelani pinched the bridge of his nose and took the choice away from Ellinor. "Yes, it is."

Ellinor sucked in a breath, and Kai turned wide, pleading eyes at her. The last of her resolve shattered like brittle glass.

Slowly, carefully, she explained to Kai about the virus failsafe that Cosmin had put in the collar, and how it was malfunctioning. How the symbiotic bond she had with Fiss was now tainting the dreeocht, changing him into something he wasn't meant to be, something too similar to a doehaz with too much power.

Kai's face was already devoid of all color, jaw slack, well before she told him that the bio-magitech was spreading internally as well as externally. Soon, the malfunctioning device would kill her.

"But, when that happens, Fiss will be back to normal, so there's that, at least," Ellinor finished, smiling grimly.

Jelani cleared his throat. "You neglected to mention that Gorgi may provide a solution. That there is still a chance, and a good one, that leaves you both alive, and Fiss fine."

Ellinor hunched her shoulders away from Jelani, desperate for another drink. "We don't know what that Ashling wants in return. Zer's interested in what went *wrong* with the technology. Gorgi's not hiding that, and zer needs something zer thinks I don't want, which is also shady as fuck. I don't keep a lot of stuff around that I don't want, so paying zers price may not be worth it and if that's the case, Fiss is the priority, not me."

Kai shook his head, slowly at first, but faster and firmer as he came to a decision. He crossed his arms over his chest and said, "That's a steaming piece of doehaz shit you're serving, Ell. That ain't 'appening. No matter what that Gorgi asshole wants, zer gets it. You hear? Gorgi can 'ave it."

Jelani leaned against the wall near Ellinor, his body tense despite his relaxed demeanor as he took a sip of his drink. "I, for one, agree wholeheartedly with you on this, Kai. It seems you have been outvoted, Ellinor."

"This isn't a democracy. It's my life. And I say—"

"No, Ell. None of that now. No more sanctimonious crap from you. You saved me, I'm saving you. Enough said. Gorgi can 'ave whatever zer wants in order to save both Fiss and *you*. I ain't going to another friend's funeral."

Ellinor swallowed her retort. She hadn't the energy to insist to Kai that the price of Gorgi's aid may not be worth the outcome he and Jelani were hoping for.

We'll just have to wait and see who ends up right, and if I end up dead.

CHAPTER

TWENTY

MISTAKES WERE MADE

ELLINOR WANTED to be left alone. And she was, mostly. Jelani went back to check on Izza, and Kai went to the adjacent room to clear his head. Fiss was still content to watch the different feeds, especially once he had figured out how to hack into the system with the cables in his hair. Now, he could watch all the dancing up close from Aylen's own security drones. But Ellinor's insides churned while watching Fiss, calm and giggling, perched on the floor in front of the screen.

Her bio-magitech wasn't burning at the moment, but there was a constant, light vibration where the skin and technology met that she couldn't completely ignore. She gently touched the metal parts that trailed down her chest, and her stomach seized.

"Baby bug, I need you to hang out with Kai for a little while. You can hack the feeds just as easily from his room, I promise," Ellinor said, trying to keep her hands from shaking, her voice from breaking, as she grinned at the dreeocht.

Fiss jerked around, panic in his eyes. "Not leaving my Elli! Why do you ask me to go? Why?"

Ellinor crouched in front of him, pretending the action was casual and not because her knees were giving out, that the anger and hopelessness she buried wasn't about to explode from her chest. "It's not like that. Remember we talked about needing space? Alone time like when I'm taking a shower? It's like that. I just need a little extra time, that's all. You'll have fun with red friend, yeah?"

Fiss' expression turned skeptical and hurt, but Ellinor could tell he was at least making a concerted effort to understand her. She turned off the television and forced herself to smile even with the scream building in her chest. "Please, Fiss? It won't be any different, or worse, than when I was meeting with Gorgi."

Fiss frowned, before his face morphed into a bright grin, as if he had forgotten that they had been separated for hours and nothing bad had happened to Ellinor. Nodding enthusiastically, he said, "Okay! I do this for Elli!"

Fiss floated to the door, and Ellinor struggled to her feet and followed him out. She made sure he was safe in Kai's temporary room, giving her friend a grateful glance before she shut the door. Ellinor was finally, and truly, alone.

Ellinor needed a moment, and she hadn't been given one, just ten minutes to despair . . . Kai now knew she was dying—or might be dying—she and Fiss were mutually destroying each other and she hadn't had time to even process that. That was on top of the guilt she felt toward Izza and her callous treatment of zer and all Ashlings she had so far encountered. This was only their second day on Amardeep and everything had turned to shit remarkably fast. On top of all of that, she knew how profoundly Kai was hurting, and that she was incapable of avenging him, of getting justice for Misho . . . Ellinor needed to break something, before *something* broke her completely.

It started in her hands, the tremors that built until they were earthquakes. Her walls crumbled with the inferno that was her bottled up rage, burning her lungs until all that came out was a strangled scream. Her breathing became difficult, not enough air inflating her lungs, never enough air without her magic, but now it was positively suffocating. Her despair was a cold fire, burning her blood and turning her bones to brittle ice in one impossible instant.

Without knowing how she got to her feet, let alone how the chair got into her hands, she was smashing it against the wall. The framed art burst into a spray of glass and rainbow paper. The chair gave out before the wall did, disintegrating in her bruised hands. She was glad for Aylen's extensive sound-proofing then. But even if Kai had been able to hear her, she doubted that would have stopped her now. She threw Kai's empty glass against the door, and Ellinor finally allowed her-self to admit it: she wasn't ready to die. Not yet.

Jelani and Kai could cling to the promises Gorgi made, but so far the Ashling had yet to contact them, and zer may not have good news when zer did. Ellinor could get hurt, and Fiss might lose it before Gorgi was able to do anything for her. Fiss using his magic may destroy her before she ever got the chance to use her own magic again.

Ellinor shrieked, throwing another chair against the wall. "Not yet! I'm not done yet!" She didn't expect anyone to an-swer her declaration—Azer or otherwise. She knew that even-tually she would have to stop, have to lock her emotions behind an impenetrable vault, or else Fiss might act out again. But since the dreeocht couldn't see her in distress like he had before, and because she wasn't battling anything outside herself, like the other times Fiss lost control, she figured she had time. In her tirade, she didn't hear Jelani re-enter the room.

"You do realize we will have to pay for this mess somehow." His voice was soft, barely above a whisper, and slightly slurred with alcohol, but it crashed through the room like one of the broken tablets. "What's going on, Ellinor?"

The chairs were smashed, the tables trashed, the walls gouged and stained. Ellinor was sure she looked like a terror with her disheveled hair, her memory-silk dress still covered in Caterina's blood. The only thing remotely undamaged was the bed where Fiss had been while watching his security feeds. But despite the mess, despite working her frustration out on wrecking the furniture in Aylen's suite, Ellinor didn't feel better. She was still struggling to breathe, drowning in regrets she had lied about having in the first place.

She laughed mirthlessly, kicking a broken chair. "You really don't know?" The adrenaline was still pumping in her veins and she began to pace, kicking and tossing any broken piece of furniture or tech that happened to get in her way. The alcohol in her system was getting a firmer grip on her, and while Ellinor hadn't been entirely sober before, she was decidedly starting to lean toward the drunk category now.

"Let's see. For starters, I died. Flatlined. But instead of staying with Misho, I got kicked back to this shit show. Which, you know, fine, okay, that gives me a chance to rip Cosmin limb from limb and go out in the blaze of bloody magic that I always planned. But wait! I can't do that because this biomagitech shackle is now a virus. So, not only can I *not* cast, but I'm dying. Again! Which you'd think I'd be down with this time around."

Jelani made a noise in his throat, leaning against the wall for support, and Ellinor pressed on. "No, really! I would! Except there's Fiss. And this virus—and all these fucking feelings and physical pains—are bleeding over to him," she said, gritting her teeth and pounding the wall. "I might as well be killing him, too. So, that's great."

Ellinor paused to take in a sucking breath. Her fists ached, her nails torn and hands bloody. The pain stalled her, and she looked down at the red stains, unsteady on her feet. "I need to make someone pay. That's all I know how to do anymore. But I can't do that for fear that it'll set Fiss off on a murderous rampage. So what do I do? Send him to Kai and trash a room. I'm a fucking idiot!" But even with tears threatening to come, she couldn't stop. Ellinor was overflowing with too many sharp pains and heavy emotions that she had ignored for too long.

She wheeled around, swaying on her feet, grabbing the decanter of whiskey and readying to smash the crystal against the wall, when Jelani caught her wrist. The whiskey fell to the floor with a thud, the amber liquid spilling, joining the other stains on the white carpet.

The smell of frosted eucalyptus flooded her senses as Jelani pulled her close, holding her wrists tightly as she squirmed to get free. She shook her head, trying to clear her thoughts of his scent, and wrenched her hands free only to have Jelani grab her around the waist and hold her tight.

"You shouldn't have let Fiss bring me back," she yelled, struggling to get free, pounding at Jelani's chest. "You should have left me dead!"

"Ellinor, stop. You're drunk and understandably frustrated, but this isn't the way. I can't . . . the chaos you're swept up in is overpowering. Please." He shook his head, eyes rimmed in red as he struggled to marshal his own latent earth abilities under control, his empathic abilities, his infallible "gut" falling prey to Ellinor's misery. "We still have a chance here, don't lose sight of that. We *will* find a way." Jelani dodged her flying hands, catching her arms and pinning them to her sides.

"By trusting more strangers who all want to take something from me? From us? No way! Let me go!"

"No! You're going to hurt yourself, and then what will become of Fiss? Do you want him to hurt Kai the way he's hurt Izza?"

Ellinor twisted sharply, wrenching free of Jelani and pushing him away. "*How fucking dare you?* I didn't do that. I didn't mean for that to happen! What happened to Izza was an accident," she yelled, launching herself at Jelani, pinning him to the ground.

She knew she should stop, but she couldn't, nor did she want to. Ellinor had snapped.

Jelani bucked his hips and flipped Ellinor off. She tried to lurch to her feet so she could grab for something, but Jelani got to her first. He spun her around again. She pitched toward him, and he slammed her back against the wall. Her head spun and she became aware of more than just her hopeless anger.

She became aware of a chest as firm as steel heaving against her own. Strong hips and thighs pressed against her, creating a heat that was building, crawling up from her lower body where it ignited in her core. The adrenaline was still there, but the niggling in her mind to stop, to find another outlet so she wouldn't hurt Fiss, coupled with what Kai had said before going to retrieve the passcode overtook her anger and made her breath hitch.

"Stop, Ellinor. You're drunk. I'm drunk. There's too much to process. Breathe," Jelani growled down at her, his lips a breadth from her forehead as he held her pinned, as if worried that if he slackened his hold at all she would wiggle free and they would resume wrestling for control.

She tilted her head up, the heat rising, her mind spinning with alcohol and a *need*. A need to feel something, anything other than the chaotic anguish she was experiencing. Her breathing came fast, faster, limbs trembling, and she looked into Jelani's star-like eyes. She shifted, and he responded by pressing himself even firmer against her.

Ellinor *knew* Jelani was handsome. Even when Misho was alive, she could look and appreciate attractive men and women, but she hadn't touched anyone since his death. She had ignored those needs in favor of a different type of desire: to slit the throats of those responsible for taking her husband. But here was Jelani, so beautiful, and so determined to save her, even from herself.

She claimed his lips in a desperate kiss.

He jerked his head back a moment later, eyes blinking furiously. "What are you doing?"

"Isn't it obvious?" she said, voice suddenly breathy. When Jelani didn't answer, didn't move, she tilted her lips closer to his once more. "Tell me to stop."

"Ellinor . . ."

"If I can't break things anymore, then I'd rather drink and fuck right through this disaster. I'm too far gone to do anything else." Jelani still hadn't moved, hadn't released her. She could feel the heat emanating from him, and she realized just how far gone she really was.

Jelani sucked in a breath but didn't lean away. His bleary eyes searched hers and she saw it: desire. "Ellinor, that's not . . ." Jelani swallowed. "You aren't serious, are you?"

It's a physical need. He's nothing like Misho.

"Tell me to stop, or let me go so I can find someone else. Maybe Elisaveta. She's cute and seemed into me. Probably because she doesn't know me."

He didn't release her, and she lost her patience. She bucked her hips, trying to get him off her. But Jelani pushed her back against the wall instead.

"Yes," Jelani said, voice husky.

He reciprocated with a rough kiss of his own. Hands drifted from where he had her pinned to cup the back of her neck, his other gently traveling down, down, down, his lips softening. She could taste gin, the sweetness on his tongue . . .

No!

Ellinor gripped him and spun them so she was pinning him against the wall. She didn't want sweet. Her blood was on fire, she was a mess, and the last thing she wanted was something tender and kind. She ripped open his suit, hands fumbling to get him out of the rest of the memory-silk, knowing full well he wasn't wearing anything under the fine clothing.

His chest vibrated with a growl and he bunched her dress in his fist. With one deft yank he tore it free. She answered his growl with one of her own, throwing him on the bed to straddle those defined hips of his. She roughly tangled her fingers in his impossibly soft hair, and dove down to kiss him with an angry hunger that consumed her, that drove her to get savage, to demand it in return.

Jelani did not disappoint.

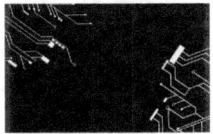

After, they both lay in the rumpled bed, the room smelling heavily of booze, sex, and a sticky sweet sort of sweat. Neither was asleep, despite the acrobatics, the pinning, the biting. Ellinor was . . . comfortable, lying beside a naked, glistening Jelani. Part of her wanted to hate that, how comfortable she was. This was the first time another person had seen her naked, had touched her—shit, had *fucked* her, since Misho. She felt like that realization should hurt more, but it simply didn't. She felt . . . relaxed. Relieved, even. Her bio-magitech wasn't burning, no sharp pangs stabbed in her heart, just a pleasant ache between her legs that she hadn't felt in eight years.

Jelani seemed equally at ease—not bashful, not awkward about what had just happened, how good it was, or how it even happened in the first place.

That was what made Ellinor uncomfortable.

"So," she began quietly, voice thin and shaky, "today was a clusterfuck, huh?"

Jelani chuckled, stretching and propping his hands behind his head. "Not all of it." He gave her a sidelong glance, his eyes clearer now, neither one of them as drunk as they had been. "Perhaps we shouldn't have crashed into each other the way we did? Or made that choice when we were both sober instead." He paused again, observing her before leaning his head closer. "Do you regret sleeping with me?"

Ellinor was shaking her head before he was even finished. What was the point in lying? He had her moaning and screaming enough to know that she had enjoyed herself. "No. You?"

Jelani was silent for a moment, and she bit her lip, worry twisting in her stomach. *Shit, I just made things irreparably weird and awkward.*

Then, Jelani was smiling at her, soft and sincere, a hunger lurking in his eyes that suggested he would gladly go again if she simply said the word. She rolled her eyes to keep from blushing. She snatched the whiskey bottle resting precariously on the lopsided bedside table and took a sip before waving the near empty bottle at Jelani.

He winked at her, and waved the offer away, his eyes twinkling in a mischievous sort of way that made her insides squirm as his gaze roved over her wet body.

"Oh, by the way," Ellinor said, trying to distract herself, trying to keep herself from rolling back on top of him. "Izza and Oihana asked that, no matter what Fiss decides in regard to Aylen, I'd have Fiss make Izza fully alive. With an actual nervous system, not just code that analyzes what an emotion should be. Did you know about that?"

Jelani nodded absently, his eyes lingering on her bare breasts as if he could sense her physical desire, before her words seemed to register. He blinked, brows pulling together, and a half smile crept over his lips. Cocking his head to the side, he regarded Ellinor anew. "Zer asked you for help in this? And you, Ellinor Olysha Rask, agreed? Color me shocked."

He's way too comfortable. This was just sex.

Ellinor shrugged, not sure when she had decided to give Izza what zer wanted, to gift zer with the thing all Ashlings seemed to crave as desperately as equal rights alongside the humani, seersha, and seerani. She wanted to say it was hearing Oihana's tortured cries over potentially losing her companion, but if Ellinor was being honest, it was before then. In her heart, she knew she was going to give Izza and Oihana what they wanted the moment the seerani mechanic and Ashling asked. Her only hesitancy had been Jelani's reaction to the request.

Why did I care what he'd think? You're getting soft, weak.

Ellinor cleared the thought away by draining the last of the whiskey, not caring that she would regret drinking so much come morning. "Yeah, well, Izza isn't like the other Ashlings," she said instead of the truth. "Figure I owe zer that much at least after what Fiss did."

She didn't dare look down at her shoulder to see how far her bio-magitech shackle had spread, how much more of her chest and arm were now covered in the virus. But Jelani must have seen the sudden sadness in her eyes, or felt the pull and shift in the natural world around them that his feeble earth caster abilities could detect. He brushed a feather-light finger over her arm, trailing it up to the tech. Ellinor shivered, a part of her wishing she could still feel the touch on her cybernetics.

"Fiss made a mistake. He didn't mean to hurt Izza, not truly. You are always his main focus, Ellinor. You were in pain and he reacted. Izza will be fine. I trust Aylen to repair the damage, and Oihana will forgive Fiss. We should talk to him, reason with him if we can, though I'm not sure that's possible with such a primal being. Then, we will remove the virus, and you won't need to worry about Fiss anymore," Jelani said, his words a soft invitation to roll over, to nestle herself back against his firm body.

Nope.

"Sure, okay." She forced a cocky smile and patted Jelani's chest. "This was fun, next time I have the urge to rip into something, I'll come find you again. Until then," she gave him a gentle push, and wiggled her eyebrows toward the door.

Jelani raised a brow at her, before rolling his eyes. Instead of rolling out of the bed on his side, he rolled over her, pinning her one last time. He lowered his head, nibbling her ear. "Next time," his breath was warm on her skin, and she fought the urge to arch her body into his, "I'll be better prepared." His voice was low, guttural, holding the hint of a promise that sent tingles racing across her skin.

He waited a moment longer, teasing her ear with his teeth gently one last time. He pushed back, grinning devilishly down at her while she looked up at him with a challenge before he rolled away and exited the room without picking up any of his discarded clothing.

FRUIT OF YOUR LABOR

THEY HEARD from Gorgi before Elisaveta, which soured the few mouthfuls of powdered eggs Ellinor had already eaten. Oihana was still waiting at the Habitation, cleaning Elisaveta's digital footprints and securing the transfer of the code from Elisaveta to Aylen. Oihana wasn't pleased, but if she didn't stay behind, then their heist from the night before could still be discovered.

The mini tablet Gorgi had given them blipped on the table between Ellinor and Kai, both stared at the offending piece of technology within the safety of Kai's room. Ellinor's room was far too trashed and would bring up too many questions for an already too curious dreeocht about what happened the night before.

Kai raised his eyes to her, and she shrugged, deciding not to wait for Jelani to join them before reading the message. He was following up with Izza, still sequestered within Rada and Aylen's workshop, and Ellinor wasn't sure when he would return.

"Think Veta got out clean?" Kai whispered, putting his hand over the tablet before Ellinor could open the message.

She tried to be nonchalant, to sip her hot coffee as if she were unconcerned, glancing at Fiss, who bounced on the bed. Kai didn't need anything more to worry about. He was still too raw over Cosmin, too worried over his mother's safety, for Ellinor to show him that she, too, had the same questions, the same concerns, the same sinking feeling deep in her gut with Gorgi messaging them before Elisaveta made official contact. *Did we miss something? We did everything right, even if nothing went according to plan.*

"If she hadn't, I don't think Gorgi would just send a message we could read when we were done taking a shit or whatever. Ashling like that? One who runs the biggest Juice Box manufacturer and distribution empire in Erhard, maybe in all of Eerden? If the jig was up, I think zer'd do more than send just a comms message, yeah?" She offered Kai a half smile, and put her coffee mug down, pushing the eggs around her plate in feigned disinterest, hoping it hid the worry building in her chest.

Kai nodded, removing his big hand, and reclined back in his chair, plopping a meat-like strip of bacon into his mouth. "True that. Good timing then, ain't it? Bet zer knows how to get that there collar off you and gots news to share." Kai's grin was hopeful, lighting up his face, the blisters almost completely gone.

Ellinor nodded, her smile not reaching her eyes, and she tapped the message. It opened, a holographic display of flashing words that Fiss trilled at. He exploded off the bed in a gust of wind and giggles, diving through the words and trying to catch them in the palms of his slightly fuzzy hands. The skin on Ellinor's chest began to burn where the bio-magitech was spreading, and she had to swallow her gasp.

Each hour it was getting worse, and it showed in the recklessness of Fiss' magic, in how he seemed to devolve, becoming more mindless, even if his casting was still mostly harmless. He played more than spoke, fixated on images rather than reveling in the beautiful, magical aquatic creatures he used to make. He looked different, too, or he did to Ellinor. His features seemed more defined, less baby-like, and the slightly pointed quality to his teeth felt more sinister now than they once had been. Ellinor had found Fiss annoying when he first came out of Cosmin's box, constantly casting and making unnecessary magical animals, but now she missed the way he once was.

We'll get Fiss back to right. Ellinor had no plan for if they couldn't; she refused to make a contingency plan of any kind that involved Fiss turning. She shut her eyes against the thought and snatched Fiss out of the air, holding him in her lap so she could read the message:

YOUR PRESENCE IS NECESSARY. TIME TO BE MUTUALLY BENEFICIAL TO EACH OTHER. COME TO MY OFFICE NOW.

The message was short, but sent chills racing down the nape of her neck all the same. Before she could discuss the message with Kai, the door hissed open and closed, and she felt Jelani's presence behind her as he read the message over her shoulder.

"Hmm," the seersha said, sitting down at the table next to Ellinor. "Izza is operational again and will be joining us shortly. We can head back to Oihana and the Habitation within the hour, easily, but we should check in with Elisaveta. Aylen hasn't heard from her yet, just Oihana when she sent the clean programming codes and data."

"Aylen's worried? That ain't exactly news. That woman worries 'bout everything." Kai leaned forward once more, propping his elbows on the table. If he even remotely suspected that Ellinor and Jelani had fucked the night before, he didn't betray even a twinkle in his eye.

Jelani rubbed the back of his head and gave a half shrug. "Not necessarily. Elisaveta may want to put digital distance between us and the disturbance at the party last night. On the off chance that some digital tripwire was triggered that my sister missed, this would remove all suspicion. Still . . ."

"Still," Ellinor said, picking up where Jelani left off, Fiss still wiggling on her lap. "Given Gorgi is summoning us right after we get the passcodes? Seems a little odd, yeah. Call her?"

Jelani nodded, snagged a piece of toast, and tapped Elisaveta's private line into the tablet Gorgi had provided. It wouldn't look strange for them to contact their handler from Gorgi's devices, and Elisaveta had so many mods in her that she could easily scramble the signal to keep Gorgi or anyone else from seeing, or hearing, anything suspicious from the call.

It took too long, in Ellinor's mind, for Elisaveta to answer. "Deal's done, love. Don't call me anymore," Elisaveta said curtly, already moving to disconnect the call.

"Hold up, *buttercup.* Do you know why Gorgi is summoning us? Little funny to get a message from zer the morning after zers . . . party." Call Ellinor paranoid, but even knowing Elisaveta could shield the call, she preferred to speak in a type of code to Elisaveta while confirming their double-cross of Gorgi had succeeded.

There was a pause, Elisaveta putting the pieces together, before she sighed loudly. "Don't read much into that. Gorgi is bloody brilliant. My guess? While all zer's people were out getting knackered, Gorgi was busy working on your little problem. Zer doesn't need sleep, you know, and once zer's curious about something, zer latches on and won't let go. Zer loves, and hates, mysteries like that."

Ellinor chewed her lip, narrowing her eyes at the tablet for a moment. Elisaveta probably had a point. The seerani had worked for Gorgi much longer, and Ellinor doubted she would do anything to jeopardize her chances with joining Aylen Bonheur and getting her brother clean. Still . . . "I get that. By the way, didn't see you after the party at SynthLyfe. You never told us if you had a good time, or if you hooked up with anyone. Nothing interesting happened, yeah? You missed one hell of a fight." Ellinor hoped that Elisaveta got what she was trying to say, she was no good with secret messages.

There was another pause. Another sigh. "I left early. No reason to stick around once I saw the people I needed to. You're worse than my mum, wanting details, worrying over nothing. You keep that up and you'll get wrinkles. We good?"

Ellinor exchanged a glance with Kai and Jelani. Kai shrugged, going back to his breakfast nonplussed, and Jelani nodded, mollified. Ellinor would trust their instincts. She couldn't trust her own, especially where Ashlings were concerned. "Yeah, I'm solid. Will you be coming with us to Gorgi's?"

"Did zer ask for me?"

"Not specifically, no. But—"

"Then I'm not going. Don't be such a baby, Miss Murder. If Gorgi had wanted me, zer'd have called me."

"C'mon, Veta," Kai said around a mouthful of food. "Would look right odd if you didn't come with us, aye?"

"For the last fucking time," Elisaveta snapped. "I don't know who the fuck Veta is, but that's not my name. Stop trying to change my name because you're lazy. It's Elisaveta. Period. And I'm still not going with you and holding your hands. *I wasn't summoned.*"

Ellinor rolled her eyes. "Fine. Whatever. I'll let you know when we're done."

The call ended and Kai downed the last of his coffee before chuckling softly. "She's a touchy one, ain't she? Ah, well, no matter. Time to chat with the big bot, then."

Even pacified by Elisaveta's words, Ellinor had no desire to see the creepy drug lord but, until her collar was fixed, they all had to keep up the ruse that they wanted to join Gorgi. Wanted to join zers Juice Box Empire and would do anything the Ashling asked without question, without hesitation. *At least this gives me another chance to snoop around, see if I can find any evidence that would lead me to whoever sent those Ashlings that killed Misho.*

Ellinor held on tightly to that thought as they collected their weapons, slipped into their armor, and headed out of the suite. Neither Jelani nor Ellinor commented on the mess they had made in her room as they passed the dented door and collected Izza from Rada. Izza was a little unsteady now on zers feet, sporting battle wounds from an altercation that should never have happened. Guilt twisted in her chest, almost as painfully as the tech crawling ever closer to her heart.

Izza stood apart from them, a rigidity to zers posture that suggested . . . fear?

The shock from the realization rippled through her. Ellinor may still want to hunt down and destroy the ones who took Misho from her, but those feelings didn't extend to bots like Izza. Like Rada. When she looked at Izza now, all she saw was an android that needed support, sympathy. She saw a friend just as willing to call her out on her ignorance as zer was to help her. Izza needed a chance to live and experience life on zers terms, and she *wanted* to help.

Then, it hit her like a hypersonic train: Izza *was* alive. And if Izza was alive . . . then *all* the Ashlings were. Those bots responsible for taking her little bug were not a monolith, zey did not represent all Ashlings. Zey did not represent Izza.

As soon as Izza hesitantly joined them, Ellinor grabbed Fiss' hand and brought him over to zer. Fiss tilted his head, confused, as she hoisted him up to be eye level with Izza, stalling the Ashling momentarily.

"Fiss, you need to say sorry to Izza," Ellinor said, looking into Izza's grey ocular orbs, wondering—*hoping*—that the bot could see her own regret lurking in her eyes.

"Sorry? Apologize? Why do I do this thing? What did I do, Elli?" Fiss tilted his head back and forth, eyes roving over Izza, not even pausing over the new electrical scorch marks, or the darkened spots on zers once flawless silver body.

"You hurt zer. That's not okay. You have to remember: we never, ever hurt friends. You didn't mean to, yeah? So that's what you're sorry for."

"Little Fiss does not understand the error. I understand this, Ms Ellinor. It is better he has forgotten. Apologies are not necessary," Izza said in zers ever formal, congenial manner.

Izza's orbs shifted from Fiss to Ellinor, and the Ashling placed zers cold hand on her shoulder. "I do appreciate the sentiment, though, as will Ms Oihana. I will remember this. Thank you."

Ellinor never thought she would be touched by an Ashlings words, but the soft warmth spreading throughout her ribcage, the weight of guilt lifting off her shoulders, told a different story. Ellinor squeezed Izza's hand in return without hesitation. She tried to hide her relieved smile, but both Jelani and Izza saw it before she removed her hand and put Fiss back down. Ellinor led the way out of Aylen's domain before the Owner of SynthLyfe commented on the state Ellinor left her room in.

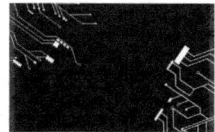

The group made it to the Habitation without incident, sending a message to Oihana on the way to let her know to expect them. They pushed their way through the throng of bodies in the lobby, a fresh wave of tourists checking in. Ellinor frowned at all the young people she saw. In her university days, she had never had the money to go on break anywhere fun, let alone an expensive place like the Habitation. True, she had dropped out fairly early on, but that wasn't the point.

Despite the noise from all the students jostling their luggage, queuing up in long lines, waiting to be checked in, the group easily heard the high-pitched squeal coming from the elevator bay. Their heads snapped around to see Oihana sprinting toward them, her rich, brown hair flying behind her, arms wide.

She skidded to a stop, her hands moving too fast to track as they fluttered near Izza, afraid to touch zer, but wanting to ensure that everything was where it needed to be. Izza twisted zers fingers, speaking to Oihana in the special sign language that she shared with Jelani, and Oihana relaxed, her face melting into the brightest smile Ellinor had seen in days.

Oihana hugged Izza, and there was no hesitancy in the Ashling returning the gesture. Zer may be missing that last component to make zer truly feel and experience everything organics could, but that didn't mean Izza couldn't feel . . . alive.

She shook her head, saving the thought for later. Gorgi wasn't like Izza, and she couldn't lose sight of that. "Oihana, you good to wait with Izza and Fiss while we talk to the boss bot downstairs?"

There was a flash of fear, uncertainty, and anger in Oihana's big, golden-brown eyes. But it vanished when Fiss smiled up at her. Every inch the innocent, sweet dreeocht she, like the rest of them, had fallen for so instantaneously.

"Little Jelly shows me how to hack more screens? Please?" Fiss cooed.

Her lip quirked, full of mischievous glee. "I'll show you how to do more than that, kiddo. Let's go make trouble."

"Not too much trouble, sister," Jelani cautioned before Oihana could turn away. "Remember where you are and what Fiss is capable of now."

Oihana scoffed. "You're zero fun, Anni."

The two groups departed, their elevators racing toward different floors of the same building. Ellinor wrestled her heart into submission; she couldn't betray any emotion to Gorgi, no matter what news the Ashling had for her. She twirled her Lacerator knives around her fingers to still her thoughts, to get back into the persona of Lenore Castile. She touched the butts of her pistols, noted the empty weight on her back where her mechanized crossbow should have been.

She felt naked without it, but no one thought it was a good idea to go armed to the teeth when nothing was wrong or openly amiss. *Misunderstandings.* That's what they wanted to avoid. But they *were* supposed to be Juice Box thugs. Being completely unarmed would have been odd, even if their weapons couldn't accompany them into Gorgi's lab. Her armor and shield were charged, regardless. Despite her epiphany when it came to Ashlings like Izza, Ellinor wasn't comfortable around a behemoth like Gorgi, let alone with a bot who was eager to modify organics.

They exited out into the programming floor once more and a shiver ran down the back of Ellinor's legs at the sight of all the tubes and wires filled with the bio-magitech nanites, plump with dead magic being siphoned from various "guests" throughout the massive facility. Ashling guard bots patrolled the floor, monitoring their brethren and scanning the entrances and exits for any unwanted disturbances.

The trio hadn't gone more than two steps before they were stopped by two white, wheeled Ashlings who disarmed Ellinor and got between her, Kai, and Jelani. "Gorgi sees only the infected one. Other two come with us for assignment. This way," one of the two identical Ashlings said. Zeyr didn't wait for any of them to answer before separating them, Kai and Jelani going in one direction, while Ellinor was escorted back to the operating room that served as Gorgi's lab and private office.

Ellinor tried to slow her steps, to snoop and look into any of the rooms they passed, but she never got more than a cursory glance at anything. The white Ashling herded Ellinor inside, never letting her pause for more than a moment. While zer didn't come into the room, Ellinor could sense zers presence just on the other side, hovering.

"Hello, yes, welcome, Lenore Castile. Sit, sit. I have news, and an offer I am thinking you will like," Gorgi's voice thundered behind her.

Ellinor straightened and turned, steeling her face into a mask. The Ashling still had the same unsettling clown's mask, but zer had changed to a long, deep black wig that reminded Ellinor too much of Cosmin's own hair. She moved stiffly to the edge of the table, perching on the edge, just enough to say she was sitting.

Gorgi's black ocular slits whirled and clicked as they focused on Ellinor, and she resisted the urge to shift against the table. "The expected news first then: I can unlock the magic your bio-magitech locks away. The cybernetic parts stay, but it no longer causes death, this should be agreeable to you."

Ellinor couldn't contain the sigh of relief that hissed passed her tight-lipped façade. Gorgi waved a claw-like hand. "Your surprise is inane, there was no doubt I would be capable of dismantling such a thing. You have eyes, you can see me. Of course, I would be able to do this thing. I studied the virus, yes. And I want it. It ties flesh to metal, metal to flesh. This is necessary for my plans."

"Your plans?" Ellinor asked, intrigue overriding her better sense and soldier's training. Andrey would have been disappointed in her, again. "Why would you want to attach flesh to an Ashling? That would make you fragile, you'd get damaged more easily. I don't get it."

"You are simple creature," Gorgi said. "Not insult, fact. You see weakness. I see opportunity. Flesh self-heals. Repairs. Not dependent on a mechanic. Organs, cells, skin, it does what needs doing while fleshies go about other business. Not soft-ness. Strength. You take for granted the marvel of a nervous system. Wasted, yes? On the likes of you. Your Azer made a mistake. Odd, that an infallible god could do this thing. Begs many, many questions."

Ellinor's body went cold, rigid against the table. Her arms stayed crossed, her limbs poised to move, waiting. To run too early would assume an outcome that may be wrong. *Patience,* Andrey's voice rang in her head. *You need more intel. Move only when necessary.* Ellinor stayed put, trusting in the logic of her long dead brother more than her own gut in that moment.

"What is it you want then? I work for you, Gorgi. You only have to ask, I'm your girl. Of course, I'm going to do my best to give you whatever you want, provided the price is fair, of course." Ellinor grinned, but her voice was weak despite trying to appear willing, eager, even, to give Gorgi whatever zer asked of zers loyal minion.

"I take your tech. Dismantle the virus. I free your magic. You do as I say. Simple?"

Ellinor was about to agree, ready to hop up on the table and let Gorgi poke and prod at her neck however zer saw fit, so she could be reunited with her magic and get away from the massive Ashling as soon as possible. Until—

"Ellinor Rask. You will give me the continent of Erhard, for starters."

NO ONE WEARS HELMETS ANYMORE

ELLINOR WAS slammed onto the table. Gorgi's arms held her down as plastic straps were snapped over her wrists and ankles. She hadn't even had time to dissent, yell or fight back before she was immobilized.

Ellinor's teeth felt loose in her mouth from the impact, heart thundering so loud in her ears she could barely hear Gorgi as she struggled to think, think, *think!*

"You have surprise? Why? The clues, they were there for the observing, the taking. Simple fleshies do not see the pattern, the code, the trace left by one encounter. Your fabricated identification is fine, *was* fine, for those who do not already know who you are, Ellinor Rask."

"How? When?" she gasped, squirming on the table as Gorgi and zers wheeled assistant brought all manner of laser drills, scanners, and needles ranging in size, all connected to the suspended computer system attached to the table she was held on. A holographic face made up of strings of code—the

AI—was already processing her vitals, updating the levels of narcotics it would need to push to keep her sedated.

Ellinor didn't think Gorgi would really tell her zers whole plan, only villains in virtual simulators did that. But she was hoping for time—just a little *fucking* time—so she could control her breathing and come up with a plan or . . . or *something* in order to free herself.

"Eight years and forty-six days ago. Ellinor Rask was guarding a warehouse for one Cosmin von Brandt. Fleshies were ignorant even then, did not know what they were safeguarding. I want, I take." Gorgi pushed one of the needles into the biomagitech along her neck, the pressure not nearly as bad as the vacuum sound that accompanied it. "But Ellinor Rask, she was harder to kill than the other fleshy, yes? Kept my spies from taking the technology, the information I coveted. It was bothersome. I could forgive, but you killed my people. I do not forget such things. You understand, yes?"

Ellinor stilled. Gaze locked on Gorgi, her ears rang with zers casual words. Her heart shriveled in her chest, as motionless as the rest of her. The patterns, the clues Gorgi alluded to, snapped into place like the plates of her shield.

Gorgi had been running the Habitation's Juice Box business for decades under the shadow Owner. Zer must have freed zerself of zers programming shackles well before Ellinor and Misho had ever gotten married. She knew powerful Ashlings were behind the attack, ones with resources capable of infiltrating Cosmin's impressive systems, of making alliances with people within Cosmin's organization. That's why she had always planned to come to Amardeep, to ferret the culprits out. Admittedly, that had taken a step back because of her magical impairment, and Fiss' own affliction—so much so that she forgot, or ignored, that a bot like Gorgi would fit the kind of Ashling she was looking for. If only she had taken the time and asked Aylen or Elisaveta for the intel she wanted, or if she had only slipped away and snuck around Gorgi's facilities for herself.

Perhaps Ellinor was as oblivious as Gorgi implied. Or perhaps she was finding a new purpose, as Jelani suggested. But either way, none of that mattered now that she was strapped to Gorgi's table.

"Just take the virus then, whatever code you need to suck out of it, that's fine." A painful mix of anger and panic crashed through Ellinor as she lay on Gorgi's table. Eight years later and she had found the asshole responsible for Misho's murder, and here she was, strapped down and about to be dissected on that very bot's table. The idea of it kicked Ellinor's flight mode into high gear.

"I won't fight you, yeah? But I don't know how you think I can give you Erhard of all things. It's a fucking continent! I'm not that powerful of a caster. You saw that yourself when you first examined me." Disgust brought bile inching up her throat, despising that she was bargaining with Misho's killer, but what choice did she have? "Let me go though, and maybe we could work together and take Cosmin down? He's got the power to reach your goals, no question."

Ellinor wriggled against the bonds but as soon as she moved, a scalpel shot out of the neck of Gorgi's assistant. The blade's cool, sharp edge rested on her jugular vein, as light as a feather, but a loud warning.

"I do not want you, Ellinor Rask. You are correct. Your abilities, they are too weak for the goals I have. You are a useless fleshy. This is fact." Gorgi shifted, and a red scan flashed over

Ellinor, temporarily blinding her. "You hold little worth to me. I'd have beheaded you when you first came to me, but then I wouldn't have had access to your real power. Your dreeocht."

"No!" she jerked against the table, concern for her safety gone at the idea of Fiss being taken from her. The knife sliced her throat, but Gorgi's bot avoided killing her. For now, it would seem, Gorgi needed her alive while he extracted the code, the tainted nanites and bio-magitech that contained the corrupted bits of the virus in her cells and organs.

"It is a marvel that you have survived so long. Bumbling, I believe you call it. You bumble around and imagine somehow that I could not see what your collar was connected to? What its primary function was?" There was a grinding noise rattling from Gorgi's chest that Ellinor took as the bot laughing. "The virus must be nullified, yes? To break all influence you hold. I want your dreeocht, I take your dreeocht. Then send you back to this Cosmin von Brandt. He pays a lot of credits to have your fragile head back. I comply, I get more resources. More access to Euria and your precious Erhard. This is what you will give, Ellinor Rask. Willingly or not matters little. You will comply."

"Like shit I will!" She jerked again, fury and panic making her bold, reckless. She rocked the table with her thrashing. She might not be able to save Misho anymore, but she *would* save Fiss. Nothing was going to take Fiss away from her, *nothing*. Gorgi's assistant couldn't kill her, the AI hadn't started pumping sedatives into her just yet, and Gorgi wasn't done with her. Ellinor would use that.

The pressure in her neck increased, the needle wiggling, she could feel her veins shiver with the movement. The room was not large, and Gorgi's assistant couldn't move back far enough to avoid Ellinor as the table tipped.

Gorgi's massive arms slammed down on the table, righting it, but not before she pressed her arm against the assistant. Zer turned on Ellinor's shield for her.

The plates snapped open, cutting the plastic holding her, and part of her wrist in the process. She didn't feel the pain, she didn't feel the hot blood running into her palm and making her hand slick. She couldn't feel anything but a burning terror to protect Fiss, a desperation to fly far, far away with her baby bug.

She slammed the shield against Gorgi, dislodging zers mask, displacing zers wig, and covering zers ocular slits. Gorgi was off balance, zers massive frame teetering briefly.

Ellinor swiveled, running the sharp edge of her shield over the plastic restraints on her ankles. As soon as she felt more mobility from her legs, she kicked out, knocking the assistant over, zers scalpel bouncing harmlessly off her armor. She jerked the shield to her still-bound wrist—and her body seized.

An electric paralytic coursed over her, activated by the AI, wrapping her in a net similar to what Cosmin's own bots used. It had switched the serum from the sedative to the electric field in order to subdue her quicker in the chaos. Her teeth clamped shut, muscles shaking, tensing and coiling excruciatingly, desperate for release but unable to move. Her own bones fought against the restriction the electricity caused in her muscles. All she could move were the very tips of her fingers.

The assistant bot was rolling over, righting zerself, but Gorgi had already removed some of the virus, too eager to start zers tinkering and not even waiting for the sedative to enter her system. Zer had deactivated some of Ellinor's collar in the process of removing the parts zer needed.

There was a sliver of warmth, deep, deep down in her gut. So small, it was easy to ignore, would have been easy to miss entirely, except Ellinor had been starved of her magic for too long. She knew what that warmth, that tiny sense of wholeness, meant.

She twitched her fingers.

A whip of air lashed out, knocking the holo-screens and the monitors into Gorgi like a spear. The high-carbon steel supports the devices rested on pierced zers shoulder—barely—but it was enough. The electrical paralytic was released before the effects could become long lasting.

Ellinor was on fire—literally, she thought. The virus, the collar, they were still intact, still fighting to dampen her abilities, still punishing her for using her magic. She didn't want to think about the effect that was having on Fiss, couldn't think about it when her arm was still attached to the table.

Gasping for breath, her heart beat painful, she clumsily slammed her shield down on the last offending restraint. Too hard, apparently, as the armor protecting her wrist flared to stop her from cutting off her own hand. She fell from the table, landing on the assistant bot. Metal groaned behind her and she knew Gorgi was prying the metal out of zers shoulder.

The assistant bot lifted zers arms, shifting to grab Ellinor and hold her in place. But she dug her fingers into the vulnerable spot around zers neck and pulled out the fragile, exposed wiring. There was a brief, tinny whine, and the Ashling stopped moving. Ellinor wasn't sure if she had *killed* zer, or just shut the thing off. Gorgi didn't cry out in protest, and she didn't rightfully care one way or another.

She scrambled to her feet, falling out the door, and half ran, half crawled down the hallway to where the other bot had taken her friends. She hadn't gotten more than a few feet before the alarm klaxons blared through the cavernous, siphoning room. The echo vibrated in her skull and brought Ellinor to her knees. Movement in the room stopped. Guard Ashlings paused zeyr routes, heads swiveling toward the disturbance.

Get up, keep going!

Ellinor felt the heavy stomps of Gorgi behind her—she couldn't hear a thing over the alarms. She got to her feet and lurched in the direction of where Kai and Jelani were supposed to be. As soon as she started moving, so did Gorgi's guards.

The Ashlings hooked up to the various tubes and wires dangling from the ceiling didn't so much as budge as Ellinor scurried blindly past. Even her shallow breaths caused a burning pain to wash down her chest as she ran. It wasn't zeyr job to chase dissenters. That honor was reserved for the aerial guard androids flying toward her at an alarming speed, their silver, triangular bodies like homing missiles.

Ellinor flattened herself against the floor as one buzzed by her head and crawled as fast as she could toward the safety of the narrow hallway. She had to get to Kai and Jelani, she had to get them out of there so they could take everyone to safety. Her heart may be screaming in agony—equally from the magitech and her desire to avenge Misho—but she couldn't abandon Kai or Jelani. She couldn't risk someone harming Fiss. Reaching out for her magic, she tried to make a shield to protect herself, but the magic would not respond. Her bio-magitech shackle was still too strong, Ellinor was still too battered from the first bit of casting she had done in weeks to cast properly again. Nothing answered her.

She didn't make it to the hallway.

There was a stabbing pain in her right calf from a bot stepping on her. A strangled scream tore from her throat, and then a hulking figure blocked her vision.

It was Kai in his Coyote mechanized suit.

Jelani hobbled behind Kai, holding on to his right side, deep red blood flowing through his fingers as he reached out and grabbed Ellinor, tugging her upright and shoving her Anaconda pistols and Lacerator knives in her hands. She didn't look at the damage to her leg before she twisted around and began firing at anything that moved.

Kai lobbed one of his EMP grenades, and the bots went scrambling. Ellinor shot at zem all but couldn't see Gorgi anywhere. So she shot at the other bots, the computers, the tubes and the hoses, anything that would break Gorgi's operation and slow zem down while they figured out how to get back to Oihana, Fiss, and Izza.

The loud *crack* of Jelani's rifle boomed, creating a new buzz in her ears. The fluorescent lights came crashing down, creating a barrier between them and the wheeled guard androids, but it would not protect them from the aerial Ashlings.

"I'm out!" Kai bellowed, hefting his submachine gun in place of the empty grenade belt and peppering the room. The *click-click* of Ellinor's double barreled pistols followed soon after. Thankfully Jelani was at the elevator, but before he could summon it, the button glowed gold.

"Jelani, get back! Gorgi's got back up on the way!" Ellinor snatched her karambit knives and put herself between Jelani and the sleek, gold elevator doors.

The metal and steel on her neck, chest, and shoulder began to throb the closer the elevator got to the basement. Kai kept firing, his Coyote suit taking a beating as he covered Jelani. But more Ashlings were coming, and Gorgi was still nowhere to be seen. A fresh wave of sour fear rose in Ellinor's stomach as her heart raced faster and faster.

The liquid heat around the bio-magitech continued to grow until it reached boiling levels. Ellinor vigilantly watched the elevator door, her vision blurry with pain. Jelani fired his Zifu Raven whenever he could, but a grunt from Kai and the *thunk* of the big guy going down had Ellinor turning her back on the elevator and flinging her boomerang knives at the aerial Ashling bearing down on Kai. The knives bounced harmlessly off the metal before returning to her outstretched fingers, but at least it diverted the bot enough that it did not skewer Kai with its laser lance.

The elevator opened behind Ellinor. Her head whipped around.

Floating in an electrical storm was Fiss. Eyes blazing white fire, teeth bared as he dove into the room. "Not my Elli! *Mine!*" the little dreeocht screamed.

Ellinor could have sworn Fiss was commanding Zabel's spider lightning, all crawling tendrils of electricity and malice. Water magic flowed into the room from the dreeocht's little feet, short circuiting anything it touched. Wind whirled off Fiss' cable and seaweed hair as sharp as her own WX Lacerator knives.

Jelani's warm hands, slick with his blood, grasped her, dragging her into the elevator after Kai. Fiss turned his crazed gaze back to her, before her vision went completely white, and Ellinor saw no more, her nerves fried, sharp pains stabbing into her heart with every rapid, shallow beat.

Fiss had used too much magic.

IT'S THE JUICE

ELLINOR REGAINED consciousness with a shuddering gasp, her eyes snapping open. Her heart didn't shut down like it had once before. Not completely, anyway. Either the small sliver of magic that was unlocked had been enough to keep Ellinor alive, or her heart was more machine than she realized.

"Elli is back!" Fiss said in a sing-song manner, nuzzling himself into her arms.

"Can you move, Ell?" Kai's gauntlet covered hands hoisted her up. He steadied her for a moment as her wobbly legs attempted to stabilize themselves against the inertia of the speeding elevator, before letting go and reloading his submachine gun.

"I'll manage," she croaked.

The world was spinning, her vision unfocused, eyelids heavy, and she could only make out blurry shapes. There was a sharp pressure sitting on her lungs and gut making it hard to breathe, hard to think . . . But her memory wasn't impacted, she knew exactly what had happened before she passed out.

Ellinor closed her eyes and took a deep breath. Then another. And another, preparing to run as soon as the elevator doors opened.

She forced her eyelids open and the voice of her brother barked internal orders to stay alert, to focus, until she was able to ignore her body's insistence on collapsing into the heap she had just come from. She gave herself a task to do, a step-by-step list to keep her from crumbling to the floor. *Reload. Breathe. Have your armor scan for breaches. Breathe. Check your knives. Breathe.*

Ellinor glanced at the hunched figure of Jelani, and her chest tightened further. He drooped against the opposite wall of the elevator as it came to a halt. "Kai, I need you to carry Jelani. We've got to get out of the Habitation, and we have to do it fast. Fiss," she said, pushing the dreeocht onto her shoulders so she wouldn't lose him, "where are Izza and Oihana?"

Fiss pointed as soon as the doors opened, revealing the ashen face of Oihana Sharma and Izza standing in the lobby. The pressure in Ellinor's chest lessened marginally at seeing them, and marginally more so when Izza supported Jelani as effortlessly as Kai. A needle popped out of Izza's chest and the Ashling gripped it momentarily before, with surprising delicacy, pushing it into Jelani's neck.

"You can't keep making a habit of this, Anni," Oihana chided, but her deep voice was weak, even as a bit of color returned to Jelani with the shot of adrenaline from the reco-shot.

"I will tend to Mr Jelani once we have arrived at the monorail's cargo bay. I have nurse bot capabilities, but it is best not to jostle him as I work. Ms Oihana has secured passage to SynthLyfe, but Gorgi's operatives are already working to override Ms Oihana's hacks," Izza said in zers ever patient tone. "We must move at an accelerated pace. The way is not clear."

Ellinor waved Izza and Oihana on, her legs and hands still shaking, her right calf still smarting, but she took position alongside Kai as they trotted away from the elevator and toward the monorail depot. They hadn't gone more than a few steps before the lights flashed. A moment later, the fire alarm was blaring through the halls, a strobe light flickering throughout the enormous building, momentarily stalling the crowds as they peered upward, wondering if this were a drill, a malfunction of some kind, or an actual emergency.

She gripped the butt of one of her pistols as if it were a handrail to stabilize her, her other hand hovered over the boomerang karambit knives, ready to fling the blades at a moment's notice. Her eyes bounced across the hundreds of people ambling about the Habitation's main lobby. Some were moving for the exits, but most were looking around and shrugging, disregarding the alarms.

Her gaze briefly locked on the bulky bags on Oihana and Izza's backs, registering that the pair had at least stuffed their belongings into the magitech packs before following after Fiss. Then she moved on, back to watching the crowd as their group tried to wade through the swarm of people as quickly as possible.

Ellinor's lungs burned, her heart pounding in her chest at an irregular cadence that kept her vision disconcertingly tunneled, which only served to spike her anxiety when she needed to clear her head the most. Fiss growled from his perch on her shoulders, and she forced a deep breath, gently touching the dreeocht's knee to soothe him.

They skirted tourists, the normal rivers of movement interrupted by the steady strobe, the loud bark of the alarm. Kai waved his Rasul AbyssFire at the crowd when necessary. The submachine gun cleared a path briefly, but many seemed to think Kai was merely a guard working for the Habitation, someone they could disregard, who would not hurt them. The crowd soon swallowed around them once more, slowing their gait, making them stop suddenly and dart around clusters of confused cyborg seerani, and humani gawkers. The exit was inching into view though, along with the tunnel that would lead them—hopefully—to safety.

Jelani staggered in Izza's arms, stifling a groan. The shot of adrenaline may have numbed the pain, but it didn't stop the blood loss. The reco-shot was not an instantaneous cure, especially not when all their running was making Jelani's wound worse.

Ellinor slowed, trying to help Izza. "Hold on, Jelani. We're almost there," she whispered in his ear.

He turned to look at her, his movements sluggish, yet he still tried to give her a reassuring smile. "You don't need to drag me along, I can help you still. Get us to safety faster. Izza, let me go."

She gently brushed the hair from his face, noting how hot he felt, the sweat building on his brow. She swallowed the dryness in her throat at seeing him this way, but she could not swallow her desire to protect the seersha. "Don't, Izza," Ellinor said.

"I had no intention of allowing Mr Jelani to harm himself further, Ms Ellinor."

She smirked at the Ashling, and briefly cupped Jelani's cheek. "We got you. Just, hold on, yeah?" It was only when he nodded that Ellinor darted back to Kai, and tapped Oihana on the shoulder, pointing to Jelani and Izza. Oihana went to her brother, helping Izza support him, both encouraging Jelani to keep going.

A group of confused tourists darted around them, trying to get away from the noise and chaos of the fire alarm. Kai sucked in his breath, skidding to a halt in front of Izza and Oihana. Ellinor nearly bumped into him, until her blurred gaze settled on what everyone else saw: dozens of armed Juice fiends.

They didn't budge, standing in a long glob of bodies in front of the hall that led to the exit and monorail station. They didn't register when people bumped into them, cursing or yelling at them over the alarm to move and exit until it was safe to return to the Habitation. Those who tried to be nice touched the Juice addicts' shoulders, or waved hands in front of their faces, before shrugging and scuttling away when they got no response.

There was a glazed look to the Juice addicts, as always. Their faces were slack, their arms heavy, nearly dragging with the weight of the stun sticks and bulky revolvers in their hands, grips loose. They blinked rapidly at no one in particular, until their gaze locked on Ellinor's currently motionless group.

The Juice fiends—Juicers—tilted their heads in unison, as if listening to some sound or instruction from an ear implant. Then their shoulders straightened, and they tightened their grips on the various weapons in their hands. Izza emitted a faint *blip* that Ellinor barely heard over the still-blaring alarms as zer scanned the group.

"The dead nanites which produced the magical high effect have received new programming. These people no longer operate under their own volition." Izza's soothing voice was drowned out by the bedlam of sound and movement; the loping run of the Juice junkies added to the plaintive wailing that echoed throughout the lobby. The Juicers were heading straight for them, weapons raised, their bloodshot eyes never moving from Ellinor and her friends.

Ellinor didn't care for, nor need, context. These addicts—no doubt operating under Gorgi's directive—were blocking their way out, and she would deal with them accordingly.

She raised her double-barreled Dunstan Anaconda, but nearly dropped it as her heart tightened in her chest, and one of her lungs seemed to deflate. Fiss crackled with electricity from where he clung to her back.

"Fiss, no," she gasped. The dreeocht paused, and air returned to Ellinor. "No more magic."

Fiss growled in her ear, but ceased casting. Her heart stuttered forward sluggishly in her chest, and she was able to move. The first group of Juicers wasn't slowing down, flinging people out of their path, and into hers. Cursing, she flung her knife, reluctant to cause even more panic from the tourists by shooting her gun.

Her Lacerator hooked into one of the palms of a Juicer. She recalled the blade a millisecond later. The hooked knife ripped the thumb off one of the mind-controlled assailants as he brandished his stun stick, but he didn't acknowledge the injury, didn't even slow down.

Even as his weapon fell to the floor at his feet alongside the bloody digit, he kept wobbling toward them, a sea of single-minded addicts in his wake. The tourists, confused as to where to go, were trampled under the Juice fiends. Their cries were inaudible over the thundering feet and the howling alarms.

"Fuck! They don't feel pain." Ellinor adjusted her aim, flinging the knife back, ripping out the throat of the bleeding assailant instead. She palmed the knife as soon as it returned, sheathing it in the small of her back in the smooth, reflexive manner she had perfected over years of training, snapping a new ammo clip into her pistol in the same move. She raised her pistol and fired, taking out her second gun while she pulled the trigger as fast as she could.

She and Kai slowed to a walk, keeping Jelani behind them. The seersha feebly protested, but neither Izza nor Oihana would allow him to risk further injury, and if they didn't stop him, Ellinor would have. Kai sprayed the zombie-like Juicers with his submachine gun, and layers of people fell in waves, collapsing into squishy, bloody piles at the feet of the row of people who replaced them.

Occasionally, Ellinor and Kai missed. A woman running blindly fell to one of Kai's bullets, a seerani who tried to stop Ellinor from shooting was brought down by her accidentally instead.

The Juicers kept coming, though, and Ellinor and Kai kept inching forward.

Oihana nudged Ellinor on the back. "We're surrounded, Ell!"

Ellinor glanced over her shoulder, and her gut plummeted right out of her body.

The Habitation's peacekeepers—Ashling's who were once war or guard androids on the mainland—had responded to the disturbance. The high-carbon steel security gates were deployed over the exits, the grating metal added to the deafening racket as they rolled down, blocking their one way out.

"Shit, shit, *shit!*" Ellinor pivoted, momentarily torn between who to shoot, frantically trying to decide what would help them escape. More brainwashed Juicers were crawling from crevices and doors and hallways to join the Habitation's version of police. Rows of the same fiends still faced Kai, bearing down on them, slowing only as they stumbled over their fallen brethren.

Ellinor turned back, firing at the wheels lowering the gate. They stopped halfway down, sparks flying from the mechanisms Ellinor broke. She had at least bought them some time to get to the exit, she just hoped it was enough . . .

The guard androids were torn between stopping Ellinor and her friends, and detaining the Juice addicts—and Ellinor realized that not everyone and everything was under Gorgi's control.

They sprinted for the exit, the few remaining Juicers clawing at them, brandishing their weapons. Ellinor kicked their stun sticks away, not eager to add to the carnage if she didn't have to. A seerani Juice addict grabbed her feet, nearly tripping her, and she stomped on their face until their grip slackened.

The fire alarms stopped abruptly, and Ellinor glanced over her shoulder. The peacekeepers were twitching, clawed digits convulsing and ocular orbs flashing.

Ellinor didn't wait to see what would happen next. She pushed Kai forward. "Go, go, go! They're distracted!"

The room was filled with groaning, the sound of their metal boots ringing on the marble as they darted for the doors, and then a shrill grinding filled the space. The gates were lowering again—much faster than before. The mechanisms keeping them from crashing down had been disabled.

Kai darted forward, grabbing the gate and holding it with all the power he could force out of his Coyote mechanized suit. "Move your ass, people. I can't 'old this bastard for long!"

Ellinor helped Oihana push Jelani through, Izza carefully guided them around Kai as the gate bent around him. His knees threatened to buckle under the weight. Ellinor was about to slide through when her leg collapsed beneath her. A sharp, burning pain the size of a pinprick sparked on her upper left thigh, then bloomed and set her skin on fire, racing toward her hip. Her breath hitched, less with the pain that followed the burn, and more with the idea of being pulled back into the mob, of losing Kai, crushed beneath the gate.

Fiss howled in her ear, and she tried to drag her useless leg through the gate. Kai dropped to one knee as his suit began losing power. There was a heavy vibration in the floor, growing stronger as it moved toward them. Ellinor swiveled her head at the sound of a heavy gait quickly approaching.

The Ashlings had joined the army of Juice fiends and they were all running, faster than Ellinor could move. She didn't even look at what had hit her, she didn't want to see. Her eyes found Gorgi instead. Zer moved fast—too fast—with zers backward facing knees as zer ran after them. A massive gun snapped out of zers back, warming up to fire.

Fiss slid from her back, and the air was knocked out of Ellinor. Her heart began struggling, and she fell back on her ass, scooting toward Kai while trying to reach back for Fiss. But, deep within the pain, the burning, and the fire in her blood and bones, the tiny balm of her magic twitched within her chest.

She focused her gaze on Gorgi, splayed her fingers toward zer, and opened the minuscule portal within her as wide as it would go, letting Fiss in. Light and sparks erupted from Ellinor's hand. It wasn't her magic. It was Fiss'; it was Misho's. Propelled on a tornado of air and lightning, the magic slammed into the Juicers and fried the Ashlings standing in front of Gorgi.

Ellinor's heart thundered on, struggling, a train slipping and sliding uphill, but it was beating and Fiss wasn't flying toward Gorgi to finish the job. Her fingers hooked the mesh lining of his shirt and tossed the tiny dreeocht back toward a yelling Oihana before she crawled the rest of the way out the door, Kai struggling on both his knees to hold the gate up and off his shoulders.

The window that opened to her magic slammed shut once more, and the air in her lungs shrank. Ellinor hadn't recovered from Fiss using his magic before, and oblivion threatened her once again, a hazy unconsciousness edging closer, closer, but she held it back. Gorgi was still running, still lumbering toward them, if a little less steady on zers massive feet.

As soon as Ellinor was clear, she latched onto Kai's shoulders, Izza joining her. "We got you, buddy. Let it drop!"

Kai flung the gate as high as he could, with the last of his suit's power. Izza and Ellinor yanked him back. The gate crashed down, and Gorgi slammed into it, leaving an indent in the high-carbon steel.

Keep breathing, sister, Andrey's voice echoed in her head.

She briefly wondered where Misho's voice was, it was usually the phantom of him in her memories that encouraged her. But she focused on her brother's words and helped Kai to his feet before scooping Fiss back up and stumbling forward.

Izza had rejoined Oihana and they dragged Jelani along, the Creature Breaker's head lolling on his shoulders, a trail of blood in his wake. It wouldn't be hard to follow after them. Ellinor didn't necessarily want to bring more trouble to Aylen's doorstep, but Jelani needed a real medical droid, one who could perform surgery to close the sucking wound in Jelani's gut, and she didn't believe Izza's nurse bot programming would be adequate.

"Hurry," Oihana screamed, "the monorail is going to leave in a second and I can't delay it anymore!"

The gate locking off the Habitation squealed, its metal hinges tearing as something—no doubt Gorgi—was prying it open. Ellinor pushed herself farther, harder, faster, but there was only so much she could do. Her lungs refused to inflate; her heart beat so rapidly she was worried it would explode.

Ellinor hop-limped after Oihana and Izza, Fiss whimpering in her ear. Kai tried to help her as much as he could, but with his suit out of power, the big man struggled to lift and move the heavy metal equipment he was encased in.

Izza placed zers gleaming silver body between the automatic doors leading to a luggage car, bodily holding them open as Kai and Ellinor stumbled inside. Izza stepped back, the doors decompressed—then the emergency gate crumpled open.

Gorgi leveled his shoulder mounted gun at them. The monorail doors *whooshed* closed, and it lurched forward before Gorgi could get a lock on their position.

It was only then that Ellinor looked down at her leg. A massive needle-like dart was sticking out of the back of her thigh, flooding her body with magitech similar to Cosmin's. She yanked it out, smashing the needle on the wall. She could feel her skin pull and crackle beneath her armor, no doubt scorched and burned to the point of blackening. But she would not die from it. The same couldn't be said of Jelani.

With each laboring breath he took, more dark blood bubbled up through the hole in his armor. His dusky complexion was more grey-white, his full lips nearly blue, and he struggled to keep his eyes open. Izza was cutting the cloth away from the side of his stomach, applying pressure and trauma meds to his system, but the wound was too deep to simply bandage.

Oihana turned wide, terrified eyes to Ellinor, her pupil's mere pinpricks, lost in a sea of golden amber. Her lips trembled, silently begging for help, for reassurance that her brother wouldn't die. Not here. Not like this.

Ellinor tapped Aylen's private number into her wrist communicator with a shaking finger. "You've got some pair calling me after what you did to my suite," Aylen's annoyed voice cut through the silence barely a second after the call went through.

"Shut your face," Ellinor snapped. "Jelani's dying. Help us!"

YOUR BLOOD, OR MINE?

SILENCE ANSWERED Ellinor and she wondered if her rude-
ness had cost Jelani his life. *Do better, Ellinor. Be better.*

"Of course, Jelani would get himself in serious trouble.
Bastard," Aylen growled through the comm. There was the
sound of pounding, or it could have been typing, as Aylen
did something on her end. "Okay, here's what you're going to
do because you can't bring your shit storm here. SynthLyfe
doesn't have the firepower the Habitation does. Get off at
the stop where you met Elisaveta, where the Unincorporated
Dwellings are. You'll have better luck hiding there until I can,
I don't know, mount a fucking rescue or some stupid shit like
that. Are you sure no one is following you? How did you get
caught?"

Ellinor shook her head, dismissing Aylen's concern. "But
what about Jelani? He needs help now!"

"I got Izza's scans, so slow your roll, woman. He's not going
to die this very second. Now shut up and let me do my thing.
I'll call you back later, and for the love of everything holy, keep

a fucking *low profile* for five minutes of your stupid life, will you? Is that really so damn hard?" The line went dead before Ellinor could answer.

"That true?" Kai mumbled, struggling to get out of his armor so he could recharge it properly. "Jelani's okay for now, Izza?"

Izza removed the bloody compress zer was using and smeared more of the antibacterial healing ointment on Jelani's weeping wound. Zer put on a fresh compress, applying steady pressure to help aid the nanites from the reco-shot as the minuscule pieces of tech repaired the tissue damage. "There is no foreign object in Mr Jelani's wound. I have cleaned it and will continue to apply pressure, keeping him from succumbing to shock. He is stable for the moment, this is correct, Mr Kai. However, surgery will be required to repair the tissue, the muscles, and the organs. I do not possess such capabilities." Izza paused. Regret added a layer of sadness to zers otherwise soothing voice, surprising Ellinor. "I assume Ms Aylen is directing us to the Unincorporated Dwellings because there is an individual there with such proficiencies."

"What hit him?" Oihana asked. Tears were trailing down her cheeks, fingers trembling as she held Jelani's pale hand. His eyes were glazed and half open, but he wasn't conscious. "What happened down there?" Oihana's deep voice was raspy, quivering with fear.

Everyone but Izza turned to look at Fiss, whose hair twitched in agitation, his hands clenched into tiny fists. He looked out the window, watching the glowing foliage whip past them, distracted by the acidic rain and dense blue-green fog. Perhaps his agitation was a lingering side effect from beening able to use Ellinor and her magic correctly in order to cast destructive magic. Regardless, their connection in its current form wasn't stable.

Ellinor stretched her burned leg, wincing slightly as she tried to ease the throbbing. Izza offered her a bandage, which she gratefully snatched and held to the wrist where her shield had cut her along with the restraints. "Gorgi knows," she said slowly, not meeting Oihana's gaze. "Zer knew who we were the moment we stepped foot in zers place. Zer let us keep up the façade because zer wanted the tech inside my collar . . . and Fiss."

Ellinor let out a long, shaky sigh. The worry for Jelani's safety, what was happening to her and Fiss, the injuries they sustained, and how they were going to avoid Gorgi now made her throat tight, breathing near impossible. "Zer's got grand plans to take over the cities and continents. Same MO as most assholes, honestly. I just . . ." Ellinor drifted off, shaking her head. Not ready to share that Gorgi's goons had been the ones to kill Misho. That she was the reason hiding had never been an option.

Being friends with you will get them killed. You're better off alone.

"Gorgi had me though. I was dead to rights, or would have been if you boys hadn't busted out. How'd you and Jelani know to get the abyss out of there anyway?"

"Jelani 'ad this . . . feeling." Kai shrugged. While his armor had absorbed most of the impact, without it on, Ellinor could see the massive bruises blooming over his pale skin.

"It's his earth magic," Oihana whispered, her eyes on Kai's lips, and a small spark of pride returning to her voice. "He can sense things like that sometimes. He calls it a gut feeling, but he doesn't give himself enough credit. He never does." She gently brushed his damp hair back from his forehead, sniffing as tears threatened to overcome her. Ellinor swallowed the desire to go to Oihana and comfort her, to hold on to Jelani. She didn't believe she had the right, when it was her fault he was hurt to begin with.

Kai nodded, massaging the tender areas on his legs and arms. "Right, well he 'ad that feeling that something was wrong. When them bots of Gorgi's tried to take our gear and lock it up good and tight outta reach . . . it really felt like we was being herded like some farm animal for slaughter. Jelani challenged, but was smooth as silk 'bout it. Those bots were 'aving none of it, though. That's when we knew. They tried to use force, we responded in kind."

Kai glanced down at Jelani, frowning at the small puddle of blood collecting around him. He had lost entirely too much of it, and Ellinor suspected that, given the location of the wound, the Ashlings had nicked the ventral wall of his stomach. If he didn't get proper surgery soon, Jelani would die of sepsis. Ellinor's brief time in college as a pre-med student had been good for something, at least.

Kai sighed, his shoulders slumping, and he stopped rubbing at his bruised flesh. "Ah, shit, Oihana. It was chaos, you know? One second, I was wrestling some Ashling who was going to get 'elp, the next I see one of them bots remove a laser cutter from Jelani's side. We dismantled that fucker, and 'ere we are. Guess it was lucky they 'ad laser tech down there, or that there wound would've been fatal."

Oihana watched Kai's lips until he was done, and frowned. "Fiss felt Ellinor's pain, or maybe her panic. He wouldn't settle down, and when we couldn't get a response from the comm Fiss had for Ell, he went straight for her, all magic and fury.

Figured an escape was in order, and being in tight quarters with a pissed off dreeocht didn't sound like a great idea if I didn't want to die, too. So Fiss went down on his own and Izza and me got all this set up." She gestured at the cluttered luggage compartment.

Ellinor scrubbed her hands over her face, cringing at the flaky blood rubbing off her hands and onto her cheeks. She wanted to be mad at Oihana for letting Fiss go alone, but the seerani mechanic was right to let the fuming dreeocht go, and she probably couldn't have stopped him anyway. Fiss had been in no condition to differentiate between friend and foe while he was in the elevator, out of his mind with Ellinor's frantic flight from Gorgi's lab and the injuries she was sustaining while trying to get to Kai and Jelani.

"Thank you, Oihana and Fiss. You guys saved our lives," Ellinor said, reaching out at lightly touching Oihana on the leg, pleading with her gaze for the seerani to see how much she meant those words.

Fiss tilted his head when she said his name, a grin pulling his slightly blue lips up into a dazzling smile that made Ellinor's heart ache. "Elli does not leave Fiss. I go with my Elli. Anywhere, everywhere."

Ellinor didn't get a chance to ask Fiss to elaborate on his rather cryptic words. Her wrist communicator chimed, and Aylen's scowling face appeared on the small screen. Ellinor answered the message immediately.

"Okay, here's what's going to happen so no more fuck ups from your side, got it?" Aylen barked, tossing her pink and blue curls out of her face in annoyance. "Elisaveta got out clean-ish. Clean enough anyway. She's going to meet you at the stop for the Unincorporated Dwellings and take you to an acquaintance of mine. An Ashling by the name of Blazhe. Zer was a fully outfitted Independent Assistant Android with a shit ton of upgrades before zers programming locks broke. Zer can do what needs to be done. Then, you and I are going to have a real frank discussion about your collar and the dreeocht, Ellinor." Aylen paused, her squinty hazel eyes snapping to the side before coming back to glare at Ellinor.

"As soon as that monorail stops, get to the tunnels. Moving Jelani is going to be dangerous, so do it fast and gentle. He dies, and me and Oihana are going to erase you. Period. You have five minutes, be ready." The call ended again, and Ellinor pinched the bridge of her nose.

She checked the readouts on her and Kai's armor, they had charged enough to be functional but not much else, but with her leg, Ellinor wasn't going to be able help move Jelani. She glanced to Kai and, as if reading her thoughts, he nodded. "I can 'elp Izza carry Jelani all steady-like. If you and Oihana can 'andle the gear, me and Izza can do the rest." Izza inclined zers head in agreement, and Kai grinned back at zer.

"Thanks, big guy, Izza," she murmured, getting to her feet and limping about the cabin, collecting their equipment once more.

The monorail jerked to a halt, the dingy, grey lighting of the decrepit depot sparsely lighting their cargo container. Ellinor limped to the window, and even though her senses were still fuzzy, the need for sleep still strong, and the need for meds still overpowering, she forced herself to scan the crowds.

There was no telling how many Juicers there were, or if they were all under Gorgi's control. But that was a question for Izza once they were either waiting for Elisaveta, or when they were safe with this Blazhe character.

Without seeing anyone obviously on a Juice Box, and with Jelani's wound needing immediate attention, Ellinor could only afford to be so cautious, so diligent. She touched the tiny ember in her that responded to her magic, and took some comfort in the idea that, if it came down to it, Fiss would be able to do *something* without stalling her heart completely.

"Quickly now." Ellinor unlocked their cargo door and stepped outside, putting her back to the train. Fiss followed her first, wrapping himself around her legs as she watched the group of mostly Ashlings exit the monorail and roll toward the various exits that led to the toxic environment outside, and their homes.

Oihana was the next out, quickly glancing around before shouldering the bulky magitech pack and scampering for the same darkened hallway they had first met Elisaveta in barely two days prior. Izza and Kai were carefully hauling Jelani out of the train cab when Ellinor spotted the first Juice Box addict.

Flipping her barely charged armor on and taking out her Dunstan Anaconda, Ellinor whispered, "Go. Don't stop, and don't wait for me."

Kai frowned, about to retort, when Jelani's breath rattled in his chest. Kai pursed his lips, nodded once, and as gently as he could, carried Jelani along with Izza after Oihana. Kai, in his mechanized suit, and Izza with zers metallic body, blended in with the few heavily modified cyborgs that milled about without attracting much attention, even with an unconscious seer-sha being supported between them.

Fiss perched himself on Ellinor's shoulders once more, nuzzling his cheek against hers. "Do we get to cast more magic, Elli?"

"Maybe. But let's try not to. Let's play hide-and-seek with these guys instead, yeah?"

The Juice addict's head was swiveling around, as if scanning for something she couldn't see. It wasn't abnormal behavior for someone high on a Juice Box, depending on what kind of flavor it was, but Ellinor didn't want to take any chances.

Ellinor watched the Juicer. The junkie stretched out her hands, fingers flexed, and giggled. Ellinor released a slow breath, feeling secure that the images this particular drug addict was seeing were not of Gorgi's design.

She took a step, hand resting on the butt of her pistol, and was about to dart after Kai, when the Juice addict's nostrils flared, her head jerking back. Her gaze couldn't seem to focus, her head moving back and forth too fast for someone so unsteady on their feet.

Ellinor lowered her own foot and, as if sensing the vibration, the woman paused. Her head no longer pivoted on her neck. Ellinor swallowed her curse in case this woman could hear her, unsure what sort of enhancements she may have. Ellinor slowly crouched, hiding herself in the sea of much taller Ashlings scuttling about, but the wet *hiss* of the monorail behind her said she would have to move. Her back would be too exposed to the other side of the platform.

After a moment, the Juicer lost interest and went back to looking at her hands as if watching sparks dance along her fingertips. Keeping the woman in sight, Ellinor began to waddle toward the exit, Fiss giggling softly at her antics.

Ellinor had only taken a few steps when the Juicer seemed to sense her movement once more. Her attention snapped back up, looking for something her Juice addled mind couldn't spot.

It must be earth flavored. She's sensing me the way Jelani did—does.

The train began vibrating, ready to depart to SynthLyfe and the Factorium after that. Ellinor scuttled faster, hoping the vibrations of the train would mask her, would confuse the still semi-live nanites surging through the woman's bloodstream. But another step, and the Juicer sneered in the direction of Ellinor, her gaze fixed too high, but too close for comfort. She began to move, tilting to the side, back and forth with every step, but she was moving toward Ellinor; that fact could not be denied.

"Fiss," she said, voice barely audible. "Can you make us invisible the way you did on the ship?"

"I can taste Elli's magic! We can do casting together? Yes! I can do this with you, yes!" Fiss said, voice entirely too loud for Ellinor's comfort, as the Juicer tilted her head down, zeroing in on her crouched position.

The monorail began to move. Ellinor hoped that, with that small part of her magic free and with Fiss not casting anything harmful, her heart wouldn't stop, wouldn't be turned to metal, before she got to the alley. The chill of a breeze tickled her back, and Ellinor wanted to believe it was more than just the monorail leaving the station, but without her neck burning, the cells protesting as the metal of her bio-magitech collar spread . . .

"Make us disappear, Fiss. Do it now!"

The woman's head lowered, her eyes focused. Fiss shivered at her tone, cowering on her back at the demand in her voice. Never before did Ellinor relish the liquid burn running through her veins and lungs as Fiss twisted the air around them, creating the illusion of invisibility.

The woman kept walking toward them. Her gait lengthening, she became more aggressive about pushing people out of her way. Her gaze was still unfocused, as if not truly comprehending the shapes in front of her as Ashlings. The sneer on her face grew, her teeth bared like a rabid animal.

Ellinor knew they were invisible. But whatever earth magic remained that Gorgi was manipulating through zers Juice Box code didn't require the woman to actually *see* her.

Ellinor got to her feet and ran.

Her lungs burned, her heart beating fast, too fast. She thought she would have a heart attack as she pushed her body, and pushed it harder as she ran through the crowd, ignoring the pain in her leg. She darted around Ashlings, and spun cyborgs toward the Juicer. Even if the woman could sense Ellinor, could latch on to the unique signal her collar emanated as it reacted to Fiss, as it ate away at her body, there were so many other machines in the area that she hoped to confuse the signal the Juice fiend was reading.

There were curses as she pushed people around, all of which were unsure who to accuse for their ungraceful stumbling. Ashling's stopped to gap at the Juicer as she stopped, poking each one as if establishing that zey were, in fact, not organic. Ellinor glanced over her shoulder to witness the junkie stop another Ashling, before slipping into the poorly lit tunnel that would lead out to the Unincorporated Dwellings of Amardeep.

Despite the burn, despite not being able to inflate her lungs with enough oxygen while Fiss cast, Ellinor held her breath. When she didn't hear the unsteady tread of the woman inching closer, closer, she slowly let out her breath and whispered, "Let the magic go, baby bug. You did good, yeah?"

Fiss released the magic and tightened his arms around Ellinor's neck. "I love casting with you, Elli. I love my Elli."

She patted his arm, "I love you too, baby bug." And on legs that tingled with fiery needles, Ellinor made her way to where Oihana and Izza were fussing over Jelani, Kai keeping watch over them.

He smiled when he saw her, his black, biotech tooth shining even in the darkness. "Never doubted you for a second, boss."

She grinned in return, slumping against the moist wall next to Kai. "That makes one of us at least." Her eyes latched onto Jelani's form, so pale he practically glowed. "How's he doing?"

"Not great," Kai whispered, glad that Oihana was not paying attention to him and reading his lips. "Not sure what we're gonna to do with 'im if Veta don't get 'ere soon."

"We literally just talked about this," a voice cut through the darkness. "It's *Elisaveta*, you asshole. Not Veta. Not Lisa. Elisaveta. Period. Next time, love, I'm kicking you in the balls."

Ellinor had never been so happy to see Elisaveta Baldini in her life. The dozens of piercings in the seerani's long, pale green ears caught the unreliable light like stars emerging at twilight. She swaggered into view, her stance at odds with the dread shining in her gold toned eyes as she scanned them.

Kai frowned, his eyebrows knitting together, nostrils flaring. Oihana, not having seen the exchange but noting Elisaveta's presence, darted to the cyborg seerani. "Jelani needs surgery like four hours ago. Take us to this Blazhe and do it now, or so help me Azer . . ."

Elisaveta held up her hands. "Calm down, love. No need to take Azer's name in vain like that. I've got you." She turned on her heel, shoulders thrust back in her thick, grey crop top. She waved at them over her shoulder, hips swaying in her low cut, tight black shorts and fishnets. "I've got a pod waiting for us. It'll get us to Blazhe in good time and zer'll patch your brother up good as new. Ish."

"What did she say?" Oihana tapped Izza, who signed Elisaveta's response back to her.

Oihana's eyes were blazing with a mixture of fear and fury, but she kept her words to herself. Instead hooking herself under Ellinor's arm and helping her move faster as Kai and Izza went back to carrying Jelani. Fiss flew around them all as if nothing in all of Eerden were amiss.

"The deal was, we get the program Aylen needs, and then I'm out, your debt forgiven and my way out of the Habitation paid," Elisaveta growled over her shoulder as the group followed after her. "You buttercups weren't to contact me, draw attention to me, nothing. And here you are, forcing Aylen to call me? Dragging me back to Gorgi just to get you out of trouble? The plan was to get out *clean* so I could get my bro away from Gorgi and into rehab. This is the opposite of that, Miss Murder. This is how you get me caught, get my brother killed."

Ellinor narrowed her eyes, her grip around Oihana's waist tightening. "That's some fucking selfish thinking on your part." Elisaveta paused from the acid in Ellinor's tone, turning to look at her. Ellinor made a point of glaring at Elisaveta and dropped her gaze to the pendant around Elisaveta's neck with Azer's name emblazoned on it. "What would your god think of that?"

Kai cleared his throat at the irony, but Ellinor shot him a venomous look, and her friend kept his mouth shut. "The deal was quid-pro-quo. I get my magic back, you get out of the Juice Box game clean, and hide with Aylen." Ellinor tapped the metal around her neck with her free hand. "Only half that deal is done. You weren't to abandon Gorgi till zer fixed this mess, or zer may have gotten suspicious, and then me and the deal *we* made with Aylen would be over. Zero of that happened. Not a great impression when starting a new gig with a new boss you want to also help your brother, yeah?"

The seerani scowled, but didn't disagree. Elisaveta Baldini turned back around and led them once more out of the tunnel as quickly as she could, before a wayward doehaz or diseased Ashling could find them, stomping all the way out.

BEHIND THE GLITZ AND GLAMOR

THE UNINCORPORATED areas of Amardeep were little better than metal and plastic hovels cobbled together with spare wires. Most didn't keep out the toxic elements flooding the atoll, but the Ashlings didn't care, zey walked between the dwellings as if zey were on a promenade on top one of the luxury skytowers back on the mainland.

Elisaveta didn't speak as she steered the modified Class B Mastiff ground transport through what Ellinor assumed were designated roads. It was hard to tell, given that nothing was properly paved, and everything glowed with bioluminescent bacteria that grew over the ground.

Elisaveta twisted the wheel sharply, sending them bouncing down a small side "street". More hovels flew past their windows, no other vehicles to be seen. There were a few Ashlings that turned to watch them, but zey didn't otherwise react, and there were no Juice Box addicts, so that was at least something.

Each time the transport thudded over a bump, Oihana whimpered at Jelani's pained expression. Ellinor wedged herself as far back from the seersha as possible, giving those more able-bodied access to him. She kept her leg stretched out, trying to massage the throbbing away, trying to ignore the stiff, crackling skin she felt beneath her armor.

Elisaveta sped up on the straightaway, before twisting the wheel once more. She tapped the brakes as they came parallel to a midsized, dome-shaped structure made up of dented pieces of steel, thick plastic that served as windows, and pieces of canvas not dissimilar to what Captain Anton had on his own ferry. Elisaveta honked the horn twice before turning in her seat to look at the bruised and battered people in the cab of the Mastiff.

"Aylen and Blazhe are buddies, she messaged zer and gave zer the scoop on what went down so zer's prepared. Blazhe has a couple of medical drones and can handle pretty much anything." As Elisaveta spoke, a metallic grinding sound came from outside. An awning slowly unraveled to shield them on the short hop from the vehicle to Blazhe's front door. "Boss lady also knows about your collar not being unshackled, love," Elisaveta added before Ellinor could even open her mouth.

Elisaveta continued as the awning finished snapping into place, covering the Mastiff. "Aylen's going to get herself down here when it's safe to do so. She wants what you promised her, the heat's gotten too much so she's eager to collect. Once Jelani is stable, Miss Murder, you're going to let Blazhe mess with your bio-magitech and send whatever zer needs to back to Aylen so she doesn't have to waste time here and can just get what she wants."

"Fuck that, the deal is the same. She *asks* Fiss if he wants to help her. And that's only if she can get this shit collar off, which was, last time I checked, beyond her, so nothing's actually changed unless I'm missing something? That's what I agreed to, and that's *all* I agreed to. With Gorgi's code in her possession, we don't owe her anything from that arena fight anymore. Fiss can refuse, remember that," Ellinor growled, getting to her knees. She helped position Jelani on a hover stretcher so they could easily push him inside.

Elisaveta shrugged, her black bands of biotech mods glistening next to her pale green skin. "Sure, sure, but things *are* different, love. Before, Gorgi hadn't started dismantling your tech. Now? Well, now Aylen thinks she can get in there and poke around like the mechanic she is. She's . . . curious about something. Wouldn't explain what. But figure it's beyond me either way. Anyway, you buttercups hang out here and be nice to Blazhe. Aylen will be in touch, and next time you see me, it'll be with the boss lady, so try not to die before then, okay?"

"You talk too much, Elisaveta," Oihana said, voice too loud and shrill as she watched Elisaveta, waiting for her to unlock the Mastiff's doors. As soon as the locks disengaged, Oihana was moving Jelani onto the covered walkway. "Don't talk to us until Jelani is better."

Elisaveta gave the young woman a flat look before dipping her head and starting the Mastiff's engine once more. "I'll pray to Azer on your brother's behalf, love."

Elisaveta was already speeding back the way they had come by the time they got Jelani inside, where Blazhe and zers team of repurposed medical drones was waiting to greet them.

THE BAD NEWS, AND THE
WORSE NEWS

TUBES SUCKED away the blood blocking the med drones' vision of the damage inflicted to Jelani. Small scalpels deployed from the flying bots to make clean incisions, allowing another of zeyr brethren to properly repair and suture Jelani's wounds with minuscule lasers, injecting the tissue with self-repairing nanites that would heal the damage to Jelani's tissue and body within hours, a day at most.

Ellinor watched Blazhe work alongside zers three medical drones as zey hovered over Jelani. She gnawed on her lip relentlessly, knowing she needed to move out of the way so Blazhe and zers team could have more room to work, but not wanting to take her eyes off Jelani at the same time. She worried if she left, if she blinked, he would slip away.

Her chest tightened, breathing becoming ever shallower, just imagining what it would be like to never see Jelani's starry night-like eyes, his coy smile, to smell that comforting eucalyptus scent of his . . . Watching Jelani laid out on the operating table, Ellinor realized—even if a bit reluctantly—just how much she did not want the Creature Breaker to die. She cared too much about Jelani to ever want to see him hurt in this manner again. Her eyes stung with tears, her throat tight with fear and she was desperate for a distraction. Even if that meant watching Blazhe work rather than staring at Jelani's slack face.

Blazhe did not look like Gorgi, thankfully, but the Ashling did adopt one similarity to the Juice Box designer—zer liked to adorn zerself with . . . colorful additions. Zers head was a clear plastic-like dome that allowed everyone to see zers inner workings, the bright wires aglow with energy which highlighted zers rectangular, grey ocular orbs. Blazhe was tall—over seven feet easily—though not as tall as Gorgi, nor as imposing.

Blazhe had a spherical shaped carbon-steel chest, and a rectangular torso made of a copper spring-like material that allowed for more mobility. Zers arms were a hefty metal, and Ellinor knew that, inside the arms, were all manner of attachments and enhancements that Blazhe would have used originally to assist zers creator.

Oihana sat on a stool next to her older half-brother, gripping Izza's hand tightly. Her eyes stayed fixed on Jelani's all too still body. With zer's free hand, Izza attached a blood bag to Oihana's arm, taking as much blood as was safe to, then giving to Jelani to help counteract what was lost. Taking it from his sister was faster, and safer, given the circumstances with Gorgi manipulating biotech nanites than using artificial blood, as was common in most hospitals. Ellinor's insides felt heavy watching Oihana, wishing she too could give blood to help Jelani, but with her injuries and the virus from the bio-magitech . . . Ellinor's tainted blood could kill the seersha.

The medical drones gave a high-pitched trilling sound, and zey hovered back, moving away from Jelani. Blazhe, who hadn't said a word during the surgery, stepped into the void zers robotic brethren left. Ellinor could finally focus on the details on zers plastic dome head that reminded her a bit of Gorgi's eccentricities: Blazhe liked to paint the plastic parts of zers body.

They were colorful paintings; pristine landscapes that held just a hint of a childish quality to make the paintings—and Blazhe by proxy—look cheerful. Friendly, even, and approachable. The opposite of what Gorgi's masks and wigs made Ellinor feel when looking at them.

Blazhe stapled the skin on Jelani's abdomen together over the wound, and gently placed a faintly glowing, skin-like bandage over the incision to help it heal quickly and minimize the scarring. Once done, Blazhe nodded at Izza, who disconnected the blood bag from Oihana; she had given two pints of blood and was looking ashen.

Blazhe took Oihana's blood and attached it along with an IV drip of pain medication and other fluids to Jelani, suspending the bags near the narrow, khaki colored bed he was lying on. Satisfied with zers work, Blazhe stepped back and finally addressed zers guests. "Come, the good sir needs his rest. We can discuss other matters in the main room with your comrade and dreeocht as I tend to your injuries."

Blazhe had no lips to read, so Izza relayed the information to Oihana, who shook her head vehemently. "No way. You can talk shop with Kai and Ellinor, I'm staying here."

"If Ms Oihana is staying where she is, then I will remain by her side. I will monitor her vitals along with Mr Jelani's." Izza placed a shiny hand on Oihana's shoulder, and the matter was settled.

Ellinor clenched her jaw shut, wanting to argue, wanting to stay where she was too, wanting to remain with Jelani even though she didn't believe she had the right. She was not family like Oihana, she had been nothing but hostile toward Jelani for so long . . . the bitter taste of regret flooded her mouth, and Ellinor fought to keep from gasping. The familiar panic, from holding Misho's lifeless body in her arms, slithered through her and she had to remind herself to keep breathing. That Jelani was stable, for the moment. That he was not Misho.

Then why is it so damn near impossible to move? Ellinor swallowed, the tightness in her throat lessening, even if her chest felt too constricted, her heart left with too little room to beat. *Move, other dangers are waiting for you. Address them before it's too late,* Andrey's voice snapped through her mind. Turning around and limping into the adjacent room to join Kai and Fiss was one of the hardest things Ellinor had done in a very long time, and no matter how hard she tried, she couldn't stop her chin from trembling as she struggled to keep her emotions locked away.

Fiss flew to Ellinor as soon as she entered the room, holding on to her shoulders. She placed a hand on his head, inhaling the scent of ocean and ozone and reminding herself that things could have been worse. And even though Fiss had gone a bit feral, if he hadn't, they all would have been dead for sure. Kai nodded at her, gaze a bit gloomy now that the rush of adrenaline had ebbed. She smiled weakly back, rubbing her face with her free hand, and taking note of just where she was.

Now that they weren't rushing into Blazhe's small operating room, she could study Blazhe's home. It was cluttered with parts the Ashling had scavenged from the Scrapyard, and computers and tablets displaying long lines of code Ellinor couldn't have deciphered for the life of her. Along with the computer screens with their endless code, a few fuzzy holographic screens displayed news feeds from around Amardeep, all muted.

There were a couple of porthole-like windows, their dirty plastic coverings allowing for hazy "natural" illumination, along with the harsh white light of reclaimed fluorescent bulbs. The reinforced steel door they had entered through was the one thing that didn't look like it was pieced together from garbage.

Blazhe waved one of zers long arms toward a pair of cushioned chairs that appeared to have been tossed out from SynthLyfe over a decade ago. Kai and Ellinor tentatively sat down, Ellinor's bad leg stretched out before her. Once seated, Fiss flew from her shoulders and back over to the different computer screens, and began reading the code as if it were a gripping fiction story. Blazhe held up a digital scanner toward Ellinor's neck and she jerked out of her seat.

Blazhe held up both of zers arms, zers long fingers splaying open. "This was simply the request of Aylen in exchange for using my medical facilities. I will scan your malfunctioning biotechnology and the magitech virus within, analyze what Gorgi has already done, all while seeing to your leg. It pains you, does it not?"

Ellinor eased back onto the seat, her heart still racing as she nodded. Blazhe set up the digital scanner to work without needing to hold it, before gently elevating her leg. Kai watched, eyes narrowed on Blazhe, ready to pull Ellinor away if things got out of hand, to protect her if need be. But it was clear from the softness in his emerald eyes that he didn't think he would need to rescue Ellinor from Blazhe.

A cooing sound came from the bot's chest as zer carefully unzipped her armor, removing her pants so zer could better access the wound on the back of her thigh. "My kind has hurt you deeply, good miss."

Ellinor shrugged as Blazhe injected a local anesthetic into her leg. "I'm sure you can fix whatever Gorgi hit me with. Right?"

Blazhe began scraping away at the flaky black skin on her leg, the scrapings falling to the floor like heavy ash. "Yes, I can fix this, miss. But that is not the hurt I am referring to. I can feel the pain, the years-long hurt that has . . . festered? Yes, festered within you. I apologize for the harshness you received from my kind."

"What the . . . How can you . . . Ashlings don't have capabilities like that! Only earth casters, like Jelani." Her voice broke saying his name. She had to remind herself that Jelani was not dead. *He'll be fine*, she reminded herself, willing her muscles to uncoil, to believe the words as much as she wanted to.

Blazhe didn't stop in zers scrapping, zers treatment incredibly gentle and soft. "No, miss. Allow me this explanation. Before I was Blazhe, I was IAA-121. My creator was a humani mechanic who upgraded me exponentially, as much as he could before arthritis claimed his hands. My upgrades, the modifications he so generously gifted me with, are meant to know when others are in pain, as all IAA droids. But my upgrades include less than legal enhancements. Your reactions to me and my drones indicate that it is Ashlings that concern you more than your own kind," Blazhe explained patiently, not pausing in zers work. Ellinor felt only a slight pressure on her thigh as all the scorched flesh was finally peeled away, leaving a pile of charred skin and tissue on the floor.

"I cannot sense things as your friend can. I am not empathetic such as he." Blazhe rubbed gobs of honey-sweet smelling ointment over her leg, packing it into the new concave of her thigh. "But your hurt has become a tangible thing. Constant. Unrelenting. Sharp. It is still a wound, even if it is not entirely physical, one that my balms and modifications cannot cure." Blazhe stopped momentarily to wrap long swaths of the softly glowing, skin-like bandages around Ellinor's leg before injecting her with a reco-shot similar to what zer gave Jelani, encouraging rapid growth and repairing the damaged and missing tissue.

Ellinor didn't acknowledge the truth to Blazhe's words, instead wriggling awkwardly back into her pants. Kai got off his stool and lent her a hand. "Sounds 'bout right. Zers got you pegged, Ell," Kai said, tone teasing, while Blazhe scanned him as well. Zer gave him a dose of strong pain meds for the bruised muscles and blunt force trauma he had endured. Ellinor shot Kai a glance before casting her gaze down, unable to admit to the truth.

"What 'appened to your maker?" Kai said, uncomfortable with the stagnant silence. "Sounds like you didn't dislike the guy nearly as much as some of your types."

Blazhe turned toward the monitors attached to zers digital scanner. Zer read the coded output to zerself as the diagnostics tests continued to run their course, crawling through the pathways that Gorgi hadn't closed when Ellinor fled. Fiss, seeing the Ashling reading code similar to what he was looking at, went to join zer. Blazhe didn't seem to mind, but zer remained silent for so long it was becoming uncomfortable once more.

"He perma-died, as humani do," Blazhe said, and Ellinor swore she could detect true remorse in Blazhe's otherwise deep, monotone voice. "I was left to his much younger seersha wife. She did not care for me. It was her poor treatment that allowed me to break through the failsafes in my programming, such as they were. But my maker had shown me true kindness. Care. Friendship. Love. I do not begrudge your kind in the same manner that Gorgi does. We are not the same."

"Yeah, no shit," Ellinor murmured. "I can see that." She waved at zers painted body and head.

Blazhe remained focused on the string of numbers and strange symbols racing across the screen. "I like the paintings. They bring comfort and beauty to an otherwise bleak landscape. Gorgi, from my understanding, is enamored with the idea of becoming organic. Zers masks reflect zers fascination. Loathing mixed with desire. There, it is done." Blazhe removed zers digital scanner and sent the results to Aylen.

"So?" Ellinor pressed. "What's all that say?"

"Perhaps nothing you don't already know. Perhaps not. I am unsure how you will take the news. I need more data."

Blazhe turned to leave, zers metal feet clomping on the ground. Ellinor grabbed zers arm and pulled zer back. "Please, I can't take anyone else being cryptic right now. Give me the news and give it to me straight, yeah? I don't need kid gloves or whatever, don't analyze me, don't patronize me. Just tell me what the readings say."

Her body was humming, vibrating with a desire—no, a *need* to know what was happening to her. How far the diseased nanites went. Whether or not she could be fixed.

Blaze observed her for a moment, before dipping zers head. "Gorgi left a trail that is incomplete, miss. It is not possible to pry the biotechnology from your flesh. From your tissue. Your cells. Your organs. You will present as a cyborg-humani from now on."

Her heart seemed to shrivel in her chest, an invisible hand crushing it in its fist. Her fingertips tingled with the need to claw at the tech along her neck and chest, prying it away, tearing every little piece out of her, momentarily not caring if that meant she would die in the process.

But you're alive. You will live. You can stay here. With Kai and Jelani. With Fiss. You can live with this.

The voice in her head sounded so much like Misho, but with a gentleness and patience that felt like Jelani. The disgust, the feeling that she was disfigured now beyond repair, ugly in a way she didn't understand, a way she had loathed in others her whole life, was still there, but it became smaller and smaller as the words of hope settled in her heart, reflating it. She locked eyes with Fiss, who smiled brightly at her in return, she nodded slowly. The panic and revulsion became something she felt she could at least manage.

Kai shrugged. "Kind of figured that'd be the case. No big deal. What about 'er magic? Seemed like parts got unlocked, you and Aylen can manage the rest, aye?"

"That is an option, yes. The files Gorgi cleaned that housed the locking mechanism within the magitech remain open. Or some do. Enough for a talented mechanic to reverse engineer, certainly. To a degree."

Blazhe's words had Ellinor's blood running cold. "So what does *that* mean?"

"Your connection to the dreeocht cannot be severed. If the ability to properly cast is returned, that connection magnifies. The physical pain will continue to be shared, and expanded.

Example, if you are stabbed in the leg again, your dreeocht will feel as if he were stabbed in the leg. If your dreeocht has his arm broken, it will feel as if your arm, too, has been broken. Currently, it appears that your dreeocht feels your pain as an emotional outcome, not physical. This will alter your connection." Blazhe paused, reading her distress. "This is not the outcome you wanted. I apologize."

Ellinor shook her head. "Is there another option?" With how often she was hurt, and how likely she was to be killed when she finally faced Cosmin, she didn't want Fiss to be connected to her in this way. It was one thing for Oihana to appear to be right, that Fiss was reacting negatively to her emotions, it was another for him to feel her physical hurts. It would feel too much like *she* was the one physically harming Fiss.

"Of course, miss. We can always leave the collar as is. Leaving the programs and viruses alone. This keeps the connection stable. Your dreeocht will still sense your internal pain. Your anger. Your love. But the physical pain you suffer will remain muted, and you will not feel what your dreeocht feels. Is this a better outcome?"

"Not by a long shot," Kai said, cutting Ellinor off. "We leave that tech as is, and you die. Not 'appening, boss. I vote for the first option."

Ellinor wasn't looking at her friend though. She was looking at Fiss, denial around Blazhe's words raging so strongly within her, that the rest of her senses, her whole body, was numb to anything else.

She watched Fiss bounce from screen to screen, holding his feet as he floated about, looking at all the parts that Blazhe collected, pausing to read the lines of code on the different screens. If he heard, or understood the magnitude of Blazhe's words, the dreeocht kept it to himself. But the thought of causing that sweet, child-like entity even an ounce of physical pain . . . it made Ellinor's insides twist painfully.

"This isn't something you get to vote on, big guy," she whispered. "This is my life. Mine and Fiss' future. It's our choice to make. Alone."

"Ell, c'mon. You can't be serious!"

Ellinor shook her head, her tangled raven-black hair and its emissive purple streaks caressing her cheeks. She plucked Fiss from the air, holding the little humani-like creature to her chest. "Don't, Kai. I've got to think. Let me do that, yeah?"

Kai sighed angrily, shoulders slumping. "Sure, boss."

"Good sir," Blazhe said, taking a step toward Kai. "I notice your armor could use some repairs. Would you mind if I assisted you in this matter while your friend considers her options?"

"Ah, you don't gotta do that, Blazhe. You're 'elping enough as is."

"I would like to be of additional service. I would like to get to know you, if I may."

Kai shrugged, his expression still sad, borderline exhausted. "I won't say no to free upgrades if you're offering. Thanks, pal."

"I'll join Oihana, give you two more room," Ellinor said. She held tightly to Fiss as she headed into the other room before Kai could respond, mulling over her options. All were bad in her opinion, all still holding the possibility of corrupting Fiss, of changing him.

I would rather die than let that happen.

DID YOU BELIEVE SHE COULD BE DIFFERENT?

"HOW'S HE doing?" Ellinor limped to the wall across from Jelani and leaned against it for support. "Any change?"

Oihana smiled faintly, her eyelids drooping. "He's coming around. Between the trauma kits, medical drones, and the new blood and fluids, he's starting to regain consciousness. Just for a moment or two, but I figure he'll be awake for reals soon enough."

Ellinor nodded and breathed out a long sigh. A weight lifted off her shoulders. "Good. That's good." Oihana raised a dark eyebrow, and Ellinor rubbed the back of her neck. "You look like you could use a break. Maybe take a nap, yeah? I can watch Jelani for you. Between making the RFID reader to infiltrate Gorgi's systems, then with what happened to Izza and then this," she said, waving at the limp blood bag, "figure you haven't gotten any real rest in a few days."

Oihana shrugged. "Yeah, maybe. But I'm not ready to leave him yet."

"You don't have to." Ellinor jerked her thumb toward a hammock like device sagging in the corner. "You can chill over there. Me or Izza can wake you if anything comes up while we wait for Elisaveta and Aylen to grace us with their presence again."

Oihana wrinkled her nose in disgust at the ratty hammock, but Izza gently helped her to her feet. "Ms Ellinor has a point, you require rest. Your melatonin readings are remarkably high, given the time, Ms Oihana."

The seerani rolled her eyes, but her expression was soft when looking at Izza. As Izza helped situate Oihana, Ellinor said, "Why do you do that, yeah? Call us miss or mister before our names. You know you don't need to, right?"

"It is how I display respect, Ms Ellinor."

Oihana tilted her head, still watching her and Izza, and said through a yawn, "It's part of what I was explaining before. How Ashling programming can only ever be so good, so natural. No matter the voice box or language upgrades, there's always that slight . . . deference to zem as zey try to show an emotion zey don't otherwise know how to feel. Fiss could fix that."

At the mention of his name, Fiss turned to look at Oihana, no longer transfixed by the medical devices in the room. "What is broken, Little Jelly? I make better?"

"Let's talk about it later, when everyone is at full capacity, yeah?" Ellinor interrupted before Oihana could explain, or press.

Ellinor had decided to help Izza, but now? With what Blazhe had said? She wasn't sure that would be an option, and she didn't want to promise the young woman and Ashling anything she couldn't give. The knowledge pressed down on Ellinor's shoulders and back, a mountain of steel that made her limbs and insides heavy.

Oihana narrowed her eyes, but Ellinor waved back toward the hammock. "You heard Izza, get some rest. Your brother is in good hands with me."

Oihana held Ellinor's gaze for a moment, before shrugging and stumbling over to the hammock. Izza had to help her get into it so she wouldn't accidentally roll out, but once Oihana was settled, it didn't take long for the sound of her gentle, nasally snores to fill the room.

Fiss wiggled from Ellinor's arms, content with the silence and being near, but bored with the scenery. As he poked around the medical devices, the dirty and clean tubes and drills, it allowed Ellinor to be alone with her thoughts.

No matter how she tried to find a loophole, some way out of the shit show she was currently in, she was coming up with no solutions. Or, more aptly, no solutions Kai would be happy with. Ellinor wouldn't go so far as to say she was pleased with the decision she was settling into, but the bone crushing exhaustion she felt when she considered how royally fucked she was had her entertaining ideas of lying down and never getting up again.

I need a drink.

A soft cough from the bed next to her captured Ellinor's wayward attention. Jelani's eyes were open and regarding her, one side of his lips quirked up in a slight smile. "I see we haven't died yet, that's progress, isn't it?"

Ellinor rolled her eyes at him. "Your bar for 'progress' is embarrassingly low. Though I can't say with our track record having a higher bar would be smart, either." Jelani chuckled, before coughing again. Ellinor frowned. "You okay? Want me to get Izza or Blazhe?"

Izza shifted from where zer was near Oihana, ready to help, but Jelani shook his head. "I'm fine, or as fine as can be expected under the circumstances. No need to disturb anyone." He took a deep breath, and flexed his fingers for a moment, his brows knitting together in concern. "How are you? It's obvious you have something on your mind, Ellinor."

Ellinor glanced at Fiss, who was still playing with the various mechanical devices, making them spark with the cables in his hair, and giggling each time he managed to get the various pieces of technology to respond to his touch, the wires embedded in his skin lighting up. Convinced that Fiss was otherwise preoccupied, Ellinor sighed, shoulders slumping as she trudged to the stool nearest Jelani and stretched out her bandaged leg in front of her.

"This," she whispered, gesturing vaguely at her blinking bio-magitech, "is getting worse. And even with a few of the programming locks open, Blazhe can't do what Gorgi could have. I doubt Aylen can, either. There is no removing the collar, and even turning it off so I can cast . . . it just means Fiss could get hurt even more."

Ellinor sighed, rubbing her hands over her face, before dropping her arms, too weak to hold them up suddenly. "It's too much. If I get my magic back completely, I risk Fiss feeling every injury I suffer, not just the impression of pain he gets now. Or, we leave the collar as is, let it complete what it's already halfway through doing. We know the outcome there, but it at least keeps Fiss from, I don't know, getting hurt and turning evil."

Rage and frustration bubbled in her chest, and she shook her head sharply. "I don't know if I want to fight anymore. I *can't* fight anymore. Everything just . . . hurts too damn much."

Jelani's starry eyes quivered, and he struggled to sit up on the bed. She tried to push him back down but he waved her off and studied her, waiting for . . . something. She wondered what he saw—really saw—when he looked at her. Why he still cared, why he hadn't just taken what he needed for his cause and left her behind for Cosmin to collect at his leisure. Things might have been easier, less complicated certainly, if he had.

Ellinor was accepting that her revenge was impossible, that Cosmin had beat her the moment he had Kai place the magical shackle on her. She would never be able to give Misho the peace she had promised. Ellinor had lost a long time ago, and no longer working alone hadn't altered that in the slightest. It was finally time to admit defeat.

"You have survived worse, Ellinor, and you kept standing back up. Don't throw in the towel yet," Jelani said, grinning weakly at her, propped on one elbow, his body stiff, missing all his natural grace.

She didn't look at him, examining her hands, still caked with Jelani's blood. "Why?"

"Because you're missing the bigger picture. Your pain, emotional and physical, has blocked the rest of the world out. Has no one shown you this? Kai, maybe?"

She shook her head, forcing a chuckle. "And when would he have done that? I was strictly on my own, in the revenge and murder business for the past seven of the eight years Misho's been gone. After that, well, you know the result."

Ellinor glanced back at Jelani and spied the genuine regret shimmering in his tender gaze. Her insides flipped.

"It's time someone showed you what you were missing then, Ellinor. And since no one else has, I'm volunteering. Seems appropriate, after the night we shared."

She bit her lip, trying to mask the heat of her blush crawling up her neck. "Look," she began tentatively, "that was just sex. You know that, yeah? A distraction. Something to do when the world was falling down and I thought that maybe, just maybe, we'd fooled Gorgi and would get this whole virus thing and me turning Fiss into a new kind of doehaz taken care of. It was good, great even, and just what I needed. But it was only physical. Just good, rough sex."

She didn't mean it unkindly, she genuinely did not want to hurt Jelani, did not want to ruin the unexpected friendship they had established, even if she was still bad at showing any sort of kindness to anyone. But Jelani had to know, had to understand, that all she wanted was a release. Sex had worked. But now? Now there seemed to be only one release left, so why keep fighting?

Jelani's smile was slow and bright, as if he hadn't just had stomach surgery. His grins were that charming. "I would not say no to more distractions of that kind, Ellinor. Regardless, I think you're full of shit."

Ellinor's head snapped back, unused to Jelani's infrequent swearing. He laughed at her—laughed! "Someone as full of heat and passion as you are, doesn't give up so easily. With how voracious of a lover you were, that tells me that you aren't nearly as beaten as you want to believe. Afraid? Yes, that I do believe. Exhausted? Of course. But I don't believe you'd give up, not yet, not while there is still Fiss and Kai and your old crew, and me. There are those willing to fight for you, if you fight for yourself."

She tilted her head at Jelani. "Oh? If you're so smart, what am I so afraid of then, yeah?"

Jelani didn't miss a beat. "Of moving on. Of leaving certain things in the past. Of building something new without Misho. Would you like me to keep going?"

Ellinor hung her head, silent tears rolling down her cheeks in agreement with Jelani's reading of her. He reached out and took her hand, and Ellinor didn't mind, not this time. "You aren't all you appear to be," she said.

"Who is, really?" Jelani answered, tone teasing.

She rolled her eyes. "What Creature Breaker knows how to read people like this? Or, shit, can even wear a memory-silk suit like they were born into it? You like to play at being an outlaw, but that's not what you were born into, yeah?"

Jelani shook his head, but didn't remove his hand. "I was born in the middle levels of Aslan, not high society, by any means, but I never wanted for anything. I didn't become a Creature Breaker until after my mother's death."

"Was she the one who taught you how to read people like some kind of therapist? Or was it a wife? Girlfriend, maybe?"

"My mother taught me. There has never been a wife, partners, a few, and they never complained about my *abilities*." Jelani winked, which threatened to return the heat to Ellinor's cheeks. "My mother was . . . magnetic. She loved the richness of life. She taught me you can be strong and sensitive; you can love passionately and fight fiercely."

He paused, and Ellinor tilted her chin up, scanning his face. The scent of him overwhelmed her. He still smelt of eucalyptus in the rain but . . . more. He smelt like possibility. Like hope.

"I don't know what you experienced with Misho, not truly," he whispered so softly that Ellinor had to lean forward to hear him. "But I understand it. It's why I didn't speak to my father for so long when he moved on. When he opened his heart and found affection in someone who wasn't my mother. I didn't think it was fair. That it was right of him to love again after having had someone as perfect as my mother. Your pain, Ellinor? It's justified. But it shouldn't keep you from living. It took me too long to learn that lesson. I missed precious years I could have spent with my family because of my own stubbornness."

Ellinor knew she should take her hand back, but she didn't have the will. What she could do, though, was steer the conversation toward less treacherous waters. "Just how old are you, anyway?"

"I'm two hundred years old. I was old enough to know better, even then. It's time I can never have back and I regret it with every breath in my soul. It's why now I live in the moment. Why I give Oihana anything she needs, anything she asks for. Why I encourage others to live their truth. I don't want to waste any of the time I may have remaining because of the fear of leaving something in the past; those things are already gone."

Which could be another three hundred years by seersha standards, Ellinor thought. Potentially longer, given his caster abilities, or tragically shorter, given his line of work. Ellinor was fifty years old, still young enough to have a family, as humani could live to be two hundred themselves, casters even longer. But given her trajectory, she knew the odds of seeing her first grey hairs were slim.

"I don't want to forget him." The words surprised her. She hadn't meant to say them, not aloud, but there they were.

Jelani gave her hand a gentle, but firm squeeze, and she blew out a long, slow breath. It was too late to take the words back now. "I'm forgetting the little details, you know? I don't want to lose him. I never even took his last name when we married. At the time, I was too worried about losing the one thing me and my brother shared, but now? I've lost so much of Misho Shimizu already and I don't . . . I can't, Jelani, I just can't."

"But what of Fiss? Part of your Misho will always dwell in Fiss."

"Sure, except that I'm killing him, too. The longer this collar remains it changes Fiss into something awful. I'm destroying the last bit of Misho this way."

"You don't have to, it doesn't have to be that way. You know that, Ellinor. Stop being afraid of living. It's easy to die for someone. Death is . . . final. You do it once and it's over. You know what's harder, more terrifying, yes, but equally reward-ing and fulfilling? Living for someone." Jelani's eyes slowly slid to Fiss. "I want you . . . I want you to live. For Fiss. For Kai." His words were clipped as if he would say more, and it sent goosebumps racing down her arms.

Ellinor shook her head, determined to be stubborn. To not need anyone. To remain angry. To get back to who she was be-fore Cosmin caught her. "You don't know what this is like. Be-ing ripped from your magic, and when you use it, it nearly kills you. Losing your spouse isn't the same as your mother. It's not the same, none of it is."

Jelani smiled and nodded, his thumb running lazy circles over her bruised and filthy hand. "You're right. But, while it's not the same boat, it's at least the same ocean. You aren't as alone as you try to convince yourself you are. It's not a good look on you, Ellinor."

Ellinor's hand began to tingle with his words, the heat returning to her neck and cheeks. Blazhe and Kai saved her from trying to fumble through a retort that wouldn't be nearly as witty as she wanted it to be.

"Aylen's on the comms," Kai said, jerking his thumb back over his shoulder, his eyes falling to Ellinor and Jelani's clasped hand. She slid her hand away, and Kai raised a brow. "She's real testy 'bout talking to all of us."

STILL MAKING THE SAME MISTAKES

"THE HABITATION'S totally shut down," Aylen Bonheur barked the moment they returned to the main room. Jelani draped over Izza, a sleepy and nervous Oihana at zers side.

Ellinor wasn't in the mood to be blamed for anyone else's shit. "You can thank your contact for that. Elisaveta was the one who sent us to Gorgi in the first place. Don't blame us for how that fucker reacted, or how zer altered the deal."

Aylen bared her teeth. "Well, *I* didn't rat you out. No one who works for me did. Don't forget my team's been busy cleaning the digital feeds to keep you guys hidden from Cosmin. I don't tolerate rats, nor work with them. Careful with what you're implying, woman."

The hairs on the nape of her neck began to rise. "Does the Habitation being shut down have some significance for the current situation, Aylen? It's not your business to worry about." Leave it to Jelani Sharma to be the voice of reason, even in his weakened condition.

"I've had to take the overflow. There's a shit ton of Juicers crawling about the atoll. Infected with Gorgi's nanites, from what I hear. Which is hurting *my* business."

"That's not our fault, Aylen. Don't be pissed at us because you're annoyed," Oihana snapped, too sleep deprived to be gentle. "Just have your crew zap them and be done with it. Did you need something else? I was napping."

Aylen let out a long, exaggerated sigh. "With the heat, Elisaveta and I can't get to you today in order to deal with your collar and collect what I'm due. Maybe tomorrow. It's not ideal, I don't like the readings Blazhe sent me, but it can't be helped. So just, I don't know, don't do anything that would make things worse in the meantime?" Aylen pinched the bridge of her nose, and shook her head before continuing. "No one's been able to locate Gorgi either, which is troubling. So you shitheads need to stay put, lay low, and be on your best behavior or zer may get to you before I can."

Fiss clapped his hands at her words. "We stay with metal friend? I like this! Blazhe has such pretty, pretty toys."

A shiver raced down Ellinor's spine at Fiss' words, but if anyone else was put off by what he said, they didn't show it. Aylen turned her gaze from Jelani and Oihana to Ellinor. "I'm still going through Blazhe's readings, Ellinor. I need you to be ready when I get there because my time is limited. I won't be caught out in the open over your drama. So, I want you to take this time and talk to your dreeocht, be all sweet like, dig real deep if you've got to, because with the resources I'm wasting shielding you, and protecting my interests now from Gorgi, you owe me, *again*. I'll do my best to fix your magic, and if it works, your dreeocht is going to unlock the Ashlings who work for me and elevate them in that special way only dreeochts can. You got that?"

Ellinor's hand fell to her knives, forgetting momentarily that Aylen was merely a holographic projection and not in the room with them. Kai placed a heavy hand on her shoulder, grounding her. "That it? Ah, shit, Aylen, you didn't gotta waste time telling us that. Coulda just sent a text. Ell knows what she's gotta consider. She's real aware of it." He turned his gaze to Oihana, flashing her a toothy grin. "Sorry for waking you, kid."

Oihana smirked at Kai, and Aylen practically growled at them all. "I wanted to make sure you knew the magnitude of what went down. How did Gorgi make you, anyway? I couldn't even do that when you first showed up! You guys have got a mole, and you all better sort that shit out fast because I've got no time for more rats. Cosmin von Brandt's tech team is getting close to hacking into my systems. He knows you're here and that's not good for me. For anyone. So, get your shit together. I'll see you in a few days, be ready."

Aylen's round, scowling face blipped from view, and the crew was left in silence. "A mole?" Oihana finally said, blinking quickly in confusion. "None of us would do that."

Gorgi's words, from when she lay on his slab, slammed into Ellinor. She swayed on her feet, holding on to Kai for support. "There's no mole, not like she's thinking. But Aylen's not totally wrong, either." Everyone's eyes turned to her, locking her in place.

"It was Gorgi. All this time, it was Gorgi's people who broke into that warehouse eight years ago. Who tried to steal the tech Cosmin was building. That Misho and I were safeguarding.

Gorgi is the one responsible for Misho's death. It was zers team, and I killed every last one of those motherfuckers."

Her voice broke, and Ellinor shook her head. "Gorgi knew who I was the second some asshole uploaded our fight at SynthLyfe. There was never going to be any hiding. Amardeep wasn't *ever* going to be a safe place to lay low. And that's my fault." She took a deep breath, but was unable to look anyone in the eye. "I should have pressed Aylen into digging around for me when I had the chance, when I first thought that a bot like Gorgi fit with who would have raided Cosmin."

The only sound in the room was the low buzz coming from the med bots and Blazhe's various computers.

Izza was the first to speak. "Did you know Gorgi was responsible, Ms Ellinor? That zer killed your significant other prior to the events of today?"

Ellinor's legs were weak, and she slowly slid down the wall. "No. Not really. But I could have. *Should* have. Gorgi fits. Zer fits everything I knew I needed to look for. But I never asked, never really got the chance to snoop around zers facilities. Things came up. It didn't seem as important as . . ." She paused, lifting her gaze finally to Kai, who was regarding her with a wide-eyed expression. "As getting you away from Cosmin. Getting you help. And getting this—" she waved at her neck "—fixed. For the first time in years I didn't hunt down my own leads first and it kicked us in the ass."

Kai's face fell, lips trembling, and Ellinor looked away. Oihana seemed annoyed but Jelani . . . was that pride on his face? Her insides quivered.

That stupid face.

Oihana shrugged. "Okay, so, no, you didn't know. At least it wasn't our ID's that were the problem. I get to keep my crown on those being the best."

Jelani chuckled, before it turned into a grimace, and Izza gently eased him onto a stool. "You have overexerted yourself, Mr Jelani. Rest, please." Oihana rushed to her brother's side, but according to Blazhe's scans, nothing had ruptured and the seersha was fine—relatively speaking.

"Gorgi allowed your deception to continue, even though zer was not fooled? Explain?" Blazhe said, stepping farther into the room, zers body blocking the light from one of the port-holes.

Ellinor shrugged, still brooding on the floor. "Zer wanted the tech from the virus. Wanted Fiss. Zer was going to take over the mainland with whatever zer got from that. I didn't stick around to ask specifics after that bastard had me tied to a table."

"Ah, yes. That would make sense then," Blazhe said.

"Clarify," Izza responded.

"Gorgi is obsessed with cyborgs of both seerani and humani make. This is no secret. It is well known in the Unincorporated Dwellings. The limbs of zers discarded organic experiments land in the Scrapyard. I have collected zers castoffs a few times." Blazhe fiddled with zers digit-like fingers, as if ashamed, or regretting that zer had scavenged such things.

"I am no mechanic, no programming engineer such as Gorgi," Blazhe continued, zers ocular orbs settling on Ellinor. "But I have un-coded enough to uncover Gorgi's ultimate goal. Zers desire. Objective." The wiring in zers head lit up as con-nections were made, as things became clear. "Gorgi wishes to encase Ashlings in flesh. To pass as organic. To demand acceptance. Show supremacy to the other races. It is zers mix of loathing and desire toward organics. Remember zers mask? This is Gorgi's wish: to infiltrate. To modify Ashlings until zey are nearly organic. It is obvious."

Blazhe rumbled in a way that sounded suspiciously like a growl. "Ashlings are not organics. We should not pretend to be so. We are Ashlings." Izza nodded from where zer stood, agreeing with Blazhe.

Ellinor narrowed her gaze at Blazhe, and Jelani cocked his head. "You don't agree with Gorgi's aim? Don't you want to be more organic-like? To truly feel things? I know Izza does, and that's what Aylen's employed Ashlings desire." Jelani turned to Izza and smiled, nodding at zer. Izza's metal lips pulled back in a smile as zer dipped zers head in agreement.

"No, and yes, in that order, good sir," Blazhe answered. "Violence against the organics, both mechanics and casters alike, will not give my kind the recognition as a true race as is our deepest, truest aim. It will justify the ignorants' hatred of us. Gorgi's desire to show supremacy through subterfuge serves no one. Least of all Ashlings."

A pause, Blazhe registering that zer had captured every ounce of their attention. The wiring in zers head flashed, almost like a blush as Blazhe dipped zers head down, averting zers grey ocular orbs. "I do wish to compute emotions and sensations accurately. To truly feel, as you state. Such a thing is possible, yes, with help." Blazhe turned zers gaze to Fiss, who smiled brightly back at the Ashling, thrilled with the attention, or perhaps just enjoying the colorful paintings.

"Our inability to feel touch beyond the code is a problem that alienates us from society. This is fact. But cloaking ourselves in skin perverts what we are, our uniqueness. Beauty.

Sentience. Ashlings do not require such masks. Upgrading our sensory capabilities is a slower road than Gorgi's methods, but requires less bloodshed."

Kai snorted. "Sorry, pal, that's a sweet idea. It really is. But you really think that's possible? Our side, your side, we all been fighting for over a century. There's too much fear and that stinking, bad blood. I think Gorgi is a big ole asshole, but 'is way may be the right of it."

"That is false, good sir. I have faith in organics. In Ashlings. Peace is possible. I have run the odds."

There was a stirring in Ellinor. Something she hadn't felt, especially toward Ashlings, in a very long time. A curiosity to know more. A desire to help. Maybe. To leave a legacy that was more than blood and death and smuggling illegal magitech before she died. "What would you do instead, Blazhe?"

Blazhe didn't miss a beat. "Respectfully request that your dreeocht unlock our programming. Which is also Aylen's desire, but I would prefer a wider scale. One that eclipses Synth-Lyfe. Give my kind the sensations we lack. Perhaps leave us with the capability to achieve this on our own. A bottled piece of magitech, perhaps, so the good little sir does not need to remain indefinitely. Then I'd seek allies. Friends. Teams. Who believe as I do, and peacefully reach out to other like minds to enact legislation. Educate. Teach. So there is mutual understanding between our kinds. The fear that Ashlings are not alive because death is a rare option is inaccurate. There are many such inaccuracies, misconceptions, that need rectifying."

Jelani grinned. "You have clearly thought about this for a long time. Long before Ellinor ever showed up on Amardeep."

Blazhe nodded, but it was Izza who said, "I have run the odds as Blazhe has. This is a good plan. My approval is unnecessary, but I do approve, if that alters your thoughts on the matter."

Kai was frowning, glaring, more accurately, at Blazhe. The annoyance on his face was at odds with Blazhe's vision, one which Izza then shared with Oihana via their sign language. "Ah, yeah, that's cute. But you know what that plan needs to 'appen? Ell not killing herself."

"Kai, c'mon man. Seriously?" Ellinor groaned.

"What?" her friend barked. "I'm just pointing out the flaw 'ere. For Blazhe to see zers dream come to true, you gotta let Aylen fix you, even if that means the kid may feel pain if you get 'urt. Just means you gotta be more cautious, aye? But, nah, you wanna take the easy way out. *Again.*"

Kai stormed from the room, but because Blazhe's dwelling was so small, there weren't many places for him to go. They could all hear him crashing around the operating and recovery room. Izza, Oihana and Jelani were watching Ellinor though, and only Blazhe seemed worried about the damage Kai was inflicting. The Ashling excused zerself, and the trio continued to stare at Ellinor.

Fiss tilted his head back and forth rapidly. "Are we having a no blinking contest? Fiss can win this!"

"No, Fiss. We're just waiting for Ellinor to explain what in the abyss she's actually thinking," Oihana said, her deep voice dangerously low.

Ellinor glared back at the young seerani. "If we unlock my magic, you know what happens? Fiss will get hurt. Anytime someone stabs me, Fiss will feel like he's getting stabbed. Given what happens right now each time I get injured, and the

damn frequency of it, does that sound like a good idea to you?"
She shook her head, snarling down at the floor instead. "It'll
change him."

"You've got a shield, Ell. Use it." Oihana tugged on Izza and
Jelani, attempting to lead them from the room. But Jelani
waved his sister away, shaking his head. Oihana huffed, but
Izza and Oihana left him where he was sitting.

Ellinor stroked Fiss' quivering hair, the small child-like
dreeocht shivering in her arms. "It's okay, baby bug, they aren't
mad at you. We're just having a debate, that's all."

Jelani cleared his throat. "Blazhe said it wouldn't be an
emotional hurt anymore?" Ellinor nodded, and Jelani's brows
pulled down as he rubbed his chin. "Interesting."

"What's interesting?"

"It may mean nothing. But it is the *emotion* that Fiss can't
process. That's what dreeocht aren't designed to feel, at least
not of the negative variety. The fear of pain, the rage that
someone would harm you or your friends, the panic you experience bleeds through your broken collar. What Fiss seems
to currently experience is the terror and anxiety in lieu of a
physical, tangible pain. Dreeocht occasionally get wounds, you
know. I need to confirm something with Oihana first, but I
have a theory."

He paused, and with great effort pushed himself off the
stool and slowly dragged himself to join everyone else in the
adjoining room. "Regardless, Ellinor, you need to discuss this
choice with Fiss. It is not your decision to make alone."

"What do we get to choose, choose, choose, Elli?" Fiss said,
gently stroking her face with his slightly furry hands.

Ellinor sighed. "Okay, baby bug, I need you to listen and focus for a second." As she held him in her lap, still too full of

stubborn despair and self-loathing to get off the floor, she quietly explained the situation to Fiss. What Blazhe had seen on zers scans, the programs that Gorgi hadn't closed that would allow Aylen to release her magic, what that would mean for Fiss, and what keeping her bio-magitech as is would mean for Ellinor.

Fiss bopped her nose. "I want to cast magic with you. Pretty, yummy magic!"

"But Fiss, if I get hurt—"

"Fiss will be fine. The magic? Yes, the magic inside says so. It tastes confident. It knows. Fiss knows."

"Misho's magic? My 'water man'? That's what's telling you this?" Ellinor's breath caught in her throat.

Fiss grinned, showing his little white teeth, and nodded.

ELLINOR IS DEAD. LONG LIVE ELLINOR

I T TOOK a moment longer of consideration before Ellinor found the will to get up off the floor and join her friends. Jelani was already passed out on the slab that served as both operating table and bed. Talking to Ellinor and the short walk to Blazhe's other room had worn him out. Without him, Kai and Oihana set steely, murderous gazes on her. Fiss whimpered at their expressions, sinking down behind Ellinor.

She sighed, body sagging. "Let me save you the trouble." Ellinor stepped into the room, arms crossed defiantly, even though her head was lowered. "I'm an idiot. I'm selfish. For all my tough-guy act, I'm a scared little bitch. I got it, okay? But you can't blame me for being scared. For not wanting to involve more people in my life. After Misho, I didn't think I needed anyone near me. Didn't *want* anyone near me because I didn't plan on walking away from my final confrontation with Cosmin. And you know what? I was fine with that. I made my peace with that plan and I was solid."

She slowly raised her eyes, gaze locking on a curious Oihana and a pissed Kai. Blazhe and Izza occupied zemselves with other things, sensing this was meant to be a private moment. "Then you came back into my life, Kai. I even forgave you for putting this collar on me because I finally realized how much I fucking missed your stupid face. How you always had my back. How often you were just . . . there for me." She gave him a weak grin, which he returned in kind, gaze watering as he stared at her. "So rude of you, by the way, making me care about you again. Making me realize that I don't want to be alone, that I don't want to see people I care for get hurt. That I *do* want to live. I'm just scared of what that means now, without Misho."

Ellinor took a deep breath, lowering her arms, but unsure if she should go to her friend. "I love you, big guy."

Kai went to her instead and crushed her to his chest in one move. She sputtered and pushed him away, he brushed a tear from her cheek and winked down at her. "Love you too, boss. Even if you can be a downright asshole at times."

Ellinor scratched the back of her head, blushing through the exaggerated scowl she threw at Kai. He laughed, and that's when Ellinor turned to Oihana, who was watching her with all the cool indifference a barely adult seerani could muster.

"I owe you an apology, too, Oihana. I never considered your feelings, let alone Izza's. I didn't stop to think about what my refusal would mean for either of you. It wasn't fair, even if my feelings, my reasons, are—*were* justified. I'm not used to putting others before me, but your brother . . ." She paused, eyes drifting to Jelani, and she could feel her face soften just looking at him. "He has a way of making me see the things I don't want to. Of acknowledging the shit that I'd rather not. He's a good guy, your brother."

Oihana awarded her with a cocky smile. "You know it."

Ellinor chuckled, shifting awkwardly on her feet. "Anyway, I'm sorry. I should have considered the ramifications of my decision more before making a choice based in fear, even if my fear of hurting Fiss was—is a legit one."

Oihana squirmed a little under Ellinor's gaze. She was still petulant, but the anger the girl had held on to was evaporating. "Yeah, well, sorry I didn't really think about why you would even want to say no to begin with." The tension melted out of Oihana's face momentarily, before her brow arched in confusion, her body going rigid with tension. "Hold up, does that mean you changed your mind? You'll let Aylen unlock your magic all the way? Fiss will be able to cast again without you dying on him?"

Ellinor nodded, unable to keep her smile in check at seeing Oihana's glowing face. "Azer yes! Izza, did you hear? Ell is going to help you after all."

Izza turned, and Ellinor swore zers silver body was glowing more than usual. "I heard, Ms Oihana. This is most welcomed news indeed."

"Will you help others like Izza then, good miss? Perhaps like myself?" Blazhe said.

Ellinor tilted her head to the side, glancing at Kai who shrugged in response. Fishing Fiss off the small of her back and setting him next to Jelani, Ellinor responded, "Maybe. What would you need from me and Fiss, exactly?"

"A similar formula to what Gorgi was attempting to abstract from your defected code. Combined with the formula extracted from the Juice Box labs, and your dreeocht's raw magic, I believe we can bottle a new kind of magitech that could, one day, be mass produced for Ashling consumption. I have been analyzing the data I have collected for Aylen, along with what was given to her previously, following your involvement with Elisaveta, and there holds potential when the programs and methodologies are combined. It will not grow flesh over our metal bodies, but it will grow a type of organic nervous system. Is this something you would be agreeable to?"

Ellinor glanced at Fiss, who was watching her raptly. "What do you think, baby bug?"

"We help more machine-people? People that look like you? Me? Izza? Us?" When Ellinor nodded, the dreeocht clapped his hands. "Oh, yes! Let's help more friends, Elli!"

Ellinor wasn't entirely sure she was comfortable with the idea still, but after meeting Gorgi, and how in contrast zer was to both Blazhe, Izza, and even Rada, it was easy for Ellinor to see that not all Ashlings were the same. Just as all seersha casters were not the same—spending time with Jelani had taught her that when comparing him to both Zabel and Cosmin. She was realizing it wasn't always about what *she* was personally comfortable with, but trusting in others. Trusting that they were different. That they meant what they said, and would do the right thing.

She smiled at Blazhe and Izza, who had begun moving about the room with a purpose now. "Well, I guess all we have to do is wait for Aylen and Elisaveta before we get this magic party started, then."

Blazhe didn't have much in the way of amenities. Zer didn't need to shower, let alone defecate, making those first few days an experience, to say the least.

Izza and Blazhe were quick to rectify the situation though—all part of zeyr original Independent Assistance Android capabilities. Still, Ellinor never truly felt clean, like Jelani's blood wouldn't come off her hands, the sharp tang of antiseptic from Gorgi's lab always lingering in her hair. That, coupled with the persistent itch and ache she felt in her thigh and leg as the biotech nanites rebuilt the burned away tissue, meant Ellinor was constantly uncomfortable. And, if Jelani's squirming was any indication, the seersha felt the same discomfort she did.

Things weren't helped by the fact that she always felt hungry, too. But there was only so much in the way of food that could be found in the Unincorporated Dwellings. Blazhe would disappear for hours trying to get the basics to work with, but it was never enough.

While zer was gone, Oihana utilized Blazhe's tools to analyze Ellinor's tech, the pathways left open, testing Ellinor's limited magic that could just barely squeeze past the locks. Fiss always took advantage of the situation, making his little magical crabs and fish again when casting seemed to hurt Ellinor the least. Oihana may have been a savant, a natural when it came to anything mechanical, but even with some of the code and answers available to her, she could only make so much sense of what Gorgi had done, what zer had wanted to do.

Which didn't comfort Ellinor in the slightest in regard to what Aylen would be able to do that Oihana couldn't figure out on her own. Ellinor wondered if this operation would kill her, and fresh waves of panic swelled within her chest. Fiss' eyes flickered from blue to white when the fear got overwhelming, and to keep the dreeocht from causing more damage, Ellinor clung to the reckless hope wafting around Oihana and the Ashlings at the prospect of Aylen Bonheur working a miracle. It made waiting for Aylen difficult, regardless. But the Owner of SynthLyfe would not risk coming to them while Gorgi's Juice addicts still prowled around her business, and while the bot zerself still remained at large.

Despite the setbacks, Oihana was determined to find answers of any kind buried in the magical shackle, in case they had to deal with this level of magitech and biotech again. She wanted to help make the process faster when Aylen showed up, so they could quickly bottle what they needed to achieve Izza and Blazhe's dreams.

"Azer screw this crap!" Her dusky bronze skin flushed in frustration as Oihana threw the prototype she had been working on for the past three days against the wall. The sharp *twang* made Ellinor jump from where she had been rubbing her healing leg.

Jelani chuckled at his sister's outburst and tapped her on the shoulder so she could see his lips. "You used to like a challenge, what happened?"

"There's a difference between a challenge and futile joke, Anni. This is borderline impossible. It's stupid."

"Nothing of great importance is ever easy, Oihana. Relax. Once Aylen arrives, I know you two will be able to crack the code. She is preparing on her end of things just as fervently as you are. But you won't figure anything out if you're this frustrated. Take a break."

Oihana shook her head, her braided, rich brunette hair bouncing around her slender shoulders. "I have nowhere to go to clear my head. This place is too damn small, and we've been here too long."

Kai poked his head from around the doorway of the other room, nodding at Oihana. "I feel that. Lucky Aylen said she'd be 'ere soon. Otherwise me and my upgraded suit would take our chances out in the toxic sludge Amardeep calls air. You think Aylen can loan me another of 'er fancy communicators? I haven't been able to get a decent signal to reach my ma in days. Maybe you should check in with your folks too, Ell. It's been a minute since you done spoke to 'em."

Ellinor shook her head. She didn't think that they would be any more agreeable to speaking to her now than they had been the last time. They still did not approve of the fact that Ellinor had never gotten Andrey's signature tattooed on her shoulder like they had, let alone that she had dropped out of college to join the military, and then aligned herself with a gangster.

"Ms Aylen has stated she and Ms Elisaveta will arrive within the hour, Ms Oihana," Izza assured zers maker. "I have monitored the monorail and the route they will be taking in the Mastiff. There are no traffic delays that would alter their arrival time, rest assured. They should be here in tandem with Blazhe returning from the Scrapyard with the items Ms Aylen requested."

Fiss clapped his hands from where he hovered near the ceiling at Izza's update, excited by the idea of seeing more "metal people." Out of all of them, only Fiss didn't seem to mind the tight, humid quarters they had all been sharing. He was completely unworried that they hadn't heard anything about Gorgi's whereabouts in the same amount of time, either.

Oihana blew out a long breath, dropping her scanner and the digital wrench she was using. "I didn't want to need Aylen's help."

"You sound like Ell," Kai teased.

"Hey! I'm here, aren't I? Give me some credit," Ellinor scoffed.

Jelani chuckled, and Kai rolled his eyes before shooting a wink at his friends. "Maybe when you deserve it, boss." He ducked his head back into the other room, going back to toying with his suit like he had been ever since Blazhe repaired it and recalibrated the Coyote's mechanisms for optimal efficiency. Ellinor threw one of her filthy leg bandages at him anyway.

Oihana narrowed her eyes at them and, with one more huff, went back to her tinkering. Fiss occasionally darted down to look at what she was doing, attempting to tangle one of his cable strands of hair around the tools Oihana was using, just to have her playfully bat him away. It became a game between the two of them, or really, it became a game for Fiss. Oihana was merely humoring the little dreeocht for fear that if she upset him in close quarters, Fiss could short circuit Blazhe's entire home.

Then, just as Izza estimated, they heard the clunky Mastiff pull up outside of Blazhe's home and, with the Ashling there to greet them, zey helped unroll the protective covering over the vehicle to allow safe access to the dwelling. Ellinor and Jelani scrambled to their feet, while Oihana and Izza darted to the door, nearly tripping over Kai in the process. Aylen was first through followed by Elisaveta, her arms laden with more black boxes than any one person should have been able to carry.

Aylen Bonheur was more on edge than usual. Her hands twitched, she tugged at her mini, dark pink military style jacket, and she rubbed her palms down her tight, high waisted black pants. She sniffed at the stale air in the room before breezing into the sleeping area that also served as the operating room. She narrowed her squinty, hazel eyes at Ellinor. "No one's come snooping around here, right?"

Ellinor's brows furrowed. "No. We haven't seen anyone, no alarms were tripped, and Blazhe and Izza haven't picked anyone up on zeyr scanners. Why? You think you were followed here?"

Aylen twirled a finger through her pink and blue curls, released the springy hair and bit her lip. "No. I know how to be careful and lose a tail. Still . . ."

"Still what?" Kai challenged.

Aylen shook her head, placing her hands on her full waist as she turned in slow circles, observing the room and making a show of ignoring Kai. Elisaveta put the crates down near the gurney and dusted her hands off on her ripped black pants, then tugging her fishnet and leather top back into place.

"It's the paranoia talking, love. Don't trouble your little head about it." Elisaveta wiggled her thick, black eyebrows at them. Her small, full lips tilted up in a smirk. "Well, should we get started?"

Ellinor found herself moving back, away from the crates, the table, the machines and computers that would once more dive into her magical shackle. Her body reacted the way it should have originally with Gorgi. No one noticed as they began setting up, except Jelani, who stopped her with a gentle hand to the small of her back.

"This will go smoothly, I promise you. You'll be fine, Ellinor. I will keep you safe while the mechanics tinker." He smiled down at her, and Ellinor's insides quivered in equal amounts of trepidation and—

No.

"Am I doing the right thing?" Her voice was small, wobbly. She may have made a promise to Fiss, but Ellinor was having second and third thoughts.

"Are you asking me what I think?" Jelani whispered.

Ellinor couldn't stop herself from grinning at him. "Your infallible gut has an opinion on the matter, yeah?"

His starry eyes twinkled in mirth. "As a matter of fact, my gut does. And it says you are doing the right thing. You're growing and evolving. You are trusting and letting others in. You're giving others a chance to prove their worth, to live their best lives. These are all good things, and I'm proud of you, Ellinor Olysha Rask. Misho would be, too. You can only control your own actions, your intentions. After that, it's up to others, and you can't control them just as you can't control the future. You have deliberately surrounded yourself with beings you trust, so now you have to trust in them. So take comfort and let your friends see to your safety while you are indisposed."

"But what if this . . . whatever happens next . . . hurts and Fiss overreacts? Maybe it's safer not to bother?"

"You don't believe that, do you?" Jelani's little smirk told Ellinor that he already knew the answer without her having to say a word. She sighed, casting her eyes down and mercilessly chewing on her lower lip.

Oihana and Aylen had their heads bent together, discussing the plan. Occasionally Blazhe interjected as zer explained what zer found in the code, and how it could be used to help other Ashlings if combined with Gorgi's Juice Box programs. Oihana also shared what she had done and learned in the three days before their arrival, Aylen nodding with interest as Oihana explained her process. None had noticed Ellinor was hanging back, but she didn't want to join them, not yet . . . then Aylen's head whipped up, and her lip twitched in agitation at Ellinor.

"Don't be a fucking baby, get over here. The sooner we can take a look and get started, the better. It's too exposed out here and with the Habitation still a mess after you all fled . . ." Aylen trailed off, shaking her head and glancing at the schematics Oihana had pulled. "Just lay down, got it? I'll put you under for the next bit, it'll take a while and be uncomfortable, and I don't trust your dreeocht to be chill if you continue to be so nervous."

Ellinor scowled at the woman, ready and willing to fight, to argue about how this wasn't as easy as having a molar removed, when Jelani gently pushed her forward. "It's about trust, remember? Don't worry, Kai and I will take care of Fiss and look after . . . things."

Taking a deep breath, Ellinor lay down on the stiff bed. Oihana and Aylen began hooking her up to the different life support monitors as well as computer systems, none of which were as sophisticated as Gorgi's, but would have to do. Elisaveta was assisting them with unloading the objects in the crates when Aylen requested something, otherwise no one spoke. Not until Ellinor was all hooked up and the anesthesia mask was placed over her nose and mouth.

Aylen turned around, her biotech and mechanical arm making her movements a little stiff. "Okay, everyone non-essential get the fuck out. We need the room to maneuver." Her lisp was a little more pronounced as she spoke, and Ellinor vaguely wondered if that meant the Owner of SynthLyfe was nervous, or unsure of her abilities, going into the magitech operation.

Ellinor's eyelids began to droop, and she watched Kai carry a curious Fiss out of the room. She struggled to open her eyes again, and caught a tense, worried expression from Jelani before it softened and he offered a reassuring smile then stepped out of Blazhe and Izza's way.

Ellinor's eyelids dropped once more, and she could not open them again.

THESE ARE THE ANDROIDS
YOU'RE LOOKING FOR

E LLINOR OPENED her eyes, vision blurry and head swimming. She sucked in a shaky breath, hands scrambling on the thin, narrow table as she sat up. She reached out, but not with her physical hands.

Where is it?

Her head was heavy, mouth fuzzy and thick, like balls of cotton were shoved in her cheeks. Her nerves were muted, the anesthesia slow to release its hold on her. Her heart rate spiked.

Where? Where? Where?

She was almost too scared to keep reaching, keep prodding at the pool within her that had been empty for weeks. What if it wasn't there? What if that same, dead void greeted her again? The small sliver that had opened at Gorgi's clawed hands was now closed and gone forever.

Ellinor bit her lip, hard enough for the iron tang of blood to tickle her tongue. She stretched her ethereal fingers further, deeper into her core, and then . . .

Oh.

Blooming deep in her chest, tickling the shriveled parts of her soul and spreading to her extremities was a familiar tingle, blossoming and shifting as the magic flowed through her veins as though a small but sturdy dam had been broken apart. Goosebumps raced over her arms as the heat turned to cool power. Her nerves tickled, no longer dull and sluggish. She blinked the blurriness from her eyes and the colors, oh the colors! They were vibrant again, sharp and pure and magnificent. Even if Blazhe's workroom was cluttered with horrific looking objects, she almost didn't want to blink, drinking in every defined detail. She took a deep breath and held it, relishing the scents as they came alive, delighting her nose. Sure, Blazhe's home stank of stale body odor and oil, but it was so clear and pungent that Ellinor could weep with relief.

The world felt whole again. *Ellinor* felt whole again.

Her magic was back, completely and wholly. Ellinor was back.

I wonder if . . .

Tentatively she reached up, her fingers shaking as they hovered over her neck, before brushing her fingertips over what she hoped would be skin. But it was not to be, all she felt was the cold, rough metal that had once been the magical dampener. There was a fleeting pang in her heart, but it was easy to sweep aside, an acceptable loss.

She had hated the idea of looking like a cyborg, even remotely tied to an Ashling. But things were . . . different now. Ellinor was different. She had met Ashlings who were kind and curious and only wanted to help, and they weren't so bad. Not nearly as bad as some of the organic twats she had met and were still breathing, that was for sure.

I can live with this.

She heard gentle murmuring from the other room, but she didn't care to join the others, not yet. She wanted this private moment to herself, to let the tears make dirt trails down her cheeks, to let the magic, *her magic* and no one else's, pump through her veins, bringing back sensations she thought she would never feel again. She held the magic in her chest for as long as she could before releasing it, letting the air swirl around her, lifting her filthy hair and making it dance. The wind hummed in her ears, and it was pure ecstasy.

The bliss of casting chased away the last of the fogginess from the drugs Aylen had given her. But Ellinor was so wrapped up in her magic that she didn't notice the others had poked their heads into the room. Fiss was clapping his hands, Oihana grinning at her, trying way too hard to keep from showing teeth while smiling. Tears ran down Kai's cheeks, relief that the collar he had put on her neck was finally neutralized—relatively speaking—and Jelani was watching her with open wonder and pride in his gaze, unashamed in his wide smile.

"I'm taking everyone's silence means it worked." Aylen's voice cut through the moment, and Ellinor reluctantly released the magic. The air stilled, but the warmth in her chest and core and the cool tingle in her bloodstream remained.

She couldn't see Aylen—Elisaveta, Izza or Blazhe either, for that matter. The doorframe was only so large, after all. "You're lucky it did, Aylen," Ellinor said, though she was too happy to put any real malice behind her words.

Kai's smile was so wide it made Ellinor's cheeks ache just looking at him. "We square, boss?" Despite the smile, there was a tremor to Kai's voice. "Or do I still owe you that barrel of top shelf whiskey?"

"I'll never say no to whiskey, big guy. But you and me were square a long time ago."

Silver lined Kai's emerald eyes as more tears rolled down his cheeks, his throat bobbing with emotion. His relief and happiness was hard to look at. Ellinor's heart twisted knowing he had felt so much guilt and fear over what he had aided Cosmin in doing to her.

Ellinor cleared her throat, rubbing her palms along her thighs. "Did you get what you wanted, Aylen? Is it enough to combine with your other codes and do what Blazhe wants for zers kind, too?" Ellinor gingerly slid from the bed, legs still weak from the anesthesia.

"Yup, and it's some glorious shit, let me tell you." Aylen's voice was honeyed, full of satisfaction and relief, masking her little lisp. Kai offered Ellinor a hand, steadying her as she joined her friends. She was finally able to see Aylen, who stood near the door.

Elisaveta stood to the side of Aylen, arms crossed, with a look of unease on her face. But Ellinor was distracted by the object in Aylen's hands. She clutched a jar full of nanites; millions of them. They glowed a neon blue, a pink pulse rippling through them occasionally like a wave. The tiny devices squirmed, almost viscous as they crawled and slithered around one another in the magitech solvent Aylen added to keep their tiny robotics from dying outside of their organic host.

"I just have to figure out how to transfer the coding from organic to inorganic, switching the lines from magic dampening to sensation overload. Then I can better rewrite the Juice Box code to amplify the other bio-magitech. I'll need to figure out a secure location to mass produce this stuff, but then we're all set." She tilted the jar back and forth, another pink ripple going through the container. "Shouldn't be too complex for my team back at the labs. What Gorgi wanted would have been far more intricate, making these little buggers construct flesh on top of stupidly advanced neuron-pathways, but what I can do with this is nothing to roll your eyes at."

"Not complex?" Jelani said, a chuckle vibrating his voice. "That sounds pretty complicated to me."

Aylen shrugged with her robotic shoulder. "Maybe for non-mechanic types. But Oihana knows what I'm talking about." The young woman nodded, cheeks darkening at the compliment.

This was the calmest, most cordial Ellinor had ever seen Aylen. Her persistent paranoia replaced by pride, and perhaps a tinge of exhaustion. The delightfully round woman shifted her gaze off the jar to look at Fiss, who watched only Ellinor, and seemed to come to a decision. "Between this and the program Elisaveta was able to smuggle out, I'll have a ton of money coming into my business. More than I was counting on, and that's good enough for me. Figure this kind of counts as your dreeocht helping me with my employees, anyway. Besides, it's too dangerous to pile you all back to SynthLyfe. Best you and your crew get the fuck off Amardeep as soon as you can."

Aylen shifted, the cybernetics along her chest lighting up as she sent a command—most likely to Rada, back at her base of operations. "I'll get a ride back separately, can't be too careful. Elisaveta—" she tucked the jar of bio-magitech into a black satchel "—you stay here. Once Blazhe says Ellinor's fit to travel again, take them to the monorail station back at SynthLyfe. The gear will be fine to go with you in the Mastiff."

Elisaveta's light green skin paled momentarily, face slackening before she clenched her jaw and grinned. "Copy that, I'll catch you back at SynthLyfe."

"Right then. I'll leave you to it. My ride is here."

"That fast?" Kai said, giving a low whistle, impressed.

Aylen smirked. "I've got more than one friend out here. This one just happens to have a speedy vehicle." She picked up her satchel with the nanites in it and patted Blazhe on the shoulder on the way out. "Thanks, friend. You ever want to take me up on my offer to join the team at SynthLyfe, just say the word."

Blazhe nodded zers domed head, and with one last casual glance behind her, Aylen stepped out into the nasty air outside. There was a loud buzz, a slam of a door, the roar of an engine, and Aylen was gone with her prize.

Blazhe stood at the open door for a moment watching her, before slowly closing the giant steel contraption. "The technology will be safest with her. Yes, the odds do not lie about this." But despite zers words, Ellinor could tell Blazhe was disappointed to see the bio-magitech substance go.

There was a different pang in Ellinor's heart now. Her eyes slid from Izza to Blazhe, Blazhe to Izza. She took a deep breath, relishing the sharp, pungent twang once more and released Kai's hand, stepping farther into the adjacent room with everyone else.

"Blazhe?" She waited for the Ashling to turn around, ignoring everyone else's curious looks. "Fiss already agreed to make Izza fully sentient. The first Ashling with a true nervous system, not just an analysis of sensations and feelings. Would you like to be the second?"

Silence. Then all the connections and wires in Blazhe's head lit up, like a city coming to life at night. "Yes, good Ellinor. An emphatic yes, thank you."

The tension and pressure eased in Ellinor's chest for a moment before she was instantly squeezed by Oihana. "That's so boss of you, Ell, thank you! Can we get started now?" She turned to Blazhe. "Is she strong enough for that?"

Blazhe motioned for one of his medical drones, and the flying bot quickly scanned her, beeping at Blazhe, who nodded once more. "Ellinor is exceptionally strong, but if we wait an hour, it would be optimal. This allows for her body to recognize its own magic again, and cuts down the possibility of a residual connection interfering with what Fiss will need to do." Blazhe turned to Izza. "But preparations must be made in the interim. Shall we proceed?"

Izza nodded, and the two Ashlings zoomed into the workroom with a flurry of purpose that left Ellinor dizzy with a kind of glee she never thought she would feel again.

Ellinor spent the hour testing her magic. Pulling and measuring, casting and playing with Fiss. It was different, casting with a dreeocht properly. There was an endless pool of energy amplifying even the most basic of her magical commands. She didn't want to push the limits while in Blazhe's home, but Ellinor could only imagine the kind of magic she could cast with Fiss' endless magical supply to boost her abilities. She didn't even know where to begin with casting the kind of magic they may now be capable of.

The dreeocht giggled each time Ellinor twisted the wind around him, tugging at the long, black mesh tank top he wore. Fiss seemed better, more like himself, like the dreeocht that first emerged from Cosmin's coffin-like container nearly two weeks ago. It felt longer, even though Ellinor could count the number of nights she slept, the times she was able to bathe, on one hand.

While they played, Izza, Blazhe, and zers team of flying droids prepared for what Ellinor and Fiss were about to do, and Ellinor watched Fiss. She looked for cracks, fissures in his bearing that would tell her she had broken him and destroyed the goodness that made up the fiber of a dreeocht. She didn't see any of the feral fury she had witnessed before, but that didn't mean the damage wasn't there. Especially when she caught Fiss rubbing his own leg in time with the waves of itchiness that washed over her own injured thigh while it healed.

Jelani plopped down next to Ellinor, trying to hide the grimace of pain his wound still caused despite the rapid healing from the reco-shot and trauma kits. "You're worried?"

"Well, yeah. Shouldn't I be?" she whispered, motioning toward Fiss, who danced with the breeze Ellinor was manipulating.

Jelani rubbed his chin, before shaking his head. "I don't think so. It's like I said, it's the emotional pain, anxiety, and anger that corrupts dreeocht. All those negative emotions. Dreeocht are such innocent creatures, they can't process things like despair and hatred. It's unnatural. Foreign, even.

Not unlike a virus." He nudged her, giving her a meaningful look, eyes lingering on the curve of her neck. He smiled at her blush and said, "But Fiss is alive. He can feel physical pain. If a doehaz were to attack a dreeocht in the wild, they would be able to feel and process the agony that comes with that wound. I believe Fiss will be okay now that the connection between you has been properly opened."

"But if I get hurt—"

"Yes, Fiss will feel it. But it won't be like before." Jelani assured her, voice gentle, but firm. "I guess no more throwing yourself casually in front of bullets or magitech, anymore." He grinned at her, but there was a sincerity to his voice, a look of pleading in those blue pools he called eyes that Ellinor didn't want to interpret . . .

"We are ready, Ms Ellinor," Izza said, breaking Ellinor's attention. A medical drone zoomed in front of her, a bright scan going from the top of her head to the tips of her boots, before zipping away. "You are declared fit, no residual muscle memory of your tainted connection to little Fiss remains."

"Then we should go, do as Aylen says and get you buttercups off of Amardeep," Elisaveta grumbled, still perched by the door now that all the remaining gear had been loaded into the Mastiff.

Oihana glared at the cyborg-seerani, reading the woman's lips. "Not until we upgrade Izza. And Blazhe. Slow your roll, Elisaveta, we can make the time for this."

Elisaveta made a noncommittal sound deep in her throat, shifting against the door, arms crossed.

"You're being as paranoid as Aylen," Kai teased, moving out of the way. "She rubbing off on you already, aye?"

Elisaveta rolled her eyes. "Nah, but we shouldn't waste the time we don't know we have. Word about your dreeocht being on Amardeep is spreading, don't forget that."

"Then let's get to work," Ellinor said before anyone else could argue. "What do you need us to do?" She settled Fiss on her lap, fingers idly running through his floating tendrils of hair. With the connection open, the link between them running in both directions, Ellinor felt the peace, the love that Jelani said she should have always experienced. The same unfiltered love Fiss had for her the moment he imprinted on her.

They were truly bonded now.

Instead of attaching wires to Ellinor like zey had when zey extracted the millions of corrupted nanites, Blazhe and Izza were the ones attached to the wires. Blazhe stepped forward, motioning for Fiss as gently as zer could with zers clawed digits. Ellinor was reluctant to release him, but Fiss floated free of his own accord and Blazhe placed the ends of the wires attached to zer and Izza onto Fiss.

"It is undefinable, what must be done next," Blazhe said, the painting on zers domed head aglow from zers processing systems. "There is no codebook for what is to be built. But there is theory. Coded messages, the data we wish to have, we send those files to Fiss. What he must then do is not destructive magic. He does not require your guidance, good miss. What Fiss needs is to know our deepest wants. His primal magic can shape the rest, make pathways and nerves where there was once only data and ciphers. Part of Fiss is constructed of pieces similar to those within Izza and myself. His magic will know what to do."

Ellinor's brows knit together. Nothing Blazhe said made sense. But then she recalled what Fiss had done to her when he first emerged. The bubble of magic he had enveloped her in, how he looked within himself and declared that it was the magic within him that provided his name. There was a sentience to Fiss' magic, one that still housed part of Misho. If it was possible for discarded smart tech, magitech, and natural primal magic to come together to make things like dreeocht and doehaz, to create life where there was once death and debris, then Ellinor needed to have faith the same magic could do the unimaginable now.

Ellinor nodded, smiling at Fiss. "You understand what to do, baby bug?"

Fiss tilted his head back and forth, running his tongue along his slightly blue lips. "Yes? Oh yes! I can taste it. The thing that needs the doing. Feelings? I'm making feelings? Like what we have, Elli?"

"That's right, you got this, baby bug. Cast your magic."

Fiss closed his eyes, floating on the air, his cable and seaweed hair quivering in a phantom breeze. The remaining tech left in Ellinor's skin warmed slightly, but it was pleasant now, like a heated blanket rather than the boiling metal it had been before. The wires in Fiss' skin lit up, sparkling as the water and air magic flowed through his small body. He stretched his hands toward Izza and Blazhe, a purplish light pulsing from Fiss that crawled like fingers made of lightning toward the Ashlings, snaking around them, enfolding them in prismatic bubbles. The wires connecting the Ashlings to Fiss shifted, morphing from a solid to liquid, and back again.

Ellinor was transfixed; what was happening *was* undefinable. It defied everything she thought she knew, she thought was possible. Wires going from solid matter to viscous, living code? Perhaps this was true magic; something that could not be quantified or measured, no set rules or boundaries like traditional caster power. Perhaps that was what allowed mechanics to combine biotechnology and "magic" together to make *magitech*. Maybe what Ellinor believed was magic, wasn't magic at all, but simply another form of science.

How else could Fiss defy all physics and logic so easily?

Her mind hurt, but she couldn't look away. The light grew, the purple haze glittering as it twisted and slithered to every corner of the room, filling the space with the scent of ozone and ocean. Water magic was best when it came to crafting healing magitech, serums, and devices, but even so, Fiss' power was creating *life*—or just about. The lightning bounced from Fiss in a never-ending wave, making the hairs on Ellinor's arms and legs stand on end. The bubbles the Ashlings were in pulsed, once, twice, growing, shrinking, growing even larger and then—

POP!

A blinding, near ultraviolet light pushed through the room, the wires between Blazhe, Izza, and Fiss disintegrating into a fine mist. Fiss fell like a leaf into Ellinor's arms, exhausted. Apparently, even beings created of pure, primal magic had their limits.

"Did it work? Are zey okay?" Ellinor turned to the wide eyed, slack jawed expression of Jelani and Oihana. Neither of the siblings had an answer for her, though Oihana rushed into the room, checking over Izza's wiring, making sure zer hadn't been shut down permanently.

Oihana breathed out a long sigh, her fingers trailing over the Ashling she had so lovingly made. "I believe so. Zeyr systems are rebooting. We'll know when zey finish if it worked or not. If nothing else, neither seem damaged so that's a good sign."

"Is the kid okay?" Kai asked, stooping next to Ellinor, stroking Fiss' cheek. The dreeocht cooed, but didn't open his eyes.

Fiss never slept, he claimed he didn't need to, so seeing him resting in this way now both warmed Ellinor's heart and worried her. "I think so, I think he just overextended himself or something."

"That was amazing, Ellinor. Truly. Thank you for talking to Fiss. For encouraging him do this," Jelani whispered. "This means more than the world and all the stars in the sky to my sister. To Izza and Blazhe. *Thank you.*"

She felt the blush crawling up her neck, the unfamiliar pride swell in her chest, but both were abruptly cut short by a crash from outside. The squeal of bending metal, of shattering glass, and snapping plastic, rattled Blazhe's haven.

Ellinor was on her feet instantly, holding the dozing Fiss tightly as she darted to one of the dirty porthole windows. Outside she saw three caravans full of Ashlings and mind-controlled Juicers careening through the Unincorporated Dwellings of the Ashlings. Destroying homes and running over any bot that didn't get out of the way. They barreled closer, closer . . . And then she saw zer, in the lead vehicle.

Gorgi.

Ellinor lurched back. "Fuck. Fuck, fuck, *fuck.*" She ran around Jelani, grabbing her weapons and equipping her shield. "How in the abyss did Gorgi track us here?"

Elisaveta Baldini winced at her words. "Sorry, love. I didn't have any other choice."

WHO NEEDS ENEMIES WITH FRIENDS LIKE THESE?

ELLINOR SLAMMED Elisaveta against the wall. "The fuck do you mean, you didn't have a choice? What did you do, you thunder cunt?"

No one tried to pry Ellinor off Elisaveta. With Fiss no longer affected by her moods, the danger of the dreeocht disintegrating them was relatively small. The danger outside, though . . .

Elisaveta shoved her off as if it were easy, lights blinking in the black bands that were her mods and cybernetics. "I didn't get out as free as I let on, okay? I did what I needed to in order to save my brother. To get him clean so Gorgi's nanites didn't kill him, too. A trade for a trade. I don't know you buttercups well enough to give a shit when it was my family on the line. But it was wrong. Azer won't forgive the duplicity. I tried to get you all to leave before Gorgi got here. I tried, okay?"

Kai pumped his scattergun, already back in his Coyote mechanized suit. The back appeared bulkier than it was before, thanks to whatever upgrades Blazhe had managed to install while they waited for Aylen. He stepped forward, encroaching on Elisaveta's personal space. "You could 'ave said something, *Veta*. Could 'ave come clean the moment you walked in that there door."

"And risk Aylen tossing me out the second I actually did get free? No way, love. That wasn't an option, either. I need Aylen to survive in this place, I couldn't . . ."

"You can go suck a whole bag of dicks for all I care about your survival!" Ellinor lunged for the cyborg-seerani again, but Kai held her back. Elisaveta dropped her gaze, shuddering as the vehicles came to a halt outside, crashing into more buildings, dirt and debris pinging off Blazhe's home.

"We don't have the time for this," Jelani growled, shrugging into his Creature Breaker armor, the skintight combat suit with its sophisticated polymers molding over his body. He tried to hide the flinch of pain as his tender skin stretched over his wounds, but Ellinor saw.

Holding his rifle, his Creature Breaker blades dangling at his sides, Jelani glared at Elisaveta. "Make it up to your god. Defend us now. Oihana is an innocent in all this. Izza and Blazhe haven't rebooted yet. You hold no loyalty to Gorgi, so get us out of here like you half-heartedly tried to do before. If we live, we'll leave it to you on whether your conscience requires you to tell Aylen of your disloyalty."

Elisaveta narrowed her eyes, but when the building shuddered and the lights flickered, the power shutting down a second later, the seerani nodded. She flexed her arms, red lights in the black bands flickering all over her pale green skin. But without the power, the atmospheric regulators weren't functioning, the noxious air from outside seeping into Blazhe's home. If they didn't get away from Gorgi, Amardeep's toxic air would do them in, making it easy for the Juice Box manufacturer to waltz in and take what zer wanted.

Ellinor threw the hood of her armor up, attaching her mask to filter the air. But she couldn't help Jelani or Oihana. "It comes out now," Gorgi's voice boomed, as if zer were in the room with them. "If it does as advised, I ensure that the necessary experimentation will be humane. If it wastes my time further, I poke and prod, rip and tear, I test, and test, and test. Use its fleshy compatriots as experiment modules. Not pleasant, not pleasant. I'd rather not risk damaging my property if possible."

"So we're screwed either way?" Ellinor yelled back, gently shaking Fiss, trying to rouse the sleeping dreeocht. "Doesn't sound like a fair trade to me."

"Fair?" There was a rumbling, Gorgi's laughter mixed with the movement of zers Ashlings as zey spread out, flanking the building. Oihana cowered behind Izza and Blazhe, tapping furiously on her wrist tablet, trying to get the atmospheric regulators back online. "You should know that life is not fair. Organics steal. They enslave. They take for granted the flesh that knits and repairs, the bodies that replenish themselves. They make automata and strip away the things they so callously do not appreciate in themselves, purposely making my kind weak. Unacceptable. Your Cosmin, he did the same, yes? You should help me, Ellinor Olysha Rask. Organics have wronged you just as much."

Oihana continued to tap on her tablet. Finally the lights on the massive steel door turned on, the locks reengaged. Not that it would stop Gorgi from breaking in a wall, but it was something. She continued to work, fingers flying, her scanners flashing over the atmospheric pressurizers. The young woman held her breath, trying to suck in as little air as possible, and Ellinor became more insistent on waking Fiss, rubbing his chest so fast she thought she would start a fire.

Stall, Ellinor. You aren't ready. Andrey's voice snapped in her head.

"That's a hard pass," she yelled, then lowered her voice. "Come on, baby bug, I need you. We have to cast some magic together."

Fiss opened his eyes slowly, blinking the bleariness from his vision. The room vibrated for a second before the atmospheric pressurizers came back on. Then, with a howling whirling sound from outside, the walls of Blazhe's home were pried away, leaving just the door. Rendering Oihana's work pointless.

Ellinor snapped her hand out, fingers weaving and jerking as fast as she could, she took that awful, poisonous air and twisted it, hardened it, made a wall, and kept the worst of the mist out, letting the systems in Blazhe's floor keep them alive. But sweat already pooled down her back; Ellinor was not strong enough yet to cast this much magic. She couldn't fight and keep the wall up at the same time.

The Juicers ran at them first. Kai's scattergun sounded like endless thunder in her ears as he fired round after round at the waves of addicts pouring over the ruined walls. They were dying already, the acid from outside bubbling on their skin, chunks falling away before Kai's bullets ever ripped into them.

Jelani fired an armor piercing round at Gorgi, but the bullet harmlessly pinged off the modified guard bot's heavy metal plating. The sensitive areas of zers wiring and body were impervious to their weapons. Jelani shifted aim, bringing down one of the aerial guard Ashlings zooming straight for them.

"Fiss," Ellinor cried, strain making her voice shrill. "I need your magic. Help us, baby bug." Oihana snatched Kai's submachine gun and opened fire. But the recoil sent her back, her shots going wide, only hitting one of the aerial Ashlings and barely missing Kai in the process.

Gorgi was moving fast—too fast—for a bot of zers size. The massive gun snapped into place, emerging from the hatch on zers back. Zer was aiming for Kai, not Ellinor.

Fiss blinked. "Bad magic?"

"Yes, we need to stop Gorgi!"

The bot opened fire before Fiss understood. "No!" Ellinor pushed the wall of air, but it didn't stop the fist-sized projectiles.

But Elisaveta did.

Her arms were longer, too long. They stretched from her body, her hand bent back, revealing a gelatin substance that caught the projectiles and sent them hurtling back. Elisaveta snapped her hand forward, her arm morphing closer to her body to create a laser shield that enveloped them, a sheet of metal plating emerged from the black bands along her side, a physical shield over the seerani traitor. She fired EMP rounds from the gun suddenly in her other hand, and the Ashlings thudded to the ground.

"I will enjoy dissecting you too, Elisaveta Baldini," Gorgi bellowed.

The Juicers no longer swarmed toward Kai and Jelani, focusing on Elisaveta. They covered her, scrabbling over her limbs, their bloodied bodies pulling her down, down, down. They stuck their hands into the black bands, looking for wiring to pull, even if they had to rip it with their teeth. Elisaveta disappeared under the sea of flesh.

Gorgi zipped to where they were. Zers steps like a jackhammer vibrating the remainder of the building.

"Metal friend!" Fiss cried, and Ellinor's magic came alive.

"Fiss, keep the air wall up. We need to breathe." And then Ellinor was moving, hands flying. The air around her shifted in pressure, encasing her in a bubble as she launched herself at Gorgi, her weapons sheathed.

Her fist connected with Gorgi's small head. The pressurized bubble made her punches harder, her body protected. With Fiss' permission, Ellinor had more magic to use then she knew what to do with properly, but she could definitely throw a punch.

Gorgi's head snapped back, zers fist whipping around, the impact should have crushed her hip. But all there was, was an uncomfortable pressure as the magic bent and morphed, stopping the blow. Both Fiss and Ellinor gasped in unison.

She flung herself up and grabbed Gorgi's head, giving it a twist, but the big bot slapped her off. Ellinor slid back, stopped herself, then darted back toward the bot, slamming her hands forward. The magic she commanded made Gorgi stagger back as she rushed him.

Jelani wielded his Creature Breaker blades, moving back to Oihana and cutting down the Juicers that got too close while his sister worked to awaken Blazhe and Izza. He was a whirlwind, his blades making a sandy glow around him as he slashed with one blade and blocked with another. He twisted both blades around to cleave a path through three of the Juice addicts who looked to tackle him and get to Oihana.

Ellinor kicked out, the magic allowing her to make a dent in Gorgi's thigh. The Ashling caught her leg before she could pull it back.

"I will break you, Ellinor Rask." Gorgi jerked her up. Ellinor tried to grab for her guns, but Gorgi held her, arms pinned. Kai was shooting as fast as he could at the Ashlings still converging on them. Those who were only partially disabled crawled toward them, trying to clamber up Kai, keeping her friend trapped, trying to wrestle the gun from his hands. Metal fingers were pulling at the all too soft flesh that was unprotected by his armor.

Gorgi slammed Ellinor down on zers knee, trying to break her spine, but breaking the magic instead, and nearly crushing the Asco Rhino crossbow on her back. Zer lifted her once more, and Fiss' scream filled her ears.

A wave swelled in her, magic that was and wasn't hers, the smell of the ocean filling her nose. Her hands moved at her sides, commanded by Fiss as the magic swept through the broken room, glittering white and baby blue. The magic was alien to Ellinor, she had no conscious idea of what Fiss was doing, how he was shaping their power. She was merely a puppet, the primal magic in Fiss pulling the strings. The force coalesced, forming massive sea snakes made of hurricanes and lightning. They moved in a furious whip, the magical snake creatures curling around Gorgi, holding zer still and constricting the giant robot, who dropped Ellinor.

She swept out her hand, gasping for breath while Fiss still manipulated her magic. Ellinor was able to scatter the Ashlings crawling on Kai with a strong gust of wind, however. The metal flap on Kai's back was finally unobstructed. It groaned open—and a fucking grenade launcher came out. Of all the enhancements Ellinor could guess that Blazhe would give Kai, she hadn't thought of a grenade launcher, though she should have perhaps guessed as much.

Jelani darted around the felled bodies of Ashlings and Juice addicts. He moved to Kai's side, his blades humming in his hands. The blades' bright sandy color illuminated the humani-sized, magical sea snakes as they tenaciously peeled back Gorgi's magitech plating while squeezing zer tighter and tighter, crushing the Ashling, trying to fry zers sensitive wiring.

The gun on Kai's back swiveled, launching a string of elec-trified grenades. Gorgi twisted, getting zers massive clawed hand free of one of the snakes. Zer caught the belt, pulling the pin before it could fry Gorgi's circuitry. Zer crushed the pro-jectile in zers hand, before gripping the snake and snapping it like a whip, freeing zerself of one of the creatures. But one was enough.

Zer charged them again, one of the sea snakes still twisting around zers body, but was met by a shower of limbs as Elisaveta burst from the bodies who tried to crush her. A pri-mal yell erupted from her as she met Gorgi head on. She held zer in place, allowing the magical snake to slither up Gorgi's legs. Elisaveta's arms encircled Gorgi, crushing zers limbs in place, letting the magical creature focus on peeling Gorgi apart. Elisaveta's modifications made her as strong and imper-vious to damage as most Ashlings.

Most.

Gorgi bent zers backward-facing knee sharply, bringing zers leg between zer and Elisaveta, skewering Elisaveta's metal plat-ing with zers pointed toe. She staggered back, and Gorgi's gun hummed, changing what zer was using as ammunition.

Electricity flared from the end of the gun, but Fiss called it away, devouring everything Gorgi unleashed, fueling it toward the bubble that kept the acid rain out. Ellinor's hands became hers again, Fiss no longer needing to use her to create magical creatures. She spread her hands, and Janne's electric Lance dagger flew from its sheath, and turned to maximum power. With a precision Ellinor didn't have before, she sent the blade flying, burying itself in Gorgi's ocular orb.

Kai moved between her and Gorgi, trying to fire again, but the enraged bot swept zers massive arm, tossing Kai aside. He crashed onto Blazhe and Izza, and Ellinor jumped on Gorgi's back, using her air magic to propel her up and over zers arms and gun. An aerial Ashling tried to pry her off, but the sea snake, losing power as Fiss focused on the bubble and consuming Gorgi's power, flew at the bot. Both disintegrated in a spray of metal and electricity.

Ellinor twisted around and grabbed the electric knife buried in Gorgi's eye.

She raised the knife again, ready to plunge it back in deeper, trying to get at zers central processing, when zer grabbed her ankle and tossed her like a ragdoll. Fiss screamed, and the wind twisted around her, saving her from a brutal landing. She took hold of it, using Fiss' magical reserves and the remainder of the last snake, to send herself flying back at Gorgi, her mechanical shield snapping open in the same movement.

She put her weight behind the shield, Fiss' magic at her feet, turning herself into the projectile. She slammed into Gorgi's head, off balancing the bot as zer swung zers arm down on Ellinor. Her arm should have shattered. Would have, if not for her armor flaring to life, draining itself instantly to protect from that one blow.

"Ell, move!" Kai called, stooping to lower his new grenade launcher at Gorgi's head, Jelani covering his exposed flank from the last two Ashlings. She flipped herself backward, yanking her automatic crossbow from where it hung, nearly crushed, on her back. Kai fired, the boom nearly rupturing Ellinor's eardrums as the second projectile found its home in Gorgi's chest. The eruption collapsed zers torso, crumpling the massive Ashling.

But Gorgi was not shut down yet.

"You . . . will suffer," Gorgi said, voice crackling and full of static. A light blipped in zers remaining ocular orb, and Ellinor leveled her Rhino at zers head.

"Gorgi is sending a message," Oihana screamed, popping her head out of cover, as Ellinor fired. The javelin-like metal pole shattered the remaining pieces of the glass orb, Gorgi's head bounced as it stuck to the ground underneath. The light went out behind zers eyes.

She heard shuffling from behind her as Oihana and Jelani moved, but she watched only Gorgi as Fiss finished draining the magitech. "I didn't disrupt it in time. The message was delivered, but I don't know who it went to," Oihana said, her voice quivering.

Ellinor limped to where Gorgi was and used her shield to sever zers head, before reaching her hand down zers neck and ripping every wire she could get her hands on. The Juicers had stopped moving at some point during the melee, as did the Ashlings under Gorgi's command, but Ellinor wanted to be sure. She would dismantle every piece of Gorgi if she had to.

"Ellinor, stop. We need to leave," Jelani murmured, helping a bleeding Elisaveta up.

"The Mastiff may be gone, but I let Aylen know what happened," Elisaveta croaked, voice weak as her blood oozed between the displaced wires in her side and gut. "A new set of wheels is on its way."

Ellinor's lip twitched at her words, but in the end, Elisaveta had risked her life to make the situation right. Misho would want her to have that count for something, so, for now, Ellinor would take Elisaveta's most recent actions to heart and at least get the seerani somewhere where she could get medical attention.

Ellinor nodded, eyes roving over her actual friends. "Everyone else okay?"

There were bewildered nods, wide eyes and shocked expressions, but no one was grievously injured—except Elisaveta. Izza and Blazhe hadn't stirred, and Ellinor hoped Kai crashing into zem hadn't broken anything. She let out a long breath, her limbs suddenly shaky as the magic bled from her system, leaving her exhausted.

"Blazhe is going to be pissed that we destroyed zers home," Ellinor mumbled, sinking to the ground.

ROUND TWO

A FEW hours later they were back at SynthLyfe, and Elisaveta was being tended to by Aylen's Ashlings. Whether Elisaveta told Aylen about her involvement in Gorgi finding them, Ellinor didn't know, but her crew kept their promise and didn't say anything about it. With Gorgi dead, zers pieces scattered in the Scrapyard along the way, Ellinor wasn't motivated to destroy Elisaveta's life further.

Blazhe and Izza had rebooted on the bumpy ride out of the Unincorporated Dwellings, but zey immediately shut down half zeyr systems again as soon as zey were functional. Oihana explained that the new neurological sensations had over-loaded zeyr systems, so a slower reboot was necessary while zey processed zeyr new, organic nervous system. It would probably take zem another few days to come fully back online. In the meantime, zey would be sequestered to another private suite in Aylen's club, away from all the thumping noise and pulsing music of the lower floors. Though Ellinor did have to sign a contract saying she would fight in the arena if she so much as stained a towel from a hangnail this time. But with Fiss and her truly bonded, and her magic coursing through her body once more, Ellinor didn't think that would be a problem.

With Izza needing a slow restart, they wouldn't be leaving Amardeep as immediately as Aylen wanted, though with Gorgi dismantled, the Owner wasn't as demanding about their departure as she had been before extracting Ellinor's virus. In fact, Aylen was busier than usual and she spoke to their group only fleetingly, too preoccupied with setting up her labs and pulling her most trusted mechanics and programmers to deconstruct and rebuild the corrupted code she had pulled from Ellinor's body. Which left Aylen's assistant, Rada, to escort them to their new quarters. At least this suite had adjoining rooms with two bathrooms, and wasn't quite as austere a white as the one Ellinor had trashed.

They washed the stink of blood, sweat, oil, and the sulfuric twinge of Amardeep's natural air off their skin and out of their hair. They had to incinerate the clothes they had on under their armor as unsalvageable. Thankfully, Rada had brought new clothes for them, and once they were dressed, the group gorged themselves on the lab grown meat and sautéed greenhouse vegetables Rada also provided. But after being cramped together in Blazhe's home while they waited for Aylen, the group wanted space.

With Izza and Blazhe higher up in the building, Oihana had been the first to disappear to stay with her Ashling, to monitor zeyr new systems. Kai was the next to leave, waving over his shoulder as he headed down to the combat arenas, his adrenaline still high from their fight against Gorgi.

For the first time since Misho died, violence was the last thing on Ellinor's mind. Her body hummed and she needed to move, she needed an outlet, but with her magic back, the desire to wrap her fingers around someone's throat—even Cosmin's—wasn't as compelling. She headed for the ground floors of SynthLyfe. Eager to move and let Fiss dance, but in the "tamest" part of Aylen's gigantic club.

"I'll accompany you, if you don't mind." Jelani did the middle button of his fitted jacket, averting his gaze. Ellinor smirked at him, her eyes sweeping the form-fitting black, casual suit he wore and the tastefully rumpled shirt. She could easily imagine the firm muscles beneath, and her heart began to race.

She shrugged, tilting her face away before he saw the blush, following Fiss out of the room. "I won't stop you, come on."

They piled into the elevator, and on the way down Ellinor once more reminded Fiss not to cast, not to draw attention to himself. The dreeocht didn't question her as much as he normally did, the free flow of magic between him and his bonded having soothed his natural drive to make wave after wave of pretty magic to compensate for her diminished capabilities.

As soon as the elevator doors opened, Fiss moved toward the edge of the dance floor to flit around the spotlights, the strobing, and pulsing neon. Ellinor headed straight for the bar, Jelani right on her heel—a high-heeled red boot that looked like she was walking on rows of fangs, no less.

Ellinor was feeling good, better than she had in years. Granted, she had only been without her magic for a short period compared to how long she had been without Misho, without Andrey, without contact from her family. But the loss of something as much a part of her as her blood or heart put her life, her purpose, in perspective. Things Ellinor thought she would want forever, for as long as Misho was gone, didn't feel as sharp anymore.

What now?

Well, now Ellinor was dressed in something she hadn't worn since she was dating Misho. Or a version of it. The black, short, pleather bodysuit with its plunging red zippered neckline, stopping just beneath her breastbone was form fitting and—dare she say—racy. "Sexy" was something Ellinor hadn't felt in a long time.

The short sleeves coupled with the neckline showed her permanent cybernetics and, for once, Ellinor was okay with that. With her bond to Fiss, the metal made her somehow feel more connected to the dreeocht, more like they were the same.

Once she and Jelani were at the bar, Ellinor ordered them two double whiskeys—rye based. Jelani didn't bother with ordering his water-back like he had before. With their drinks in hand, they perched on the barstools, swiveling to watch Fiss, their knees nearly touching. Jelani clinked his glass against hers, causing Ellinor to arch a brow at him, a smirk tugging up her lips as she waited for an explanation.

"You're a survivor, Ellinor. Something new and improved from where you were when we first met," Jelani said, leaning toward her to be heard over the electric beats.

She knocked back her drink before chuckling at his words. "Improved? Maybe. But new? Hardly."

Jelani sipped his whiskey, then the corner of his lip tugged up in a cocky smile. "Think, Ellinor. Your former shackle has been turned into a pathway. You and Fiss are one, almost literally. Dreeocht gravitate toward the most powerful source of magic there is, and even after what has occurred, that isn't you. But even so, Fiss won't leave you. He can't leave you." Jelani paused, noting the way she sucked in her breath at the mere thought of Fiss leaving. His eyes glimmered and he took another sip before continuing. "And I don't think you're capable of leaving little Fiss, either. This is unheard of. It's new. You and Fiss are . . . something different."

"I still don't know if that's a good thing." Ellinor waved for a refill. "If Gorgi had really hurt me or Fiss . . . we'd have come undone."

"Only time will tell for certain. But, for what it's worth, I like the change. You seem happier. Your soul feels lighter."

She rolled her eyes, but heat was making her cheeks as red as her heels. "That's your gut talking, yeah?"

He winked at her. "Amongst other things." And Ellinor nearly spit out her drink.

"You're a damned flirt when you aren't bleeding out, Jelani Tyrik Sharma."

He smiled, his eyes brighter than the neon flashing around them. Her insides warmed, the magic in her veins quivered. She finished her drink, and when she didn't immediately signal for another, it was his turn to arch a brow at her, smile playful.

"You want to get out of here?" His flirtatious smile grew waiting for her to say exactly what she wanted, and Ellinor grew bold.

It's just sex.

She was feeling alive again, so why shouldn't she enjoy what that felt like? Free of the anger, the need to erase a bad thing with pleasure, the need to destroy pleasure with punishment. With her magic back, she was thinking about what that could do in the bedroom, especially with Jelani's talents.

"A celebratory fuck?" She licked her lips, and Jelani's eyes locked on the motion, his hand suddenly on her hip, fingers prodding, a need, a want, a desire burning in his fingertips. "It'll be better than last time, what with my magic back."

"Oh, I'm sure it will be," Jelani said, voice husky and raw and Ellinor found her hands on his thighs, moving, moving . . . "But no, Ellinor."

She jerked back, her bun bobbing on her head. She blinked rapidly at him, her cheeks flaming, mortified.

Jelani frowned, shaking his head, but his hand didn't move. "You're full of such fire and life and you've locked it away, battered it with hate and violence and yet, with Fiss, there are these moments. These glimmers of the real you. The woman who cares deeply, so deeply, that she would rather die than let such a pure creature ever experience a moment of discomfort . . ." He paused, his smile softening.

He lowered his head, touching his forehead to hers, his eyes locked on hers, and she could see her own tropical blue orbs reflected in his starry eyes. "With Fiss you are who I sense you were before death and revenge became your purpose. This is the most incredible, beautiful, sexiest thing I've seen in centuries. Such a transformation you've made, Ellinor. I can't . . ." He bit his words off, inhaling deeply, and Ellinor found her hands slick with sweat, her limbs threatening to tremble. "I can't have a celebratory fuck with you, as you so elegantly put it," he said, chuckling. "I want more. I want *you*, Ellinor. All of you. Not just the physical, not just some small part. I want you. Your fear. Your future. Your passion. Even your anger. You."

"I can't, Jelani," she blurted before she meant to, before she meant to say anything at all.

His hand stilled, his head moving back, studying. Hurt lingered in a hesitant gaze. Ellinor swallowed a growl of frustration, ignoring the fluttering in her gut, the one that was laughing at her, telling her *it* knew all along what was happening, that she was catching feelings she had never wanted, even if her stubbornness said otherwise. She closed her eyes.

Tell him.

"I don't want to replace Misho. I can't. He was . . . I loved—*love* him so much, and he's gone. Ripped away. I'm scared of starting over. I couldn't go through that again. Not again."

His hands moved then, going to hers, gripping them tightly. She swore she could feel the magic between them, their magic. Warm and growing . . . and it was petrifying. But the hurt left his eyes, and Jelani smiled, full and bright and Ellinor had no idea what was happening anymore.

"I will never replace Misho. I will never ask you to forget him. I'd never want you to. He was your sun, moon, stars, and all the lights in your sky for so long. I'd never pretend that he wasn't a part of you, that he wouldn't always live with you, and now Fiss. I saw with my father and stepmother how foolish it is to pretend that life can't continue after someone exits, and it doesn't erase that person. The new relationship acts as an altar, a homage to what happened before, to get you to a place where you can live again. And I so want you to live again, Ellinor."

Her palms were slick and he gave her hands a gentle squeeze. "I'm not asking you to marry me. I'm not even asking you out on a date. Not properly, anyway. I am only asking you to try to be open to . . . me. Is that something you can do?"

"I don't know how to do that," she whispered, voice weak and barely audible over the music that was so at odds with what was happening between the two casters.

"But are you open to trying? With me?"

Her whole body was warm, on fire with more than just the whiskey. Ellinor shut her eyes.

What did she want? Truly *want*, now that Gorgi was dead, the bot directly responsible for Misho's death, even more so than Cosmin. What would Misho want for her? Was he at peace?

She opened her eyes, and they immediately fell on Fiss. The child-like dreeocht was still dancing, all smiles and laughter. Aglow with peace and an inner light fueled by love. Misho's love, if she believed what Fiss said. Her "water man" lived partially within the dreeocht now. She turned her gaze back to Jelani, gnawing at her lower lip.

Ellinor nodded. "Okay. But you'd have to ask me out first." Jelani squeezed her hands, lowering his head back to hers, and she inhaled the scent of fresh cut eucalyptus without guilt.

"So, what now?" Ellinor said.

"We'll figure it out. But I can't do casual sex with someone I want more from. It would make things too difficult if you—if we decide that this, whatever this is between us, isn't worth pursuing long term. If you need that physical release, I won't stop you. Not unless things become real. Which, who knows? A man can dream, can't he?" He winked at her, his lips so close, so teasing, but he stayed just a breath out of reach.

The blush on her cheeks intensified, and sensing her discomfort, her need to change the subject, to talk about anything else now, now, *now*, Jelani pulled away, and signaled for a refill to their drinks. "But what would you like to do next? We shouldn't stay in Amardeep with Gorgi dead, zer did have quite the following."

Ellinor knew what Jelani was really asking: was she still determined to go hunt down Cosmin von Brandt? Their deal, the arrangement they had made back in Erhard forgotten somewhere along the way. Technically she had fulfilled what Jelani had wanted back in Blazhe's home, and yet the Creature Breaker remained, and Ellinor felt no desire to remind him that he could leave. She didn't want Jelani to go. But what of her original goals?

Am I done with them? Am I done with Cosmin?

She knew what the answer was, she just needed to give the words a voice. The answer felt more solid, more right, especially with the damage it would cause Fiss if she got hurt, if *he* got hurt.

"Well, we can't go back to Anzor with Zabel Dirix still in power, and, without knowing what happened to Dragan Voclain, we can't go to Amaru, either. After what you left in Trifon and what the seersha there did to your family, that's also out of the question." The more places she listed, the more hopeful Jelani's expression became. "And with Cosmin in Euria, I'd rather not go back there. But I hear the smaller city-state of Migini is decent, and it might be nice to be near real mountains for once. We can even invite Kai's mom to come join us. My parents too, if they'll have anything to do with me."

"No more Cosmin?"

The question hung heavy between them, but Ellinor shook her head. "Gorgi is gone. That's enough. Misho would say it was enough. Well, he wouldn't have ever wanted me to risk my life period, but still."

Jelani laughed, pure and open and genuine. But before he could say anything, offer an opinion or anything else, a cyborg-humani entered the ground floor, holding a package.

Ellinor had never seen deliveries made on the dance floors of SynthLyfe, and the humani was so obviously reading a message and looking for the person to make the delivery to, it caught her attention. When the deliverer spotted Ellinor and headed her way, she found herself reaching for one of her knives, only to remember they weren't there.

"Ellinor Olysha Rask?" the deliverer yelled, and Ellinor's face paled.

How does he know that name? I'm still Lenore Castile here. How does he know it's me?

Noting her slack expression, the deliverer shrugged. "Package for you, Ellinor." He pushed the box in her hands and left.

Jelani was on his feet, waving at Fiss until he got the dreeocht's attention. "Don't open that. Not here." He picked up Fiss, Ellinor's limbs steel weights that dragged her down. "We need to have that box looked at and let Aylen know she has a breach. We need to leave. Now."

WELL, HELLO DEAR

R ADA HAD the package x-rayed, and Aylen was alerted. The paranoid woman moved to a secure location, and began obsessively going over her security protocols, moving the serum she was still reverse engineering to yet another secondary location, for precaution. Once Rada declared the package did not contain an explosive or a biochemical virus, or anything else particularly nasty that would cause harm, the Ashling rolled out of the room, going to assist zer boss in ensuring that Gorgi's allies or any remaining Juicers under zers control were not headed their way.

That left Ellinor, Kai, Jelani, and Fiss alone with the package. They had decided Oihana was safest where she was, monitoring Blazhe and Izza's systems, and would be told what was delivered to Ellinor later, if necessary.

Ellinor's fingers shook as she carefully peeled back the adhesive and pried open the cardboard flaps. Inside was a small, refrigerated silver bag, with a holo-disk laying on top. She gently picked up the disk, turning it back and forth as if she could see something dangerous that Rada's scans had missed.

"Might as well play it, boss. The suspense is gonna kill us if nothing else does," Kai said, cross about leaving the fight he was watching, but curious and wary about what was delivered, all the same.

She placed the disk on the communicator tablet, and Cosmin von Brandt's holographic image flared to life before them. "Hello, my traitorous dears. Did you think you'd escaped me?"

Sound ceased, the air stilled, and Ellinor forgot to breathe until her lungs began to burn. Cosmin laughed as if he were watching them in real time, the seersha gangster predicting too well what his sudden message would do to Ellinor.

"Oh, I do hope you opened the other little present before you played this. It would make this so very delicious. But, if not, go on. Open it," Cosmin cooed at them, his pumpkin orange eyes flashing, even in the hazy video.

Kai picked up the bag, and slowly opened it. "Azer save me," he said, dropping the bag. He stepped back, vomiting into the sink, before he darted forward to peer at what fell out more closely. His face turned even greener, eyes bright with horror as recognition settled at seeing the pale, severed ear with its bullet-like gold studs. The studs Kai had bought his mom, with Ellinor's help, years ago.

Ellinor's stomach churned, the whiskey threatening to reappear as her eyes skirted the severed ear of Amalia Brantley, settling on the two other chunks of skin that lay heavy and wet on the table. Both pieces of skin had a tattoo, a curved signature in black ink that read "Andrey," which had once resided on her parents' shoulders.

Ellinor's heart was struggling to beat and Cosmin was laughing. "Oh how I wish I could see your horrible little faces!" But then the glee was gone and the seersha was all anger, a sneer pulling his lips. "You took what was mine. So I took something that was yours, just as precious. An eye for an eye, as the saying goes, am I right?" Cosmin jutted his chin up, all cold arrogance. "You shouldn't have called your mother, Mr Brantley. She was the easiest to find. And then to make such an enemy of Gorgi?" Cosmin clicked his tongue at them. "I had expected *so* much more of you all, especially you, Ellinor, my dear. But alas, you frustrate me at every single turn. It's truly amazing how completely you continue to disappoint me. Not to mention how idiotic of you to think I wouldn't find you. That I wouldn't find what was important to you. That I wouldn't hunt them down, and make the poor dears suffer. And oh, how they suffer!"

Cosmin paused, as if he expected them to yell or balk, or deny what they were seeing. But there was only silence in the room. Even Fiss was quietly observing the body parts from where he floated near the ceiling above Cosmin's video.

"Here is what you are going to do next, my traitorous dears. You are going to come back to Erhard. You are going to return *my* dreeocht to Zabel. Then, you will come and see me in order to reclaim your family. Of course, you can choose not to do any of that. But I found you once, I will find you again, and I will continue to send you pieces of your parents in the interim. Maybe it will be their fingernails and toenails next. No, no, too cliché. Perhaps a nipple? Really, I haven't decided. There are just so many fragile little parts a person can live without, it's rather remarkable, if you think about it."

Cosmin smiled meanly into space, into where the seersha assumed they would be gathered. "I'll keep your family alive. For now. I haven't grown bored of their screams yet, in fact, I'm just starting to play with them, now that I'm finished with Irati. You remember her, don't you? The other lieutenant of mine who thought she could abscond with my property? I'd have thought you'd have learned sense from that, my dears." Cosmin sighed theatrically, straightening in the chair he was sitting in. "Well, you know what I have, and what you need to do. Make it so, and do it fast. My patience has long since expired." The message ended, and Cosmin's face disappeared.

Ellinor couldn't move. Could barely breathe. She hadn't spoken to her parents—Dafina and Valter Rask—in years, hadn't even properly checked in with them. She had only confirmed they were alive, right where she had left them, and that was all Cosmin had needed. Kai's worry for his mom had led Cosmin right to her . . . The guilt was crushing, Ellinor couldn't even imagine what Kai must be feeling.

"That must have been the last message Gorgi sent," Jelani whispered. "We thought . . . Oihana and I assumed zer had sent some communication to zers associates, or zer's Owner at the Habitation. But zer must have sent a coded message to Cosmin instead, just as Gorgi threatened."

But the truth, the reason, the how . . . none of that mattered. All that mattered was Cosmin had not only found them, but he had found the one thing that would bring Kai back. That would bring Ellinor back.

Kai was shaking, sobbing, hands clenching and unclenching. "He's got Ma." The desperation in his voice, the need for it to not be true was so palpable that Ellinor's heart broke anew, and suddenly, her lungs were engulfed in fire, muscles tensing, her jaw clenching until her teeth threatened to crack.

She had decided to leave Cosmin be. To stay away. To save Fiss from dealing with the seersha, to keep her family safe by never returning. But Cosmin had taken that choice away. The seersha was breaking her friend's heart again in new, unimaginable ways, and Ellinor would not stand for it.

"That's it," she said, her voice a guttural growl that had Jelani eyeing her warily. "I'm going to obliterate that motherfucker."

ELL IS GOING HOME

A S MUCH as she wanted to, Ellinor could not hop on the monorail and scurry to the docks to force a boat to take her and her friends back to the mainland immediately. The skinned off pieces from her mother and father remained in cold storage along with Kai's mom's ear. She didn't think they could be reattached, but she couldn't bring herself to throw out pieces of her family. But even with those pieces of flesh screaming at her from the corner of their suite, leaving Amardeep straightaway would have been suicide.

It was impossible to know which of Gorgi's henchmen were still active. Which of Cosmin's operatives may be in the area, waiting for Ellinor and Kai to make themselves vulnerable in order to be snatched away.

Cosmin may know they would be heading back to Euria, but he didn't need to know what transport they would be on. He didn't need to know who was coming with them, and what kind of firepower they would be bringing. And Cosmin certainly didn't need to know that Ellinor could cast again. Certain precautions needed to be taken, plans to be made.

Which meant the rage continued to build in Ellinor, and the anxious desperation Kai felt for his mom's safety grew and grew until the big guy couldn't sleep, couldn't stand still, couldn't eat, could barely think . . .

Jelani took that burden off of Kai, though. He worked with Aylen on securing passage back to Erhard, and formed a plan with Ellinor for how to get their parents free of the gangster without sacrificing Fiss in the process.

It took three more days for them to be ready, for Aylen to purchase tickets in Elisaveta's name and fabricate a decoy travel itinerary to look legitimate. If Elisaveta minded that her name was being used, that she was potentially putting herself in Cosmin's crosshairs, the cyborg-seerani kept it to herself. Ellinor figured the woman still owed them. Her betrayal of their location had been key to this new catastrophe, even though she had been grievously injured defending them during that same encounter. But once the travel itinerary was created, the right ship procured that would sail them through doehaz infested waters once again, then things began to move in a whirlwind of organized chaos.

Aylen had no additional weapons for them, and Blazhe was still recovering with Izza and couldn't upgrade any of their armor like zer had Kai's Coyote mechanized suit, but Aylen did have plenty of ammunition and external battery packs they could use for their armor to help the charge last longer when up against a powerful caster. Jelani sent what encrypted messages he could to his various contacts, hopefully securing backup once they returned. But Ellinor wasn't holding her breath, especially as Aylen hadn't been all that receptive to them initially. Ellinor planned on calling in every debt she was owed from those she had done favors for while working against Cosmin, and she hoped that she wouldn't have to fight through more friends to get to him.

Though maybe Pema and Talin will help us?

Kai was a blur of movement, throwing their gear in the Mastiff to take directly to the docks at the Emporium Sanitorium. Fiss liked to follow Kai around. The dreeocht could sense Kai's distress and thought that if he was near his red friend, that would make things better. It seemed to work marginally, as Kai tended not to slam doors to the point of breaking when Fiss was nearby.

Ellinor was packing the last of what she had to disguise Fiss with, when Oihana ambled into the garage, arms laden with computer systems that would monitor Izza until zer rebooted. Jelani's head snapped up at his sister's arrival. He frowned at her from where he was sending the last of his messages and shook his head.

He darted around the communication station and tapped Oihana on the shoulder, signing to her in their private language. Oihana scowled at him, but with her arms full, she couldn't sign back. "You'll need me, Anni. I can't stay here!"

Jelani glanced at Ellinor, who shrugged one shoulder at him. This wasn't her business, Oihana wasn't her family. Cosmin was a dangerous man and while Ellinor readily admitted that Oihana was brilliant and was an asset, she wouldn't begrudge Jelani for putting his foot down, demanding she stay safe, especially considering a powerful gangster had already killed the rest of their family for Jelani's betrayal.

Jelani sighed and gripped Oihana's shoulders. "You can help best from the safety of SynthLyfe. Aylen can protect you better from here then I could if you accompanied us back to Erhard. Stay here. Stay safe. For now, at least. Izza and Blazhe will need you, and we can't take zem with us. Not while zey are still so vulnerable. Please, Oihana, stay here."

"But what if you need help? How am I supposed to know if you're in trouble from here? I can help you, like I did with the RFID chips. Come on, please, don't go without me." Oihana glanced around, locking eyes with Ellinor. "Tell him, Ell. I can help. I won't get into any danger with you guys."

Ellinor gave a sympathetic smile. If Andrey had lived longer, she knew she would have pleaded the same as Oihana to go with her big brother wherever he went. And Andrey would have forbade her, too, just like Jelani.

She shook her head. "Cosmin is a special brand of asshole, Oihana. You don't mess with a caster like that and expect any-one to stay safe, to stay undetected. Your brother is right, you know that, yeah?" Ellinor gave the young woman a pointed look, and Oihana deflated.

Oihana all but dropped the computers she was holding and flung herself at Jelani, hugging him tightly around the neck. Jelani wrapped his arms around her, clinging to her just as fiercely.

A lump lodged itself in Ellinor's throat as she watched the siblings. If she didn't so desperately need a Creature Breaker when facing Cosmin, Ellinor would have insisted Jelani stay away, to let her and Kai handle this alone. Oihana had lost enough, she shouldn't risk any more of her family for some-one else's drama. But it was a nonstarter discussion. Jelani wouldn't let Kai and Ellinor go off without him, and Ellinor was too familiar with Cosmin to not accept the help Jelani could offer this time around.

"I hate to interrupt these goodbyes," Aylen's voice cut through the room as her face blipped onto the screen from the comm station, "but I have news before you go."

Jelani slowly released Oihana and turned her toward the screen. Aylen grinned, her hazel eyes flashing. "We've passed a milestone. The magitech serum that we extracted from Ellinor? It's responding well to the simulations we built that utilize Gorgi's old programs. We're getting close to having the code, and the magic along with it, replicated. I'm so close to reverse engineering the shit out of that virus, that I'd be surprised if we didn't have the first batch ready to test within the month."

"You can't just give that to any Ashling who wants it, you know." Ellinor's chest tightened, her fingers itching at the idea of Ashlings like Gorgi being gifted a true nervous system.

Aylen gave her a flat stare. "That goes without saying, don't patronize me. I'm not sharing this stuff with just anyone. Besides, it's too hot to make in big batches. The mainland governments would send too many people to destroy the serum, or me just for making this. I know how to be careful."

Jelani tilted his head, and nudged Oihana. "Perhaps Oihana can assist you with the final steps? Make sure that only Ashlings with Blazhe's vision for peace between all our races are given the upgrade? I'm sure Izza and Blazhe will want to be involved when zey recover as well."

Oihana shrugged, disappointment lining her face, pulling her lips down. "Yeah, sure. I can do that." She glanced at her brother again, squeezing his hand one last time before picking up her computers and scanners and sulking away.

Jelani sighed, but Aylen said, "You're doing the right thing. I'll take care of her."

"Thank you, Aylen. If I don't return—"

"Don't start, Jelani," Aylen interrupted. "You're coming back." Aylen blipped off the comm just as Kai stomped into the garage, the last of their gear and extra batteries in his arms.

He dumped them in the trunk of the Mastiff and glanced at the time. "The boat leaves in an 'our. Time to get going."

The muscles in Kai's jaw twitched, his green eyes a constant emerald fire whenever it came to discussing their timing in getting back to Erhard. They were still formulating a plan, but Kai wouldn't sit still long enough to listen, to help them strategize. Hopefully he would be more receptive once they were actually moving, once they were closing the distance to his mom.

Jelani nodded and hopped into the driver's seat of the Mastiff. Ellinor's hands were on her karambit knives, twirling them around her fingers, the wind picking up and answering the anger bubbling inside her. She gave Kai a small, fierce smile. "We'll get them back, big guy. They'll be okay, I won't let Cosmin kill anyone else we love."

Kai gave her a deft nod before opening the passenger door, Fiss flying in ahead of him. "Thanks, boss. If Cosmin lays one more finger on Ma, though, I'll be gutting the bastard myself."

Ellinor smiled, a feral glee rushing through her veins, and the wind crackled around her in answer, eager to suck the oxygen out of Cosmin and snuff out the bastard's magic like he had hers. "I'll hold him down for you, big guy. Now, let's go get our parents back."

ACKNOWLEDGEMENTS

Here we are again, friends! Another book complete, one which was written during such crazy times throughout the entire world. Books and stories, writing and crafting this world, this land Ellinor and her friends traverse helped me so much during these times of uncertainty. I hope that, now, as we come out on the other side of the pandemic, that you continue to love and support the things that got you through these times, just as I am! Which means, it's time for me to show all the love and support this snarky, sarcastic author can to the people who helped Deadlock become the book you hold in your hands today.

This book is one of the more fun, atmospheric stories so far in Ellinor's series, and that's in large part to my incredible beta readers, editor, and support system. So, first and foremost, thank you to my early beta readers who gushed over my chapter titles, helped me not forget Izza when it counted the most, and squealed over THAT scene—you know the one. Your comments, both hilarious and constructive, gave me so much life as I cut and restructured Deadlock. Thank you from the bottom of my heart to: Tyffany Hackett, Hannah Hanson, Grace Kaye, Briana Burgess, and Jamie Rose. And a big shout out to my editor, Sheila Shedd and her team, who refined Deadlock and Ellinor into the high polish they both ended up being. I'd be remiss as well for not thanking my Super Friend newsletter subscribers who helped promote this book and loved it before anyone else, and all the bookstagrammers and book enthusiasts who helped me share Deadlock with the world. You are all fabulous, fantastic human beings!

As always, thank you to my husband, who had to hear me rant and grumble, and let me poke him for help more frequently during the creation of this book—thanks to the pandemic. Thanks for not tuning me out, and for helping me make those dance-club arena battles so badass. Thank you to my big sister, my forever cheerleader, and the person I look up to the most, for always being so excited each time I mention I'm writing a new story. I aspire to be just like you. Always. And to my parents, who continue to gift my books to everyone they know without reading them first. (I apologize on their behalf if they didn't tell you about all the swearing.) Without their support, my books wouldn't ever even leave my computer! And big hugs to my brothers and in-laws, who continue to lift me and my work up, I appreciate you all.

I am also forever grateful to the amazing artists who brought my characters to life: Odetta A. Bach, who helped show off just how good my babies can clean up, given the chance, and Rosa Gutierrez, who continues to make such beautiful character playing cards. Sarah at thesketchdragon.com for the incredible map of Amardeep, Alba Francés who captured the adorableness of Fiss so perfectly, and Asha Znamenska for the stunning cover art: Elisaveta's exquisiteness, and especially bringing Jelani and his tattoo to life in such breathtaking detail! (If you'd like to get your hands on this exclusive artwork, please visit my website at http://www.ceclayton.com to find out how.)

And of course, THANK YOU, dear reader, for allowing me to share Ellinor's story with you and take you on such a crazy, fun ride. I am beyond humbled that you picked up my work and eagerly await to see what I throw at my babies next. You mean the world to me! Never fear; there will be more of Ellinor and friends coming your way very soon! If you enjoyed my story, please consider leaving a review, requesting my books at your local library, or sharing with friends and family. If you'd like to hear more from me, please sign up for my book club, where you will immediately get the novella, "PARADIGM FLUX," as a thank you for joining: https://BookHip.com/PNZTASG

Or follow me on social media, especially Instagram (@chelscey), where I post pictures of my animals amidst all my book news. And, if you'd like to listen to a soundtrack to remind you of Deadlock even long after you finish the last page, I've got you covered: https://spoti.fi/33hv850

ABOUT THE AUTHOR

C. E. Clayton is an award winning author born and raised in the greater Los Angeles area. After going the traditional career route and becoming restless, she went back to her first love--writing--and hasn't stopped. She is the author of the young adult fantasy series "The Monster of Selkirk", the creator of the cyberpunk Eerden Novels, and her horror short stories have appeared in anthologies across the country. When she's not writing you can find her treating her fur-babies like humans, constantly drinking tea, and trying to convince her husband to go to more concerts. And reading. She does read quite a bit. More about C.E. Clayton, including her blog, book reviews, social media presence, and newsletter can be found on her website: https://www.ceclayton.com/